Jessica Sorensen lives in Wyoming with her husband and three children. She is the author of numerous romance novels. All of her New Adult novels have been *New York Times* and kindle bestsellers.

Keep in contact with Jessica:

jessicasorensensblog.blogspot.co.uk
Facebook/Jessica Sorensen
@jessFallenStar

The author that everyone is talking about . . .

Novels by Jessica Sorensen

The Ella and Micha series

The Secret of Ella and Micha
The Forever of Ella and Micha
The Temptation of Lila and Ethan
The Ever After of Ella and Micha
Lila and Ethan: Forever and Always

The Callie and Kayden series

The Coincidence of Callie and Kayden
The Redemption of Callie and Kayden
The Destiny of Violet and Luke

The Breaking Nova series

Breaking Nova
Saving Quinton
Nova and Quinton: No Regrets
Delilah: The Making of Red
Tristan: Finding Hope

The Destiny of
Violet & Luke

JESSICA SORENSEN

sphere

SPHERE

First published in Great Britain in 2014 by Sphere

A CIP catalogue record for this book
is available from the British Library.

ISBN 978-0-7515-5262-1

Printed and bound in Great Britain by Clays Ltd, St Ives plc

Papers used by Sphere are from well-managed forests
and other responsible sources.

MIX
Paper from
responsible sources
FSC® C104740

Sphere
An imprint of
Little, Brown Book Group
100 Victoria Embankment
London EC4Y 0DY

An Hachette UK Company
www.hachette.co.uk

www.littlebrown.co.uk

*For everyone who marches to the
beat of their own drum.*

Acknowledgments

A huge thanks to my agent, Erica Silverman, and my editor, Amy Pierpont. I'm forever grateful for all your help and input.

To my family, thank you supporting me and my dream. You guys have been wonderful.

And to everyone who reads this book, an endless amount of thank-yous.

The Destiny of
Violet & Luke

Prologue

Luke

(Eight years old)

I hate running, but it always seems like I'm doing it. Always running everywhere. Always trying to hide. I hide just as much as I run, but if I don't then bad things will happen. Like getting found. Or getting forced to do things that make me sick to my stomach. Getting forced to help *her*.

"Come out, come out wherever you are," my mom sing-songs as I run out the front door of my house. Her voice is slurred, which means she's been taking her medication again. She takes her medication a lot and it doesn't make any sense to me. I have to take medication sometimes, too, but because I get sick. Whenever she takes it, it seems to make her sicker.

She used to not be like this, well not as bad anyway. About a year ago, when my dad was still around she would act normal and not take medication. Now, though, she does it a lot and I think she might be going crazy. At least she seems that way compared to everyone else's moms. I see them picking up my friends from school and they always look happy and put together. My friends are always glad to see them and they don't run and hide from them, like I do all the time.

I race around to the back of the house, running away from the sound of her voice as she chases after me, looking for me. She's always looking for me and I hate when she does—hate her sometimes for always making me run and hide. And for finding me. I usually hide underneath the bed or in the closet or somewhere else in the house, but she's been finding me quicker lately, so today I decided to hide outside.

As I make it to the back porch stairs, I slam to a stop, panting to catch my breath. There's just enough room for me to duck down below the decaying boards and hide underneath. I pull my legs up against me and lower my head onto my knees. The sunlight sparkles through the cracks in the wood and down on me. I'm nervous because if the sun can see me, then maybe she might see me, too.

I scoot back, closer to the bottom step and out of the sunlight, and then I hold my breath as I hear the screen door hinges creak.

"Luke," my mom says from up on the top step. She shuffles across the wood in her slippers and the screen door bangs shut. "Luke, are you out here?"

I tuck my face into my arms, sucking back the tears, even though I want to cry—she'll hear me if I do. Then she'll probably want to hug me better and I don't like when she does that.

I don't like a lot of things she does and how wrong she makes my life feel.

"Luke Price," she warns, stepping down the stairs. I peek up at her through the cracks and see her pink furry slippers. The smoke from her cigarette makes my stomach burn. "If you're out here and you're ignoring me, you're going to be in trouble." She almost sings it, like it's a song to some game we're playing. Sometimes I think that's what this is to her. A game that I always lose.

The stairs creak as she slowly walks down to the bottom step. Ashes from her cigarette scatter across the ground and all over my head. A few land in my mouth, but I don't spit. I stay as still as I can, fighting to keep my heart from beating so loudly as my palms sweat.

Finally, after what seems like forever, she turns around and heads up the stairs back to the house. "Fine, have it your way, then," she says.

It's never my way and I know better than to think so. That's why I stay still even after the screen door shuts. I barely breathe as the wind blows and the sunlight dims. I wait until the sky is almost gray before I peek up through the cracks in the stairs. If I had my way I'd stay here forever, hiding under the stairs, but I'm hungry and tired.

I can't see or hear her anymore so I lean forward, poke my head out from under the stairs. The coast looks clear so I put my hands down on the dirt and crawl out onto the grass. I get to my feet and brush the dirt and the rocks off my torn jeans. Then, taking a deep breath, I run around to the side of the house and hurry quickly up the fence line until I make it to the front yard.

I've never liked where we live that much. Everyone's grass always looks yellow and all the houses look like they need to be repainted. My mom says it's because we're poor and this is all we can afford thanks to my dad leaving us and that he doesn't care and that's why he never comes to see me. I'm not sure I believe her since my mom's always telling lies. Like how she promises me time and time again that this will be the last time she makes me do things I don't want to do.

I stand in the front yard for a while, figuring out where to go. I could climb through my sister's bedroom window and hide out there until she gets home, then maybe she can help me. But she's been acting strange lately and gets annoyed whenever I talk to her. She's lucky because Mom never seems to notice her as much as she notices me. I don't know why. I do my best to blend in. I don't make messes, keeping the house clean and organized like she likes it. I keep quiet. I stay in my room a lot and organize my toys in categories, just the way she likes them, yet she's always calling for me. But Amy seems invisible to her.

She's so lucky. I wish I were invisible.

I decide to go for a walk down to the gas station at the corner where I can get a candy bar or something because my stomach hurts from hunger. But as my feet touch the sidewalk, I hear the front door swing open.

"Luke, get in here right now," she says in a frenzy, snapping her fingers and pointing to the ground below her feet. "I need you."

I freeze, wishing I were brave enough to take off running down the sidewalk. Just leave. Never come back. Sleep in a box because a box seems so much nicer than my sterilized house. But I'm not brave and I turn around and face her just like she wants me to. She's holding the door open, her hair pulled up messily on top of her head and she's wearing this purple tank top and plaid shorts that she always wears. It's pretty much like a uniform for her, except she doesn't have a job. Not a good one anyway where she has to wear a uniform. Instead, she sells her medicine to creepy men who are always staring at her or Amy when she walks out of her bedroom.

She crooks her finger at me. "Get in here."

An unsteady breath leaves my mouth as I trudge to the front door, a nauseating feeling rising in my stomach. It happens every time she needs me. I get sick to my stomach at the thoughts of what she's going to make me do creep inside my head.

When I reach the stairs, she moves back, not looking happy, but not looking sad either. She holds the door open for me, watching me with her brown eyes that remind me of the bag of marbles she made me throw away because they didn't look right. Once I'm inside, she closes the door and shoves the deadbolt over. She fastens the small chain and then clicks the lock on the doorknob before turning around.

The curtains are shut and there's a lit cigarette on a teal glass ashtray that's on the coffee table, filling the room with smoke. There's a sofa just behind the table and it's covered in plastic to keep "the dirty air from ruining the fabric," my

mother told me once. She always thinks the dirt in the air is going to do something to either the house or her, which is why she rarely goes outside anymore.

"Why'd you run off?" she asks me as she walks over the sofas and flops down in it. She picks up her cigarette and ashes it, before putting it into her mouth. She takes a deep inhale and seconds later a cloud of smoke circles around her sore-covered face. "Were you playing a game or something?"

I nod, because telling her I was playing a game is much better than telling her I was hiding from her. "Yes."

She takes another drag from the cigarette and then stares at the row of cat figurines on one of the shelves lining the living room walls. Each row on the shelf is organized with figurines, according to breed. She did it once when she was having one of her episodes from too much medication, the one that makes her stay awake for a long, long time, not the stuff that makes her pass out. The glass clinking together and her incoherent murmuring had woken me up when she was rearranging the figurines and when I'd walked out she was moving like crazy, frantically trying to get the animals into order or "something bad was going to happen." She knew it was—she could feel it in her bones. I think something bad already did happen, though. A lot of bad things actually.

"Luke, pay attention," my mom says. I tear my gaze away from the figurines, wishing I was one of them, so I could be up on the shelf, watching what's about to happen instead of taking part in it. She switches her cigarette to her other hand and then leans to the side, grabbing her small wooden "medication box." She sets it on her lap, puts the cigarette into her mouth one last time, and then places it down so she can turn on the lamp. "Now quit messing around and come here, would ya?"

My body gets really tight and I glance over my shoulder at the front door, crossing my fingers that Amy will come home and interrupt us long enough that I can find another place to hide. But she doesn't and I'm stuck out here. With her.

"Do I have to?" I utter quietly.

She nods with chaotic frenzy in her eyes. "You need to."

Shaking, I turn back around and trudge over to the sofa. I take a seat beside her and she pats me on the head several times like I'm her pet. She does that a lot and it makes me wonder how she sees me; if I'm kind of like a pet to her instead of her kid.

"You were a bad boy today," she says as her fingers continue to touch my hair. I hate it when she does that and it makes me want to shave my head bald so she won't be able to touch me. "You should have come when I called you."

"I'm sorry," I lie, because I'm only sorry I was found. I need to find better hiding spots and stay in them long enough that she'll stop looking for me, then maybe I can become invisible like Amy.

"It's okay." She strokes my cheek and then my neck before pulling her hand away. She places a kiss on my cheek and I shut my eyes, holding my breath, trapping in a scream because I want to shout: *Don't touch me!* "I know deep down you're a good boy."

7

No, I'm not. I'm terrible because I hate you. I really do. I hate you so much I wish you were gone.

She starts humming a song she made up as she removes the lid from the box and carefully sets it aside. I don't even have to look inside it to know what's in it. A spoon, a lighter, a small plastic baggie that holds this stuff that looks almost like brown sugar, a thin piece of cotton, a half a bottle of water, a big rubber band thing, and a needle and syringe that she probably stole from the stash I use to give myself insulin shots.

"Now you remember what to do?" she asks, and then starts humming again.

I nod, tears burning in the corners of my eyes because I don't want to do it—I don't want to do anything that she tells me. "Yes."

"Good." She pats my head again, this time a little rougher.

I don't watch her as she opens the baggie and puts some of the brown sugary stuff onto the metal spoon along with some water, but I can pretty much visualize her movements since I've seen her do this a lot, sometimes twice a day. It really depends on how much she's talking to herself. If it's a lot then she brings out the needle a lot. But sometimes, when she gets quieter, it's not so bad. I like the quieter days, ones where she's either focused on cleaning or stuck in her head. Or I'll even take her being passed out.

She heats the spoon with the lighter as she mutters lyrics under her breath. She actually has a beautiful voice, but the words she sings are frightening. After the spoon is heated enough, she ties the rubber band around her arm, I sit on the couch beside her, tapping my fingers on my leg, pretending I'm in there instead of here. Anywhere but here.

I hate her.

"All right, Luke, help me out, okay," she finally says after she's melted her medication into a pool of liquid and sucked some into the syringe.

I turn toward her, shaking nervously. Always shaking. Always nervous, all the time. Always so worried I'll do something wrong. Mess up. She instantly hands me the syringe and then extends her arm onto my lap. She has these purple marks and red dots all over her upper forearm from all the other times the needles have gone into her. Her veins are really dark on her skin and I don't like the sight of the needle going in just as much as she does like it. Like a routine, I point the needle toward her arm near where all the other dots on her skin are.

My hand quivers unsteadily. "Please don't make me do this," I whisper. "Please Mom." I don't know why I even try, though. She'll do anything to get her medication. And I mean anything. Dark things that normal people wouldn't do.

"Deep breaths, remember?" She ignores me as she wraps her free arm around the back of my neck. "Remember, don't miss the vein. You can mess up my arm or even kill me if you're not careful, okay?" She says it so sweetly like it's a nice thing to say and will make me less nervous.

But it makes things worse, especially because part of me wishes I'd miss the vein. I have to take a lot of breaths before I can settle down inside and get my thoughts from going to that dark place they always want to go, reminding myself that I don't want to hurt her. *I don't.*

When I get my nerves under control the best that I can, I sink the needle into her vein, like I've done hundreds of times. Each time it gets to me, like I'm sticking the needle in my own skin and feeling the sting. I wince as her muscles tense a little underneath the poke of the needle. As I push in the plunger, the medicine enters her veins and seconds later she lets out this weird noise, before sinking back on the couch, pulling me down with her. I hurry and pull the needle out before we fall down completely onto the couch cushions.

"Thank you, Luke," she says sleepily, patting my head with her hand as she holds me against her. Her throat makes this vibrating noise, like she's trying to hum again, but the noise is trapped like I am.

I press my lips together, staring at the wall across the room, barely breathing. After a while, her arm falls lifelessly to the side, her hand hitting the floor as her eyelids flutter shut and I'm temporarily freed from her hold.

I sit up, sucking the tears back, hating her for making me do this and hating myself for doing it and being secretly glad she's passed out. I toss the syringe down on the table, then I push to my feet. Using all my strength, I rotate her to her side because sometimes she throws up. I have a house full of quiet now, just how I like it. Yet, at the same time I don't like it because the emptiness gets to me. What I really want is what all the other kids have. The ones I see at the park playing on swings while their parents push them higher. They're always laughing and smiling. Everyone always seems to be, except for me. Every time I get close I always remember this feeling I have inside me right now, this vile, icky feeling, mixed with hatred and sadness that makes me sick all the time. It always wipes the smile right off my face and I don't even bother trying anymore. Happiness isn't real. It's make-believe.

I throw the syringe and spoon into the box, wondering if my life will always be this way. If I'll always carry so much sadness and hate inside me. I'm shaking by the time I get everything into the box and I feel like I need to flee somewhere—run again. I can't take this anymore. I can't take living here. With her.

"I can't take it!" I shout at the top of my lungs and ram my fist into the coffee table. My hand makes this popping sound and it hurts so bad tears sting at my eyes. I cry out in pain, sinking to the floor, but of course no one hears me.

No one ever does.

Violet

(Thirteen years old)

I hate moving. Not just from house to house, but from family to family. I hate moving my legs and arms, moving forward in my life, because it usually means I'm going to someplace new. If I had my way, I'd remain motionless, never moving forward, never going anywhere. The thing is I always have to, it's not a choice, and I never know exactly where I'm going or who I'll be stuck with. Sometimes the families are fine, but sometimes not. Drunks. Religious freaks. Haters. Wandering hands.

The family I'm staying with now always tells me everything I do is wrong and that I should be more like their daughter, Jennifer. I'm not sure why they took me in to begin with. They seem pretty content with the child they have and I'm just a decoration, a flashy object they can show off to their friends so they can get told how great they are for taking in such a messed-up child. I'm the unwanted orphan they took in, hoping to fix me and make their family appear wonderful.

"It was so nice of you to give her a home," a woman with fiery red hair tells Amelia, who's my mother at the moment. She's having one of her neighborhood shindigs, which she does a lot, then complains about them later to her husband. "These poor children really do need a roof over their head."

Amelia glances at me, sitting in a chair at the table where I was directed to stay the entire party. "Yes, but it's hard, you know." She's wearing this yellow sweater that reminds me of a canary that was a pet at one of my foster parent's homes that never stopped chattering. She arranges some crackers and sliced cheese onto a large flowery platter and then heads for the refrigerator. "She's kind of a problem child." She opens the fridge door and takes out a large pitcher of lemonade. She looks over at me again, then leans toward the redhead, lowering her voice. "She's so angry all the time and she broke this vase the other day because she couldn't find her shoes...but we're working on fixing her."

Angry all the time. That's what everyone seems to say; I'm so angry at the world and it's understandable considering what I've been through, yet no one wants to deal with it. That I probably have too much rage inside me. That I'm broken. Unstable. Maybe even dangerous. All the things that no adult wants in a child. They want smiles and laughter, children who will make them smile and laugh, too. I'm the dark, morbid side of childhood. I swear they're waiting around for me to do something that will give them an excuse to get rid of me and they can tell everyone they tried but I was just too messed up to be fixed.

"And her nightmares," Amelia continues. "She wakes up screaming every night and she wet the bed the other night. She even came running into our room, saying she was scared to sleep alone." Her eyes glide to the tattered purple teddy bear I'm hugging. "She's very immature and carries that stuffed animal around with her everywhere...it's strange."

I hate her. She doesn't understand what it's like to see things that most people can't even admit exist. The ugly truth, painted in red, stuck in my head, images I can't shake. Death. Cruelty. Terror. People taking other peoples' lives as if lives mean nothing. Then they leave me behind to carry the foul, rotting truth with me. Alone. *Why did they leave me behind?*

This teddy bear is all I have left of a time when ugly didn't consume my life.

I turn my head away from the sound of her voice and stare out the window at the sunlight reflecting against a lawn ornament shaped like a tulip, and hug the teddy bear against my chest, the one my dad gave me as an early birthday present the day before he died. There are little red, heart-shaped beads on the tulip and when they catch in the light they flicker and make dots dance against the concrete on the back porch. It's pretty to watch and I focus on them, shoving my anger down and bottling it up—trying to stay in control of my emotions. Otherwise all the feelings I've buried will escape and I'll have no choice but to find a way to shut it down—find my adrenaline rush.

Besides, Amelia doesn't need to repeat what I already know. I know what I do every night, just like I know what I am to them, just like I know in a few months or so they'll get tired of me and send me to another place with a different home where everything I do will annoy those people, too, and eventually they'll pass me along. It's like clockwork and I don't expect anything more. Expecting only leads to disappointment. I expected things once when I was little—that I'd continue to grow up with my mom and dad, smile, and be happy—but that dream was crushed the day they died.

"Violet," Amelia snaps and I quickly turn my head to her. She and her redheaded friend are staring at me with worry and a hint of fear in their eyes and I wonder just how much her friend knows about me. Does she know about that night? What I saw? What I escaped? What I didn't escape? Does it make her afraid of me? "Are you listening to me?" she asks.

I shake my head. "No."

She crooks her eyebrow at me as she opens the cupboard above her head. "No, what?"

I set the teddy bear on my lap and tell myself to shut off the anger because the last time I released it, I ended up breaking lots of things, then got sent here. "No, ma'am."

Her eyebrow lowers as she selects a few cans of beans out from a top cupboard. "Good, now if you would just listen the first time then we'd be on track."

"I'm listening now," I say to her, which results in her face pinching. "Sorry. I'm listening now, ma'am."

She glares at me coldly as she stacks the cans on the countertop and takes a can opener out from a drawer. "I said would you go into the garage and get me some hamburger meat from the storage freezer."

I nod and hop off the chair, taking the teddy bear with me, relieved to get out of the stuffy kitchen and away from her friend who keeps looking at me like I'm about to stab her. As I head out the door into the garage I hear Amelia saying, "I think we might contact social services to take her back…she just wasn't what we were expecting."

Never expect anything, I want to turn around and tell her, but I continue out into the garage. The lights are on and I trot down the steps and wind around the midsize car toward the freezer in the corner. But I pause when I notice Jennifer in the corner, along with a boy and two girls who are messing around with bikes in the garage.

"Well, well look what the dog dragged in," she sneers as she moves her bike away from the wall. Her bike is pink, just like the dress she's wearing. I used to have a bike once, too, only it was purple, because I hate pink. But I never learned how to ride it and now it's part of my old life, boxed away and sold along with the rest of my childhood. "It's Violet and that stupid bear." She glances at her friends. "She always carries it around with her like a little baby or something."

I keep the bear close and disregard her the best that I can, because it's all I can do. This isn't my house or my family and no one's going to take my side. I'm alone in the world. It's something I learned early on and becoming used to the idea of always being alone has made life a little easier to live over the last several years.

I hurry past her and her friends who laugh when she utters under her breath that I smell like a homeless person. I open the freezer and take out a frozen pound of hamburger meat, then shut the lid and turn back for the door. Jennifer has abandoned her bike to strategically place herself in front of my path back to the door.

"Would you please move?" I ask politely, tucking the hamburger meat under one of my arms and my teddy bear under the other. I dodge to the side, but Jennifer sidesteps with me, her hands out to the side.

"Troll," the boy laughs and it's echoed by the cackling of laughter.

"This is my house," Jennifer says with a smirk. "Not yours, so you don't get to tell me what to do."

I hold up the hamburger meat, fighting to keep my temper under control. "Yeah, but your mom asked me to get this for her."

She puts her hands on her hips and says to me with an attitude, "That's because she thinks of you as our maid. In fact, I overheard her talking to my dad the other day, telling him that's why they're fostering you—because they needed someone to clean up the house."

Don't let her get to you. It doesn't matter. Nothing does. "Get out of my way," I say through gritted teeth.

She shakes her head. "No way. I don't have to listen to you, you loser, smelly, crazy girl."

The other kids laugh and it takes a lot of energy not to clock her in the face. *You were taught to be better than that. Mom and Dad would want me to be better.* I move around to the other side but she matches my step and kicks me in the shin. A throbbing pain ricochets up my leg, but I don't give her the satisfaction of a reaction, remaining calm.

"No wonder you don't have any parents. They probably didn't want you," she snickers. "Oh wait, that's right. They died...you probably even killed them yourself."

"Shut up," I warn, shaking as I step closer to her. I can feel anger blazing inside me, on the brink of exploding.

"Or what?" she says, refusing to back off. The boy on the floor stands up and starts to head toward us with a look on his face that makes me want to bolt. But I won't. I'm sure they'll chase me if I do and in the end I'm going to get blamed for this incident.

"What do you mean, she killed her parents?" he asks, wiping some grime off his forehead with his thumb.

Jennifer grins maliciously and then turns to him. "Haven't you heard the story about her?"

"Shut up." I cut her off as I move so close to her I almost knock her over, then raise my hand up in front of me, like I'm going to shove her. "I'm warning you."

She keeps talking as if I don't exist. "Her parents were murdered." She glances at me with hate and cruelty in her eyes. "I heard my mom saying she was the one who found them, but I'm guessing it's because she did it herself because she's *crazy*."

I see the image of my mom and dad in their bedroom surrounded by blood and I lose it. I quickly shove the image out of my head until all I see is red. Red everywhere. Blood. Red. Blood. Death. And a stupid little girl who won't walk away from it.

I throw the hamburger meat down on the ground, not concerned about what happens to me, and grab a handful of her long blond hair and yank on it. "Take it back!" I shout, pulling harder as I circle around to the front of the car, away from the boy, dragging Jennifer with me.

She starts to cry, her head tipped back, tears spilling out of her eyes. "You evil bitch!"

"Let her go!" the boy yells, running around the car at us. "You crazy psycho." He turns to the other girls and tells them to go get someone and then they take off running, looking at me like I'm crazy, too.

I know it'll be just moments before Amelia comes out and then not too long after she'll call social services to come take me away. I'm trembling with anger and hate all directed toward Jennifer, because she's the one here in front of me. No one else. My vision blurs along with my head and my heart and it feels like I'm back at my childhood home walking into the room again, seeing the blood...hearing the voices...

I'm trembling so much my fingers have no strength left to hold on to Jennifer and I release her. She immediately stumbles forward into the front of the car. Regaining her balance, she spins around and shoves me so hard I fall to the ground and my head bangs against the wall.

"You psycho!" she shouts, her face bright red, tears streaming out of her eyes. "My mom and dad are so going to send you away."

I stare at the space on the floor in front of her feet, hugging my teddy bear, motionless.

She lets out a frustrated grunt and then stomps her foot on the floor before running out of the garage.

Moments later, Amelia comes rushing in, shouting before she even reaches me. "You're done here! Do you understand?"

19

"Yes." I don't have a single drop of emotion left and my voice sounds hollow.

"Yes, what?" She waits for me to answer her with her arms crossed.

I don't reply because I don't have to anymore. I'm finished with this home. There's no erasing what just happened. I can't change the past just as much as I can't control my future.

She gets livid, her face tinting pink as she tries to contain her fury. She tells me I'm worthless. She tells me that no one will want me. She tells me I'm leaving. She tells me everything I already know.

"Are you even listening to me?!" she shouts and I shake my head. Fuming, she snatches the bear from my hands.

That snaps me out of my motionless trance. "Hey, that's mine!" I cry, jumping to my feet and lunging for the bear. My shoulder bumps into her arm as she moves it out of my reach.

She moves back and tucks her arm behind her back. "Consider it a punishment for hurting my daughter."

"Your daughter deserved it." I panic. If she does anything to that bear I won't be able to take it. I need that bear or else I can't survive—don't want to. *Why did I survive?*

"Well, when you're ready to apologize to Jennifer, you can have it back." She heads toward the door to the house where Jennifer is standing with a smile on her face, expecting an apology.

"Sorry," I practically growl, wanting the damn bear back enough that I'll do whatever she asks at the moment. "Please, don't take it away." Desperation burns in my voice. "It's all I have left of my mom and dad—it's all I have of them." I'm begging, weak, pathetic. I hate it. I hate myself. But I need that bear.

Jennifer grins at me as she crosses her arms and leans against the doorway, her cheeks stained red from the drying tears. "Mom, I don't think she's really sorry."

Amelia studies me for a moment. "I don't think she is either." She frowns disappointedly, like she's finally seeing that she can't fix me, then turns for the door with my bear in her hand. "You can have it back when I see a real apology come out of that mouth of yours. And you better make it quick because you won't be here for very much longer."

"I said I was sorry," I yell out with my hands balled into fists at my side. "What the hell else do you want me to say?"

She doesn't answer me and goes into the house with my bear. Jennifer smirks at me before turning for the house, shutting the lights off and then closing the door on her way inside.

I'm suffocated by the dark. But it's nothing I can't handle. Seeing things is much harder than seeing nothing but the dark. I like the dark.

I slide down to the ground and lean back against the wall, hugging my knees to my chest as I let the darkness settle over me. A few tears slip out and drip down my cheeks and I let more stream out, telling myself it's okay, because I'm in the dark, and nothing can be seen in the dark.

But after a while I can't get the tears to stop as what

Jennifer and the other kids said plays on repeat inside my head. I think about the last time I saw my parents lying in their coffins and how they got there. The blood. I'll never forget the blood. On the floor. On me.

More tears spill out and soon my whole face is drenched with them. My heart thrashes against my chest and I tug at my hair as I scream through clenched teeth, kicking my feet against the floor. Invisible razors and needles stab underneath my skin. I can't turn off the emotions. I can't think straight. My lungs need air. I hurt. I ache. I can't take it anymore. I need it out. I need to breathe.

I stumble to my feet and through the dark, until I find the door that leads to the driveway. I shove the door open, sprint outside into the sunlight and race past the cars parked in the driveway and toward the curb. I don't slow down until I'm approaching the highway in front of the house where cars zip up and down the road. With no hesitation, I walk into the middle of the road and stand on the yellow dotted line with my arms held out to the side. Tears pool in my eyes as I blink against the sunlight, my pulse speeding up the longer I stay there and that rush of energy that has become the only familiar thing in my life takes over.

It feels like I'm flying, head-on into something other than being moved around, passed around, given away, tossed aside, forgotten. I have the unknown in front of me and I have no idea what's going to happen. It feels so liberating. So I stay in place, even when I hear the roar of a car's engine. I wait until

I hear the sound of the tires. Until I see the car. Until it's close enough that the driver honks their horn. Until I feel the swish of an adrenaline rush, drenching the sadness and panic out of my body and mind. Until my emotions subside and all I feel is exhilaration. Then I jump to the right where the road meets the grass as the car makes a swerve to the left to go around me. Brakes screech. A horn honks. Someone shouts.

I lie soundless in the grass, feeling twenty times better than I did in the garage. I feel content in a dark hole of numbness; a place where I can feel okay being the child that no one wants. The child that probably would have been better off dying with her parents, instead of being left alive and alone.

Chapter One

Violet

(Freshman year of college)

I've got my fake smile plastered on my face and no one in the crowd of people surrounding me can tell if it's real or not. None of them really give a shit either, just like I don't. I'm only here, pretending to be a ray of sunshine, for three reasons: (1) I owe Preston, my last foster parent I had before I turned eighteen, big time, because he gave me a home when no one else would; and (2) because I need the money; and (3) I love the rush of knowing that at any moment I could get busted—so much that it's become addicting, like an alcoholic craves booze.

"You want a shot?" the guy—I think his name is Jason or Jessie or some other J name—calls out over the bubbly song beating through the speakers. He raises an empty glass in front of my face, his gray eyes glazed over with intoxication and stupidity, which are pretty much one and the same.

I shake my head, my faux smile dazzling on my face. I wear it almost like a necklace, shiny and making me look pretty when I'm out in public, then when I go home I can take it off and toss it aside. "No thanks."

"You sure?" he questions, then slants his head back and guzzles the rest of his beer. A trail drizzles from his mouth down to his navy blue polo shirt.

I'm about to say *Yes, I'm sure,* but then stop and nod, knowing it's always good to blend in. It makes me look less sketchy and people less edgy and more trusting. "Yeah, why the hell not." I aim to say it lightly even though I loathe the fiery taste of hard alcohol. I rarely drink it, but not just because of the taste. It's what I do when it's in my system, how my angry, erratic, self-destructing alter ego comes out, that makes it necessary that I stay sober. At least when I'm sober, I have control over the reckless things that I do, but when I'm drunk it's a whole other ballgame, one I don't feel like playing tonight. I already have a barely touched beer in my hand and have no plans on finishing it.

Jessie or Jason smiles this big, goofy, very unflattering smile. "Fuck yeah!" he practically shouts, like we're celebrating and I want to roll my eyes. He lifts his hand for me to high-five and I slam my palm against it with a frustrated inner sigh, even though it's a good sign because it means he's veering toward becoming an incoherent, drunk idiot.

It's always the same routine. Get them drunk and then I can get more money. It's what Preston taught me to do and what I do pretty much every weekend now, hitting up the parties around the nearby towns. Never in the town I go to college in, though. That would be too risky and way too easy to get noticed according to Preston.

I'm wearing a tight black dress that shows off what little curves I have, along with my leather jacket, and thigh-high lace-up boots. My curly black hair that's streaked red hangs down my back, hiding the dragon tattoo and two small stars on the back of my neck, each star drawn to represent the people who have loved me in life. I usually wear my hair down because guys always seem to like to run their fingers through it, like they get their kicks and giggles from the softness. Personally, I have no opinion about it, although a lot of girls seem to gush over guys playing with their hair. Let them touch it if they want, just as long as I get paid at the end of this charade.

J, as I'm going to call him because I honestly can't remember his name, pours two shots of tequila, spilling some on the countertop. When he hands it to me I slam it back without so much as flinching, filling up my mouth with the disgusting drink, then I quickly move my beer up to my lips, pretending to chase the shot with it, when really I spit the tequila into the bottle. I smile as I move the bottle away from my mouth and set the empty shot glass down on the counter. Preston would be so proud of me right now, since he taught me that little trick as a way to stay sober when everyone else is getting drunk to avoid mistakes with the deal. And I'm glad, because mistakes with Preston never go over well.

"Another?" J asks, pointing a finger at the glass.

I decide it's time to move on from shots and on to taking care of business. I dazzle him with my best plastic smile as I set my beer down on the counter. I stained my lips a bright red before I left and my dress is low-cut enough to show a sliver of my cleavage, created by a push-up bra. It's all a distraction, a costume to keep them focused on something else besides the deal. Distractions equal mistakes.

I grab the bottom of his shirt and bat my eyelashes at him as I lean in, trying not to scrunch my nose at the foul scent of alcohol on his breath. "How about you take me to your room?" I breathe against his cheek. "So we can take care of some business."

He blinks his blue eyes through his drunkenness, alarmed by my bluntness. Most people are. And that's what I love about it. Throw them off. Never let them know what's really hidden in me. Never let anyone in because no one really wants to get in, not for good reasons anyway.

"Okay," he slurs, dropping the bottle of tequila down onto the countertop, and then he drags his fingers through his clean-cut blond hair.

I keep smiling as I grab a lime slice from off the counter and shove it into my mouth. I suck the juice off so that I can get the damn tequila taste out of my mouth. It tastes bitterly sweet, but better than the burn of the alcohol. After I'm done with it, I discard it onto the counter and scoop up the bottle of tequila.

"Lead the way," I say to J and he gives me another one of those goofy drunk smiles of his, probably thinking he's going to get lucky after we make the deal. Most guys do which is why Preston loves having me do this for him. *You're a distraction*, he always tells me. *A very beautiful, enticing distraction.*

Deep down, I know I could do it. Fool around with J and probably feel fine afterward. I can turn off everything I'm feeling in the snap of a finger and put it away, only bringing it out when needed. I wouldn't feel a single part of it, which makes doing things I don't necessarily want to do easier. Plus J's not that bad looking, although he's a little too athletic and preppy for me. He's tall, with broad shoulders, and lean muscles, his entire body screaming that he spends way too much time at the gym. I wonder if he's a jock, but I'm not going to ask him. Just like I'm not going to fool around with him.

He takes my hand, his palms clammy, and he leads me through the crowd of college-age people packed in the townhouse living room, where a game of beer pong is going on. A few of the girls shoot me dirty looks, like I don't belong with a clean-cut guy like J who's wearing a collared shirt and a watch that probably cost more than all the money I've spent in my entire life. And I'm fine with it, too high on the thrill of what I'm doing—what I'm about to do. The danger. The instability. The adrenaline.

When we reach the hall, we disappear out of the sight of all the judgmental eyes and lucky for me, J's not doing that great. His feet can barely carry him as he stumbles his way to the last door in the hall, hauling me with him.

"Whoops." He giggles like a girl as he turns the doorknob. "I'm sorry."

I have no idea what he's sorry for, but I just smile. "It's fine."

He grins again, stealing the bottle of tequila from out of my hand. He tips his head back and knocks back a mouthful, gagging as he moves the bottle away from his lips. Then he aims it at me.

Not having my beer to spit it back in, I grab the bottle and set it down on a small bookshelf nestled in the corner. "Let's take a little break from drinking, okay?"

"Sure," he says, trying to stun me with an award-winning smile. "How 'bout we just get ya in here and get ya out of those clothes of yours." His gaze scales my body and I briefly contemplate clocking him in the face. I know that look way too well, just like I know what he wants way too well.

I give him a little shove so he stumbles across the dark, empty bedroom. I follow him as he continues to stagger back and then lands on the bed. I shut the door and lock it without taking my eyes off him as he lies there on the mattress. Soft moonlight filters in through the window and lights up the dazedness on his face.

"Come...here..." He props up on his elbows, working to keep his head up.

I saunter toward him, glancing around at the clothes scattered around the large room decorated with a dresser set that matches his king-size bed.

"How about we talk some business," I tell him, positioning myself in front of where his legs hang over the edge of the mattress.

He shakes his head determinedly, and then flops his hand toward the leather belt looped through his slacks. I watch him fight with the buckle for a while and then growing impatient, I finally unhook the buckle myself, and jerk it from his belt loop.

"I knew you'd like to play rough." He laughs and starts to sit up, his fingers seeking my waist. But I gently shove him back by the chest so he's lying flat on the bed.

I toss the belt onto the dresser. "I didn't come here to play."

"Preston promised you'd take…you take…" He blinks around the room, looking lost. "That you'd take care of me first."

I roll my eyes. *Damn it, Preston.* I hate when he promises stuff. If he'd just be vague about what was going to go down, then I wouldn't get in so much trouble when I don't follow through. Then again, most of them can't remember that much about what happens anyway.

"I will, baby," I lie, cringing at my endearing term, but doing what I have to do to smooth things over. I reach for my jacket pocket and take out the small bag of pills. If I'm lucky he'll try one and then quickly pass out. "But first I need you to pay up."

Shifting his weight to the side, he snatches the bag out of my hand and then scoots back so he can sit up. He totters as he sits up straight, then when he gets settled he opens the bag. He glances inside it, pretending like he's checking to see he's not getting ripped off, even though it's too dark to count the pills.

"You got the cash?" I scan his room, his stereo on the nightstand, the open closet overflowing with clothes, and the closed armoire in the corner. I can't see a wallet anywhere, so I'm guessing he's got it tucked in his pocket. Things just got a little complicated if he decides to be a pain in the ass about paying.

"Cash comes after we play," he says, but I shake my head, ready to be done with this deal. I'm about to tell him to pay up, when he has an abrupt burst of energy. He throws the bag of pills aside and his fingers quickly jab into my waist. He jerks me toward him and I lose my balance and fall down on him as he collapses back onto the mattress.

He starts sucking my neck, his wet tongue placing sloppy kisses all over my skin as his hands start to wander up my leg toward the bottom of my dress. His breath reeks of tequila and cigarettes. "God, you smell so good." His fingers pinch down into my skin and it kind of stings. "I bet you like it wild... you sure as hell look like you do."

I roll my eyes. If I had a penny for every time I heard that, I wouldn't have to be here dealing.

Turning my head, I lean to the side and try to slip out of his grip. His hold on me starts to loosen, but he continues to kiss my neck, his hands moving all over my ass and slipping between my legs. I'm starting to get bored, my mind wandering to homework, finals, moving back in with Preston in a few weeks.

J moans against my mouth. "I'm so hard for you right now, baby." He rubs the evidence that he is against my leg and runs his fingers through my hair.

I get a little annoyed by his pet name and that I've become a humping post. I'm about to gently knee him in the balls and get rid of his hardness for him, ending this tiring situation, when he stops kissing me and slumps backward. He mutters something about me being a cock tease and then his head flops against the mattress. His eyes drift shut and seconds later he's passed out, his chest rising and falling as he breathes loudly.

"Thank God." I slip out from his arms and climb off him.

Although the situation has gotten more complicated, I'm glad he passed out. After a lot of deliberating on what I should do, I decide it's best to leave it up to Preston so I take out my phone and dial his number.

"What's up, beautiful?" he asks after three rings.

I climb off the bed and pace in front of it. "I got a dilemma."

"What'd you do now?" he asks in that flirty tone he uses on everyone. Even guys. It's just how he is and I know he really doesn't mean anything by it. Besides, he's eight years older than me.

"I didn't do anything." I glance over at J. "Well, not really… J…that guy you were having me deliver to, passed out."

"And?" I can hear the laughter in his voice.

"And I want to know what you want me to do." I stop pacing and look down at J with his legs and arms sprawled out to the side. "Do you want me to just grab his cash or really screw him over and take the pills, too?"

It takes Preston a while to answer. I can hear voices in the background, which probably means he's at a party. "What do you think you should do?" he finally asks me.

"I know what I want to do," I answer, biting on my fingernails, a bad habit of mine I can't seem to break. "But I mean, it's really your thing. I'm just doing it as a favor to you and I'm done once I finish paying for my tuition. You know that."

"A favor to me, huh?" he deliberates. "How disappointing. All this time and I thought you were doing it because you secretly were in love with me."

I roll my eyes at his twisted sense of humor. "You did not."

"I did, too."

"Did not."

"Did—"

"Stop." I cut him off because this could go on forever and J is starting to stir. "Look, I really want to get out of here. I've got a final to study for. And a life to get back to." The last part is kind of a lie, but it sounds like a good point to make in theory. "So should I take the pills and the cash or just the cash?"

He pauses. "How much does he have on him?"

I sigh and pat the front pockets in J's slacks, but they're empty. Pressing the phone between my cheek and my shoulder

I use both my hands to rotate him on his side and then I check his back pockets and find his wallet in one of them. I take it out and step away from the bed, opening it and counting the money inside.

"There's a hundred bucks in his wallet." I frown, knowing what it means.

"Well, isn't that interesting, since I told him it was going to be two hundred bucks for a bag," Preston replies in a calm voice.

"So you want me to take the pills, too," I say flatly. Sometimes when I'm doing something I'm not totally comfortable with, like stealing from an unconscious guy, my conscience tries to wake up on me.

"I think it's only fair," he replies simply. "Especially since he was obviously going to screw you over."

"Maybe he has the money somewhere else," I suggest, but even I can hear the doubt in my voice.

"Or maybe he was just going to try and fuck you over," he says. "Literally."

I blow out a breath and take the cash out of the wallet, feeling the slightest bit guilty. Then I drop the wallet onto the bed, reach over J, and snatch up the bag of pills. I put the cash and pills into my pocket, then head for the door.

"Give me like a half an hour and I'll be at your house," I tell Preston, opening the door.

"Sounds good," he replies as the music in the hall drowns

over me. "And, Violet, remember, I'm a nice guy and everything but don't try to screw me over." He always says this as a warning, reminding me that business comes before our friendship…our foster-parent bond…whatever the hell we have. He used to not be this intense when I was younger, but now he'll say just about anything. It makes me nervous and uncomfortable, but I never say anything about it, worried I'll lose the only family I have.

"I remember." I step out into the hall, but halt when I spot a group of guys I'm pretty sure I've scammed before, standing at the end of the hall. "Look, I got to go." I hang up and stuff the phone into my jacket pocket.

One of the guys with a really thick neck points at me, saying something, and the rest of their gazes wander in my direction.

"Hey, I know you, don't I?" the tallest one says as he strolls down the hall in my direction. "You're that girl, right? The one who sold me the stuff at that party a month ago. The one that fucking screwed me over." I spot anger in his eyes at the same time I note the thickness of his arms that can easily hurt me. For a moment, I just stand there, letting the group of them get close to me, feeling the beat of my heart accelerate inside my chest, alive and thriving—finally awake.

But when they're almost within arm's reach, I whirl around and run back into the bedroom where J's sleeping. I lock the door and then search through the dark for a solution.

"Open the door, you fucking cunt!" One of them bangs

on the door as they shout loudly over the music and J lets out a loud snore.

It's not the first time I've been in this kind of situation, and I doubt it will be my last. I wonder what my mom and dad would think of me if they were here now? Would they be ashamed? But they're not here and there's no one else in the world that really gives a shit what I do with my life. I can't just wait around here and wait for something—or someone to show up and miraculously help me. I'm in this on my own, which is for the story of my life.

Striding over to the window, I pry it open and pop the screen off. Tossing it onto the floor, I lean over the edge and look down the two-story drop to the wooden fence right below the window. It's not that far of a fall, but if I land on the fence things could go badly, like one of the pieces of wood could get lodged in my body or I could land the wrong way and hit my neck or head on it. They're such morbid thoughts, but my mind always goes to that dark place. The what-ifs of death. Those random occurrences that no one can control. Most of my life has been based on one random occurrence of death.

I know if I jump, either I'll safely land on the grass just over the fence or I'll mess up and get hurt, maybe even killed if random occurrences really hate me. Either way, I don't care what the hell happens to me, so I climb up onto the window-sill, letting destiny take over as I slide my legs over the edge. I hear the lock on the door click and open. My time here at this place is up.

My heart speeds up and I breathe in the rush of knowing that something tragic could happen to me. It makes me feel alive and without any hesitation, I jump.

Luke

(Freshman year of college)

My night has been filled with shot after shot. Empty glass after empty glass. I knock back one after another as the sound of the music vibrates inside my chest. With each scorching swallow of Bacardi, tequila, Jäger, I feel more at ease, letting all my worries and the fact that I haven't checked my blood glucose slowly erase from my mind. My tongue becomes numb. My lips. My body. My heart. My mind. It's a fucking beautiful state of mind to be in and I wish I could never leave it—most days I don't.

After I lose count of how many shots I've downed and how many asses I've had grind up against me, I ditch the club with the woman I've been dancing with for the last two songs, debating what to do—fuck, wander around, go find a place to gamble. There's a familiar burn inside my chest as I drown in a sea of alcohol, where nothing bothers me. I relax and breathe the cool night air and just exist without all the weight of my past inside me. I've been drinking more frequently, especially since my past has been forcing its way into my life again. Stuff's been happening with my sister, Amy, specifically questions about her suicide that happened eight years ago. I thought it'd been put to rest, but it was brought up a month or so ago, questions mainly about what really drove her to throw herself off the roof that night. Plus, on top of it, my dad's decided he wants to become a huge part of my life again, after being pretty much absent since I was five. It's bullshit and I don't want to think about it or deal with it. I just want to get trashed, fuck as many women as I can, and live my life the way that I want to.

I lose track of how much time has gone but somewhere along the lines I stop walking and end up with my back against the tree. I'm not aware of too much going on but there are three things I'm sure of: (a) It's nighttime, since I can see the stars, (b) I feel very relaxed and in control at the moment, and (c) there's a blonde kneeling down in front of me with her mouth on my cock.

I have a fistful of her hair as she sucks me off, muttering something incoherent every once in a while. As she moves her mouth back and forth I feel myself verging closer to exploding and I let myself go as I approach it. It's the only few moments of peace that I have, where I don't have to think about the past, the future, just the God damn moment. Once I'm done, though, the silence of the night tears at my chest as there's nothing left to do but think. I'm back to that place where my past and who I am haunts me. The only thing that gets me through is the fact that my body is numbed by the potent amount of alcohol in my bloodstream.

I zip up my pants as the blonde gets back up to her feet. She mutters something about that being amazing, biting her lip as she tracks her fingers up my chest, looking like she's waiting for me to return the favor. I'm not going to, though. I only do things for myself and no one else. I spent too much time when I was younger living under restrictions, never living for myself, never enjoying things, and I refuse to go back to that place again.

I shove her hand off and head down the sidewalk, hoping she'll just stay behind. But she follows, her high heels clicking against the concrete as she rushes to keep up.

"God, it's such a beautiful night," she says with a contented sigh.

"If you say so," I say. "Don't you need to go back to the club and catch a ride home?"

"You said you were going to take me home," she reminds me, rushing to keep up with me.

"I did?" I sway as a maneuver around what looks like a bush in the middle of the sidewalk…no, that can't be right. I bump my hip on a fence and stumble off the grass and back onto the sidewalk

"Yeah, you said you'd love to give me a ride." She braces herself by grabbing my shoulder, then giggles. God, I hate gigglers. I really need to start paying more attention when I pick them up to avoid getting stuck with a Miss Fucking Giggles.

"I'm pretty sure you misunderstood me." I move my shoulder out from under her hand, stepping back onto the grass, and causing her to miss a step. She looks stunned, but still grins at me as she adjusts her boobs in her dress, pushing them up so they bulge out. I'm sure she does it on purpose, trying to remind me what she's giving me if I take her back to my place, but what she doesn't realize is that I've already had it. A lot. And I don't care about what she gives to me as much as I care about what I took from her back behind the tree.

There's a party going on in one of the townhouses nearby and music booms and vibrates the ground. We're walking in the ritzier side of town, made up of two-story townhouses, the yards matching, and the sidewalk is lined with trees and a fence. I'm not even sure how I got here, nor do I know the way back to my dorm. Sometimes I wonder how the hell I get into these messes.

I really need to stop drinking.

I laugh at my own absurd thought as I stop to retrieve my cigarettes from my shirt pocket. The only time I can actually deal with the chaotic aspects of life is when I'm drunk, otherwise I panic for some structure. I never had structure when I was a kid. I had a crazy mom who did crazy shit and dragged me into her crazy world, making me feel crazy with her. I still have nightmares about some of the stuff I saw or heard her do and I need order, otherwise the vile, sick feeling I experienced when I was a kid owns me.

I pop a cigarette into my mouth and light the end with a lighter I dig out of the back pocket of my jeans. I deeply inhale and blow out a cloud of smoke, then I start walking again,

41

zigzagging back and forth between the sidewalk and the grass just to the side of it, running into the fence a few times.

"Where are we going?" the blonde asks as she tugs on the bottom of her dress, hurrying to keep up with me.

I graze my thumb on the end of the cigarette and ash it onto the ground. "*I'm* going to my place."

"That's cool," she says with a slight slur to her speech, not taking my not-so-subtle hint. "We can just walk wherever."

She doesn't look that drunk and she only drank girly fruity drinks at the club, but her voice is portraying otherwise. She's putting a lot of trust in me at the moment, to get her wherever it is she's going and whatever it is she's looking for. Maybe sex. The best orgasm of her life. A fleeting escape from reality. Maybe she's looking for love or someone she can connect with. From the needy, I'll-do-anything-you-want look in her eyes, I'm guessing it's the latter. And if it is, she's not going to get it from me.

I consider my two options. I can take her back behind a tree again and just bang the shit out of her until she's crying out my name and I get a few more moments away from the helpless, drowning feeling inside me—get the control I need. Or I can call my friend and roommate, Kayden, to come pick my drunken ass up, because I'm getting exhausted.

I'm battling my indecisiveness when I hear this strange swooshing sound coming from above me. I look up just in time to see something tumble out the window of the townhouse we're passing.

I stagger back onto the grass as it falls toward me and stick out my arm to push Blondie back. The tips of a pair of clunky boots clip my forehead and I stumble over my feet as something lands on the grass in front of me and rolls down the shallow incline toward the sidewalk.

"What the hell," Blondie says as she rolls her ankle and her foot slips out of her shoe. She quickly works to fix her hair, smoothing her hands over it.

Catching my breath, I shake my head, which is going to hurt like hell in the morning when I sober up. Usually when I'm this wasted my heart goes still, but my pulse has forced its way through the multiple shots I hammered back and suddenly I feel sober.

Blowing out a tense breath, I focus on whatever the hell just fell from the window as I mentally tell my heart rate to shut the fuck up. At first I think I'm seeing things, so I blink my eyes a few times at the...person...a girl lying on her back, groaning as she clutches her ankle.

"God damn it...that hurt," she moans, rolling to her side.

My heart is still racing and I move my hand toward my mouth to take a drag, hoping nicotine will settle it down but realize I've lost my cigarette somewhere. "Shit, are you okay?" I drag my fingers through my cropped brown hair as I glance up at the window she fell from, then back at her, wondering if I should help her up or something.

She releases a grunting breath as she gets up on her hands and knees and pushes to her feet. Her legs wobble as she gets to her feet, then she limps forward, trying not to put weight on her right ankle. "Yeah, I'm fine." Her voice is tight, and normally I'd back off from her leave-me-the-fuck-alone attitude, but she just fell out of a fucking window and a painful sense of déjà vu hits me square in the chest as I wonder if Amy fell the same way.

"Did you hurt your foot or something?" I follow after her as she limps down the sidewalk. Blondie calls out that she can't find her shoe, but I ignore her, walking after the girl. I'm not even one-hundred-percent sure why other than I'm worried she might be hurt or that she might have been trying to hurt herself on purpose, like my sister Amy did, only she never walked away from it.

"I'm fine," she says and then picks up her pace when a guy shouts something out the window she fell from. "Now go away."

I look down at her ankle, hidden under her boot. It's obvious it's causing her pain by the way she won't put pressure on it. "You shouldn't be putting weight on it if it hurts. You could fuck it up more."

At the corner of the sidewalk, she veers to the left, and steps into the light of the lampposts surrounding the parking lot. I finally get a good look at her and recognition clicks. She's got long black hair with streaks of red in it that match the shade of her plump lips. She's wearing a leather jacket over a tight black dress and her boots—the ones that put a lump on my head—go all the way up her long legs, stopping at her thighs.

"Hey, I know you," I state as we step off the curb. "Don't I?"

"How should I know?" She peers over her shoulder at me, giving me a once-over. I can tell she does know me, by the recognition in her expression, just like I'm almost certain I know her.

She continues to hobble toward a row of parked cars and I walk with her.

"Wait... I've seen you around at UW... We have Chemistry together." I make the connection as she stuffs her hand into the pocket of her jacket. "And I think you're Callie Lawrence's roommate?" I point a finger at her. "Violet... something or other?"

She shakes her head as she removes her keys from her pocket. "And you're Luke Price. The stoically aloof and somewhat intense man-whore/football player who dorms it up with Kayden Owens." She stops in front of a battered up Cadillac. "Yeah, we know each other. So what?" She extends her hand toward the lock on the door, holding the key, but I grab her arm and stop her.

"Wait, 'stoically aloof'?" I ask, slightly offended. "What the hell does that mean?" I've crossed paths with her quite a few times, but never actually talked to her. I've heard Callie say she's intense, which I'm getting right now. But people say that

45

about me, too, and it's for a reason. A dark reason I don't like to talk about. I wonder if she has a reason, too, or if she's just a bitch. Plain and simple.

"It means whatever the hell you want it to mean." She jams the key into the lock and unlocks the door, glancing over the roof of the car. "Now will you please let go of my arm?"

I'd completely forgotten that I was touching her and I instantly let go, tracking the line of her gaze to the sidewalk and a guy heading toward us. When I look back at her, there's panic in her eyes, but when she notices me staring at her, the look quickly disappears and is replaced by indifference.

"Is that guy messing with you?" I ask. "Because if he is I can kick his ass if you need me to." I cringe as I say it because most of the time when I start swinging punches I have a hard time stopping.

She seems shocked for a very intense split second but then again the look vanishes. "I can take care of myself." She leans into the car and falls into the driver's seat. She puts her hand on the steering wheel and takes a breath before looking up at me. "Look, I'm sorry I kicked you in the face during my fall." She carefully pulls her leg in, wincing from the pain. "I didn't mean to."

I touch my finger to my forehead, feeling the forming lump. "It's not a big deal," I tell her. "But I'd really like to know why you...fell out the window." I'm not sure if "fell" is the right word. She could have jumped. On purpose. For so many reasons.

"I didn't fall…I jumped." She stares up at me and I see something in her eyes. I have to search my hazy brain for what it is, but finally I get there. Detachment. Like she feels and cares about nothing. For a brief second I envy her.

Before I can say anything else, she glances through the windshield at the guy who's reached the border of the parking lot and then she slams the car door. She revs the engine and I have to jump back as she peels out of the parking lot, driving away like her life depends on it and all I can wonder is what the hell she's running from.

Chapter Two

Violet

I'm supposed to be sleeping, but I'm too excited to sleep. My sixth birthday's tomorrow and I can't wait to see all my presents. My dad already gave me one, a really cute purple bear with a pretty bow on the front of it. He told me that I was too special not to get one of my presents early, but that I'd have to wait for the rest tomorrow.

It's really late and I can see the moon outside my window, looking like a half-eaten cookie. The stars sparkle like the glitter on my pajamas and my nightlight in the corner of my room keeps flickering. It was the Fourth of July today and I can still hear some of the fireworks the neighbors must be setting off.

I lie in my bed staring at the glow-in-the-dark stickers on the ceiling, some shaped as hearts, some as stars. I try to close my eyes, but it's not working. Finally, I decide to get out of bed and go down to my toy room in the basement. Maybe if I play with my toys for a while then I can stop thinking so much about all the toys that I'm going to get tomorrow.

Taking my new teddy bear and the flashlight I keep in my nightstand drawer, I tiptoe down the stairs. I pause at the bottom, staring at the window in the living room where I can see showers of red and silver sparks glittering in the sky. It's so pretty and I stop at the bottom of the stairs to get a good look at them. When the colors fade, I turn for the basement door and open it. A lot of the kids I know are afraid of the basement, but mine's not that bad. My dad even let me paint my favorite flowers on the walls and I get to keep all my toys down here, too.

I don't flip on the light, instead I use my flashlight because I'm not supposed to be out of bed this late at night, but the moon and fireworks shower light through the window. Once I get the flashlight turned on, I skip down the stairs to where my toys are stacked in boxes around the room. There's also a chair in the corner by a bookshelf where I have a ton of books. I love to read about anything. Princesses. Monsters. Magical kingdoms. I asked my dad once if stuff like that really existed and he told me of course and asked what fun would life be if fairy tales weren't secretly real.

I go over to the bookshelf, deciding I'll read for a while, and maybe that will help me fall asleep. My favorite one isn't on the shelf, though, so I go to the storage room where there are more books stacked on the floor. My dad loves to read, too, and we have so many books that there's really nowhere to put them. At least that's what my mom says.

I set the teddy bear down on the floor and shine the light on the first pile of books I come across. They're all my dad's books so I kneel down in front of the next stack, reading over the titles. Finally I find it, but as I'm pulling it out of the stack I hear a noise coming from my toy room. It sounds like scratching or scraping maybe and my mind instantly goes to the possibility that maybe it's a monster or a dragon or something else with claws. My hand shakes a little as I stand up and turn back toward the room. When I step into it, I feel the wind hit my cheeks. I shine the light around and notice one of the windows is open. I don't understand why. I didn't open it and I don't think it was open when I came down here. What if it was a monster?

I sweep the flashlight around the room at all my toys as I start back toward the corner. Then the light lands on something tall... I hear voices. Ones that don't sound like they belong to a monster, but just people. But that's what they end up being.

Terrible, horrible monsters.

❧

I wake up gasping for air, clutching my blanket, my heart thrashing inside my chest, my lungs desperately seeking air as I hold my teddy bear tightly against me. It's like I'm drowning and for a moment I actually think I'm buried beneath the water. It's how I've woken up every morning for the last thirteen years. I used to breathe as loud as possible, but I've had to train myself to be quieter since I have a roommate now. As my eyes open to the sunlight, my breathing ragged, I quickly roll over and bury my face in the pillow, smothering the fear and panic out of me. I grip handfuls of blanket, reminding myself that I'm not drowning, that it just feels like it. That monsters don't really exist. That it was just people. Really terrible people who did something really fucked up and never got caught. Never had to pay. Just went on living, hiding their evil fangs and claws, while I was left to wander the world alone.

I breathe in and out until my face becomes hot and the scent of the fabric softener in the pillowcase overwhelms my nostrils, then I turn to the side, facing the wall, sliding the bear aside. I can sense that my roommate, Callie, is awake and I don't want to see her looking at me. She's got music playing on the stereo, some girl bellowing out lyrics to a poetic song. It's not really my kind of music. I like the rougher kind that will drown out the thoughts inside my head and the emptiness in my heart. But the soft beat of this one is kind of soothing, I guess.

I lie there with my head on the pillow, staring at the wall, deciding if it's worth moving today or not. My body feels like it's been run over by a truck, like every single one of my limbs is dislocated and my organs have burst open. I'm fairly sure I'm okay, though, except for my ankle. Last night it was so swollen I could barely get it out of my boot. I landed very awkwardly

51

when I jumped out the window and I'm pretty sure I felt something pop. There's nothing I can do about it, though. I won't go to the student health clinic and see a rent-a-doctor and I'm not going to go to a real doctor. I don't have the money for that and I don't want to get into debt more than I already am over tuition. I hate owing people things. It makes me dependent and dependency leads to getting hurt. It's going to suck, though, when I have to go to my part-time job, waitressing at Moonlight Dining and Drinks.

After a while, Callie turns down the music and then I hear her moving around, rustling through papers, opening and closing drawers. Then it gets quiet.

"Violet," she says and I tense. When we moved into the dorm, we kind of established without really talking about it, a no-talking-to-each-other-unless-necessary rule, so it's weird she's speaking to me. Plus I think she thinks I'm a prostitute or at least a slut because I created a rule that when I tie a red scarf onto the doorknob, she can't come into the room. Really, I'm just dealing, but she doesn't need to know that. It's better if she just thinks I'm a slut, even if I'm still a virgin.

I remain motionless, even when I hear her walk up to the side of my bed, hoping she'll give up and leave. It's not like I hate her or anything. Callie actually bothers me less than most people, but that's because she rarely talks. She never really asks me for anything, either, like privacy in the room, but sometimes I willingly give it to her because I don't want to walk in on her again with her football player boyfriend. Those two like each other too much.

Finally she leaves and shuts the door behind her and I'm free to breathe as loud as I want to. I roll over to my side, wincing at the pain in my ankle. Damn it, it hurts, but I'll live. It could have been a lot worse and I sort of wish that it had been. A little more dangerous, maybe landing closer to the fence instead of kicking that football player in the forehead. I wonder if his head's okay. I did kick it kind of hard, but not on purpose. Usually when I kick a guy I have a good reason to, but this time he was just in the wrong place at the wrong time. Or maybe I was.

I check the clock over on the desk and realize it's later than I thought. My chemistry class is going to start soon. I need to get up and moving. I carefully sit up in the bed, slowly as my muscles ache in protest. I'm still wearing the dress I had on last night because I was too tired when I got to my dorm to bother changing into my pajamas. The fabric reeks like cigarettes and booze, which usually happens whenever I go to a party. The stench of partying, no matter where it takes place, always seems to embed itself into my clothes and my pores. I need a shower, but I don't have time.

I slide my foot over the bed and flinch at the tender throb in my ankle. It looks horrible, twice as swollen as it was last night and it's starting to turn a light bluish purple. But I'm going to have to tough it out. Shutting my eyes, I push myself up, letting a little weight fall onto it. "Motherfucker," I curse as the pain swells through my leg and I collapse down onto the bed. A few inhales and exhales and then I try again, but the pain is too unbearable. I'm trying not to lose it, but I can't miss class. I want to accomplish something for once and that's getting good grades and eventually doing something with my life other than wandering around, pushing my limits. I've managed to attend all of my classes this entire semester and it's probably the longest amount of time I've spent in one place, besides Preston's house. That's an accomplishment for me and I've had few of those throughout my life, unless you can count the record number of times I got into fights or got passed around to foster homes.

Sucking up every amount of strength in me, I force myself to try again. Shifting my body upward, I straighten my legs and get my feet underneath me. I take gritted breaths as I steady myself through the pain and limp over to my closet. One foot in front of the other. I can do this.

I grab my boots, but then decide against wearing them and reach for the one pair of flip-flops that I own. I wiggle my uninjured foot into one and then bracing my hand on the door frame of the closet, I struggle to wiggle my injured foot into the other. Not only does it hurt like a bitch but my foot is too swollen to fit in it.

Giving up on the shoe, I collect my book from the desk and then put some deodorant on. I comb my fingers through my hair and twist it up in a bun on the back of my head. I've looked a lot worse than wearing a day-old dress and one shoe before, like the time I traded my shirt for a can of food and a pocketknife during one of the brief times I lived out on the streets and had to walk around in this weird tube-top bra for a while.

I hobble over to the door and maneuver it open, relieved when I make it into the hallway. Now if I can just make it to the elevator then all will be golden. Putting all my weight on my good leg, I gradually move down the hall, ignoring the stares and whispers as I pass people, heading to the elevator. I internally celebrate when I make it onto the elevator and it takes me to the bottom floor.

After a lot of struggling and holding on to walls, I finally make it outside to the yard surrounding the McIntyre Building, the dorm where the University of Wyoming puts most of the freshmen. I check my watch dragging my foot across the sidewalk as I move toward the grass and realize that I'm going to be late. I try not to flip out and put more weight on my ankle so I can pick up the pace. I breathe through the pain, reminding myself that I'm as tough as nails. But then I step into a divot in the lawn and my ankle rolls awkwardly.

I trip to the side and drop my book. "Damn it!" I shout, bracing my hand on a nearby tree as the pain spreads up my leg.

People walking down the sidewalk stare at me like I'm a nut job and I'm briefly thrown back to Amelia's garage, surrounded by Jennifer and her friends. I hate how I feel just from remembering it. The sharpness. The little self-worth. I'm not

that person anymore. I'm strong, shielded, and unbreakable. Yet the memories get to me, force my shield to drop. I want to run to that one thing that helps me turn it off, box up my emotions and lock them silently away inside me. But I'd need to move in order to do so. *Fuck*.

"Knock it off, Violet," I mutter to myself, my skin damp from exertion. "You're letting stuff get to you. Suck it up."

I push back from the tree but then immediately return my hand to it. Shaking my head more at myself than anything, I slump back against the tree. I'm frustrated. I'm not going to make it and panic claws at my throat as disappointment in myself seeps in. I need a way to fix this…make the violent flood of emotions go away. Now.

I search the grassy area beneath the trees looking for a distraction from what's going on inside of me. There's a group of guys across from me playing Frisbee. I could pick a fight with them, see if I could get them to actually hit a girl, but fighting is usually a last resort, because it causes very little adrenaline to surface anymore. Or I could pick a fight with that creeper over by the tree, taking pictures of me with his camera, the ginormous flash blinding me even from this distance.

I lean forward, squinting to get a better look at him. The last time someone was taking a picture of me like that was right after my parents died and every damn reporter in the country wanted to get a picture of the girl who survived the slaying of her parents. But it's been ages since that happened and no one seems to care anymore.

The longer I stare at the guy, the more he backs away through the trees, clicking his camera repeatedly, and I start to drift forward, with a threatening look on my face.

"Well, you look like shit," someone says from beside me and I stop. "I can see you didn't take my advice and stay off that damn foot."

Luke Price suddenly appears at my side in the shadow of the tree next to me. I've seen him around school and last night when I kicked him in the face, but I don't really know him other than what I told him last night, plus the fact that he seems super intense. He's wearing a black T-shirt with a small hole in the hem and his jeans have a small hole in them, too. He's got cropped brown hair and intense brown eyes that automatically make me picture him as a fighter or boxer or something. But as far as I know he's just a football player, another jock that's probably walking in his father's footsteps.

He reaches up to scratch the welt on his forehead from the impact of my boots and I notice he has a leather band on his wrist that has the word "redemption" on it. I wonder if it means anything to him. If he's been saved from something?

"Well, if it isn't Mr. Stoically Aloof." I aspire to sound disinterested but the soreness in my leg and my anxiety is straining my voice. I glance back over to where the guy with the camera was lurking but he is gone. Shaking my head, I turn back to Luke, forcing myself to be the normal, indifferent Violet that I strive to be. "God, you really know how to charm a girl."

He eyes me with this illegible expression. "Who says I was trying to charm you?"

I'm not sure if he's aiming to be a flirty douche or just a douche, but either way I'm done talking to him. I need to get myself calmed down anyway. I inhale and blow it out as I glide forward, but freeze as blinding pain radiates through my leg and I start to fall toward the ground.

"Shit." Luke hurries forward with his arms out in front of him. "Let me help you."

I stick out my hand as I stagger back against the tree. "I got it. I don't need your help."

He stares at me with condescending doubt. "Yeah, I can see that."

"I just need a breather and I'll be good to go," I insist, portraying confidence on the outside that I lack on the inside. I've pretty much given up hope that I'm going to make it to class today and the anxiety is only escalating. The ideal thing for me to do now is to go back to the dorm and take care of the problem the only way I know how.

He crosses his arms, his lean muscles flexing, and presses his lips together, either to conceal his irritation or amusement—I honestly can't tell from the intensity dripping off of him. "Where are you trying to go?"

"I'm not *trying* to go anywhere." I press my palms flat against the rough tree bark. "I'm *going* to go to class."

He crooks his eyebrow. "To chemistry?"

"Yeah," I say. "The class you're supposed to be at, too, I'm pretty sure."

"Yeah, I'm running late." He gives a fleeting glance at the sidewalk and then his gaze lands back on me. "And now I'm going to be even later thanks to you."

"No one said you had to stop and talk to me." I square my shoulders, preparing to march my way across the yard with my head held high, showing that I do have some dignity left in me, even though I know I'm not going to make it all the way. I can pretend though, at least until he leaves.

I make it five amazing, dignified steps before my knees give out on me. Then Luke steals all the dignity I have left as he rushes forward and catches me in his sturdy arms. Even though it would have hurt worse, I would have rather face-planted into the grass and injured myself, than let my pride be wounded like it is now.

"What are you doing?" My flip-flop scrapes against the grass as I endeavor to get my feet back under me. "I said I got it."

"Sorry, but you obviously don't," he replies simply, tucking his arms underneath mine as he helps me to my feet.

I consider shoving him as one of his hands slides down my side and to my waist, but then I realize he's doing it to support my weight. I'm not sure what to do. I don't ask for help with anything—I'm not that weak anymore—but technically I'm not asking Luke for help right now. He's just doing it on his own, which isn't the same. At least that's what I tell myself to make this situation feel better. Besides, he's become a very good distraction from the emotions stirring in my chest before he showed up. I'm starting to settle down, calming on the inside. No one's ever done this to me before, except for maybe Preston and his ex-wife and my ex-foster mother, Kelley, and those instances were few and far between.

"Now are you going to let me help you back to your dorm or not?" His fingers gently press into my side.

I dither, then place my hand on his shoulder so I can lift more weight off my foot. "No, but I'll let you help me to class." I catch a hint of his scent; cologne mixed with soap and a splash of tequila.

He gapes at me. "You need to stay off your foot."

"No, I need to go to class," I argue, then hold my breath because the scent of his cologne is delicious. "It's important."

"Why? It's just one class."

"Because I don't miss class. Ever."

He searches my eyes for God knows what, a sign of sanity maybe, but then he gives up and nods. "All right, Violet..." He waits for me to give him my last name, but I only shake my head. I don't like saying my real last name because then I remember that I'm the only living person left carrying it. I could use my made-up one, but I don't like giving that one out either since it seems like I'm giving someone an open invitation to know me. "Okay, then Violet with no last name. Let's get you to class."

Then for the first time in thirteen years, someone actually helps me. And the odd thing is he willingly does it.

Luke

I help Violet to class, bearing as much of her weight as she'll let me, but she seems pretty dead set on letting me help her as little as possible and keeps putting weight on her ankle. It looks like shit, purple and blue, swollen up so big she couldn't even get a shoe on and I seriously just want to pick her up so she won't put any weight on it at all, plus I'll be able to move at my pace not hers. But I can tell there's no way she'll let me and honestly, I'm not that chivalrous. If I was acting like my normal self I'd have left her out under the tree.

It was a complete fluke that I crossed paths with her. I'd taken one too many shots of tequila this morning and my head was too foggy for me to drive to the university. So I had to walk and just happened to pass by when Violet was leaning against the tree. She looked like she was struggling and all I could think about was her falling out the window...my sister Amy jumping off the roof...suddenly I was walking over to her.

We end up being late and she's upset about it. She doesn't seem like the kind of person who would care so much about being on a schedule or getting good grades, but neither do I. My need to control my life, my grades, is an obsessive habit I developed early on to fight the constant loss of control that

61

always surrounded me when I was at home. I wonder what her reasons are.

I don't sit by her in class, not just because I don't want to come off as some obsessed guy, but there aren't any vacant desks beside her. I sit at an empty desk a few rows behind her and I try to concentrate on what Professor Dotterman is saying instead of what Violet's doing, but it's hard.

I thought about her a lot last night, even in my drunken stupor, which completely defeated the purpose of getting drunk. But she never did explain to me why she jumped out the window. I want to believe she wasn't trying to end her life, but knowing what I know—knowing what happened with Amy—I can't help but think about the deeper meanings behind her jump.

The longer I watch her, the more I analyze her. She's extremely stubborn—that much I understand—even going as far as refusing to stretch her foot out comfortably in front of her. She's sitting straight up in her chair, with her feet planted firmly below her. I think I might have met my match for the Stubbornest Person in the World award. It's an award I've pretty much been winning since I was sixteen when I decided to stop trusting people and doing only what I wanted. I'd spent way too much time giving other people everything they needed and finally I turned sixteen and got my driver's license. Suddenly, I had the freedom to go anywhere whenever I wanted and it didn't matter who was with me. I had myself and that was all that mattered. No one controlled me or had power over me and I've been making sure things stayed that way ever since.

Violet kind of seems like that. I've never met anyone who was so determined to do things on their own. But it's not like I'm about to ask her why. She gave me a dirty look just from me asking her last name and she'd probably try to kick my ass if I asked her anything personal. Although, the idea of her trying to kick my ass is sort of enthralling. It's not my usual thing. I like things easy and uncomplicated, because my life was too complicated when I was younger. For some reason, though, challenging Violet is becoming appealing. Then again no one's ever really tried to challenge me, too afraid to go up against the intense image I purposely send out.

I can tell Violet tries to look tough, but beneath the diamond stud in her nose, the red streaks in her hair, and the tattoos on the back of her neck, she's fucking gorgeous—even though she's wearing the same dress she had on last night, she has no makeup on, and her hair isn't done. She also doesn't have the muscle to do any damage, her long and slender legs and arms better suited to wrap herself around me, than hit or kick my ass.

I roll my tongue in my mouth at the idea of her legs and arms wrapped around me as I pin her underneath me and thrust deep inside her. It's got me curious about trying it and I'm seriously debating taking a break from the slutty, lacking-in-substance women that I've been hooking up with since I was sixteen.

In the middle of my thoughts, Violet casually glances over her shoulder. It's obvious she's trying to discreetly look at me, but I'm already looking at her, so it doesn't work. Her eyelids lower a little, like she's going to scowl at me, but instead she gives me this cocky look like she knows I was looking at her first. I'm not sure how to react to this, because usually I'm the cocky one. Pissed off at myself, I decide to stop being obsessive since I barely know anything about her, other than she likes to jump out windows and hates getting helped.

I start penning notes, seeking some structure amid my mess of thoughts. I can handle chaos when I'm drunk, because I'm too drunk to notice, but right now I'm too sober to deal with a girl who literally came crashing into my life.

I remain focused on the lecture for the rest of class and when the professor lets the class go I seriously consider letting Violet fend for herself. But as I walk by her, I notice her staring at her ankle with her book tucked under her arm and her eyebrows furrowed. As much as I only take care of myself anymore, when I picture her jumping out the window, either by accident or not, I find myself stopping beside her desk. I stick my elbow out, giving her the option of taking it. She looks up at me, giving me a real glimpse of her green eyes in the daylight. They're insanely big and beautiful, surrounded by long black eyelashes, but there's something missing from them. Emotion. Most of the time, when I look into people's eyes, I can get a good glimpse of what they're feeling, but with Violet I can't see anything, like she has a shield up.

Her fingers wrap around my arm and she tugs herself to her feet. When she gets her balance, I slip my arm around her lower back and settle my hand on her side. I feel her muscles constrict, but her face remains blank. Then she leans her weight on me, her hair brushing my cheek, and we walk out of the classroom.

We don't talk as we head down the crowded hallway, lazily winding through people. At first I think our silence is because I can't think of anything to say, but then it starts to become some sort of challenge over who can be the most stubborn, at least to me it is. If I talk first, I lose. If she does, then she loses.

We push out the door and cross the quad toward the sidewalk. It's the end of April, the sun is shining, and the air is a little chilly, but tolerable even without a jacket. Only a few more weeks and the semester will be over. Then everyone will return home. I'm trying to find a way out of it, though. The idea of going back and living with my mother is fucking unbearable. And my dad . . . he's preoccupied with other things at the moment, like his wedding. Besides, I've seen him maybe eight times since he walked out on my mom and me and half of those have been this year. The idea of asking to live with him aggravates me because I don't want to need anything from him. I want to be on my own here in Laramie. I could get a job now that football isn't going, but I fucking have the worst people skills and I tend to make people skittish, which makes getting a job really hard. Plus, I'd have to get an apartment unless I take summer classes. I need a little break from school, but I also need a roommate to afford living anywhere and Kayden's going to be gone all summer with Callie. I don't have much in the line of friends besides the guys I play football with and I really don't want to live with any of them. I can barely stand living with Kayden and he's been my best friend since we were kids. I could go gamble a little bit, take some risks, see if I can get a bigger cash flow, but ever since I lost a big hand during a game back in March, I haven't had enough to ante up for a game worth playing. Not unless I want to throw down all my cash, which I sort of want to do because I miss owning the game, cheating my way to the top. It's what I'm good at, at least most of the time, that is unless I lose the card I'm hiding like I did during the game in March.

The rest of the journey with Violet is interesting. She keeps glancing at me with arrogance and sometimes intrigue. It feels like she wants to say something, yet she never does, and the more she does it the more insane it drives me. When we get on the elevator at her dorm and the doors shut, Violet clears her throat and I think she's finally going to speak. She peeks at me from the corner of her eye and I tilt my head to the side, waiting for her to utter the first word. But instead she hits me with that arrogant look like she did in class and I'm thrown off by her cocky attitude again. I almost break down and ask her what the hell that look is about. Lose our silent battle, just like that. Let her win. Let her have that kind of power over me. She's got me all riled up and I'm cursing myself for not taking more shots before I left my room this morning.

For a brief second, I seriously contemplate pushing the emergency button and stopping the elevator, so I can push her back against the wall and kiss her fiercely before pulling away and leaving her. Regain a little of my control and power over the situation.

But as the elevator continues up and my arms stay at my side, I realize that I can't go through with it and honestly I have no idea why. She's messing with my head and I don't know what else to do besides stare at my reflection in the shiny steel doors for the rest of the elevator ride. When the doors open, I let out a breath of relief, glad we're coming to the end of this strange, silent journey. As we approach Violet's dorm room toward the end of the hall, I spot Kayden and Callie standing in front of the door. They're smiling as they talk to each other and they make it look so easy, so natural, like it's as simple as breathing. But even breathing is difficult for me sometimes.

Callie says something and Kayden laughs, but when he sees me walking up the hallway with Violet his expression fills with inquisitiveness.

"What's up?" he asks as we walk up to them. He glances from Violet to me, then his eyebrows arch, his eyes widening a little.

Callie steps out of the way as Violet moves out of my arm and drags her foot as she moves up to the door. "Are you okay?" Callie asks, looking down at Violet's ankle.

"Yeah," Violet answers with indifference as she punches in the code to their room with her finger. The lock beeps and she shoves the door open, tossing her book aside as she starts to shut the door behind her. I'm about to call our stubborn challenge a tie, when she pauses with the door still open a crack, her eyes sparkling with life for the very first time, and says, "Thanks, Mr. Stoically Aloof."

"You're welcome, Violet with no last name," I tell her and then she shuts the door.

Callie and Kayden instantly look at me and I work to keep a smile off my face.

"What the hell was that about?" Kayden asks, slipping his arm around Callie's shoulder. She's a tiny little thing and he has to lean down a little to reach her.

I shrug, not wanting to get into it. "She hurt her foot and I helped her back to her room."

Callie gives me a wary look. "How'd she hurt it?"

I shrug again. "I'm not sure."

One of the things I like about both of them is that they respect privacy and so they don't press.

"Where are you headed?" Kayden asks me, pulling Callie in to give her a kiss on the top of her head. "Back to the dorm?"

I start to back toward the elevators, stuffing my hands into my pockets. "I was thinking about hitting the gym. It's been a while. You want to come with me?"

Kayden nods. "Yeah, I'm down." He glances at Callie. "You want to come? I'll help you with your kickboxing skills." He winks at her and she rolls her eyes, smiling.

"Whatever. I totally kicked your ass last time," she says,

reaching for the key code on the door. "I can't anyway. I have to study for my biology final."

Kayden looks disappointed and I look away as he leans in to kiss her. As much as I'm happy for them, I sometimes miss my best friend not being whipped. I start to head toward the elevators to wait for him there when Callie calls out my name.

"Wait a minute, Luke," she says and I slowly turn around.

She's walking toward me with Kayden at her heels. When she reaches me, she snags my arm and hauls me past the elevator while Kayden waits behind, like he knows she wants to talk to me alone.

"How are you doing?" She tucks some strands of her brown hair behind her ear, seeming uneasy. "With the stuff with your sister, I mean."

I swallow hard. "I'm doing okay." It's always been hard dealing with the fact that my sister killed herself when she was sixteen, but a month ago I found out that Caleb Miller, some douche Amy used to go to school with, and who used to be friends with Callie's brother, raped her during a party a few months before she threw herself off the roof of an apartment complex. I guess the police found some journals written by Caleb about what he'd done, but Callie was the one who told me. Although she didn't flat out say it, I think Caleb might have done something similar to her.

When she first told me, it took me a while to process what it meant—that maybe Amy killed herself because of it. It's frustrating to feel so much rage inside me every time I think about it. Caleb's lucky he vanished, otherwise I might have tracked him down and beat the shit out of him, like Kayden did once. Or maybe I'm the lucky one, because sometimes when I get going, when I feel that much heat and tightness in my chest, I have a really hard time not swinging.

"Are you sure?" She touches my arm, then quickly pulls away. She's a sweet girl, but sometimes she's a little skittish. "Because I'm here if you ever want to talk. I know it's hard, especially since Caleb never got caught…he's just out there living his life…" Her eyes well up, but she quickly sucks the tears back.

I force a smile. "I'm not much of a talker, but thanks for the offer." I learned at a young age that trying to talk about what was bothering me was pointless. I once told my mom I didn't like that she was doing drugs and she only did more. I told my dad once during his yearly phone call that I hated my life and he told me that a lot of people do. When I found out about Amy's death, I went on a silent streak for about a week because it seemed like if I said anything to anyone they'd tell me to suck it up. I found serenity in the quiet and I seriously wish I'd never spoken again, at least about anything important, but my mom wouldn't let me mourn so easily and wanted to talk. About Amy.

"Neither am I," Callie says. "But sometimes it does help."

"Thanks, but I'm good for now."

She smiles and hers is real, not forced like mine. "How's your mom doing with all this?"

I internally cringe. My mom showed very little reaction when she found out and I'm not the least bit surprised. She barely paid attention to Amy while she was alive and after she died it was like she'd never existed. She threw all her stuff away days after it happened, saying horrible things about Amy choosing to leave us in the most monotone voice. She did sing a song at Amy's funeral, but the lyrics were crammed with madness. Not too many people heard it, though, since hardly anyone came to the funeral and those that did blamed the insanity on my mother's mourning.

When I told my dad about Amy, during our yearly phone call, he started to cry. It pissed me off. How dare he cry when he wasn't around to help and maybe some of this stuff could have been avoided. He'd abandoned us in that house with my mom and her craziness, letting his two kids get sucked right along into it.

"My mom's fine," I lie to Callie, inching around her to head toward the elevators. It's nice of her to care, but it doesn't make it easy for me to talk about my mother.

Callie seems wary by my offish answer, but drops it and steps out of the way so I can scoot by. Kayden's waiting for me at the elevator and when I approach him, he hammers his finger against the button.

"I'll call you later," he says to Callie and then kisses her.

I look in the other direction again, ready to get away from this whole affectionate thing they've been obsessed with for months. Affection is overrated. I've never wanted it and will

71

never, ever go looking for it. The one person that showed me affection made it seem wrong and it's one of the reasons I won't get close to anyone, not even Kayden. Yes, we know stuff about each other, but we've never had a heart-to-heart. I've never had a heart-to-heart with anyone and I plan on keeping it that way, no matter what it takes because the last thing I want is anyone to find out about my past and how screwed up my thoughts are.

Chapter Three

Violet

Right after my parents were murdered, I used to come up with reasons why their lives were taken. The police's theory was that it was a freak accident when we were getting robbed—for some reason the robbers thought no one was home. My parents had woken up in the middle of it and saw them. Panic ensued. Then gunfire. They never caught who did it and as far as I know these people are walking around in the world, living their lives while my parents were left to rot.

It drives me absolutely insane when I think about it, but sometimes my mind opens up on its own. Thoughts of the people I pass on the street. It could be any of them and I worry that maybe they'll recognize me. Even though I'm not sure, there's always that question in my mind if one of them saw me that night, because they looked right at me, but never said a word. It's something that's haunted me to this day

I always wonder what I'd do if the murderers were actually caught. Freak out. Celebrate. Be filled with overpowering hate toward them because now I had a face to link with the event. Be terrified. I'm not sure and every time I analyze it too much, my habit kicks in and I seek comfort in the one thing that can give it to me. Danger. Pushing death. Parasuicidal. Adrenaline junkie. Insane. There's so many different things it could be called and I honestly don't know which one it is. All I know is what I do—what I need—to get through my life.

I haven't been doing it over the last few days, though, since I can barely limp around let alone walk. It's becoming an inconvenience and making me feel weak. But my ankle's refusing to heal, so I have no option other than to hobble around in pain. The worse part was work. I've never been that great of a waitress, since my dazzling people skills are lacking. Add pain to the lack of people skills and my supervisor, Johnny, was threatening to tell our boss about my bitchy attitude toward the costumers. Thankfully I charmed him with a dime bag and that seemed to smooth things over.

I'm headed to the nearest McDonald's to feed my junk food addiction, wearing a pair of cutoffs and a FROM AUTUMN TO ASHES T-shirt I've worn so much the letters are starting to fade. My hair was untamable so I pulled a beanie over it and I'm still sporting the flip-flops. Not my greatest of fashion moments, but I've never tried to claim to be some sort of fashionista.

It's hot and my ankle is swelling from all the weight I'm putting on it, but I'm starving and I don't have Preston's car anymore because he only lends it to me when I'm dealing, so my only form of transportation is on foot. I'm counting how many blocks I have left in my head...five or maybe it's six...

My phone rings and I answer, knowing the ringtone belongs to Preston. Part of me doesn't want to answer it because I know he's going to want me to do something I probably don't feel up to and I won't tell him no, because I owe him for taking me in when no one else would.

Before Preston came along, I was living with Mr. and Mrs. McGellon, a foster family who liked to lock me in the basement for hours whenever I smarted off or did something wrong. I would have been okay with sitting in the dark listening to the drip of the pipes, but I've hated basements ever since I was six. One time when Mr. McGellon threatened to put me down there, I'd shoved him out of frustration and when Mrs. McGellon threatened to call the police, I took off. I lived on the street for about two weeks, and then got busted when I stole some food from a grocery store and ended up spending time in juvie anyway. After I got out, when no one else wanted to take me in, Preston and his wife stepped up. They were young and I think social services was looking for a reason to get rid of me at that point, so they more than willingly turned me over to them. Still, they were there for me.

I answer the phone and put it up to my ear right before it goes to voicemail. "What's up?"

"Kelley's getting remarried," he announces in an irritated tone.

"What do you mean she's getting remarried?" I drag my

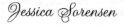

foot down the sidewalk. "I thought she left you because she felt trapped."

"Wow, thanks for painfully reminding me why my ex-wife packed her shit and left," Preston says, his voice dripping with sarcasm. "Jesus, Violet, sometimes you're too blunt for your own good."

"Blunt?" I pause at the end of the sidewalk. "You've always told me what a liar I was."

"You're a liar when it comes to you," he replies. "But with everyone else, you're blunt. I swear to God you like witnessing people in pain."

I cross the street and trip onto the curb. "Maybe, or maybe I've never been taught to censor myself."

"You're so full of it right now. You know exactly what you're doing so don't try to pretend you're all naïve and innocent." His voice drops an octave. "And speaking of innocence, have you finally lost yours yet?"

I fidget uncomfortably, tugging the bottom of my T-shirt down, glad he can't see me right now. "Don't be a creepy old man."

"I'm not that old, Violet," he says. "And besides I was just making sure you're okay and that no guys have fucked you over. Asking about your love life would have been Kelley's job but since she ditched us, I gotta step in and play the part."

I shake my head. "Play the part of my foster mom?"

"Sure. Why not?"

"You're such a sick freak."

"Coming from the girl who refused to eat anything but pork 'n' beans for two straight weeks when she first showed up at my house."

I swing around a couple holding hands blocking the sidewalk. "What can I say? I was missing the foul taste of prison food."

"You weren't in prison," he clarifies. "Just juvie. Don't try to make yourself sound more badass than you are."

"Hey, I'm badass," I protest, not bothering to wind around water spraying on the sidewalk from some sprinklers in a yard. "I could kick your ass."

He snorts a laugh and it gets under my skin. "Okay, I'll tell you what. The next time you come here for a visit and we have some time, I'll take you in my bedroom and you can try to show me how tough you are."

I wipe water droplets off my arms. "Why would we have to go into the bedroom?"

His laughter drops to a deep throaty sound. "Think outside of your naïve innocent brain, Violet, and maybe you'll get it."

"I'm not naïve or innocent, just a little slow," I say, catching on to what he meant. "And FYI, you're disgusting and it's never going to happen." I don't like it when he talks to me like this, but if I say anything serious about it, he'll probably get upset. I saw him get that way with his now ex-wife Kelley and when Preston gets upset, he gets violent.

"Whatever. Don't pretend like you're not getting turned on," he says.

I'm not. At all. I've never even been turned on before, at least from what I can remember and it seems like something I would. When I lived with Preston he wasn't so flirty like this, but once I hit eighteen and was officially considered my own guardian our relationship sort of shifted, especially when Kelley left him. He's never actually tried anything with me, just talked a lot of talk, and I don't say anything about it. I don't want to lose him—he's the only thing close to a family I have. Even Kelley doesn't talk to me anymore.

"I gotta go," I lie. I still have three or four more blocks to go, but I want to end this uncomfortable conversation. "I'll call you later."

"You better." The deep throaty tone of his voice vanishes. "I have stuff for you to do and you still need to pay me back for the eighth I fronted you the other night and you know I don't take money, only work."

I tense, worried I've upset him and that he'll get angry and I'm going to lose the only family I have. Then I'll be totally alone. "I know. And I'll call you back. I promise."

"Good girl," he says and then we say good-bye and hang up.

The tension raveling in my body makes me want to throw myself into oncoming traffic and see how much I can get my heart rate up and shut the tension down. Just thinking about it takes me from worry to terror and excitement. I'm starting to wander sideways toward the curb, wondering if I'd die instantly if I got hit, when a truck pulls up, backfiring when it slows at the curb.

I keep ungracefully strolling up the sidewalk, not wanting to deal with any more perverts today, when I hear a familiar voice say, "Still putting weight on that ankle, huh?"

I speed up, taking long strides, but the radiating pain in my ankle forces me to slow down. "What can I say?" I call over my shoulder. "I'm a rebel. I like to walk on the wild side."

Luke inches his beat-up truck along beside me, driving up the wrong side of the road toward traffic, but luckily no one's coming. He has the window rolled down and his arm resting on the windowsill. "Well, you're only rebelling against yourself since it's your ankle."

I shake my head, but a smile pushes its way through and manages to push out the tension the conversation with Preston created. I need to put a stop to this thing I've got going with him. I enjoy bantering with Luke a little too much and I found walking in silence with him too amusing as well, especially since he didn't crack under my silent pressure like a lot of people would have. Plus, he helped me and no one's ever really done that before, except Preston and Kelley and a couple of other people that breezed through my life.

I halt at the edge of the curb and Luke taps the brakes to slow down his truck. "What do you want?" I shield my eyes from the sunlight as I look over at him.

His intense gaze relentlessly holds mine. "I want to see if you need a ride somewhere."

I elevate my eyebrows as I lean forward and rest my arms on the edge of the open window, just inches away from his.

"That's really what you were doing? Cruising up and down the streets looking for me, hoping that you can give me a ride."

He presses his lips together, looking entertained by something I said. "No, I was heading to the gym but then I saw you hobbling around like an old lady and thought *Hey, maybe she'd like someone to help her out so that she can make it to wherever she's going by sometime today.*"

I struggle with this one. There aren't too many people in the world who have made me smile and the majority of them are dead. Luke's getting close and I don't like it—don't like how little control I have over my reaction. If he keeps it up, I'm going to have to jack his truck and drive a hundred down the highway, just to clear out all the feelings that come with that damn smile.

"Maybe I enjoy walking around like an old lady." I slant so close to him I feel the heat of his breath and notice how long his eyelashes are. But I'm only doing it to mess with his head.

He doesn't move away and his intensity goes up a notch, his expression flaring with something I can't quite interpret, which is disconcerting. "Okay, I guess I'll leave you to your hobbling." He leans back into his truck and looks ahead, throwing me a curveball.

I'm not sure how to respond. I miss a beat, which doesn't happen too often, and maybe that's why I do what I do next. "Wait." I touch his arm as the truck starts to roll forward. The touch startles both of us and I draw my hand away. "I'm going to McDonald's. It's like a few blocks up. If you want, you can give me a ride."

Again he looks like he's going to laugh. "Okay, then hop in and I'll give you a ride."

Wallowing in my own stupidity over the fact that I get vaguely enthused over the fact he's helping me out again, I round the front of the truck, and hop in.

The door's hinges squeak as I shut it and Luke shakes his head in annoyance. "Sorry, my truck's a pile of shit." He reaches for a pack of cigarettes on the dashboard.

"It's not a piece of shit." I roll down the window and let in the warm spring breeze. "It's just rustic."

His eyebrows furrow. "You have an interesting vocabulary." He pops a cigarette into his mouth.

"Is that a compliment?" I relax back in the seat. "Coming from Mr. Stoically Aloof."

He cups his hand around the cigarette and then ignites it with the lighter. "Yeah, you're going to have to explain that one to me because I don't get it."

At the beginning of school, during one of my English classes I had with Luke, the professor told us to describe something in the classroom that we thought would be difficult to describe. For some reason I thought of Luke, the guy who always sat in the back with his arms crossed and this I-don't-give-a-shit look on his face. He almost seemed unapproachable or maybe just offish or perhaps it was something else. He had friends, though, so it didn't make any sense. After a lot of analysis, I'd come up with "stoically aloof," and although I'm not sure I nailed it correctly, every time I've crossed paths with him, the nickname pops up in my head. But I'm not about to tell him this.

"Not telling you is what gives it its appeal," I tell him as he tosses the lighter onto the dash.

He takes a deep drag from his cigarette and then smoke encircles his face. "So you're not going to tell me ever?" He holds on to the steering wheel with one hand and pulls back onto the road in the right lane and then drives down the road.

I give a one-shoulder shrug. "Maybe one day, but not right now."

He shakes his head, but a trace of a smile touches his lips. "Fine, but I think I should be able to give you a nickname, too."

I rotate sideways in the seat, bringing my knee up on it, curiosity sparking inside me. "Oh, I'm really interested to hear this. Let me guess. Crazy Bitch. Psycho Jumper. Old Lady."

The corners of his lips turn up. "As much as I think all of those are great choices, I'm not going to give you one just yet. I'm going to wait until I find the perfect one to fit your... charming personality."

I make a face as I roll my eyes. "Ha, ha, you're hilarious." He actually kind of is, though, and I have to work to restrain a smile.

His smile broadens, and I feel my heart spastically skip a beat. But then the happiness fades as he hurries and sticks his hand out the window to ash his cigarette. "Shit, I forgot to ask if it was okay to smoke in here."

"It's your truck," I say, turning forward in the seat and putting my foot back on the floor. "You can do whatever the hell you want."

"Anything I want, huh?" He cocks his head, studying me as he pauses at a stop sign. We're leaving the residential part of town and now gas stations and small stores line the street. "What if I said I wanted to drive like a hundred miles an hour in the wrong lane."

"Then I'd say go ahead." I kind of wish he would, that way I'd get my much needed dose of adrenaline and these unfamiliar emotions Luke's creating inside me, ones I haven't felt in a long time—if *ever*—emerging inside me would be suffocated. I'm not even sure exactly what they are; whether I find him attractive, annoying, comforting. Regardless, I don't want to feel anything for him and I need to get rid of whatever it is that I'm feeling.

He continues to hold the cigarette out the window, some of the ash drafting back inside the cab of the truck and landing on the gray Henley he's wearing, the sleeves rolled up. He's contemplating something deeply as he looks at me, perhaps actually doing what he said. I wait with a hint of anticipation. Just the idea that my life could potentially be put into danger settles me.

Eventually he concentrates on the road, leaving me marginally disappointed. "So where are you from? Laramie? Or are you just living here for school?" Such a casual question, which doesn't fit the intensity in his eyes.

"Where are you from?" I counter his question with a question, hoping to divert his attention away from me.

"Around," he says with a twinkle in his eyes.

Okay, this is harder than I thought. "So besides the fact that you like to walk around with blond sluts in the dark and force your way into people's lives, what do you like to do?"

His gaze slides from the road to me. "I thought you already knew what I did—play football, help damsels in distress, walk around being stoically aloof."

I stare impassively at him even though a laugh tickles the back of my throat. It's been a long time since I've even tasted the brief glimpse of laughter. "Touché, Luke Price."

He presses his hand dramatically against his chest. "Did I just win a conversation?"

"You say that like we were playing a game."

"Weren't we?" There's a challenge in his brown eyes and I feel something awaken inside me, something I'm not sure has ever been fully awake.

"Maybe," I shift uneasily at the fact that I'm actually feeling something besides numbness, yet I don't know what it is. "But I wouldn't count on winning just yet."

He inhales from the end of his cigarette again, then smoke eases out of his lips. There's a ghost of a smile on his face, but the shadows in his eyes leave Luke Price unreadable, a mystery, exactly what I strive to be myself. I could press him for more details about his life, where he came from, what makes him tick, but I'm guessing the shadows are there for a reason. And if I go digging into his life, he just might try to dig through mine. And I don't want him or anyone else to get to know me, because it's a waste of time. In the end he'll leave me. Everyone always does.

Luke

"You know I'm not really a fan of hamburgers," I say. We're sitting at a table in McDonald's on opposite sides with a tray of food in between us. I'm trying to keep the conversation light since it was getting heavy in the car. She's got my thoughts all tangled up. Not only is she a girl who jumps out of windows, but she got way too excited when I said I'd drive down the wrong lane going a hundred miles an hour. It's like she wanted me to do it and again I can't help but wonder what's going on in that head of hers. It's almost becoming an obsession—needing to know. And that makes me instantly back off.

"You sound like you're a vegetarian," Violet remarks from across the table, unwrapping her hamburger.

"Nope, just a guy who doesn't have much of a taste for burgers." I grab a handful of fries and plop them into my mouth.

She raises her eyebrows and takes a bite of her hamburger. "I think it's weird."

I'm not even sure how I ended up here with Violet. I'd

been heading to the store because I'd run out of tequila and Jack Daniel's and I needed it more than I needed air. I'd just gotten my dad's wedding invitation, along with a call from him, asking me to be his best man.

"I'm trying to decide if you're kidding," I'd replied, because he couldn't be serious. Best men were supposed to be friends, like each other, know each other.

"I know it's kind of late notice, since the wedding's in a couple of months," he said. "But I'd really like you to be the one standing beside me."

I shook my head, balling the invitation up in my hand. "I'm not even sure I can come to the wedding."

"Oh, I see." He sounded so disappointed, but I wasn't about to give into him that easily. "Well, could you just do me a favor and think about it?"

I tossed the wedding invitation into the garbage. "I guess."

"Thank you, Luke." He sounded so sincere. "And if you ever need anything or want to talk, I'm here."

I should have just let it all out then, everything I wanted to talk about. How he abandoned us and left me to be destroyed in that house. I should have finally told him what he left me with, what happened, what my mom made me do. But I didn't say anything but good-bye, too afraid of what he might say or wouldn't say, and then I hung up.

As I was driving down the road toward the nearest liquor store, I saw Violet limping on the damn foot, completely disregarding my advice to stay off it. I should have just driven by her, let her limp around, like I should have during my walk to school the other day. We keep crossing paths, but it's not that big of a town or school so it's not that surprising. We've always probably crossed paths a lot, but the thing is I've never really paid attention to her before. And now, all of a sudden, I'm hyperaware of her. Part of me is still curious to know what the hell was going on that night she jumped out the window and the other part . . . it has a lot to do with my messed-up issues with women and control—the obsession with getting her underneath me.

So instead of a shot of Jack I settle for a chicken sandwich, fries, and a Coke. Not much of a trade-off, but I can always hit up the liquor store on the way back.

Violet takes a bite of her hamburger and then sets it down on the tray. She adjusts the beanie on her head a little lower, so it's covering more of her hair. She doesn't have any makeup on again and she's wearing this faded T-shirt that looks about ten years old. I'm starting to wonder if that's just how she is, low maintenance. But when she jumped out the window, she was all dressed up. I'm not even sure why I'm analyzing it— her. She's far from my type. I usually go for the slutty, prissy girls who like to look pretty. I'm not even sure why I prefer that look, other than girls like Violet look more intense, and if they're anything like me they've got too much going on inside them, which is the last thing I want. I want no strings attached. I only want girls who can suck my cock and smile about it, without asking for more. And without any annoying giggling either.

"What?" Violet asks, dabbing her mouth with a napkin. "Do I have something on my face?"

I rip my gaze off her and open up my chicken sandwich. "No, I was just spacing out." I take a bite of my sandwich. "Sorry."

She reaches for her fries with an undecided look on her face. "So I have a question."

"Okay..."

"About you."

I slowly chew my food. "I'm not really sure I want to hear your question now."

She picks a pickle off of her burger, pulling a repulsed face. "Well, I'm still going to ask it."

I grab a handful of fries from the tray that's on the table between us. "Go ahead and ask but it doesn't mean I'll answer."

She props her elbows onto the table with her burger in her hand. "Why haven't you ever talked to me before? I mean, we've walked past each other probably a hundred times, but never so much as acknowledged each other and then suddenly you're stalking me."

I pick up my soda and sip from the straw. "First off, I'm not stalking you. I just can't seem to get rid of you."

"You didn't have to stop to pick me up."

"Yeah, I did."

"Why? You don't know me—you're in no way obligated to help me."

"I know, but I wanted to."

"Why?"

I shrug, setting my drink down. "Why not?"

She gives me a funny look, like I'm the most confusing person in the world, when really she should be looking at herself like that. "I don't get it. Why would someone like you help someone like me?"

I open up the bun of my chicken sandwich to pick the tomato off. "What do you mean someone like me and someone like you?"

She points at me. "You as in a football player who has friends." Then she points at herself. "And me as in the loner girl who could probably kick your ass."

I choke on a laugh and my mouth full of food almost shoots out of my nose. "You could not kick my ass," I cough, and then take a swallow of my drink.

She scans me over while scooping up some fries. "I beg to differ. I think you're not as tough as you try to look."

"Do you really?" If only she knew what really lay inside me. "Because most people think I am and for a good reason."

"I think it's all for show," she replies nonchalantly and I can't tell if she's being serious or not. "I think that deep down you're just a softy."

"Are you trying to pick a fight with me right now?" I set my sandwich down on the tray and crack my knuckles. "Because I'm not going to fight a girl."

"That's such a typical guy answer." She hurries and takes a drink, but I detect a hint of a smile before her lips wrap around the straw.

"You know what I think?" I cross my arms on the table and lean in, cocking my head to the side as I observe her closely. "I think you like arguing with me and that's why you're bringing this up."

Her shoulders lift and descend as she takes a bite of her hamburger. "Maybe, but maybe I'm being serious."

"You know that as a football player I have to tackle guys, right? It takes strength to do that."

"Maybe you just run, though," she counters. "Maybe you're just good at running."

The way she says it reminds me so much of my past and it's like a kick to the stomach. "Maybe I'm not, though. Maybe I suck at running." I sound choked and I decide it's time to cut this conversation short, my brain seeking that potent taste of Jack and Tequila mixed with nicotine. I glance at my watch, pretending to check the time. "I just remembered that I have to meet Kayden somewhere in like a half an hour, so I'm going to have to take you back."

She balls up the wrapper for her hamburger, acting nonchalant, but her shoulders are stiff. "Sounds good to me. I was done anyway." She seems irritated and I have no idea why, other than she seems to be able to read through my bullshit and test me, which most people can't and won't even try. I'm supposed to be a closed book. A mystery. That way no one can see who I really am. It's the way I've been living for years and it's comfortable. Not ideal, but nothing is ideal.

We don't talk as I collect our garbage and then walk next to her as she limps out to my truck. I try to offer her my arm and open the door for her, but she denies my offer, moving to the opposite door and pushing it open.

During the car ride, she barely says two words to me. I should be happy about it. That way there's no room for sudden questions and statements that will set me off, however I find myself missing the bantering thing we had going and the way she pushed my buttons. By the time I drop her off, all I want to do is ask her to stay, talk some more, let me get to know her. But I don't understand why. I've never wanted to get to know anyone before. I've never even been out on a date. Each woman I've been with, I've only been with once. Just sex. That's all it's ever about. And I've never wanted anything more.

Until now.

Chapter Four

Violet

There was more than just one person at my house the night my parents were killed, but one person sticks out in particular. She was tall, with long hair and eyes that glowed in the moonlight. She wore these bright yellow shoes with pink flowers on them that reminded me of a character in a fairy tale. In the book she would be a fairy or something, while in real life she was the evil villain. When she first snuck into the house she was quiet, but on her way she was loud and erratic, a mess of emotions.

"Why, why, why," she kept repeating and then would add, "I can't feel my hands."

The guy told her, "Shut the fuck up and quit tripping. You need to get your shit together, now." Over and over again until, finally, he slapped her.

She only laughed, this crazy laugh and then she started singing this song, "Lean into me. Lean into me. Take. Help me. I need to understand. Help me. I can't do this without you."

The guy slapped her again, this time harder, and it shut her up for a moment. As he did it, I swear she looked right over at me hiding in the corner behind a box of toys, yet she never said a word. It's all I could really see of her—her eyes— everything else was masked in the shadows. I'll never forget the song she sang, the lyrics engraved into my mind deeper than letters and dates in my parents' headstone. Even when I'm listening to other music, always hoping I'll stumble across the song they belong to, I'm thinking about the song. The sound of her voice . . . so disturbingly beautiful. I told the police about the song and the shoes and they looked at me with sympathy in their eyes, telling me they'd do everything they could to find the person. I was six and confused and really did believe they'd bring the bad guys in. And sometimes, when my imagination got the best of me, I'd secretly tell myself that once the bad guys were behind bars, my parents would come back to me again.

But neither ever happened and eventually the case was closed, like the lids on my parents' coffins.

৵

I called in sick for work tonight and I'm blowing off dealing, even though it's Saturday night, the best night for hitting up parties. Preston doesn't always have me screw his costumers over, sometimes he just sends me to deal straight up, which is what he asked me to do when I dropped his car off last weekend. I'd agreed, but that was before I realized that it was nearing finals week, and I need to study. Plus my ankle is still a little black and blue and it's not ideal for walking around in boots or heels, which is required attire when dealing— Preston's rules.

I haven't talked to Luke since he took me to McDonald's, but I have passed him a couple of times in the halls and the campus yard. I caught him a couple of times staring at me, but he always looks away when he notices me noticing. I think I upset him with something I said while we were at McDonald's. But I'm known most for unintentionally insulting people— and sometimes intentionally—so I'm not surprised. What I am surprised about is how much I've thought about him over the last few days and how I kind of sort of wish that he'd talk to me and I've even almost lost my sanity a few times and thought about going up to talk to him.

I don't like it. At all. I don't think about guys—or people in general—for extended amounts of time or worry about talking to them. It's a waste of brain space. But he seems a little different from the long sequence of people I've met in my life, mainly because he's helped me out and hasn't asked anything from me in return. There's no clear reason why, but I'm waiting for one to surface, because he has to want something from me. If he's helping just to be nice then it means my theory that people only help others to help themselves is ruined.

And maybe it's that slight difference that makes me so drawn to him. Maybe it's because he does, in his own strange way, seem nice. And I hate to admit it, but I also think it might be his eyes, too, but I'm blaming that on the fact I'm a female and I don't think there's any woman out there who wouldn't be drawn to his intense eyes just a little.

I'm lying on my stomach on my bed with my Philosophy book opened up in front of me, along with my Calculus book, so I can rotate between the two subjects. I've got some Green Day cranked up fairly loud since Callie's out, a bag of Sour Patch Kids and some Doritos in front of me, along with a thirty-two-ounce Dr Pepper. Between the sugar, caffeine, and loud music, I've hit a super zone where studying has become like breathing. My eyes feel like they're bleeding, though, and my head's starting to hurt, but it feels good to know I'm trying so hard it hurts.

I could take a study break, but I'm not going to. School was always sort of my thing and maybe it's because it was my escape from whatever home I was living in. I almost flunked out when I lived on the streets and then went to juvie but when I got my shit together, I vowed never to mess up in school again.

Suddenly Green Day is overlapped with a little Rise Against as my phone starts to ring. Blowing out a breath, I lean over to the iPod dock and turn the stereo down, then I pick up my phone and answer it.

"I can't do it tonight," I tell Preston, sitting up on the bed and rubbing my eye. "I have to study."

"Who said I was calling for that?" he replies. "Jeez, you didn't even fucking let me say hello."

"I know, but I know what you're going to say and I can't. I have finals coming up."

"But you told me last Sunday that you could."

"I know." I sigh heavily. "But I forgot how close it was to the end of the semester."

He pauses and I hear a flick of the lighter in the background as he lights up a cigarette. "Violet, I don't want to make you do anything you don't want to, but I need you to go out tonight." His voice is calm, but firm. He's getting irritated and I've seen what can happen if he gets too upset. "I was there when you needed me. I gave you a place to live and put a roof over your head when no one else would. And I let you live your life however you wanted."

"Preston…I…" I waver. I want to stay in and study, but I don't want him to be upset with me. And he has a point. He did help me out when no one else would—when no one else wanted me. "Okay, I'll do it," I finally say, frowning at my study stuff on the bed.

"That's my girl," he says, flawlessly changing from intense to flirty. "Take the bus over to my house and get the stuff. Then I'll let you use my car."

"Okay," I tell him, trying to hide my disappointment. "But am I just dealing tonight or do I have to screw people over?"

"Just dealing," he tells me. "After what happened last weekend I think it'd be good if you took a little break."

"I'm sorry I screwed up."

"It's okay. Just don't do it again." He hangs up and I sigh, getting out of bed to get dressed.

I decide on a black backless, floor-length dress that will hide the fact I'm going to wear flip-flops. Then I tousle my fingers through the waves of my hair and sweep it to the side, then put some lip gloss on and outline my eyes with kohl eyeliner. It's not my best presentation, but I'm only dealing tonight and I honestly am too exhausted to put any more effort into my looks. But hopefully I'll be up to Preston's standards, otherwise I'm going to be on the shit list for a while.

❧

I arrive at Preston's house a little after eight, which is a little later than he'd probably like but I had to wait around for the bus. I knock on the front door to the house that I called my home for three years before I went to college. It still looks the same; green shutters, nasty brown siding that used to be white, and set of rusty metal stairs that lead to the front door. The yard's nice, though. There's even flowers growing in it and the flourishing trees make me think of the trees that enclosed my old childhood home.

"Come in," Preston calls out after I knock again.

I turn the doorknob and then gather the bottom of my dress so I can step over the threshold without stepping on it. The air always smells pungent in the house, but I think that's because someone's always smoking something. Like Preston right now. He's got a cigarette in his hand, smoke snaking out of his lips, and a candle burning on the kitchen counter, which is diagonal from the front door.

"Well don't you look beautiful," he says, his eyes scroll over my outfit and I feel myself let a relieved breath out of my lips. I hadn't even realized I'd been holding it.

"Thanks. I do try my best." I swish the skirt a little as I make my way across the living room and to the kitchen. I pull out a barstool and take a seat, propping my feet up on the bottom bar.

Preston's wearing a plaid shirt that's unbuttoned and shows a series of tribal tattoos on his chest and ribs. His sandy blond hair is a little long, running down to the bottom of his chin and he has a five o'clock shadow, but he usually does. His jeans are missing a button so I can see the top of his striped boxers and when he steps back from the counter, I notice he's barefoot.

"Wow, you sure dressed up tonight," I joke, folding my arms on top of the counter. "Aren't you throwing a party or something? You usually do on the weekends."

He glances at me as he puts the cigarette into his mouth. "Not tonight," he says, smoke snaking from his lips. "I'm getting a little tired of people at the moment."

"Getting too old for those crazy kid parties, huh?" I tease, then zip my lips together when he glares at me.

He grazes his thumb across the end of the cigarette,

holding it over a coffee mug, and spills the ashes inside it. "I'm not that much older than you, Violet."

"You're ten years my senior," I argue in a playful tone. "Which does make you old."

"Eight years your senior," he corrects. "I'm only twenty-seven . . . don't be adding years on me."

I shoot a conniving grin at him. "When you get that old, does it really even matter anymore if I add a year or two?"

He shakes his head with forced annoyance as he extends his arm over the counter and grabs the ashtray next to my elbow. He puts his cigarette out in it, then his hand moves for the front pocket in his shirt. "So I'm going to have you stick to herb tonight," he says, taking out a small baggie of weed out of his pocket. He tosses it down on the counter in front of me, getting down to business. "And I heard that the cops were going to be out a little heavier around town, so be careful."

"How do you know that?" I ask. "Is your friend Glen tipping you off again? He's such a dirty copper."

" 'Dirty copper'?" He chuckles under his breath. "I think you've been watching a little too many cop shows, Violet. No one talks like that."

"I don't watch cop shows," I lie, tracing one of the many cracks on the countertop. "I read that expression in a book."

"What era does the book take place in? 1930?"

"No, 2012."

"You're such a liar," he says, crossing his arms as he slumps back against the counter. "You seriously are the worst I know and one day it's going to get you into trouble."

"I don't lie all the time." I pick up the bag of weed. "I just make things colorful when they're gray."

"You are the most entertaining girl I know, Violet Ha…" He trails off, probably remembering the one and only time I yelled at him—when he called me by my last name.

I quickly change the subject before it can get to me. "So, are you going to let me crash here for the summer or what?"

A flirtatious smirk curves across his face. "You know you're always welcome here. I'll even share my bed with you."

I roll my eyes. "Thanks, but I think I'll take my old room."

"What? I'm not good enough to share a bed with?"

"No, I'm sure you are, but you know I don't share a bed with anyone."

He leans over the counter. "I know and I'd really like to know why."

I give a one-shoulder shrug. "For the same reason I don't share anything else. Because I don't like people touching my stuff." That's not entirely true. I used to hate sleeping alone— being alone in general.

After I found my parents murdered, I stayed in the house with them for twenty-fours hours, and it was the longest twenty-four hours of my existence. The longer I stayed in the house with the bodies the farther I sank into the loneliness and myself. I kept telling myself to get up, but I knew once I did that it'd be over. That I'd have to say good-bye. Finally the silence broke me down, though, and I had to move.

I didn't cry right away after the funerals. It'd taken a few days and then I couldn't stop. It went on forever and I just wanted someone to comfort me. And I hated sleeping alone with the nightmares filled with loneliness. I tried to get someone to hold me, hug me, help me not feel so alone, but in the end, no one wanted the job. And finally I decided not to be so weak. I made myself be strong. Be okay with being alone. Be okay with only having myself.

"Earth to Violet." Preston waves his hand in front of my face. "You're spacing off on me."

"Sorry." I go to put the bag of weed in my pocket, but realize I forgot my jacket. "Shit, I don't have any effin pockets in this dress."

Preston cocks his head to the side and strands of his hair fall into his liquid blue eyes. "Personally I like the dress..." He looks me over and I try not to let his penetrating gaze make me uncomfortable, but it kind of does. "I have an idea." He rubs his scruffy jawline as he winds around the counter and I turn in the barstool to face him. He sticks his hand out. "Give me the bag."

I drop it in his hand and he folds his fingers around it and reaches for my chest. I flinch, but don't say anything, focusing instead on keeping my breathing even as his hand brushes the top of the dress.

"You're not wearing a bra." He bites his lip, his hand lingering on my chest for a moment, then he moves it toward my hip, reaching around to my back where the dress opens up and my bare skin shows. He barely slips his fingers underneath the fabric and then tucks the bag just beneath the waistband of my thong, my skin blazing with heat at the contact of his fingers. It's not like I'm innocent. Guys have groped me and I let their hands wander wherever they want as long as it's nothing more than business. It's easy to ignore everything when they're just a face, think of something else, like how much laundry I have to do. But if there's the slightest spark of emotion then I push away.

The idea of connecting with someone emotionally and intimately never has appealed to me. Emotions haven't in general. They serve no point other than to lead to disappointment when you realize you're feeling something for someone who doesn't reciprocate. Preston knows this about me and it makes me sort of question why he would touch me like this. He can joke with me all he wants, but touching is off limits with people I have some sort of relationship with whether it be foster dad or friend, whichever he is to me... it sometimes gets confusing.

I'm battling to get oxygen into my lungs without gasping as my head swirls with confusion and the urge to ram my fist into his jaw.

"Just don't get too crazy with your dance moves," he says, withdrawing his hand and winking at me. Then he circles the corner of the kitchen counter. "There's a party in Fairtown," he tells me, carrying on the conversation as if nothing happened as he digs through his cupboards for something. "You should hit it up. That town's full of potheads."

I swallow the anger down and force my voice to come out as upbeat as a cheerleader on crack. "Okay, sounds good." With my back turned to him, I squeeze my eyes shut, reminding myself to breathe, reminding myself that he's all I got and when faced with the choice of being entirely alone or taking this, I choose this.

Chapter Five

Luke

I have a beer in my hand and a few shots in my system, building my safety net for the night. Without them, I'd feel like I was helplessly falling nowhere. I know it's a dangerous road I'm headed down, especially because I'm a diabetic. There have been a few instances where I pushed my body's limits and doctors have told me that if I don't stop, I could end up dead. The problem is that living without alcohol is a life I can't live.

It's Saturday night and I'm checking my computer for listings of apartments for rent. As usual, nothing turns up, nothing affordable anyway. It's the wrong time of year, summer break approaching, and all the college students are looking for places to live so they fill up quickly. If I had more money saved up, it'd be easier, but I don't. I'm starting to debate whether I can look past my resentment toward my father and ask him if I can come live with him or at least stay at the beach house. But the idea of asking him for help, when I got so little of it growing up, makes me feel weak. I want him to have to work to be my father. I don't know for sure how much he knows about what went on, but what I do know is that for years there wasn't enough contact from him for me to even tell him. The only thing I can do is let the memories haunt my head, which they do pretty much every night when I close my eyes, unless I'm drunk. When I'm drunk, nothing is in my head.

I get a text as I'm shutting the computer. I pick my phone up off the desk and swipe my finger over the screen. It's from Seth, Callie's best friend. I sometimes hang out with him and his boyfriend Greyson, since they both like to party as much as I do.

Seth: R u going out tonight?

Me: Aren't I always?

Seth: Where u headed?

Me: Probably to the Red Ink up on 6th street. Why? You got something planned?

Seth. Not yet. Red Ink, huh? You must be looking for a skank tonight.

Me: Tonight? Don't you mean always?

Seth: You know, rumor has it you've been hanging out with the biggest skank on campus.

Me: What? Who?

Seth: A bitchy roommate with a dragon tattoo on her neck. Goes by the name of Violet.

I scratch at my head, wondering where the hell he heard that from, but then it clicks.

Me: Did Callie tell you that?

Seth: Well, she didn't use those words per se since Callie
would never use those words, but she said she saw
you helping Violet around campus...what's that
about?

Me: Nothing. I was just being a nice guy.

Seth: Since when r u a nice guy.

He has a point. I'm not usually a nice guy, but for some
reason Violet momentarily brought it out of me. I'm not feeling like a nice guy right now though. I feel pissed off about my
living situation and all I want to do is get trashed out of my
mind and go find a girl to fuck so I can get rid of this feeling,
like I'm falling into a bottomless pit.

Me: I thought I'd try something different for a
little bit.

Seth. How's that going for you?

Me: I think I'm deciding to quit it before it becomes
a habit.

Seth: Good for u. U gonna do it cold turkey?

I shake my head. This could go on forever.

Me: I'm headed out. R u and Greyson down
or not?

Seth. Yeah, as long as we can get a cab. Neither one of us
wants to be DD tonight and I'm doubting u do either,
since u never offer.

Me: Sounds good. Callie and Kayden coming?

Seth: They went out somewhere . . . I think up to that
rock. They're becoming obsessed with it and each
other, lol.

Me: Yeah . . . meet u out in front of my dorm in ten?

Seth: Sounds good :)

I check my blood sugar levels and grab my glucose tablets,
just in case, then put my phone into my pocket and grab my key
card and wallet. I toss my empty beer bottle into the trash and
get another one out of the mini fridge, ready to get the hell out
of here and start drinking even heavier. That's what I love about
spring and summer, when football's not really going on and I'm
free to get trashed as much as I like without having to worry
about practice. It makes the noise and memories in my head just
a little more bearable. It makes breathing bearable. Life bearable.

I started drinking when I was thirteen. I wasn't with my
friends or anything, just sitting at home after my mom had
passed out on the sofa, not from heroin but from booze. She'd
made me sit with her as she drank gulp after gulp, forcing me
to hold her hand and coddle her like she was a sick person taking medication to numb the pain. As she started to doze off,
she'd wrapped her arms around me and held me tightly against

her, telling me that I would always be her little boy, and then sang a song to match her words. I hated when she did this, especially because I never felt like her little boy, even when I was seven. At that point in my life I knew our whole relationship was wrong, the things she made me do for her, like crush up her pills and the way she was always touching, but I was too ashamed to say anything and honestly I knew even then that nothing was ever going to change until I was old enough to get out of that damn house.

Finally, after holding me for way too long, she'd passed out into a deep sleep and I was able to slip out of her arms and be free for a moment. She'd left the bottle of whiskey out on the coffee table and I can remember sitting there, wondering what it tasted like, wondering why my mom needed to drink it all the time. So I picked it up and took a swig. The alcohol felt like it singed my throat and when it hit my belly it burned like fire. I was fascinated with the way it felt inside me, how the heat smothered out the wrong inside me, so I kept taking swigs until I passed out completely and for a moment, the wrong in me drifted asleep. After that, I'd always take a few drinks after she passed out and the more I did it, the more the rage and helpless feelings living in me became tolerable. And now I have a hard time functioning without it.

I'm about to head out when I get a call from my dad. I stare at my phone as it rings and rings, deciding whether I want to answer it or just silence his call. Finally, I hit talk and put it up to my ear, attempting to sound in a better mood than I am.

"Yeah," I say, pressing the phone between my ear and my shoulder so I can unscrew the cap off the beer.

"Hey," my father replies and there's music in the background. "You answered."

"Yeah, but I'm headed out so I can't talk for long." I tip my head back and guzzle a mouth full of beer, feeling the slightest bit better as it liquefies my throat.

"Oh, okay." He sounds disappointed. "I was just calling to check in on you."

"Why?"

"Because you're my son and I worry about you."

"Why? You didn't when I was a kid. Why start now when I'm an adult?"

He pauses and the noise gradually gets quieter. Then I hear a door shut and silence fills the connection. "Luke, I know I haven't been a very good father to you, but I'm trying to make that up to you now."

I grit my teeth. "I'm twenty years old. It's a little late to decide you want to be my father."

"I've always wanted to be your father," he says, nervousness creeping into his voice. "I just had a lot of stuff going on and I wasn't in the right place to be a good father."

"Well, I wasn't in the right place to be without a father." I head for the door, ready to bail out on the conversation because it's getting a little too heart-to-heart for my taste.

"Luke, I'm sorry." He sounds like he's about to cry, which makes me feel a little bad for him but then I get pissed off at myself for feeling sorry for him. "If there's anything I can do to make it up, I will."

I pause with my hand on the doorknob, biting my tongue, arguing with myself over how much pride I really have. Then I think about going home to Star Grove with my mother, the house covered in plastic, her begging me to help her. It makes me want to puke. "There might be one thing that you could do."

"Name it and it's yours."

I take a long breath. "You could let me stay at the beach house for the summer. I know you and Trevor are going to be there but I was hoping I could take one of the extra rooms or something." Trevor is my father's fiancé. I guess part of the reason why he left my mom was because he was struggling with the fact that he was gay. It took him years of drinking to finally accept that he was and come out to the world. It was about the time he reentered my life, but it was a little too late. Amy was already gone and I'd been around my mom enough that I only felt hatred for him for leaving me with her. I honestly don't really know how I feel about our relationship now. Confused maybe. I mean, Trevor and him both seem like nice guys but the fact that he left me to be responsible for shooting up my mother is what I'm most pissed off about.

He pauses long enough that I know he's going to say no and I want to hammer my fist into the door, enraged with myself because I knew I shouldn't have asked. "Luke . . . I'm so sorry, but Trevor and I are putting the beach house up for sale.

We're trying to get a house near work and we need a down payment."

"Could I stay with you in your apartment then?" I almost sound like I'm begging and I grip on to the doorknob tighter.

Again he pauses way too long. "We only have a studio apartment right now and it's overcrowded with Trevor's art, but when we get the new place in a couple of months you can definitely come out and stay with us for as long as you want. We'd love to have you."

I shake my head as my pulse pounds in my eardrums. *I need to get out of here. I need a drink. I need to not have so much damn noise in my head.* "Never mind," I say, then I hang up. I let go of the doorknob, step back, and kick the bottom of the door hard enough that my boot leaves a dent in it. "Shit." I press my hands to the side of my head, taking ragged gulps of air. Now on top of everything else, I'm going to have to try and explain to Kayden why it looks like a boot went through the damn door, although he has broken a few pieces of furniture himself.

I can't take this anymore. I knew I shouldn't have asked my father for anything. I wish I could hate him, then maybe it'd be easier to feel so much anger toward him.

❧

I party with Seth and Greyson at Red Ink until around nine or ten, downing shot after shot, my dad and my approaching homelessness becoming a dwindling problem. When we're pretty trashed out of our minds, we get a cab to drive to a house out in this town in no-man's-land...Fairtown I think...because Seth heard there was going to be a "raging party." When we get there, there are so many people it's hard to even move through the house. I end up losing track of Seth and Greyson in the crowd, but instead of looking for them I head straight for the drink area in the kitchen.

After I slam down about five shots of Bacardi, I head for the living room where the couches have been shoved aside and the stereo's booming some pop song. I'm not a fan of the music but it's danceable and there's some slutty-looking girls that are barely dressed, totally bangable and easy, at least from what I can tell—my vision's a little distorted right now. But I'm only looking for a distraction to get me through the night, so I can fall asleep in peace, something I rarely do.

I make my way out there and a short curvy brunette instantly comes up and starts rubbing up on my leg. I blink my eyes until I can kind of make out her face and then figure she'll do. I get behind her and she backs her ass up into me as we rock to the slow, sultry beat of the song. As she leans her head back, I sweep her hair to the side and slide my hand up to her rib cage as she tries to seduce me with her best seductive gaze. What she doesn't get, though, is she doesn't have to try. I'll take her back to her place and fuck her, just like she's hoping. I'll give her what she wants and in exchange I'll get a few moments of silence where I can be free from the reality of my life and all the twistedness inside me won't feel so sickening.

"You smell really good," she says, batting her eyelashes with her head tipped back against my chest.

"I smell like cigarettes and Bacardi," I call out because she's so full of it. The whole room smells like sweat and beer.

"Well, maybe I like that smell." She bats her eyelashes at me again as she slips her hand behind her and starts to rub my cock.

It's starting to feel really good when she starts doing this weird thing with her hips, then she spins around and strikes some kind of cat-clawing pose with her hands out in front of her. "I used to be a stripper," she tells me, shimmying her hips.

"In Fairtown?" I don't even try to hide my disgust. The town is pretty much a trailer park out in the middle of nowhere and I'm wondering if my drunk vision is making her seem a lot more attractive than she really is.

She nods her head, doing a little twirl and her hair whips me in the face. "Yeah, for like a year." She starts to back up and then comes at me again, shaking her tits, which are big enough that they bounce up and down. Then she starts whipping her head around as she swings her arms out to the side.

Any possibility of me getting hard dwindles and I'm about to tell her I'm going to get a shot, so I can get away from the whole nasty stripper dance she's got going on, when I hear laughter from behind me.

I glance over my shoulder and my heartbeat speeds up just a little. Violet is standing behind me, trying to restrain her laughter, her lips smashed together so tightly they're turning blue. I haven't talked to her since our McDonald's trip, where we sat down and had lunch like we were a fucking couple or something, which we're not because I don't do relationships—get involved. But I've seen her around on campus. I've been trying to avoid her as much as possible, trying not to look her way, otherwise I'll get drawn into whatever the hell is pulling me toward her. It's been a struggle, though, and a couple of times I've even found myself drifting in her direction.

Now she's the one who's drifted toward me, and I like it that she's here. I hate that she has that much power over me, that I'm feeling things for her … feelings I'm still trying to figure out.

I frown as she opens her mouth to say something. I'm sure she has some sort of snarky remark on the tip of her tongue.

But she moves around to the front of me and says to the brunette, "Mind if I cut in?"

"Are you being serious?" the brunette asks then glances at me, waiting for me to respond.

"I'll catch up with you later maybe," I say to the stripper, being evasive to avoid any confusion later.

She shoots me a glare, putting her hands up in front of her. "Don't bother. I've got plenty of other guys waiting in line to get with this." She rolls her body and shakes her tits again and Violet covers her hand with her mouth, choking on her laughter as the brunette stomps off.

Once she disappears in the crowd, I quickly take Violet in. Her red and black hair is swept to the side and has this sexy wave thing going on. Her green eyes are outlined with black and her lips shine even in the inadequate light. She's wearing this long black dress that flows all the way to her feet. It's different from what most of the other girls here are wearing, in the sense that it covers up a lot more. But she's not wearing a bra and even though her breasts aren't as big as the brunette's they're more attractive, her nipples perking through the thin fabric and making my cock rethink its deflation.

"So are you going to stare at me all day?" she asks, biting on her thumbnail, scanning the crowd instead of me. "Or actually dance with me?"

I rip my gaze from her tits and focus on her eyes. "I thought you were joking about that." I scroll over her body, taking my leisurely time, enjoying her slender frame. "You don't really seem like the dancing type and plus you shouldn't really be dancing on that ankle."

"I can dance, swollen ankle or not," she says neutrally, finally looking at me and again I'm taken aback by how detached she looks. "But you don't have to. I was just giving you an easy out from Bust-a-Move over there as a thank-you for helping my crippled ass around."

"Who said I needed an out?" I question, concerned over the fact that I've actually missed bantering with her. "Maybe I was into Bust-a-Move."

She holds up her hands and starts to back away from me. "Fine. I'll let you be. I was just trying to do something nice, which I don't do a lot."

I let her take two more steps back before I reach out and wrap my fingers around her arm. She may be trying to pretend like she doesn't give a shit, but I think she might. "I got nowhere else to be," I say, pulling her toward me, figuring dancing with her might keep me distracted for a minute or two.

"Oh, lucky me. Luke Price wants to dance with me. Swoon." She feigns a dreamy look, then tops it off with a roll of her eyes.

"Hey, you're the one that asked me to dance," I remind her as she reaches me. I slide my hand from her arm to her side and then around to her back. Then I guide her even closer, until heat builds between our bodies. *Good, fucking God.* I nearly moan when I realize that her dress doesn't have a back, at least from halfway up.

I casually slide my palm down her back, checking to see where the fabric starts. I seriously fucking lose it as I feel the softness of her flesh all the way to her waistline, where I finally touch fabric. I detect a slight shiver on her part, but her expression remains emotionless, her gaze locked on me as she places her hands on my shoulders.

We begin to move to the song together and I realize that she wasn't lying about being able to dance. Her hips sway softly against the grip of my hands, the front of her body grazing against mine. Each time our chests brush together a small breathy noise escapes her lips and it's sexy as hell and turning me on, my cock getting rock hard. *Jesus, I'm going to lose it if I don't calm down.*

After half of the song plays, she leans in toward my ear and whispers, "So why are you here, Luke Price?"

"Luke Price?" I grip her hips tighter as I turn my head toward her. "What happened to Mr. Stoically Aloof?"

She shrugs, wetting her lips with her tongue as she traces her finger up and down the back of my neck. I wonder if she's even aware that she's doing it, but I'm definitely aware—too aware. "I thought I'd give the nickname a break tonight," she says.

Our faces are inches apart and the heat of our breaths mix and make the already damp air even damper.

"Why are you here, Violet with no last name?" I maintain her gaze as I lean away just a little so I can get a better look at her.

The intensity in her expression mirrors my own and I wonder just how much I'm getting into just from dancing with her. She's a challenge, secretive like myself, and that only makes me more curious. About her. About her secrets. About getting to know her. It gives her so much power over me, because I want to know her and she won't let me. And I usually don't want to know things about most people.

"For the awesome company, obviously," she jokes and her lips quirk a little like she's going to smile.

"Well, obviously." I'm getting uncomfortable with the way my heart keeps speeding up every time she starts to smile and I'm debating on whether to leave or not. Yet at the same time I'm so turned on by the feel of her hips in my hands all I want to do is stay and keep touching her. My attraction to her ends up controlling me as my hand travels from her hips to her back and I press on the small of it, luring her even closer to me until her chest is pressing against mine. "How's your foot?"

Biting her bottom lip, she glances down at her feet and I realize she's not wearing shoes. "It's doing okay, I guess."

"Okay, so where are your shoes?"

She shrugs, returning her attention to me. "I had flip-flops on, but they were annoying me so I kicked them off somewhere."

Through my irrational alcohol-filled mind I somehow rationalize thinking it's okay to ask, "About the other night when you…you know, jumped out the window. What was that about?"

Her body goes rigid, but her expression is calm. "What was what about?"

I turn my head away from her gaze and stare out into the crowd. "Why'd you jump?"

"It's a long story," she says evenly and I feel her eyes on me. "Why are you asking?"

I meet her gaze again as the music switches to a more bumping song. I want to tell her the truth—that I'm worried about her. That I know the darker reasons of why someone would jump out a window. That even though I barely know her, I can't stop thinking about her. That she's controlling my thoughts way more than I'd like. But instead I say, "Just curious. It's not every day a beautiful girl falls out the window and kicks me in the face."

She doesn't react, like she doesn't even notice that I just complimented the crap out of her, at least in my book. "I got into a little bit of a mess. The only way to get out of it was to jump out the window," she says indifferently.

A thousand questions tumble through my mind. "What kind of a mess?"

She chews on her bottom lip nervously and then sighs, annoyed. "Why do you care so much about this?"

I shake my head and shrug. "Because...I'm worried that...that you might have done it...on purpose." I almost mumble the last part and I'm not sure if she heard me or not.

"Worried about me? Really?" She seems skeptical at the possibility.

"People worry about people all the time," I say.

"No they don't," she insists and her eyes briefly flicker with anger. "And besides, you don't even know me."

"Well, this is me trying to get to know you." What the hell is wrong with my drunken mouth tonight? It's like it's got a mind of its own. "Look, maybe—"

She covers my mouth with her hand and shakes her head. "No more questions, okay?" Without giving me time to answer, she spins around, turning her back to me. I think she's going to leave, but instead she leans back against me, pressing her back into my chest.

Then she starts to dance. And I mean really dance, leaning just to the side to keep her weight off her ankle as she hypnotically rocks to the rhythm. Her hips move from side to side, matching the beat perfectly. The movement brushes her ass up against my cock and I start moving with her, grabbing at her hips, delving my fingertips into her, and her back arches. The more the song goes on, the more into it we get. Sweat beads out skin and there's so much contact and friction between our bodies it seriously feels like we're veering toward sex. Then she does this little move where she gradually, but gracefully lowers toward the floor. Her body slides down mine until the back of her head brushes against my cock, which is rock hard. Then she pushes back up, dragging her body up mine again. By the time she's standing upright, I'm about to grab hold of her, take her to the nearest room and fuck her until she screams out my name. I need to get back control over the situation.

I get distracted, though, as she lets her head fall to the side and her arms come up and wind around the back of my neck, her movements owning me. I get a glimpse of the back of her neck and the dragon and two stars tattooed on her skin. I haven't fucked very many girls with tattoos but good God I need to start because it's mind-blowingly sexy. I slide my palms around to the front of her stomach and I crush our bodies together. Heat blares through me as the smell of her blends with the alcohol in my system and it makes the hunger and overpowering need inside me feel like it belongs there.

Her hair is swept over her shoulder and her neck is just inches away from my lips. The desire to suck and bite at her skin is intoxicating and without contemplation over what I'm doing or what it'll mean, my lips part and my tongue slides out along her skin. It's not like I've never licked a girl's neck before. I have many times, just like I've kissed and fucked many times. Usually it drowns out any noise inside my head, but right now I can still hear all of it, if not more. It's louder. Sharper. More potent and I'm afraid I'm going to lose myself, lose control. But it's almost like my mouth is being magnetized to her skin and I start sucking on her neck, nipping and grazing my teeth gently along it. With the way her muscles tense, I half expect her to turn around and punch me in the jaw. I sort of wish she would so I'd walk away...at least I think I would...I might actually want to stay more. But instead her head falls to the side, giving me access to devour the taste of her.

My hand wanders up her ribs, across her breast, her nipple hardening underneath the thin fabric. I graze my thumb across it and then move my hand all the way up to the hollow of her neck. She groans as I press my fingers gently into her collarbone and leans back against my chest, putting her weight against me. Reality starts to blur away as I move my hand down her body to her leg and start pulling the fabric of her dress up, desperate to slip my fingers inside her and make her groan louder.

"God, you're so beautiful..." I breathe against her neck as

my hand reaches her upper thigh. "We should go back into one of the rooms…"

She starts to slant her head toward me, our lips briefly brushing, and desire floods my body at the spark of contact. I grip handfuls of her dress, opening my mouth to devour her, when suddenly she pushes my arms from her and moves away from me.

She peers over her shoulder at me, her cheeks a little flushed, but her expression emotionless. "Thanks for the dance," she says and then putting her hands up above her head, she makes a path through the crowd, eventually disappearing into a swarm of sweaty, drunk bodies.

I stand in the crowd, shaking my head at myself, dumbfounded by my own idiocy. "God, you're so beautiful? We should go back into one of the rooms." Yeah, it wasn't my best line ever but Jesus, she runs off more than anyone I've ever known.

After analyzing her for way too long, I decide that it's not my fucking problem—*she's* not my fucking problem. I need to move on, cut whatever it is that's drawing me to her, get over my developing obsession with the mysterious girl who jumps out windows and seems to show up wherever I go. Leaving most of my thoughts of Violet behind, I shove through the crowd and push to the kitchen where the counters are lined with bottles and bottles of alcohol. There are so many choices it's like Christmas. I select a bottle of Crown Royal and slam back another shot... or two... or three... or four... until they all blur together and I can't think anymore.

When I'm almost gone, veering on blacking out, I find the first decent-looking girl I come across and flirt with her until we're heading back to one of the rooms. It doesn't take long after the door shuts before our clothes are off and I'm thrusting inside her. The headboard bangs against the wall as I pin her hands down to the side of her head and she screams out, not my name because we never got that far. Her head is tipped back, her neck arched, her skin beaded with sweat. As I stare down at her, thrusting our hips together, all I think about is how I can do anything to her right now. For a second it feels right. I don't feel so helpless and fucked up inside. So controlled by the things around me and my past. I feel drunk and high on this girl under me, who's ready to give me whatever I want. For a brief moment I have control over everything. There's not all this noise inside me, reminding me of the bad and horrible stuff that makes up my past. I feel content and still inside. Then I'm pulling out of her and the wholeness inside me empties out. The girl rolls over to her side and moments later she passes out. The control I felt over the situation is dissipating and I feel like a helpless kid again, which is so fucked up. I climb out of bed and get dressed, and then I leave her behind, hoping I never cross paths with her again. As I exit the room, the control fleetingly rises again, but once I step out into the living room again it's all gone. Leaving me to try and outrun it again.

Violet

After I leave Luke on the dance floor, I hurry for the back of the house, trying not to run, but I can't help but walk quickly. The guy I was working before I headed out to Luke catches me by the arm as I'm crossing the kitchen.

"Hey, where'd you go?" he asks as he reaches for a beer on the counter. "I thought we were going to go somewhere and talk."

"We will, but I have to take care of something first." Before he can respond, I jerk my arm out of his hold and leave him behind with his jaw hanging open. I burst out the back door and then stare at the small lake a little ways out in the backyard. There's a dock stretching out over it and that's where I head, pushing past the crowd and to the grass, the sounds and lights of the party disappearing the farther away I get. The closer I get to the water, the quicker I walk, the pain in my ankle tearing at my muscles. When my bare feet brush the wood of the dock, I run as fast as I can toward the edge. My heart thrashes in my chest, my blood pumping furiously. It wants to escape the adrenaline rush, but me, I embrace it, bask in it as the adrenaline pours through me like liquid fire, burning away everything I feel at the moment; the want, the desire, the way I let Luke touch me and how I let myself feel when he touched me. He wasn't just groping me. What was going on inside my body was very real. Too real. So real I actually briefly considered going back to a room with him and letting him do whatever to me because I wanted him to.

When I reach the end of the dock, I gather every ounce of energy I have left and jump, releasing all the oxygen from my lungs until I'm empty of air. Empty of everything. Seconds later, I crash into the water and the cold water floods over my body, drenching my dress, my skin, my hair. It weighs me down, drags me under, and I don't fight back. I willingly let it take me over.

I remember when I finally realized that my parents weren't coming back. That they were dead and the blood I saw all over them wasn't just in my imagination. That the images of them lying on the floor, their bodies still, and their eyes open wasn't just a picture I'd drawn up in my head. It was real. The reality that I was alone started to seep in and even at six years old I knew that nothing would ever be the same.

I'd never be the same.

It was hard to feel it, the blunt truth that I didn't have parents anymore. There was a lot of pain. A lot of razors slicing at me from the inside. Needles stabbing at my veins. A hole rapidly growing inside my heart. I felt it—I felt everything. I'd wake up sometimes at night clawing at my skin, trying to dig the feeling out of me, but all I'd ever get were cuts and scratches.

The first couple that took me in thought I was crazy. I heard them talking about it once, that they worried I'd hurt them or myself and why wouldn't they after what'd I'd seen. Death. Violence. Murder. The morbid part of life—it was branded into my head, which meant I was going to become morbid myself. It confused me and I think I actually started to believe that it might really happen, that I changed into a violent person. Between the idea that I'd end up hurting someone and the constant pain inside me, I decided to give up feeling all together. Turn it off. Shut down. Self-induced numbness.

It was hard at first, especially at night when my mind seemed insistent on remembering everything. But one night when I woke up from a nightmare, panicked and my head a little muddled, I'd gotten confused and thought I was back at my old house. I'd run out of my room, miscalculating where the stairs started and I ended up tripping. I nearly had a heart attack as I fell down the stairs, the carpet scraping at my back and legs, my life flashing before my eyes. When I finally reached the bottom, I stared up at the ceiling feeling the adrenaline pounding through my body and all the pain and fear I'd felt from my dream was replaced by a rush of energy. For a second, I couldn't feel the razors or needles or the hole in my heart. My mind and body were content. It was the first real moment of peace I'd felt in a while and it was silently and painfully beautiful.

After that, it became a habit. I'd wake up in a panic and run out of my room and fall down the stairs. I was intentionally doing it and I knew it was insane, but it was making me feel better. My foster parents were heavy sleepers and didn't notice at first, but I did wake them up occasionally. At first I played it off as being sleepy and confused but by the sixth or seventh time they started to wonder if something was up and they started asking questions. So I told them the truth, hoping they'd understand. They looked at me with fear in their eyes and two weeks later I was moved to a new home. After that, I stopped telling the truth and I found different ways to get my adrenaline rushes. Running out in front of cars, standing on top of buildings, letting myself sink into the water until my lungs felt like they were going to combust.

I know what I'm doing is dangerous, but I don't care. It's better than feeling the razors. The needles. The unhealable hole in my heart.

The water is cold but not very deep and I reach the bottom quickly. I let myself sink to the ground, my knees pressing against the muddy bottom. My arms float to my side, my hair in my face. Above my head, the moon glows distortedly and beautifully through the ripples in the water. Everything is silent. The water. The night. The emotion inside me. I shut my eyes. I let myself start to drown. I stay as still as I can until my lungs ache to burst. Until I become light-headed. Until I feel myself start to leave reality. Until I'm at the point where I'm about to no longer exist. Then I push upward. Bubbles float from my mouth as I rise, kicking my feet. I stretch my arms up and moments later I burst through the water, gasping for air. Adrenaline is drowning the inside of my body as my lungs fight to breathe—fight to stay alive. Water drips down my hair into my face as I lie back and float in the water, staring up at the moon, my chest rising and falling, up and down, my body half above the water and half below.

Chapter Six

Luke

I was seven when I realized that there was something really wrong with my home environment. It wasn't something I'd slowly discovered. It was suddenly forced on me when my mother showed up in the middle of the night after being gone somewhere for hours. She was freaking out, chattering about being sorry. I think she was high out of her mind and it looked like there was blood on her hands and clothes, but when I asked her about it—even though I was scared shitless of her answer—she only hugged me for hours, rocking me like a baby, and told me everything was going to be okay. The thing was nothing was ever okay from that point on. It's still not okay, but livable, as long as I have enough alcohol in my system that the fucked-up parts of my life don't feel real. As long as I have control over the things that I do I'm fine. The problem is that lately the control I've worked so hard to get is slipping from my fingers.

School ends in a few days and it's getting close to the day

when I should be heading home, back to the hellhole where nothing feels right and I feel like a God damn kid again. Kayden's already got most of his stuff packed, his side of the room covered in taped-up boxes. He is over at Callie's dorm helping her out right now and I haven't even gotten started on my side, the bed still made, my clothes still in the dresser. I'm seriously contemplating lighting it on fire and living in my truck. I haven't even bothered talking to my father since our last conversation. He's called a few times, but hasn't left any messages.

"Look, I'm sorry I'm breaking your heart or whatever," I pace the length of my small dorm room between the two beds with the phone pressed up to my ear, shaking my head at pretty much every word she utters, "but I'm seriously going to stay here." I'm so full of shit. I officially have nowhere to stay. All the apartments for rent cost too much money. At this point I've been searching for a roommate, but I can't seem to find one. It's just the wrong time or something and I fucking hate it because I don't want to go back to my hometown, Star Grove.

"Lukey," she starts. I hate it when she calls me that and even now it makes me feel nauseous. "You need to come home and take care of me. I've started taking my medications again and I need your help."

"Which ones?" I say disdainfully, kicking at the leg of my bed, the need to pound a hole into something rising in me like a flame burning toward a pool of gasoline. "Your heroin? Your crushed-up pain meds? Coke? Whiskey? Which one is it, Mother?"

"You act like I don't need it," she says, sounding hurt. "I do. I need it, Lukey. I need it more than anything otherwise I think too much and bad stuff happens when I think too much. You know that."

"Bad stuff happens regardless of what you're on." I slam my boot into the leg of the bed over and over again, the bed slamming into the wall, and my foot starts to hurt. *Fuck!* "And you know I'm too old to believe that shit, Mother. I know you're just doing drugs for the same reason that everyone else is in the world and that's to escape whatever it is you're running from. It's not some doctor prescription like you convinced me it was when I was six."

"But it is, sweetie." Her voice is high-pitched as if she's talking to a child. "The doctors just haven't realized I need it yet."

I hate her. I hate myself for hating her so much. I hate the hate inside me and how out of control it makes me feel. I hate that every time I get even remotely close to anyone, I think of all the horrible things she made me do—the hell she put me through. "You know what I think," I say and storm over to the wall. "I think you've done too much of it and now you've lost it." I pause, wondering how she's going to respond. I'm usually not so blunt with her, instead avoiding her at all costs. But the moving back is getting to me.

"You think I'm crazy?" she asks in a subdued voice. I hear rustling in the background and I don't even want to know what she's doing. "Is that what you think? Does my little boy think his mother is insane?"

I press my fingertips to my temple, the muscles in my arms tightening with my frustration. "I don't know what I'm saying."

"You're sounding like all the rest of them," she says and something loud bangs in the background.

"All the rest of who?" I ask, rolling my eyes.

"The neighbors," she whispers and then pauses. "I think they've been watching me...And there's this car parked out front...I think it's the police watching me again."

"The police aren't watching you again—they never were. They just questioned you once for God knows what, you never would tell me."

"They are, too, Lukey. They're after me again."

I shake my head and the list of what "medication" she's been taking becomes shorter because there are only a few of them that bring out her paranoia. "No one's after you and you want to know why? Because no one cares."

"You care about me, though." Panic fills her tone. "Don't you, Lukey?"

I sink down on the bed and lower my head into my hands. God, I wish I could just say no. Tell her I hate her. Rid my life of her. But I can't seem to bring myself to say it aloud, always bound by that stupid little kid that lives inside me, the one that always helped her, felt like he had to because no one else would. "Yeah, sure."

"That's my good boy," she tells me and I feel the burn of approaching vomit at the back of my throat. "Always taking care of me. I can't wait for you to come home. We're going to have so much fun."

I know what her version of fun is—cleaning the house together, having me help her with whatever drugs she's taking, sit with her, listen to her sing, be her best friend and enter her insane world of drug-induced ranting. I can't go back and live with her. In that house. In my room. With the insanity. Her telling me she needs me. Needs. Needs. Needs. Just going back for Christmas was enough and I wasn't even there that much. If I end up with her there I can probably get a job and party a lot just to avoid going home, but in the end I'll have to go home. I never want to go back. I ran away from all that shit when I was sixteen and I can't go back. I need to get out of going home no matter what it takes. "I have to go." Before she can say anything I hang up.

I toss the phone aside on the bed and rock back and forth, breathing back the impulse to scream and hit something. I know if anyone walked in and saw me like this they'd think I'd lost my mind, but I can't stop the wave of anger and panic once it surfaces like this. Only three things do it for me. Sex and alcohol and violence.

I keep rocking and rocking but the rage inside me rises and mixes with the vile feeling of shame I always carry with me. I feel a wave of rage building and building as it makes its way through my body toward the outside of me. If I don't do something soon I'm going to end up destroying the room. Finally, I can't stand it any longer. I jump up from the bed and storm for the wall again. This time I don't stop. I just bend my arm back and ram my fist against the wall over and over again, heat and rage blasting through my body. After the fifth slam of my fist, I'm trembling from head to toe and there's a fist-size hole in the wall and each one of my knuckles is split open. Kayden was already worried about fixing the door and now the wall's messed up. I'm really on a roll. I need to get out of here because it still feels like I need to hit something. Kick something. Beat the shit out of something. I need to get the anger building inside me out, before it takes control of me, and there's only one way to do that and it requires a lot of physical pain and alcohol, but I want it. More than anything.

Violet

I'm in a super shitty mood today, the invisible razors and needles I haven't felt in a long time are back, slicing at my skin as my irritation builds. At first it was a slow-building irritation, over life in general. I tried to tell myself over and over again that it was nothing—that I was just in a mood. But I think it might be something deeper, like the fact that I find myself missing a certain someone.

I never miss anyone. And all I want to do is turn it off, yet at the same time I don't.

It's confusing and slightly annoying

As I'm packing my boxes, telling myself to stop thinking about him, my phone rings and the song playing means it's an unknown number. When I answer it the person breathes heavily and then hangs up.

"Seriously," I say to the phone, before setting it down on my bed. I move over to the desk, searching through the papers stacked on it, wondering if any of them are mine. As I'm reaching the bottom stack, my phone rings again, same ringtone, unknown number.

I glare at the phone as I pick it up. I don't even get to hello this time, before the caller hangs up. It happens again and again and finally, after the seventh or eighth I tell the person off.

"Look, if you don't stop calling me," I say, "I'm going to track you down and cut your balls off."

"What if I'm a girl?" he asks with a hint of laughter in his tone.

I sit down on my bed and cross my legs. "Then you really need to stop taking so much testosterone since your voice is lower than a normal dude's voice."

He laughs, like I was amusing, but I'm being serious. "You're funny."

"I'm not trying to be."

"Well, you are."

I shake my head. "What the hell do you want? And who are you?"

"I'm looking for Violet Hayes," he says.

I go rigid. I don't recognize his voice—he shouldn't know my last name.

"Who the hell is this?" I start to grow nervous as I glance around my empty room. It's been a long time since I've felt uneasy with being alone, but the old feelings are emerging, the feeling that someone is watching me, waiting to hurt me like they should have done twelve years ago.

"The Violet Hayes who was part of the Hayes murder case," he says.

I hang up on him and chuck the phone across the room. It dents the wall and I think I broke it until it rings again. I let it ring and ring, then it silences as it goes to voicemail. But then it starts ringing again, until finally I can't take it anymore. I get up and track the sound of the ringtone to the corner of the room, where I find the phone wedged between the leg of the desk and the wall. I bend down and fumble around until I get a hold of it.

"What the hell do you want, asshole?" I practically shout in the phone as I stand back up.

"Is this Violet Hayes?"

"Oh my God, are you being serious? I don't want to talk to you, whoever you are, so stop calling."

He pauses. "This is Detective Stephner. I need to speak to Violet Hayes."

I hesitate as I wander back to my bed. "Did you just call me?"

"No…" He sounds lost and gives an elongated pause. "I'm calling you to see if you can come meet with me. I'd like to talk to you about your parents' murder."

It takes me a second to answer. "Why?" I ask cautiously.

"Because I'm reopening the case," he responds in a formal tone. "And I want to see what you can remember about that night."

"Why are you reopening the case?" I ask, wondering if maybe they found something, feeling a spark of hope. "Did you find something?"

"No, but we're hoping to," he says and all of my hope simmers out.

"Well, I remember what I told the police thirteen years ago, which isn't a hell of a lot, since I was six and emotionally fucked up," I say, telling myself not to get my hopes up but I can already feel the emotions pressing up, the ache connected to the loss of my parents. "So I don't really see the point of me coming down there and wasting my time, you asking me the same damn questions and shoving the same damn mug shots at me even though I told you I barely saw the killers since it was dark."

"I understand your frustration, but answering some questions could help solve your parents' murder," he points out and I hear him shuffling through papers.

"No it won't," I say, flopping down on the bed on my back, holding the phone to my ear. My muscles are starting to tighten just from the suggestion of going down to the police station and chatting about something I'd laid to rest a long time ago. Case closed. They said so themselves and even though I didn't like it, I accepted it. Moved on. Lived what life

I had. "They couldn't solve it thirteen years ago and you're not going to solve it now."

"I'd appreciate it if you'd come down," he tells me, sending me a silent message through his firm tone. You're going to meet me—it's not a choice.

"Fine, but I live in Laramie now, not Cheyenne," I say in a tight voice. "And I'm in the middle of moving, so it'll have to wait a few days." I'm making up excuses on purpose.

"How about next Monday at seven? Downtown at the Laramie police station?" he asks without missing a beat. "Does that work for you?"

I frown. "I guess."

He says good-bye and then I hang up, lying on the bed. I chew on my fingernails, not liking the emotions tormenting me in the quiet. I'd shut that door a long time ago and now I was just supposed to open it up so I could tell him the same things I already told the police thirteen years ago. I'm sure he has all that in his file, so why is he bothering me?

I check my voicemail seeing if creepy, deep-voice guy left a message. He didn't and an unsettling fear stirs in my stomach. For the first few months after my parents died, I had this overwhelming fear that the people were going to come back to finish me off. It was like I constantly felt I needed to look over my shoulder; if I saw a shadow at night in my room, I thought it was them breaking in. But I managed to get myself out of that place and land where I am now. I worked hard not to be afraid of anything and I refuse to go back to that place.

I barely budge from the bed, drowning in my emotions, and I start to debate my options for a much-needed hit of adrenaline. I have these pills that I've taken a couple of times and at the right dose they can put me into darkness and I can still get out. They're hidden in the computer desk drawer, beside the prescription bottle that holds the stash of weed Preston gave me to make quick sales, right within arm's reach. Such an easy escape from everything going on around me. It's not my favorite route to go, because it's easier for someone to walk in and find me. I don't want to be found. I want to remain lost because it's the only thing that's become serenely and painfully familiar.

But then Callie and Kayden walk in the room with boxes in their hands, ready to pack up the last of her stuff, and I force myself to shove my bed-binding emotions down and move again.

After packing for a while, Callie and Kayden start making out with each other. They actually think they're in love and the concept is ridiculously absurd to me. I sort of feel sorry for them, because one day down the road they're going to break up and it's going to hurt. They'll cry. They'll become depressed. They'll eat lots of ice cream or whatever people do when they mourn the loss of a relationship.

I remember one foster home I lived at when I was about fourteen. The Peircesons, a husband and wife that lived in a townhouse in this decent subdivision where each house was a duplicate of the other. I remember, when I pulled up to it, thinking it was pretty and that worried me because I was anything but pretty. I wore dark clothes, chains for a belt, and I had more studs in my ear than I could count on my fingers. I was going through a misunderstood phase and wanted everyone to know it. The Peircesons were decent, but the husband seemed a little uninterested in having a teenager around. At first, it seemed like my stay there was going to be boring, until I was out back one day on the porch and the next-door neighbor came out, talking on her phone. There was a tall fence, so she couldn't see me at first, but I could hear her talking dirty to someone on the phone, telling them she would spank them. The conversation got me interested the longer it went on and by the time it was over I was laughing, something I hadn't done in a while.

The lady must have heard me, too, because when she hung up she peeked her head over the fence. She seemed a little annoyed at first that I was eavesdropping, but her annoyance turned to intrigue when I showed no remorse for listening.

After that, I started hanging out with her during the three hours I had between when school ended and the Peircesons came home from work. She taught me how to light her cigarettes for her and told me the ins and outs of men, even though I told her I'd never fall in love. Her name was Starla, although I never really believed it was her real name, but it seemed fitting. She ran a phone chat operation from her house, which meant she told guys she was doing dirty things to herself, playing into their fetishes while they jerked off. She actually had a part-time job as a saleswoman at a car dealership, living a double life. She reminded me of a starlet from the 1940s when she was at home, her blond hair always curled, she wore a lot of silk, and sometimes even a feather boa. She told me she dressed like that because it made her feel like the sexy seductress she played on the phone. When I asked her why she enjoyed talking to men like she did, she told me it was because it made her feel like she had control over them. That she'd had too many heartbreaks and spent too many nights crying over ice cream and this helped her stay away from that. What was amusing about the whole thing is usually she was cooking dinner or reading a magazine, even watching television when she was talking dirty to the guys. She never actually did any of the stuff she said.

"You like that, Biggie," she'd said once into the phone as she walked around the living room cleaning up the garbage laying around, while wearing her silk robe and slippers. I was hanging out on her couch, waiting until it was time to return home to the boring Peircesons, watching reruns of *My So-Called Life*, this nineties television show that got canceled after one season, but I found highly entertaining.

I giggled when she called him Biggie and she'd glanced over at me, smiling as she rolled her eyes. "Creeper," she mouthed.

I laughed again. "Aren't they all." Then I grabbed a handful of chips out of the bag on my lap. A lot of the guys liked her to call them their special nicknames and I was guessing this one asked for her to call him Biggie, probably because he wasn't.

"Oh yeah, I like that," she said, picking up a few empty glasses off the coffee table. Then she whisked out of the room and I'd returned to my show.

A few minutes later, after the guy had probably finished himself off, she'd come back into the living room, smoking a cigarette. "Men are exhausting," she said, plopping down on the sofa beside me. The whole house was crammed with gold-trimmed antique furniture, none of which matched, and the teal walls were hung with pictures of bands and actresses she'd met. I loved her place because it was different. Every place I'd lived looked pretty much the same as the others and most of those turned out to be crappy.

"Then why do you work for them?" I'd wondered curiously, kicking my feet up on the coffee table.

She glanced at me as she reached for an ashtray on the coffee table. "Oh my dear, sweet, innocent Violet. They work for me, honey."

She always used endearing terms and it annoyed me, yet I let it slide with her.

I stuffed a few more chips in my mouth. "You know, I seriously wish you would be my foster mother."

She smiled sadly, leaning forward to put the cigarette out. "I can't be a foster mother, Violet. I can barely take care of myself."

I chewed on the chips as I stared at the television screen. I didn't get it because it seemed like she took great care of herself, no attachments, doing whatever she wanted. It sounded like such a great life, but maybe she was just saying that because she really didn't want to be my foster mother.

"So what's up with the girl with the red hair?" she asked, changing the subject as she reached for the chips. "She seems obsessed with gorgeous eyes right there."

"I don't think she's obsessed." I silently shouted at the emotions stirring inside me to shut up, that it doesn't matter if I have a mother or not because it wouldn't fix anything—fix me. "Just addicted to him."

"That might be even worse than being obsessed."

"What do you mean?"

"Addiction is dangerous," she said and then patted my head as she rose to her feet. "Especially with men." She'd gone back into the kitchen and moments later the phone rang. I sat on the couch listening to her talk about spanking some guy wondering if she was addicted to guys or whether they were addicted to her. What was the difference?

Even though my time with Starla was fleeting, since the Peircesons quickly got tired of having a foster kid, I learned a lot from her. Not just about manipulation, but about gaining power. Plus she never gave a shit about what she did, even though a lot of people would have looked down on her if they found out about it. She would say stuff that most wouldn't and I idolized her for it.

"Would you guys knock it off?" I ask Callie and Kayden as

I stuff the last of my shirts into the boxes. Callie and Kayden are rolling around on the bed together and I swear I'm about two seconds away from getting a live porn show.

They barely hear me as Kayden lies down on top of Callie and starts sucking on her neck. I give up on making them stop, scooping up the last of my packed boxes. I still have a few more things to box up but I need a break from all the PDA so I head out of the dorm room and carry the last box down to Preston's car. He let me borrow it this morning so I could get my stuff to the house a little easier and thankfully my ankle's healed enough that I'm not walking like I need a cane.

It's mid-May and the temperature is pushing ninety-something. As I toss the last box into the trunk, I pull my hair up into a messy ponytail and then tie the bottom of my T-shirt so that it sits above my waist. I have cut-offs on and my combat boots, the ones with the broken buckle. It's hot and I seriously wish that someone would create a law that we could be allowed to walk around naked when it's this hot.

Unfortunately if I stripped down and paraded around the campus naked, I'd probably get arrested. Given the right time and my mood, though, I'd probably be glad to be handcuffed and thrown into a police car. Plus, it might get me out of going down to the police department on Monday.

❧

When I pull up to Preston's trailer house, there's a party going on. I'm a little irked because he knew I was moving back today and it's going to be a pain in the ass trying to get my stuff in the house with a bunch of annoying drunk dumb-asses hanging out in the living room.

I park the car as close to the front door as possible, but there's a line of cars blocking the driveway. People are standing all over the front yard, on the driveway, and on the steps leading to the front door. Most of them are older, but some are about my age. Plastic cups and cigarettes in their hands. I haven't lived here for nine months and apparently I've forgotten what it was like and why I decided to live in the dorms. Living here is like having to deal at parties all the time.

Sighing, I get out of the car and adjust my hair into a more secure ponytail as I bump the door shut with my hip. Some guy wearing an oversize hoodie whistles at me and I shake my head and disregard him as I weave around the people toward the front door.

"What's up, baby? You come here to give me another show," a douche named Trey calls out as I walk by him and through the front door. He's in his midtwenties and when I was staying here he used to walk into my room all the time pretending to be lost when really he was trying to catch me changing, which he did once. I'd have locked the doors but there aren't any locks on any of them, except for the bathroom.

"I'll give you another show," I say, shutting the screen door. "Just as long as I can give you that painful knee-to-the-nuts reminder of what happens after you steal a show?"

His eyelids lower as he puckers a kiss at me and then laughs like he's the most hilarious person on earth. "It's a deal."

I let the screen door slam shut in his face. Cigarette smoke and the pungent scent of weed engulfs me as I squeeze through the crowded room. "Kryptonite" by 3 Doors Down blares from the stereo and some weirdo tripping in the corner is pretending to play air guitar. When I first moved in with Preston things weren't like this, but that was because of Kelley. Yeah, they were dealers and sometimes I think that was part of the reason they adopted me, so I could go to all the high school parties and sell stuff for them. I wasn't a fan of it, but I didn't care, either, so I did what they asked because they gave me a home. But they never brought their dealing or their clients home like this, Kelley would never have allowed it.

I head down the hall toward Preston's room, knowing he's probably in there doing something highly illegal. I pause at the door and knock, but the music playing in his bedroom is even louder than the music in the living room. After the third knock I turn the knob and open the door, hoping he's not having sex or anything. He's not but there are four guys on the bed with him and they're circled around a blue bong shaped like a vase and there's a guy and a girl on the television screen, the guy ramming her from behind as she moans and whimpers. I've seen porn videos here and there, but not under circumstances where I paid attention to it. But right now, I can't seem to take my eyes off it. The guy looks so content in this really intense way and so does the girl, but there's no emotion toward each other. They're just there in the moment. I wonder if that's what I look like all the time. Just there in my life.

Finally I blink my eyes away from the screen and fix my attention on the bed. One of the guys has his mouth to the mouthpiece of the tall, slender glass bong and a lighter in his hand, about ready to light up. He says something to Preston and then Preston looks over at the television with this euphoric look on his face.

I'm deciding if I really want to stick around just so I get high off secondhand smoke tonight and sit around watching porn with a bunch of guys, when Preston notices me lingering in the doorway. His bloodshot blue eyes light up as they scale my body and then he says something as a languid smile spreads on his face, but the music's too loud for me to make out his words.

"What?" I shout, cupping my hand around my ear.

He turns the music down that's playing from an old stereo, the smile still on his face as he waves me over to him. The other four guys suddenly notice me, and their undivided attention is unwelcomed on my part. I know there's something wrong about the situation, but it's hard to determine what exactly the wrong part is because I've seen so much wrong that sometimes it starts to seem right.

I let out a breath, knowing I'm going to have my hands full with five stoned, horny guys in the room. I walk over to the bed and when I reach the edge Preston's fingers spread around my waist. Pressing his fingertips into me, he guides me to his lap and sits me down on it. I still have my shirt tied up so his hands are on my bare skin and I'm pretty sure I feel his hard-on pressing against my ass. I'm not enthusiastic about the situation so I casually start to slide off his lap, but he only constricts his grip and secures me in place. It stings and I wouldn't be surprised if he leaves red marks on my skin. It doesn't feel like he's being friendly at all, but territorial. Pins and needles prick at my skin as I feel the confusing, indecipherable emotions tied to the moment, to Preston. He means something to me—this means something. I tap my fingers on my leg, trying to figure out what to do.

He leans closer and puts his scruffy chin on my shoulder. "Why are you so tense? Is it the weed or the video?"

I force one of my infamous plastic smiles as I rotate my head toward him. "I'm just tired. I spent all day packing and I still have to go back and finish up." I don't mention the thing about the detective because I don't want to talk about it at the moment.

"Well, I'll help you unpack the car," he says, his hands wandering from my waist to the top of my thighs as he glances at the television screen. "That should help, right?"

One of the guys across from me, wearing this really grungy beanie, elbows the blond guy to the side. They exchange an underlying look, then the blond one's eyes drink me in. I'm getting a little nervous, but also the thrill of what could happen arises and the two painfully mix. The pins and needles fizzle but I'm not sure whether I'm relieved or terrified anymore.

I nod, without taking my eyes off the blond guy. "Yeah . . . that should help." My adrenaline's speeding, soothing and pulling at my emotions, an internal tug-of-war. Do I like it? Hate it? Do I want the danger to accelerate? Or do I want to run? Be weak. Let the pins and needles win.

After the argument goes on and on in my head, I finally give up and maneuver my legs to the side, lowering my feet onto the floor. I'm still uncertain how I feel about my emotions at the moment, but a break from the smoke, Preston's hands, and the porno movie might clear my head.

"I'm going to go start getting boxes out of the trunk," I tell him as I slip out of his arms. Thankfully he easily lets me go and then follows me out of the room, one of the guys shouting out for him to take it easy on me. I don't say anything as I wind back through the living room and then go outside, ignoring Trey when he asks me for a show again. I put one foot in front of the other, shoving people out of my way as I walk swiftly down the driveway to Preston's Cadillac. I pop the trunk, go around to the back, and then stare down in it with my hands on my hips wondering what to take out first, instead of focusing on what just happened, the way Preston touched me, and my confusion over it.

"Hey, what's up with the power walk?" Preston weaves to the car and then his feet scuff against the dirt as he moves up behind me. "You took off like the house was on fire."

"No, I took off like a person who wasn't comfortable watching porn with a bunch of dudes stoned out of their minds." I keep my tone light and my chin tucked down, avoiding eye contact.

His arms wrap around my midsection and he presses himself against me, lining his body with mine. "Let's unload the trunk later." He rubs against me and I go stiff as a board.

"I need to unload it now," I tell him, leaning into the trunk to grab a box.

His arms leave my waist and his hands cover the top of mine. He presses them roughly against the edge of the open trunk and pins me down with my back slightly bent over. Anxiety surges in my body, but I'm still managing to get pissed off through the storm of needles. It's one thing to cop a quick feel, but this is too much.

"I need help with a problem," he whispers in my ear as he thrusts his hips forward, pressing his hard-on against my ass.

"Go jerk off in the bathroom then." My voice comes out uneven and I cringe.

One of his hands slides up my arm and he cups my breast. "I took some E, Violet, and it's so fucking amazing…everything feels so amazing…*you* feel fucking amazing." He starts palming my breast like it's some kind of stress ball.

"Well, that seems like a dumb-ass move, especially if you mixed it with weed, too." I'm a little uneasy but don't show it. I've seen what mixing drugs can do to people and it's unpredictable, which makes Preston at the moment unpredictable. And when he gets that way, I've seen him get violent.

"I did though…couldn't help it…and God it feels so good." He moans, grabbing my breast so hard it hurts.

I use my free arm to jam him in the ribs and nudge him away from me. His hand leaves my breast as he wobbles backward and I seize the opportunity to turn around. "Look, I'm sorry you popped a pill that makes you want to screw everything that moves. But that's not my problem. It's yours. I'm not going to help you."

He crosses his arms, the sun is shining behind him and casting a shadow over his face as his jaw clenches. "What if I'd said that to you four years ago when social services asked us to take you in? What if Kelley and I had turned her away because you were bad…what if we wouldn't have helped you?…You're acting really ungrateful."

"I'm not ungrateful. I'm really grateful that you and Kelley gave me a home when no one else wanted to, but…" I shift my shoulders uncomfortably as I release an uneven breath from my lips. "But I can't have sex with you."

"Why? We could be fucking amazing together." He reaches for me, but I protest, stepping back. He sighs and brushes his hair out of his eyes. "What's your problem? And don't try to feed me that no-one-ever-loved-me-so-I-can't-stand-being-touched-by-someone-I-know bullshit. I know you want to be with me, you just won't admit it."

"That's not what it's about and you know it," I say through gritted teeth, my pulse hammering. I was barely in the mood to be around people after the call from the detective and now I have to deal with the horny asshole version of Preston, the one that wants to touch me, feel me, make me feel things I'm not comfortable with.

"How do I know it? I don't know anything about you," he replies, adjusting his man part with his hand, wincing. "Everything that's come out of that mouth of yours is a damn lie."

I walk backward, making my way to the driver's seat. "Go fuck yourself. You're acting like a jerk."

He storms for me like he's going to tackle me. "I'm acting like someone who just took some E and wants to get laid." His hand drifts for me again and he grabs my hip. "Come on, Violet, let me fuck the shit out of you. You won't have to feel a thing. I promise." He looks like he's about to orgasm, sheer ecstasy on his face.

"I have no idea what that means," I say, squirming from his grip, my skin burning as he digs his fingers into my skin. But I manage to get my arm loose, reach for the door, and yank it open. "But I'm leaving."

He shakes his head and then moves for me with his arms open, like he's going to hug me. I jump out of the way and bang my hip on the door. My eyes pool with tears from the pain as his hands miss me and he loses his balance and falls into the driver's seat. He reaches for the keys, chuckling under his breath, and I realize that he was never going for me in the first place. He removes them from the ignition and slides out of the seat, twirling the key chain around his finger as he gets to his feet.

"Have fun walking wherever it is you were heading." He backs down the driveway, with his hand stuffed in the pocket of his low-riding jeans, grinning like an asshole. "Face it, Violet, you have nowhere else to go, so you might as well come with me, baby."

I curl my fingers inward, and then flex them, telling myself not to open my mouth, but he's worked his way under my skin way too much and my control over my mouth snaps like a thin rubber band. "Have fun beating yourself off because face it, no one wants to be with you."

It's the wrong thing to say, but either I'm too pissed off to care or I'm seeking the danger of the moment to stop feeling the hurt that I'm feeling—I'm conflicted over my reason. As Preston rushes toward me, I calculate how much strength it's going to take to bring him down and if I have the guts to do it to him. Even though he's jacked up on sex pills and pot, a bad combination, and isn't thinking clearly, doesn't mean he's going to see this my way when he's sober.

His hands move for my shoulders and I prepare to lift my foot to kick him in the balls, when his arm suddenly veers to the right and seconds later his fist collides with my jaw.

It lets out a loud pop and my ears start to ring. "Ow… fuck," I groan, clutching my jaw as my head falls forward and my shoulders slump.

"God damn it, Violet, why couldn't you just give me what I want for once!" he shouts, his voice cracking. "I gave you everything when no one else would and yet all you are is a pain in my ass!"

The blinding pain spreads through my cheek and I can already feel it swelling. Even though tears sting at my eyes, I feel alarmingly content, my heart beating at a consistent rate.

I raise my head up with dispassion on my face and slowly lower my hand from my cheek. He's breathing ravenously as he takes me in, his chest puffing out and then sinking in, his eyes wide, his pupils dilated, his face red and damp with sweat. I don't say anything because there'd be no point. I just turn around and walk down the driveway. He doesn't say anything, but I glance over my shoulder when I reach the street at the end of the driveway, and he's still standing by the car watching me.

I turn to the left and walk down the highway, not bothering to move over when cars zoom by at sixty-five miles an hour. The breeze that gusts over me as vehicles pass by calms the panic in my chest that's been there since I got the call from the detective. Just the idea that they could swerve to the side and take me out, throw me out of this world, is enough to distract my body from what it's feeling and my mind from what it's thinking. When I arrive at the edge of town, which is just a bunch of farmhouses, I retrieve my cell phone from my pocket. It's getting dark, and I'm getting tired of walking but my list of contacts consists of Preston and a few guys I frequently deal to.

I'm about to stuff my phone into my pocket, when it starts singing the ringtone that belongs to any unknown number. I hate that I'm slightly disappointed that it's not Preston's ringtone and when I answer it I sound grumpier that I want to.

"Hello."

There's a long pause.

"Seriously, again." I shake my head, about to hang up.

"Violet Hayes?" he asks in the somewhat familiar deep voice.

"I think we've already established that that's who I am." I glance around at the flourishing trees around me, the tall grass in the fields, the ditch to the side of the road. All places where a creeper can hide.

He laughs softly in the phone. "Yeah, I guess."

"But what we haven't established is who you are," I say, picking up my pace.

He draws out the silence forever. "Can we just call me a friend for now?"

"Can't do that," I say, trying to shake the uneasiness of the situation off. "I don't have friends."

"I'm sorry to hear that," he replies, sounding genuine. "It's no fun not having any friends."

"It sucks about as much as everything else." I veer down into the grass as a car whizzes by, more nervous than I prefer.

"Does your life suck...do you not like it?"

"Okay, this conversation is getting a little too personal for me," I say. "So please stop calling."

"Violet, I want to talk to you," he says, quickly. "I need to.

154

Please, it's important. Can we meet somewhere? Just you and I? Just talk?"

I laugh insultingly. "You seriously think I'm going to meet some creeper who randomly called me and knows my last name all by myself?"

"You're not afraid, are you?" he asks, his voice lowering. "You don't seem like the type that's afraid. You seem like the type that doesn't give a crap, at least from what I've seen."

I stop walking, glancing around up and down the road. "What did you just say?"

"I just said you seem tough."

"No, you said 'seen'...who are you?"

There's a pause and then the line goes dead.

"Shit." I hammer my finger against the end button and hurry up the side of the road. It's too far to turn back to Preston's but it's also a fairly long walk back to town. I start running and I'm not ever sure why. It was just some creepy guy... some creepy guy who's been watching me.

I try not to think about the fact that the case is reopening and that the calls started coming in around that time. There can't be a connection. It's too random. Then again, my whole life has been based on random events.

I keep walking, trying not to think too much, knowing I'll only get worked up and there's nothing I can do about it at the moment. I know there's supposed to be a bar somewhere on this road where a lot of college kids hang out because the owner doesn't card very often, but I'm not sure where exactly. After about an hour of walking, my dorm is still about five or so miles away and I'm exhausted, hot, and my cheek is starting to hurt pretty bad.

"Stupid asshole." I place my hand over my cheek, not really sure if I'm referring to Preston or the guy on the phone. My steps are beginning to lag along with the high of being so close to the traffic. Finally, I arrive at civilization in the form of a rundown bar called Larry's Palace, the one I've heard people talk about. I'm sure they'll have ice and a place for me to sit down for a minute and if rumors are correct, I won't get carded.

I open the door and instantly get overwhelmed by the musty scent of beer and peanuts. There's loud music playing from a jukebox, neon lights glowing from the signs flashing in the windows and some girl, probably barely eighteen, is dancing around a pole on a stage wearing a bikini that hardly covers anything.

I note that almost everyone in the place is male and that this bar is actually a strip club. I sigh, disheartened.

I decide to make it quick and walk straight up to the bar. The bartender is one of the few females in the place. She's also the most dressed one, wearing a white T-shirt that's a little too small for her.

"Can I get some ice?" I ask politely, crossing my arms on the counter.

She eyeballs my swollen cheek. "How old are you?"

I sink into a barstool and point over my shoulder at the stripper on the stage. "Probably older than that girl you have on stage."

She narrows her eyes as she reaches for a glass cup under the counter. "Do you want water with your *ice*?"

My fake smile is shining on my face. "Just ice straight up."

She rolls her eyes at me as she retreats to the back of the bar. She scoops some ice out of a bucket and then drops the glass down in front of me, before heading to an older guy with salt-and-pepper hair sitting down at the end of the bar.

I pick up the glass and press it to my cheek, wincing at first from the sting but then letting out a relieved breath as the cold begins to soothe the heat. I prop my elbow on the counter and rest my head against my hand as I listen to some guys cheer from behind me. There's a mirror behind the counter, giving me a good glimpse of how bad I look at the moment. My mascara is running down my flushed skin and my hair is a little frizzier than normal because of the heat. My cheek is so puffy it looks like I'm carrying a giant jawbreaker in it and the skin is tinting purplish blue.

The song switches to a more upbeat one and if it's possible the guys in the bar get even noisier, cheering for more. I decide it's time to take the glass and bail because I have a long walk ahead of me and very little patience left. I hop off the barstool while the bartender's distracted by the old dude at the end of the bar. I'm headed to the door when I notice that the cheering has shifted to shouting. I glance over my shoulder just in time to see a chair flying through the air and then it smashes into the stage. It causes a domino effect and suddenly everyone's shoving up from the seats and the stripper takes off running from the stage. I've never actually seen a bar fight...or a strip club fight, but the idea of jumping in makes my pulse beat faster. It speeds up even more when I spot the guy in the middle of the room getting held back by two guys that look large enough to be bouncers.

Luke Price. He's wearing a long-sleeved gray shirt with the sleeves pushed up and there's blood staining the front from a trail dripping from his cut lip. His jeans also have blood on them and his boots are untied. His arms are being held back as a thinner, but taller guy stands in front of him rolling up his sleeve. Luke looks like he's relishing the fact that he's getting his ass kicked. I kind of understand it, although I usually try to avoid the actually physical part of a fight, just letting it work up to almost getting there then bailing.

There's a thin guy wearing a tight black shirt and steel-toed boots standing in front of Luke and he says something to him. Luke laughs as he slams his head back, crashing it into one of the bouncer's faces, the taller one with a more rounder gut. Blood gushes from the guy's nose as he releases Luke. He starts cursing as he clutches his nose, blood dripping down his hands and arms. The bouncer begins to raise one of his arms to punch Luke.

I feel this wave of something, not adrenaline, but close to it, and suddenly I'm shoving through the crowd toward Luke, carrying so much energy in me it's hard to know what to do with it. I don't help people out. Ever. But with Luke I feel obligated because he's helped me out more than once.

A few guys give me a look like I'm insane as I squeeze by them, but I'm too amped up on shock and adrenaline to care. With each step, the emotional aspects of tonight slowly erase the confusion Preston put in me. The way he hurt me, the feelings that surfaced from his words and his inappropriate touching. By the time I reach Luke and the bouncers, I'm so silent inside I feel like I could do anything.

Luke's attention darts to me as I step through the last of the bodies and out between him and the thinner guy standing in front of him. The taller and rounder bouncer is hunched over, his nose bleeding all over the floor and the other one has wrapped his arm around the skinny guy's neck. The thin guy has a puffy nose and a swollen eye, which I'm guessing is why Luke's knuckles are scraped.

Luke looks at me curiously, his gaze lingering on my cheek, before gliding up to my eyes. I can tell he's having a hard time focusing and standing, probably because he's beyond drunk.

"Who the hell are you?" the thin guy asks then spits blood on the floor, his boots crunching against the glass and peanut shells as he turns toward me.

I glance from him to the big guys and then at the thinner one, realizing I should have created a plan before I walked into this mess. Thankfully, being in the middle of guys pumped up on alcohol and testosterone is giving me even more silence from the earlier emotions Preston—the entire shitty day—put in me. I feel high, like I'm flying and could fall at any time. Blood is pouring through my veins and roaring in my ears. It's like I'm invincible and it feels like I could do anything.

I fix my attention back to the thin guy with barbed wire tattoos on his arm. "I'm here for him." I hitch my finger over my shoulder at Luke and give the skinny guy one of my best charming smiles.

The skinny one frowns, unimpressed, and crosses his arms. "Your friend broke the rules and he's got to pay for it." He leans to the side to look at Luke. "No touching the dancers." He points to a sign hanging on the wall to my right that matches what he just said.

I look over my shoulder at Luke again, fighting an eye roll. "Really? You couldn't have just gone home and jerked off."

He shakes his head, his brown eyes darkened by the alcohol I can smell flowing off his breath. "I couldn't wait that long." He has this silly, drunk, innocent look on his face that actually makes my heart miss a beat and I don't like it.

I'm seriously debating whether or not just to let him handle this on his own, but then remember how he helped me to and from class and gave me a ride to McDonald's. My shoulders slump as I turn around to face the skinny guy, doing the one thing that I'm good at. Bullshitting people.

"Look…he's really sorry he broke the rules, but can't you just let him go?" I ask with a sweet smile.

The thin guy narrows his eyes. "I was just going to kick

him out but then he fucking sucker punched me in the nose when I asked him to leave. He gets a freebie for touching, but I'm not about to let some idiot punk get away with punching me."

My eyes sweep the crowd of people watching us, racking my brain for an idea. "So you're just going to hit him and let him go?"

The thin guy shrugs. "Haven't you ever heard of an eye for an eye? He hit me so I hit him, then he can walk out of here."

The idea of watching this guy ram his fist into Luke's not-too-bad-looking nose makes me squirm. I should do something... for him... and for me maybe, too. I've had a crappy night and testing my boundaries in a fight seems so much better at the moment than feeling the weight of the crappiness. It'd take my mind off Preston, the detective, the fact that I'm probably homeless.

I feel my heart pitter-patter with excitement as I dive head-first into the mess with no regard for my future. "Look..." I pause so the thin guy will give me his name, but he doesn't catch on. I inhale quietly through my nose and exhale through my lips, preparing myself to create one of the best lies I've ever come up with. "You can't kick my boyfriend's ass. He does this sometimes, you know. But he just found out that we were going to have a baby." I rub my stomach, blowing it out a little. "And he's been really stressed working two jobs so we can move out of the apartment and get a house." I take a deep breath and let it out, releasing the tears I only let flow when I'm playing a part. "Plus, he has a drinking problem and I don't really know what to do anymore but he's the father of my child and I need him, you know?" I let tears drip out of my eyes and the thin guy shifts awkwardly. "You can't hurt him otherwise he's going to have to miss work and we can't afford it."

I'm not sure if he's buying it or not but he's definitely not comfortable with the crying. Most guys aren't, which makes my ability to cry at the drop of a hat spectacularly good luck. And I don't mind the crying, just as long as it doesn't have any emotion behind it.

"Please just let him go." I finish it off with a heart-wrenching sob, letting my shoulders curve inward as I cover my face with my hand. "Please, I can't deal with this right now... everything's just too stressful."

The whole room is so quiet you can hear a pin drop and some of the guys start to wander back to the tables, over the drama. I glance up and the thin guy is staring at me like I've just escaped from a mental institution.

Then he shakes his head and throws his hand in the air exasperatedly. "Just let him go so he can get the fuck out of here. I'm too old to deal with this shit."

The large guy shoots him a harsh look. "What about setting an example? You want things to go back to what they were pre-Ted?"

"Ted was a moron who had no idea how to run a strip club," the thin guy says, cupping his hand over his puffy nose and wincing.

The large guy shakes his head in disgust, but releases Luke

and steps away toward the stage. Luke stumbles forward and bumps his shoulder into mine as he grabs on to my arms to hold his balance.

"Sugar dearest," he whispers, his fingers digging into my arms as he laughs in my ear.

I grab on to his arm, helping him get his feet firmly under him. Then holding on to each other, we wind around the tipped-over chairs, broken glass crunching under our shoes. Some of the guys are watching us, but others have already forgotten, staring at the stage. Luke leans his weight on me, gripping at his ribs, and I wonder if he got punched there.

Once we're outside and safely behind a row of trucks where no one can see us through the bar window, I step away from him and his arm falls from my grip. The sky is a sheet of black, the stars twinkling, and neon lights in the windows of the strip club light up the ground around us.

"So what was that about?" I ask as he trips to the side, fighting to stand up straight on his own.

He glances over me with unresponsiveness, his body tottering to the side. "You're kind of crazy, Violet with no last name."

"I'm crazy." I point at myself as I gape at him. "I'm not the one who groped a stripper in a sketchy club in the middle of nowhere that has bouncers with their own special rules."

He shrugs with his hands out to the side, tripping over his own feet. "She stuck her ass in my face. I didn't touch her. She touched me."

I raise my eyebrows accusingly as I fold my arms. "Is that really what happened?"

He wavers as he blinks his glazed-over eyes and then braces his hand on the bumper of a lifted pickup beside him. "I might have put my hand on her, too."

"Why would you do that? Why not just go grope one of those skanks you always have hanging around you?"

His mouth dips to a frown. "Because I wanted the bouncers to hit me."

"What? Why?" Actually, I can think of a few reasons, but that would imply Luke was like me and I doubt that's possible.

"So I could hit them back," he replies with a casual shrug.

Now I'm more curious than concerned. "Why would you want to get hit?"

He wipes some blood off his forehead that is coming from a cut on his hairline and then winces as he pulls his hand back, flexing his fingers. "I didn't want to get hit. I wanted to get into a fight."

Okay, now I'm just confused because that sounds like something I would do and I've never met anyone who has a weird obsession with danger like I do. I want to know if that's why he wanted to get hit. If it was because he wanted the thrill of an adrenaline rush. If Luke is like me for whatever reason. "But why would you want to get into a fight? For kicks and giggles? Or do you just like getting your ass kicked?"

He grabs at the bottom of his shirt, shaking his head. "You ask a lot of questions."

"*I* ask a lot of questions?" I watch him as he tries to get the bottom of his shirt up high enough so that he can wipe his lip. The low lighting around us is enough to highlight his stomach muscles and I can see how ripped he is and that he has tattoos. *Jesus.* I've seen muscled and tattooed guys before, but I've never had this much curiosity and draw toward them.

He nods his head exaggeratedly as he continues to fight with his shirt to wipe his lip, pulling a face at the uncooperative fabric. "Yeah, you do."

Blinking my gaze from his muscles, I shuffle forward and snatch hold of the bottom of his shirt. I move the fabric up to his lip and he gets this goofy grin on his face.

"I knew it." His speech is slurred and his breath reeks of booze and cigarettes. He gazes over my shoulder at the road where it sounds like a semi truck is driving by, the headlights reflecting in his eyes. "Knew that you wanted me."

I snort a laugh and stretch his shirt far enough that I can wipe the blood from his lip. "I don't want you and I think you know I don't." But as I say it, I actually picture what it would be like to press my lips against his, blood and cuts and all. In fact, it might be a bonus, make things more intense and wrong—making *him* more intense and wrong. My stomach warms and coils just thinking about it.

He winces, his relentless gaze eating me up as I smear the blood from his cut lip. "Not even a little bit." He seems slightly saddened, which amuses me.

I let go of his shirt and step away from him, the weird

stomach sensations simmering down now that I put the space between us. "Maybe you should stop talking before you say something really stupid." But the inside of me doesn't match my words. I feel the smallest acceleration in my pulse and my stomach starts doing the weird warm, coiling thing again.

"I only say the truth when I'm drunk," he tells me, stepping forward. "And the truth is," he leans in toward me, passion and Jack Daniel's dripping off him, "That you drive me fucking crazy." His pupils are large, the brown in them blending in with the black. "Rubbing up against my dick one moment and the next moment you're running off all because I say you're beautiful and I want to fuck you."

I stifle a laugh, completely entertained now. "Actually, I think you said that we should go back to one of the rooms." I hold my hands up to my side, pretending to be innocent, and trying not to laugh at him as his face contorts in perplexity. "Maybe you just wanted to cuddle or something. Some guys like that."

His eyes narrow as he moves back and leans his hip against the bumper for support. "You think this is funny." He pats his back pockets and then starts to panic, standing up straight as his hands dart around to his front pockets. He promptly relaxes as he pulls out a pack of squished Marlboros and then fumbles to open it. "It's not funny..." He plucks one out and then goes to put the end in his mouth, but drops it on the ground. Cursing, he bends down to pick it up and doesn't bother to brush the dirt off before he puts it into his mouth as he stands back up.

"It's not funny at all." He snatches his lighter out of his back pocket and then drops the pack on the ground and cups his hand around his mouth. He flicks the lighter over and over but can't get it to light. Grunting, he kicks at the dirt with the tip of his boot and then curses some more. I feel like I'm witnessing a drunken tantrum and it's ridiculously hilarious.

I haven't laughed in a while, but I find myself laughing under my breath as I snatch the lighter from his hands. "Here, let me help you."

"I don't need your help or anyone else's," he insists, annoyed, but still doesn't bother stopping me as I move the lighter up toward the cigarette in his mouth and flick it. The flame burns as the paper crinkles, but he starts blowing instead of sucking and it doesn't light. I try again and then again.

"Would you stop blowing on it so hard?" I flick the lighter again and the flame poofs up.

"Shouldn't I be saying that to you?" he retorts in a lazy tone and his bleary-eyed gaze is unyielding. "Hey, what happened to your face?"

I put the flame from the lighter up to the end of the cigarette. "I got into a fight with the wall and the wall won."

He crooks his brow, blowing too hard again and it burns out. "A wall?"

"Yeah, a wall." I give up on lighting the cigarette and pluck it from his mouth.

"Hey," he protests as I put the end of the cigarette into my mouth. I gag at the potent taste of Jack Daniel's on it as I light it up and take a deep inhale. I quickly puff out the smoke and do it a few more times, getting light-headed and then I hand it over, the end glowing orange through the dark.

"There you go, nicotine addict," I say as he takes the lit cigarette from my fingers.

He puts it in his mouth and sucks on it. When he exhales the cloud of smoke, he looks more calm and relaxed. "You sucked that like a pro."

"Well, I've had a lot of practice," I tell him and then laugh a little when he busts up laughing, hunching over and holding the cigarette out to the side, the cherry bright through the dark.

"And I didn't mean it like that." I shake my head with a somewhat real smile on my face. "I just meant that I had this foster mother who liked to smoke when she cooked and sometimes when her hands were full she'd have me light her cigarette for her." He stops laughing and I realize I've just told him more about me than I've told pretty much anyone besides the people who've taken me in.

He quiets down, putting the cigarette back into his mouth. "Foster mother?" He blows out smoke. "You grew up in a foster home?" He pauses, considering something. "What was it like?"

"All rainbows and sunshine—I was completely showered with love. Can we drop the subject?"

"Was it weird or good having different parents all the

time?" he continues, clearly not registering that I want to change the subject.

A sinking feeling moves through my body, so weighted and heavy I nearly collapse to the ground. "So where's your truck?"

The lights from the strip club's signs flash in his eyes as he stares at me. "I think I parked out back...why?"

I head for the back of the building, motioning for him to follow me. "Because I'm going to drive you back to campus."

He staggers after me, surprising me when he hitches a finger through a back loop on my shorts. At first I think he's going to jerk me back to him, but all he does is hold on to me for support and balance, trusting me to get him where he needs to go, which is weird.

"How'd you get here?" he mutters in my ear.

I lead us around the corner, ignoring the blast of heat when his knuckles graze the skin on my back. "I walked."

"From where?" he asks, flicking his cigarette to the side, little orange sparks dotting the gravel.

"From nearby," I lie and speed up when I spot his truck parked crookedly at the back of the club in front of a cluster of trees beneath one of the lampposts. "Were you drunk when you got here?" I ask.

He steps up to the side of me, releasing my belt loop and grabbing hold of my arm. "No."

"You parked like you were drunk." I stiffen, not liking the

way he's clinging on to me for support. It's causing a mixture of emotions from panic to desire and those damn heated stomach sensations to surface again.

"Well, I wasn't." He stares at his truck like he barely recognizes it. "I was just distracted."

I'm not sure if he's telling the truth or not, but I lead him the rest of the way to the truck. The doors are unlocked and I help him into the passenger side, letting him put his hands onto my shoulder to boost himself in. God, he owes me big time. Just thinking about him owing me a favor thrills me way, way too much. I need to get my head out of Luke land and get back to the place where it's only me and me alone.

Once he gets settled in the seat, I close the door and round the front of the truck, deciding where I'm going to go when I get him back to his dorm. Walk back to my dorm and then what? I don't have hardly any of my stuff and I'm pretty much homeless, at least in a couple of days I will be.

When I open the driver's door, Luke is already lying down in the seat. I nudge him over and then hop in, slamming the door. "Where are your keys?"

His eyes are shut, his arms flopped over his chest, looking like he's asleep. "I think...I think in my...pocket."

I rest my hands on the steering wheel. "Can you please get them out?" I ask as nicely as I can because he's wasted and doesn't really know what he's saying, but my patience is wearing thin.

He moves his hand slowly for his pocket and pats himself down. "Hmmm...that's weird...They're not there."

This night is quickly becoming the night of ill-fated events, but I'm not going to put it down as my worst. "Then where are they?"

He shrugs, kicking his feet up on the door. "I have no idea."

Sighing, I pat down his pockets myself, causing him to laugh and squirm. The only thing I can find is what looks like an insulin monitor thing with a strip sticking out of it and also a pen-shaped object.

"Oh good, you found it…" he mutters, taking it from my hands. But his fingers falter and he drops it on his stomach. "Damn it, I'm all…I'm all…" He sighs the longest sigh in world's history. "Violet…can you…can you check my blood sugar for me?"

I pick up the monitor and pen object and flip on the interior light, examining them. "How do I do that exactly?"

He extends his arm over his head toward me and points his finger. "Just put the pen up to my finger and push the button."

I'm a little uneasy about helping him, but put it up to his finger, and push the button like he asked. It pricks his finger and blood pools out of it.

"Now put the strip up onto the blood," he says, yawning.

I do what he asks and move the strip on the monitor up to his finger. He dabs his blood on it and his eyes shut, like he barely knows what he's doing. Then he pulls his hand away and flops it down on his stomach as the machine beeps. "What's it say?" he asks.

I glance down at the beeping screen. "Sixty-eight."

"Shit," he mutters, forcing his eyes open. "Can you get my pills out of the glove box?"

I reach over him, flip the handle of the glove box, and dig around the papers and past the flashlight until I find a bottle of vitamin pills. "These ones that say 'glucose' on them."

He bobs his head up and down with a lot of effort. "Those would…be the…ones."

I unscrew the cap. "How many do you need?"

"Three…"

I'm kind of worried. Luke's drunk and I have no idea about diabetics and what happens if they don't get the right meds. What if I do something wrong?

"Are you sure it's three?" I ask.

He bobs his head up and down. "Yeah…three and I'll be…good…"

I swallow hard and pour three into my hand, then put the cap back on, and put the bottle away, shutting the glove box. I nudge him gently with my arm. "Luke, here. Take them."

His eyelids flutter open, bloodshot, with zero comprehension. He gradually lifts his hand up and scoops the pills out of my hand, opening his mouth and dropping them in. His neck muscles work as he forces them down his throat. "Thanks."

"You're welcome," I mutter, confused by the momentary exchange of gratitude. Such a foreign concept to me.

I stare down at him as his eyes drift back shut and then I lean over to turn the light back off, deciding to just lie back and shut my eyes, sleep until morning and then ask him where the hell he put the keys. But as I lean back, I feel a shift on Luke's part and suddenly I'm being grabbed and he's pulling me down between the back of the seat and him.

"Holy shit," I gasp, startled because it seemed like he was barely awake a few moments ago.

I start to get up when he flips us over, putting his body on top of me. I freeze as he stares down at me, the lights from outside barely illuminate the cab.

"God, you're so beautiful," he mutters, tracing a line up my cheekbone. "It drives me so crazy how beautiful you are."

It takes me a second to remember that I've never actually been pinned underneath a guy before. I'm always either standing or taking the top. I've never lay in bed beside one. Never touched a guy before just because I want to. Never kissed while feeling any sort of emotion behind it. It takes me another second or two to realize that this moment is going against all of my previous experiences. Because I'm pinned below him, being touched, and feeling something I desperately want to run away from. I don't do normal feelings. There's no point. Letting someone in and giving yourself to someone else has no purpose but heartache. I should shove him off and bail before he does.

But as he breathes heavily, leaning down, his lips inching nearer, I remain stationary. Frozen by fear and want. The contact of his lips only heightens the fear and desire, the two feelings mixing so persuasively that I start to weakly tremble as the walls I worked so hard to put up begin to crack. I try to keep my mouth closed as he works to kiss me, not wanting to give in, not wanting to give any part of me to him, knowing that eventually he won't want me anymore. But as my body warms below him, I can't help it and my lips readily part. Seconds later, his tongue slides into my mouth and he groans against my lips. It sends vibrations through my body and I shiver.

"Jesus, this feels so much better than I imagined..." he moans as his fingers tangle through my hair, tugging at the roots and it feels so good. "I need this...God..." There's an alarming amount of panic in his voice as he breathes heavily. It's deafeningly quiet around us and I'm about to say something, when his tongue slips back into my mouth more forcefully and his movements fill with desperation. I can barely keep up with him, gasping for air as his hands travel restlessly across my body, over my legs, my stomach, my breasts. I'm crushed between him and the seat, pinned down and I don't do anything to escape. And I don't want to because for a fleeting, unfamiliar, passionate, overwhelming moment, I feel safe with him over me. And I haven't felt safe in a very long time.

I kiss him back, but don't touch, feel him with my tongue, keeping some sort of boundary between us. I don't think of anything else, but the taste of his breath, the blinding heat of his body. His scent: tequila, cologne, and a splash of cigarette smoke.

Then suddenly as quickly as he started, he stops, sliding to the side and nearly falling onto the floor. I turn over and look at him, his chest descending and rising as he breathes. He's passed out and I'm left wide-awake. I lay there for an eternity, watching him sleep, knowing once I sit up I'm probably going to panic over what I just did. Reluctantly, I sit up and face the consequences of my choices, let them hit me square in the stomach.

I open the door to turn the interior light on and search the floor, the glove box, and the visor, for the keys. I want to get back to the dorm before he wakes up. I get out of the truck, leaving him in it, and backtrack to the bar, searching the ground for the keys. The farther I move away from the truck and into the dark, the less safe I feel, yet I keep going because it's familiar. I continually curse myself for what I just did as I hunt for the keys behind cars and in the gravel, taking my cell phone out to use the screen as a light. That was not a no-strings-attached kiss. It had meaning behind it and I can't stop thinking about doing it again, even though he probably can't even remember doing it. It's a bad place to be and I need to get away from it.

All I end up finding on the ground is the pack of cigarettes Luke dropped. I pick them up and tuck them into my pocket. The only other place to check is in the strip club and I don't think it's a good idea to go back in there.

I drag my hand across my face, deciding whether to stay here and help Luke or bail out on the situation and hitchhike back to campus. I've hitchhiked a few times, wandered around a desolate highway more than once, and slept in the streets.

But something is pulling me back to the truck, almost like I feel guilty for leaving him there. I don't know where the feeling's coming from. I've never cared about anyone before, but then again no one's ever given me a reason to care about them. And no one's ever made me feel safe. I don't want safe—I need danger—because it's easier.

As a car zooms by, I realize that just like everyone else who's ever entered my life, Luke is just someone who will be gone by morning when he wakes up with a hangover, unable to remember what happened between us. So I hike up the road beneath the stars and the moon, with my arm out to the side and my thumb up. The possibilities of what could happen float through my mind like they always do. I could get run over. Picked up by some creeper, maybe the one on the phone. Be beaten. Murdered like my parents. Is death in the cards for me tonight? Is that what I'm searching for?

Eventually, a sleek red car slows down and pulls up beside me. The headlights light up the darkness in front of me as I open the door and climb in. The cab smells like pine trees and there's garbage on the floor. The driver, a thirty-something, slightly overweight, bald guy, smiles at me as he turns the steering wheel toward the road. The imaginative side of my brain wonders if he's the guy who's been calling me.

"Where you heading to, sweetie?" he asks as he flips on the brights, the road ahead getting brighter, yet it feels like I'm falling farther into the dark.

I stare at him, noting that his voice doesn't sound like

the guy's on the phone. I wonder what he'll want from me in exchange for the ride. Will he want me to suck his dick? Will he hurt me if I refuse? Try to hit on me? Or is he simply just a nice guy giving a girl in need a ride. "I'm not sure," I mutter as he drives down the road.

"Not a problem, gorgeous," he replies. "I know just the place where we can go, if you want to have some fun?"

I don't respond and contentment settles in my chest as I step farther and farther into the unknown, just like I have been since I was six.

Chapter Seven

Luke

I open my eyes to the stained ceiling of my truck and my body feeling like it's been run over. My head is throbbing and my eyes sting against the sunlight shining through the window. It's not the first time I've woken up in a situation like this and I'm sure it won't be my last.

I know not to sit up quickly otherwise I'll end up hacking up my lungs, so I take my sweet time getting upright and then move for my pocket where my cigarettes should be, but they're gone. I start to feel the anxiety of addiction stir awake as I reach for the glove box where I keep an extra pack for emergencies just like this. Once I get one lit up and the smoke saturates my lungs, I feel a little bit better and I quickly check my blood glucose. Something about doing it registers a memory of Violet...helping me check my blood glucose...Violet giving me pills. I rarely let anyone know I'm a diabetic, not wanting to reveal my weakness, and if someone does find out, it's usually by accident. If I'm remembering correctly, which it's hard to tell, I'd willingly asked her for help and she willingly gave it.

I'm so confused and all I want to do is get out of here and go take a shower, wash last night off me. I pat my pockets, not surprised that my keys aren't there—I have a thing for losing keys when I'm drunk. But my phone's gone too and that pisses me off because I don't have an extra one of those. Irritated at myself, I gradually climb out of the truck and head for the gas tank where I hide a set of spare keys for situations just like this.

Last night's events start to crash over me. I drove out here because I'd heard rumors of how the bouncers like to get rough with guys if they messed with the strippers and I wanted a fight without the worry of cops getting involved. What I didn't plan on was Violet walking in and saving my ass. I can barely recollect anything about it other than her leading my stumbling ass out of the club and to my truck. I have no idea where she went afterward or why she'd shown up in the first place and I'm not sure whether to track her down and thank her or get pissed off at her for ruining my brawling moment.

As I open the gas tank and remove my spare set of keys I take a long drag off my cigarette, the sweet taste of the nicotine calming me. Rubbing my eyes, I climb back in the truck and drive toward my dorm. At first I'm planning on just going straight to my room, but I keep thinking about Violet and how I have no idea where she went last night. The strip club isn't in the best part of town. What if something happened to her?

Why do I care? I don't usually care about girls that come in and out of my life, and I definitely shouldn't care about Violet. I don't do relationships at all. Letting someone in like that, means actually *letting* someone in, letting them be a part of my life, which means giving into things they want, letting them have control over things. I don't want to let people into my life so I can slowly go back to that place I lived in when I was a kid, doing things I hated, hating the person that I was and hating the person who made me that way.

Apparently I'm not thinking clearly, though, and I make a last-minute right instead of left when I arrive at the intersection and turn into the parking lot to the side of her dorm building. It's the tallest of the dorm buildings at the University of Wyoming and it blocks the sunlight flowing over the mountains. The yard in front of the dorm is pretty much empty, the few people wandering around look like they're only there to clear out the rest of their stuff. The inside of the building is even emptier. And quiet. It reminds me that I only have a day or two left to get my stuff out and move to wherever I'm going.

When I get to Violet's dorm room, I expect it to be cleared out like the rest of the building. But I hear some extremely angry music playing through the door that I doubt Callie's listening to and I knock.

The music turns down and then Violet opens the door. Her damp hair runs over her bare shoulders in waves and again she has no makeup on. The outline of her red lacy bra is visible through her top and she has a floor-length black shirt on.

Her cheek is also really swollen and red, but her expression is neither surprised nor happy to see me. Just neutral like always. I want to look equally neutral but my body comes alive at the sight of her and for some reason the idea of kissing her seems so tempting and oddly familiar.

"You're alive," she jokes flatly with an arch of her eyebrows as she stands just inside the doorway.

"Don't act too happy to see me." I lean against the doorway with my arms crossed, aiming for relaxed but I'm too hung over to get all the way there. "What happened to your face?"

She touches her cheek with her fingertips. "I told you last night that I got into a fight with a wall."

My forehead creases as I attempt to recollect her telling me. "I don't remember that...and I don't really think that's what happened. I didn't..." I trail off, squirming uneasily as the weight of her gaze becomes almost unbearable. "I didn't hit you, did I?" I've never hit a girl before, but, shit, I was really wasted and upset last night and I can't remember hardly anything.

"No." She doesn't seem alarmed or upset or anything really. Just indifferent. She moves back, leaving the door open and I'm not sure if she wants me to come in or not. "Where'd you find your keys?" She changes the topic as she roams over to a desk in the corner, which is cleared off. Her entire room is actually; the beds only have a mattress on them and the posters on the walls have been taken down. She must be leaving soon, probably to go back home or wherever it is she came from.

I swallow the lump in my throat, thinking about how I have to go back where I came from soon, too. "I keep a spare set in the gas tank."

She glances over her shoulder, elevating her eyebrows. "And you couldn't have told me that last night when I couldn't find them?"

I shrug and finally cross the threshold, stepping into her personal space. "I swear I did, but then the next thing I know I'm waking up in the truck by myself, the sun is up, and you're gone."

She pulls the desk drawer open and reaches inside it. "Yeah, I'm not one for sleeping in trucks with guys who like to hog the entire seat."

I sit down on the mattress, wishing I'd gotten a shot or two in before I came here. At least then, my headache would be gone. "You could have put me in your car, you know, and driven me back with you." I'm half joking, because I don't really care. I've slept in the front seat of my truck more than once and I'm sure I'll do it again.

She retrieves a prescription bottle out of the drawer, reads the label, then tosses it into an open box on the floor. "I didn't drive back." She grabs her iPod off the dock on the desk, the last thing left in her room. She throws it into the box and then leans over the desk to unplug the dock.

"Then how'd you get back?" I ask as I stare at her ass. God, the things I'd like to do to that ass.

"I hitchhiked." She stands back up, drops the dock in the

box, and kneels down on the floor. She adds a purple teddy bear from her bed, then gathers her hair out of her eyes, and grabs a roll of tape from the desk. She folds up the top of the box and stretches a line of tape over it, sealing the last of her stuff.

"You hitchhiked?" I say, unfathomably. "Are you serious?"

She presses down on the strip of tape, securing it in place. "It's not that big of a deal." She chucks the tape aside and then stands up and pretends to check to make sure she's packed up everything, when really I think she's avoiding looking at me. "Do you see anything else lying around?"

I continue to gape at her. "So let me get this straight. Last night after you put me in the truck, you walked down the highway until some guy picked you up and gave you a ride here."

Her eyes land on me. "Who said it was a guy?"

I scan her body over. So God damn sexy it's ridiculous and her skin is so ridiculously soft...an image of me touching her in the truck pushes up in my head. Me lying on top of her. My hands all over her. *Is it real or from a dream?* "Am I wrong?"

She narrows her eyes, ready for a fight, but then puffs out a breath, surrendering. "Yeah, it was. So what? Nothing happened." She thrums her fingers on the sides of her legs as she looks around the floor.

I get to my feet. "You should have just stayed in the truck. Do you know how dangerous hitchhiking is?"

"About as dangerous as starting a fight at a strip club when

183

you're by yourself." She walks over to the box and picks it up, steadying it in her arms. "And you're welcome for saving your ass." She props the box on her hip and then looks at me like she's waiting for me to say it.

"You shouldn't have hitchhiked," I say instead, and then snatch the box from her, gazing at her lips, recognition clicking in my head...kissing her, drowning in her taste.

At first she looks like she's going to snatch the box back from me, her hands rising toward it, but then she drops them back to her side as I move out of her reach.

"And thanks for pretending that you were pregnant with my child and crying over bills," I say and then the rest comes rushing back to me. I kissed her. In my truck. I felt her and tasted her because I needed to and wanted to. And she helped, not by kissing me but by checking my blood sugar. Shit. "And for helping me with, you know, the pills and stabbing my finger with the needle." The last thank-you is harder to say.

The corners of her lips quirk as she folds her arms over her chest. "I'm surprised you remember what happened at all." She pauses, like she's waiting for me to say something about the kiss.

I back toward the door with the box in my hand. "I'm actually good at drunk remembering." I wink at her, trying to play it off, because I can't go there. I've never stuck around afterward and had to endure the awkwardness of the morning after. Granted, we didn't have sex, but still I touched her breast and slid my fingers up her legs.

She offers me a small smile. "I'm sure you are."

I feel this heat swell inside my chest at the sight of her smile and it feels both good and bad at the same time. I've never flirted with a girl like this before. I usually give them like an hour and use little effort, just enough to charm her, get laid, and leave. Building too much of a connection defeats the purpose of what I'm trying to accomplish with sex and that's to control a few moments and forget all the moments I didn't have control. Things have crossed that line between Violet and me, especially after last night. I can't have sex with her without feeling bad afterward, which means it would be next to impossible to bail after I got what I needed from her. But the thing is I want to slip inside her so bad it's seriously becoming hard to control.

"I have a question," she says, grabbing a bag off the bed and draping the handle over her shoulder.

Her tone makes me wary. "Okay."

"I thought," she starts but then reconsiders. "I mean, I thought diabetics were supposed to give themselves shots."

I get a little uneasy as we veer toward two subjects I hate. My diabetes and needles. "Yeah, it doesn't do any good when there's alcohol in my system."

"But usually you use a needle."

"Yeah." My throat feels thick.

"Does it hurt?"

"Sometimes it does," I say, sounding choked. "Depending on my mood."

She observes me briefly then drops the subject.

"So where's the box heading?" I ask, patting the bottom of the box.

She hugs her arms around herself as she glances over her shoulder at the window. "Outside, I guess."

I nod, and then head out into the hall. She follows me, shutting the door behind her. As we walk to the elevator I try not to think about the fact that after I get done helping her, I'm going to have to go back to my own dorm and figure out what to do with my stuff—figure out where I'm going. When we get outside, I glance around the parking lot. There are hardly any cars left on campus.

"So which car am I putting the box in?"

She stops at the edge of the curb and bites her lips as she looks at the road to the side of us. "You can just set it down here."

I lower the box onto the concrete, lost. "Is someone picking you up or something?"

"Or something," she mutters and plops down on the box. She props her elbow on her knee and her hair falls to the side of her face, veiling her expression from me as she lets the handle of the bag slide off her slumped shoulder and to the ground. "Thanks. You can go now."

I lean forward and try to catch her eye, but she won't look at me, so I have no fucking clue what she's thinking. I want to know and that's not a good thing because it gives her some control over me.

I begin to back up the sidewalk and force myself to walk away, go back to my Jack Daniel's, and women who don't interest me enough to pull me back to them. But right as I'm losing sight of her, I spot her lowering her head onto her arms, looking so defeated I know I can't leave her like this.

I backtrack my steps and halt beside her. "Violet, where are you going?"

Her chest rises and falls as she sighs deeply, keeping her face buried in her arms. "I have no idea."

I feel the faintest acceleration in my pulse as I crouch down beside her and sweep her hair out of her face. "Do you need me to take you somewhere? Because I can. As a thank-you for last night." *What the hell am I doing?*

Her eyes are closed, her face angled toward me. "I don't need a thank-you," she says. "I just need a ride...somewhere."

Despite my initial reservations, the least I can do is give her a ride as thanks for getting me to my truck and not letting my dumb-ass get beat last night and for helping me get glucose pills in my system. "Okay, where do you need to go?"

"Just outside of town." She opens her eyes and her pupils shrink as the sun hits them, absorbing any emotion with it. But for a concise instant, I see something in her: the very familiar feeling of helplessness—the same thing that drove me to the strip club looking for a fight. "It's on one of the back roads just off the freeway...you take the road where the strip club is," she says.

"Why were you walking down that road last night? And what made you stop at the strip club?"

"A freakish coincidence," she states, searching my eyes for something.

"A coincidence?" I stroke my finger across her cheekbone and she doesn't flinch or move away, staring at me like she stared up at me last night. "I'm not buying it."

"Okay, you caught me. I was stalking you," she jokes dryly, then shuts her eyes again. "I have a headache," she mutters, breathing in and out.

I watch her sink farther and farther into herself, her lips part as she forces air into her lungs. It's like watching someone break apart and I'm not sure if I want to fix her, try to catch the pieces, or step back and let them fall all over the ground. God, the look is tearing my heart in half. Needing to make her feel better, more than I need to make myself stay under control, I start to lean in toward her, to either kiss her or hug her…needing to touch her again…comfort her. She holds completely still, her expression neutral but her eyes widen. I still have my hand in her hair and I pull gently on the roots, causing her breathing to quicken. Her chest rises and falls and images of the things we could do together pour through my mind; things like what we did last night in my trunk. I could touch her again and remember it more vividly—soberly. Suddenly I realize I'm thinking of us *together*. I'm not thinking of just me getting off. I'm thinking of getting her off. This is no longer just about me anymore. I snap out of it, untangle my fingers from her hair, and straighten my legs to stand up. "Do you want me to carry your box to my truck?" I ask, trying to get my shit back together. I refuse to go back to that place I used to live with when I was a kid and my mom controlled everything I did. And getting involved with someone, means giving up total control.

She watches me with her head still on her arms, her eyes scaling me, then she sits up, running her fingers through her hair as she rises to her feet. "No, I can get it." She bends over and scoops the box up. Even though I can tell it's a little heavy for her, I let her carry it to the truck, putting a much-needed boundary line between us. It's the line I put up between most of the people that breeze through my life, to keep people away, to keep me safe from ever having to go to that place I lived for so many years. The one where I feel lost. The one where I'm weak and have no control over anything.

Violet

I think he might have almost just kissed me. I could feel it in the electricity in the air and through his energetic pulse in his fingers. I'm glad he didn't otherwise I would've had to hurt him and I don't want to hurt him. Go figure. I'm too upset to keep my anger under control today and I'm too lost over last night with him. I don't even know if he can remember it, the electric kiss that, at least for me, had feeling behind it. And if he's forgotten, then I'm going to forget, too.

Forgetting is a good thing. I wish I could do that with everything; what happened with Preston, that I have no home,

189

and that come Monday I'm going to have to drag my ass down to the police station and face my parents' reopened case alone, like I've done with everything in my life. All I want to do is stand on the top of a building and inch my way to the edge, feel the adrenaline of knowing I could fall and everything would end.

The longer I sit in the truck with Luke, the more I want to taste the adrenaline rush instead of having this unsettling feeling about going to Preston's house and facing whatever's waiting there for me. By the time we're pulling up, I'm contemplating if I should just grab my boxes and bail. Just leave before Preston can tell me to. Go live in the ditch just a little ways down the road.

"Thanks for the ride," I mutter to Luke as he parks the truck behind Preston's Cadillac.

Luke stares through the windshield at the trailer house and the people passed out in lawn chairs on the front porch. "Whose house is this?" he asks as I flip the door handle.

"A friend's." I swing my legs out of the truck, preparing to jump out.

He snags me by the elbow. "This is where you're living for the summer?"

I don't look at him, face forward, torn on how much to say. "I don't know where I'm living."

"Seriously?"

"Yep." I bend my arm and wiggle it out of his grip, making sure to look straight forward as I kick the truck door shut.

I grab my box out of the bed of his truck and trek up the driveway, my long skirt dragging in the dirt behind me. The entire yard is littered with beer bottles and cigarette butts. There's vomit on the lawn and gravel and the front door to the trailer is agape. As I approach the Cadillac, the screen door swings open and Preston appears in the doorway with his hand cupped around his cigarette as he lights up. Once he has it lit, he blows out a cloud of smoke and looks over at me. By the lack of surprise in his expression I bet he saw me pull up, but what I can't tell is if he's still mad at me.

He doesn't say anything as he trots down the stairs. He kicks some bottles out of the way with his bare foot as he makes his way down the rocky path over to the driveway. When he reaches the front of the car, he glances down the driveway.

"Who's that?" he asks, nodding his head at Luke's truck.

"Someone," I say without looking back as I pause at the trunk of the car, debating on how to go about this as I drop the box beside my feet. I don't want to let it go. I want to allow myself to get angry at him, because he deserves it, but I also feel that stupid gnawing guilt. I owe him, for giving me a place to stay.

"Don't be a bitch." He grazes the pad of his thumb across the bottom of the cigarette as he approaches me. He doesn't have a shirt on and the cargo shorts he's wearing hang low on his hips, the top of his boxers peeking out. The bags under his eyes and the redness in them scream that he's hungover and irritated.

"So you're still pissed," I say, through hooded eyes. "Good, so am I." I sidestep to the left to get to the driver's door so I can pop the trunk open, but he moves with me, blocking my path.

"I'm not pissed," he says, blinking his bloodshot eyes and then rubbing his free hand across them. "I'm just confused what the hell happened—why the hell you took off like that."

I cross my arms. "Because you were being a horny asshole."

"I was high," he argues, spanning his arms out to the side of him. "People do all kinds of crazy shit when they're high."

"You tried to get me to fuck you."

"I was on E… of course I did."

I gape at him. "So what? I'm just supposed to forgive you because you were high?"

"I'm not asking for your forgiveness." He scratches at his arm as he glances down the driveway where I can hear Luke's truck running. *Is he still there?* "And what did you do? Run off and fuck the first guy you came across."

"Does that sound like something I'd do?" I ask, lifting my eyebrows.

He sucks a drag from his cigarette. "How the hell should I know? You never tell the truth. You barely show any sort of reaction when I ask you to pretend to be a slut to sell drugs for me." He leans in, moving his arm out to the side of him and I cringe, thinking he's going to hit me. "You let me put my hands on you however I want without so much as blinking an eye." He suddenly cups my breast with his hand. "I can't tell if you like it or if you want me to stop and when you say stop it doesn't even sound like you mean it."

I shuffle back and his hand falls from my breast. "I'm telling you to stop right now and I mean it."

"You're saying to stop, but there's nothing in your eyes that's matching your words." He marches forward and grabs my breast again, this time rougher. "I think that you secretly like it but you don't want to admit it."

The intensity of the moment is making me very mellow. I want to see him explode, so I can feel more adrenaline and more sedated from my emotions even after the fact that he hit me and is now fondling my breast. It's obvious he's crashing and unstable and it makes the situation dangerous. I love it.

"Is this because Kelley is getting remarried?" I ask. "Or are you just going through a midlife crisis?"

His face reddens as he hunches over, lowering his face so it's right in front of mine. His breath is searing hot and a large vein bulges in his forehead. "I'm not that much fucking older than you are, Violet! So stop with the age shit!" he shouts, the muscles in his neck tensing.

A surge of energy instantaneously crashes through me, my chest lifting and descending as I catch my breath, my heartbeat booming in my ears. It feels like I could do anything at the moment and maybe I will—maybe today is the day that I'll take that extra step and finally fly away from all of this. As I rack my mind for something absurdly reckless I could do, he shifts his fingers from my arm and yanks me with him as he stomps toward the house. I should probably pull back and run... Maybe when I get in the house I'll finally run away... or when he hits me again. Beats me. Would he beat me? Do I care? I'm not sure. About anything.

"Violet, are you okay?" The sound of Luke's voice slowly penetrates my thoughts and my adrenaline surge deflates like a balloon.

"I'm fine," I say through gritted teeth as Preston glares at him from over my shoulder.

"Who the hell is he?" Preston's nails pierce my skin as he glances from Luke to me and there's a slight hint of uneasiness in his expression, like Luke's presence unsettles him a little.

"My stalker," I lie, not as amused as I want to be. The fact that I have nowhere to live, no one to count on, no one to help me is catching up with me.

"What?" Preston's jaw drops as he blinks at me. "He's stalking you?"

"No, he's just a guy." I blow out a breath and then raise my voice. "Who won't leave me alone."

"Who won't leave you alone? Seriously?" Luke suddenly appears beside me, startling me by his abrupt nearness and how much anger is in his eyes. "*You* keep on showing up wherever I go."

I angle my head to look up at him. "Because you look for me." I know he really doesn't, but I don't want him to think I want or need him.

"I didn't look for you any of the times I ran into you," he protests and then his eyes cut to Preston as he folds his arms across his chest, his lean arms flexing. "And I sure wasn't looking to drop you off at some old pervert's house this morning."

I feel this wave of heat in the air, but I don't really believe that it's a rapid increase in temperature so much as a spike in the excitement in my body. I feel it at the same moment that Preston releases me from his hold, his attention darting from me to the house, like he's considering walk away, but ultimately it lands on Luke.

Luke stands beside me, unbothered as Preston hesitates and then inches closer to him. I'm not sure if Luke's protecting me, or just looking for a fight, but it's kind of obvious that Luke's making Preston a little nervous. I wonder if Luke would continue helping me if he knew what was going on in my head, how invigorated I feel over the fact that at any moment they could start swinging and I could get caught in the middle.

"You think some punk kid is going to scare me?" Preston says with an off-pitch laugh. "Wow, that's a new one."

Luke licks his bottom lip, which is still swollen from last night's fight. His knuckles are crusted over with blood and there's dried blood on his shirt. He also has a cut on his forehead that looks like it needs some peroxide on it. He looks pretty beaten up already and for a split second I actually care enough that I consider taking his arm and pulling him away, to protect him from getting hurt, even though I'm not sure things would go down that way. But then he moves forward

and lines himself up with Preston, his hands balling into fists. He's taller than Preston and sturdier in the chest. He also seems more willing to throw a punch or two, more rough and ragged.

"Do you think some old dude scares me?" Luke's eyes flare with the tone of his voice. "Especially one that likes to hit women?"

At first I'm confused because Preston hasn't hit me, but then I remember how he did last night. Luke must have put two and two together.

Preston glances at my cheek without turning his head. "You told him I hit you?"

I shrug, even though I didn't. "Maybe."

Luke starts to open his mouth to say something, the muscles in his arms flexing. Preston flinches, like he thinks Luke's going to hit him and cranks his arm back and sucker punches Luke right in the jaw. I cringe, tripping backward at the sound of the pop, remembering the pain I felt when he did the same thing to me. Like me, it doesn't look like it bothers Luke, only pisses him off. Without missing a beat, Luke slams his fist into Preston's face. Before Preston can even register what happened, Luke is driving his fist again toward Preston, this time connecting with Preston's ribs. Preston swings right around and hits Luke in the gut. Luke's face contorts in pain, but it doesn't faze him, and before Preston can catch his breath Luke brings his knee up and rams it into Preston's stomach, knocking the wind out of him. I'm torn on whether to run to Preston and break up the fight or let Luke hurt him. This whole thing has gotten out of hand and I still owe Preston for giving me a roof over my head when no one else would. I want to help Luke, too, though, because he's helped me more than most.

I can feel an ache inside my chest just thinking about the idea of him getting hurt. But I also just stand and watch them fight to see how far they'll go, how dangerous things will get. I'm so fucked up in the head and I don't think I can make a decision at the moment, even though it feels like I need to. It no longer seems like it's about me, but more about them brutally beating each other up, maybe to death. And what if they do get hurt? Or one of them dies? Then what? Am I responsible? Do I care? Do I want to care about either of them?

I remain motionless, observing their movements, hearing each crack as their bones collide, their rapid breathing, the way the sunlight hits them. I hear my own breathing, the way I'm gasping for air, the way my heart races faster with each desperate breath. The sunlight starts to flicker in and out of focus as my vision spots over. This has happened to me a couple of times and if I don't do something quickly, I'm going to collapse.

I try to step forward and unlock my knees, but I can't get my feet to budge. My legs, arms, and tongue are numb and rubbery and it feels like an elastic band is wrapped around my forehead. I try to open my mouth to say "stop," but the world tips to the side and I fall with it. I manage to get my hands down before I slam into the ground, but the gravel scrapes my knees, and my palms open. Warm blood oozes out. It's been a while since I've had an adrenaline overload, at least a few years.

The first time was a little harder to deal with. It was right after I found my parents. I'm not sure why I did what I did when I found them. I was old enough that I should have known better and called the police right away. But I remember hiding for what seemed like forever, even after the people snuck out the window. I remember how full the moon was and how even though I didn't fully understand what was going on, there was this excruciating ache in my chest caused by the deafening silence of the house. I think it was sunrise when I finally dared to go upstairs. It was about the time my dad usually woke up for breakfast, but the kitchen was empty, so I went up to their room, telling myself that I was just going to wake them up.

The first thing I noticed was that the door was wide open, not cracked like they usually left it, and then I noticed the blood droplets on the carpet. Seconds later I saw them. It felt like I'd been kicked in the gut, the wind knocked out of me, fingers wrapped around my neck. I couldn't breathe. I wanted to die. I'm not sure whether it was the lack of air or my rubbery knees that kept me on the ground for so long, trapping me there, looking at my parents soaked in their own blood. Or maybe it was the fact that once I moved, my life would start moving again while theirs would stay frozen. Forever.

I jerk away from my thoughts as the sounds of Luke and Preston fighting stop. Did one of them end up killing the other one? Or did they just kill each other?

"Violet, are you okay?" Luke's voice, so close, startles me.

I keep my head hung low, taking quiet breaths. "I'm fine."

His shadow moves over my line of vision in the gravel and then his arms are slipping underneath mine. He lifts me to my feet and helps me get my balance, holding me in his arms. I'd shove him away, but I'm too drained at the moment to do anything but lean against his chest. His arms encircle my waist and for the briefest of moments I don't feel completely alone. The look Preston's giving me, however, counteracts the sensation. His harsh expression cuts into me like the rocks cut into my hands.

"Get your fucking stuff and get the hell out of here," he says, spitting blood onto the ground. His lip is cut open, his eye swollen shut, and there's a giant welt on his rib cage.

"Gladly," I reply in a composed tone, but on the inside I want to grab on to him and beg him not to leave me. Tell him I need him.

He wipes his arm across his lip, rubbing away the blood. "And don't come crawling back to me when you're homeless and living out on the street, because I won't take you back."

"I won't come back," I assure him with a harsh glare as tears try to shove their way out my damn eyes. Fucking traitor eyes. I inhale and exhale over and over again, sucking them back until I feel woozy.

"Violet, let's go," Luke says softly. The steady beat of his heart hitting my back is both soothing and terrifying.

Shaking his head, Preston stomps back toward the trailer

199

house, kicking the door before opening it up and disappearing inside. Luke's arms relax around me as I stand there in his grasp with my arms lifelessly to my side. I can barely breathe, let alone talk, knowing that soon life is going to catch up with me and so is the painful reality that I have nowhere to go. I have no car, and only two hundred bucks to my name, which will maybe get me a hotel room for a few days. Then what?

"Are you okay?" Luke's voice is soft and conveys caution as his arms loosen around me.

"You keep asking me that," I say as I stare at the shut door of the trailer. My eyes are burning with tears that almost escaped and my throat feels dry.

"That's because you haven't answered me." His breath caresses the back of my head.

"I'm fine," I say. "So you can stop asking."

He pauses and then slides his arms away from my waist and winds around to the front of me. His lip is bleeding and his shirt's torn, but other than that I don't see any new damage on him. "Do you need anything? Water?" he asks, his lips tug upward as he studies me intently. "A sedative, maybe?" He pats the pockets of his jeans. "I could give you a hit of my cigarette... that might help calm down the anxiety a little."

"I don't have anxiety," I tell him. "I'm completely calm."

He frowns with disbelief and starts to back up toward Preston's car. "I know what a panic attack is, Violet, and I know that the only reason you're calm right now is because you're exhausted from one."

I don't want him to be able to see so much of me, yet as he backs away, still looking at me, it seems like he's seeing what's hidden underneath my steel skin. He bends down and picks up my box of stuff, then carries it toward his truck. When he drops it into the bed, I force my feet to move forward, knowing I can stand in the same spot all I want but ultimately I'm going to have to face the bleary future I created for myself. Swallowing the lump in my throat, I head to the driver's side of the Cadillac and pop the trunk, then weave around to the rear end of the car.

Luke's boots crunch against the gravel as he hikes back up the driveway, lighting up a cigarette. I start piling the boxes out of the trunk, stacking them beside me. Luke silently starts picking them up and carrying them to his truck. By the time I'm finished unloading the trunk, he's taken care of most of the boxes. I pick up the last one, head down the driveway, and set it in the back of his truck. Then we climb in and I crack the window as he puffs on his cigarette and smoke fills the cab.

He places his free hand on the shifter and his other on top of the wheel with the cigarette positioned between his fingers. "So . . . where do you want me to take you?"

I shrug as I stare at the trees lining the yard. "I have no idea."

He's silent for a second, then backs the truck down the driveway. He doesn't say where we're going, what we'll do when we get there. Everything is so unknown. Just the way that I like it, yet at the same time it scares me because I'm not walking into it on my own. Luke's here with me and I have no idea why. No one's ever helped me out before, not like this. And it terrifies me because I actually want him to be in this moment with me, helping me.

Chapter Eight

Luke

It took a lot of energy not to beat the shit out of the guy who was getting rough with Violet. The surprising thing was, as cocky as Violet has always been, she actually seemed afraid of him. She was pretty much going to let him drag her into that house and do who knows what to her, so I intervened, even though I didn't want to get involved in her obviously messy life. I don't intervene for just anyone. Maybe Kayden or Callie or even Seth, but for some insane, erratic girl I met only a few weeks ago, no way. Yet I did and now I can tell I'm going to get even more involved because she has no place to go.

The strange thing is she almost looked excited about it. About the old dude yelling at her, getting rough with her, and then when we started to fight. I'm not sure if I imagined it, but if I didn't, it makes me wonder: Does she like starting trouble? Or is there some other reason?

"You can just drop me off downtown," she says, gazing out

the window as I drive down the highway toward the center of Laramie.

I flip on the blinker to switch lanes and pass a car moving at a snail's pace. "Drop you off downtown where?"

She shrugs, resting her forehead against the glass. She looks exhausted, probably from the panic attack that she insists she didn't just have. But I've seen them before, had a lot myself, especially while I was growing up.

I merge back into the right lane and flip the visor down to block out the sunlight. "Violet..." *Stay out of it.* "Do you have someplace to go or are you..."

"Homeless?" she asks as she twirls a strand of her hair around her finger. "I was supposed to live back there, but obviously that's not happening." She lets out a tired sigh, pushes away from the window, and rotates in the seat to face me. "I'm good, though. You can drop me off downtown and I'll find a place to crash."

"Where?"

"Somewhere."

I slow down as we reach the city limits where seemingly identical houses start to line the streets. "It sounds like you don't have anywhere to go." My gaze locks on her.

"I can take care of myself," she insists.

"I never said you couldn't." I downshift the truck and the engine rumbles in protest as I get ready to turn toward the side road that goes past the park and leads to downtown. "I'm just asking if you have somewhere to stay."

At first, rage crosses over her face and I seriously think

she's going to hit me, but then she recomposes herself, detachment possessing her eyes. "No, I don't," she says, then she fixes her attention on the window again. "But like I said, I can take care of myself."

I'm about to turn down the road that will lead us to the center of town where I can drop her off and let her go, which is what I need to do. She's unstable and erratic; the last thing I need in my life since I can barely take care of myself. And she has this control over me and makes me do things for her without even asking. I hate it, the way I'm drawn to her, yet I can't seem to stop the feeling.

All I can keep picturing is myself at eight years old, gasping for air, wanting to be able to breathe, but it seeming so hard. I looked a lot like Violet did when she collapsed to the ground and I felt that way when I took off for that strip club yesterday. We're both stuck in the same situation, not having anywhere to go, and it really doesn't make any sense why I'd try to help her when I can't even get myself out of the situation. Yet right at the last second, I straighten the wheel back out and keep heading straight, toward my dorm. I don't know why I do it, other than there's this part of me that wants to help her—wants to understand her.

She doesn't ask me where I'm going and it doesn't seem to faze her when I pull up to my dorm building and park the truck near the entrance doors. There are only three cars left in the parking lot and a couple sitting in the shade under the trees.

I turn off the engine and wait for her to say something, but she continues to stare out the window. She's making this difficult. I'm not used to being the person who works to open closed doors. I'm the one who wants to hold them shut.

"So you can crash in my dorm until I have to leave tomorrow," I tell her, my eyes widening at my words as I slip the keys out of the ignition. I pause, get myself together, before I look at her. "You're welcome."

That gets her to turn her head toward me. Her green eyes burn and I lean back in the seat. "I'm not going to fuck you, if that's what you're thinking," she says bluntly.

I tuck the keys into my pocket. "It's not even close to what I'm thinking." Well, it wasn't until she brought it up.

"Then what are you thinking?" Some of the harshness evaporates as she studies me.

"I honestly have no idea. You've seriously got my head fucked up and all over the place," I admit.

She seems pleased over this. "Why?"

"Because I have no idea what you're thinking and that's not normal for me."

"What are you? A mind reader?" she asks, sarcasm dripping from her voice.

"No, just observant."

"Well, maybe you can't tell what I'm thinking because I don't have a whole lot going on inside my head."

I almost smile as I recline against the door and rest my elbows on the windowsill. "I don't think that's even close to the truth. I think you have a lot going on inside your head. More than most people, which is why you had a panic attack."

"It wasn't a panic attack," she contends, resting back against her door. "I just got caught up in the excitement."

I touch my split lip with my fingers and wince from the sting. "You think watching two guys beat the shit out of each other is exciting?"

"Maybe." She pulls a regretful face as she admits this, bringing her legs up on the seat. "Does that make you afraid of me?" she wonders.

I'd laugh at her, but I am kind of afraid of her. Afraid of how she makes me feel, the way I get swept up with her, the fact I'm thinking about her and not just myself, something I promised myself I'd never do in order to keep control over my own life. *Me and me alone.* "So Kayden moved out." I switch topics to avoid the pull I'm feeling toward her, the needy ache, to kiss her, feel her, be with her. *Complicated,* I remind myself. "You can crash on his bed, but tomorrow I can't help you."

She sits up, slides her knees toward her chest, and wraps her arms around them, hugging them against her as she rests her chin on her knees. She looks so vulnerable and helpless, the armor she wears chipping away. I can't seem to think about anything else but how easy it'd be to hit on her, play her until she gives in to me. I'd lay her underneath me and fuck her over and over again until I got this stupid obsession I have for her out of me.

"Where are you living for the summer?" she asks,

slamming me away from my thoughts. "Are you staying here or going home or something?"

I lean away from the door and open it up without answering her, ready to escape the conversation. Then I hurry and hop out of the truck and head up the sidewalk, hearing the truck door open.

She quickly rounds the front of my truck, skittering in front of me with her arms out to the side of her. "That's not fair," she says with a frown. "You know my sad little story, at least part of it, and it's only fair I get to know yours."

"The only thing I know is that you were going to live with some old pervert who likes to hit you and now you have no place to live," I clarify and dodge around her, heading for the entrance doors.

She walks across the parking lot beside me. "Do you have someplace to live?"

I rake my hand over the top of my head. "Does it really matter?"

"Maybe."

"That seems like your go-to answer." I bite my tongue, deciding whether to shout at her to back the fuck off or run like hell. "Don't flip this to being about me."

"Why?" she says, spinning around and walking backward in front of me. "You know I'm homeless, so why's it a big deal if I know you are?"

I stop at the curb, feeling something force its way up inside me. I've never been asked questions like this. People are usually too afraid of me and that's the way I like it. And if it was any other girl I'd probably think she was just trying to get an invite home with me, but I'm starting to understand Violet enough to know that she's probably getting a kick out of being a pain in the ass.

"You're right." I throw my arms up in the air exasperatedly. "I have no fucking place to live." I breathe heavily. "There, are you happy?"

She shakes her head, pieces of her hair blowing in the warm breeze as she looks over at a couple laughing beneath the trees. "No, not really."

"Me neither." I glance around the campus yard, scanning the trees, the few cars in the parking lot, my boots, looking anywhere but at her, otherwise she'll pull me into her, like she's been doing since she made me care enough to follow her to her car after she kicked me in the face.

"So now what do we do?" Her eyelids flutter against the sunlight as I glance up.

"You're asking me what we should do?" I arch an eyebrow at her. "Really?"

She looks around defenselessly and I wish she'd bring back that detached attitude so I wouldn't feel such a need to help her. "I'm running out of ideas, but if I have to I'll sleep on the streets," she says.

"You're not going to sleep on the streets…we'll figure something out." I close my eyes when I realize I said "we'll," like we're a couple, which we're not. We're just two strangers

209

who keep crossing paths and can't seem to get rid of each other. "If we have to, we can sleep in my truck."

"Yeah, I've seen how well that goes. You're a serious seat hog." Humor laces her voice.

"You can sleep sitting up," I retort, opening my eyes. "Or sleep in the bed of the truck."

"Wow, what a gentleman," she jokes with a small smile and the tension around us crumbles.

"I'm not trying to be a gentleman," I say, fighting a smile. "And I'll never try to be one."

"Good, because I don't want you to try. Guys who claim to be gentlemen are full of shit."

"Okay..." I say. "I'm glad you don't want me to be a gentleman."

She grins and it reaches her eyes and reduces the hideous swelling in her cheek. It must hurt like hell. "I think I won that one."

I can't help but smile and it feels strange and unwanted, yet it's there. "Were we playing a game?"

"Aren't we always?" she counters, plucking strands of her hair out of her mouth as the wind blows through her hair.

Again, she throws me out of my element, but instead of continuing to lose whatever game we're playing, I surrender. "We should go get something to eat," I tell her. "Because I have absolutely nothing in my room but a bottle of vodka and a lemon." I glance down at her hands, the palms covered in dry blood. "And we need to pick up some peroxide and Band-Aids."

She folds her fingers into her palm as she chews on her lip. "Are you giving up our game?"

"What game?" I fake forgetfulness. "I'm just hungry. It's like one o'clock and I haven't had anything to eat. And the peroxide is for you—your hands look like shit."

She looks down at her palms, cut up from the rocks, blood oozing out, and then back up at me. "Haven't had your hangover food yet, huh?"

"Yeah, and I'm dying. I need to get some tacos in me."

"Tacos? I thought you said you didn't like hamburger?"

"Tacos are about ground beef. Not hamburger."

"Potato, *potato*. It's pretty much the same."

"It is not," I argue as I turn around and we start back toward the truck. "It's completely different."

"Maybe you should go get cleaned up first." She runs her thumb down the side of my lip and the connection sends uninvited emotions coursing through my body. I have to clench my hands into fists, just to keep myself from grabbing her and crashing her lips against mine. She withdraws her hand and wipes her thumb and her finger together. "You have blood on your face and clothes."

I shrug, smothering the desire to jerk her hand back to me, rip her clothes off and bend her over the hood out of my truck. "I'm fine with looking like a man who just beat the shit out of someone, but if you're too embarrassed to be seen with me, you can sit in the truck."

"'A man who just beat the shit out of someone'?" she

211

muses, stopping at the passenger door of my truck, her hand hovering above the handle of the car door. "Or a guy who just got his ass kicked?"

I can't tell if she's toying with me or not, but it's both irritating me and exciting me in ways I didn't know were possible. Half the damn time I have no fucking clue whether she's being serious or not. Being a control freak, this should send me running, yet it's having the opposite effect when it comes to her.

I decide to give her a taste of her own intense medicine, throw her off a little, regain the upper hand and hopefully scare her away. "Are you saying that I'm not tough?" I position myself in front of her, trying to get her to back up into the truck, but she stays still. "Or that I'm not a man?"

"I'm not saying either," she says with a fervent look in her eyes that nearly sends me soaring through the roof. The more intense I get the more excited she gets, which makes me want to get even more intense. "Although, I'm guessing that despite that fact, you're still about to show me that you're both of those things."

"Is that what you want me to do?" My voice comes out husky. This isn't working out how I want, my plan of keeping her away backfiring on me. I take a step forward and then another, until I'm pretty much stepping on her feet. She still doesn't back up and it frustrates me even more. "For me to show you how tough I am or how much of a man I am?"

She presses her lips together, her gaze unwavering, eyelashes fluttering. "I don't want anything from you, Luke. I'm just simply saying what's in my head. And the longer you're around me, the more you'll realize this."

The longer I'm around her? Fuck. I reach a hand around the side of her and grab the door handle of the truck. "So you don't think I'm tough?" I ask.

"I think *you* want to show me how tough you are and how much of a man you can be," she says.

I put my other arm on the other side of her, so she's pinned between my arms. Most girls in this position would back up into the door, but she stands firm, refusing to let me control her like I desperately want to.

"And how would I show you?" I drop my voice to a husky growl, intentionally this time.

"I'm sure you have your ways," she replies, her gaze flickering at my mouth as I lean forward and our bodies press together.

It takes every ounce of strength not to seize hold of her hips and gently shove her back. Instead, I lean farther in, our lips inching closer. "I do have my ways..." I lick my lips and feel the sting of the cut. It reminds me of everything I just witnessed; with her, with me. I know if I kiss her it'll more than likely lead to me jerking the door open and throwing her down on the truck seat, right here in broad daylight. I wouldn't care who saw us. I never do. I'd just want to get this God damn need to regain control out of me, the need she's putting in me. But then what would happen after it was all over? Would we go get tacos and come back to my dorm and hang out? Yeah, that doesn't seem at all possible, but neither does screwing her and then bailing. I'm too far into her and I'm not sure how to get away or if I can get away at this point.

I clench my hands into fists as I fight the urge to shut my eyes and kiss her until she can barely breathe. I feel weak the moment I flip up that handle and start to pull the door open because I'm choosing to feel the vile, pathetic feelings of my past—how I did things I didn't want to do, how my mother messed with my head, how I had no control over my life. I was a puppet. I was weak. I don't want to be that person ever again.

I wait for Violet to move out of the way so I can get the door open, but she doesn't budge and I'm the one who ends up stepping back, losing again. It's an unsettling place I've arrived at and I don't know what to do with it beside drink myself into a stupor and hammer my fist through anything that gets in my way. My body is actually shaking as my mind craves the burning, blissful taste of alcohol.

"So where are we going to get tacos?" She sidesteps around me and hops in the truck, tucking her skirt in as she brings her legs into the truck.

"You pick," I say as I shut the door.

She smiles a plain, fake smile, not even giving me the benefit of a real one. "It doesn't matter to me," she says as I climb into the cab. Then she kicks her feet up on the dash and flops her head back against the seat, looking as calm as can be.

I have to wonder if she really means it. If nothing matters to her, and if she's beginning to matter to me.

214

Chapter Nine

Violet

We go get tacos, stop by a drugstore, go to the electronics store to pick up a new phone for him because apparently he lost his last night, then go back to his dorm. The conversation is as light as air, which makes it complicated, in my book. It's too easy to be around him and it's not supposed to be that way with anyone. Things are supposed to be hard so it makes it easier to keep up my wall and stay detached, so if and when he decides to exit my life, it'll be like he was never really there at all.

But I can feel my wall collapsing, especially when he didn't kiss me while we were by his truck. He could have and I could tell he wanted to. I probably would have let him, too, if only to taste the rush of adrenaline that was forming at the tip of my tongue the second he leaned into me. The way I was hyperaware of his body heat and my own was unfamiliar and it terrified me. All I wanted to do was silence the fear awakening inside me, but the closer he got to me, the quieter I got on the

inside. He was my escape from my emotions, yet he was putting them in me at the same time. It was the strangest feeling and I had a difficult time deciding what to do. So I just stood there and let him decide and eventually he moved back and I was left relieved and disappointed.

I'm still analyzing why. The only conclusion I can come up with is that all the stress of being homeless and going to the police department tomorrow has caused my head to crack open and I'm not thinking clearly.

Only minutes after being in his dorm room, he leaves me alone in his room to take a shower. He has packed up hardly any of his stuff, which makes me wonder what he's going to do when morning comes around.

I douse a cotton ball with peroxide and press it to my hand, feeling it sizzle against my dirty, scraped skin. I now have $7.56 less than I did, all because Luke didn't want me to get an infection. I was fine with the risk, but he insisted it was unsafe. I almost laughed at him. If only he knew just how unsafe life can get for me.

I flop back on the bed that doesn't have a sheet on it, just a mattress, the one that was Kayden's I'm guessing, and stare up at the ceiling, rotating the cotton ball around on my hand. It burns and makes my palm ache, but I let it soak into me as I figure out my next step.

I've never had a friend before, if that's even where Luke and I are moving toward. Preston and Kelley were the closest to friends I ever had, but they were more like my crazy babysitters/landlords than anything. There was no one actually caring enough about me to convince me to buy peroxide and Band-Aids, to clean some cut up and properly take care of myself. There was no one who would beat someone up simply because they were groping my breast. Luke had hammered his fist into Preston's face without even so much as a second thought.

My heart starts to pump harder as I think about it, the way he did it without any hesitation, when the dorm door opens and Luke enters. He's wearing a towel wrapped around his waist, his skin still a little damp from the shower. His lean muscles carve his stomach along with a massive welt he probably got from the fight. He's got a serious set of tattoos. Most are sketched in dark ink and tribal shapes except for an inscription that's too small for me to read from this far away.

I drape my arm over my head, unable to take my eyes off him. "I like your tats."

He sets his dirty clothes down on the dresser and shuts the door with his foot, his brow curving upward. "Was that a compliment?"

"Perhaps."

He sinks down on the made bed across from me and disappears out of my line of vision. "You have some of your own, on the back of your neck, right?"

"Yeah, two of them," I say, returning my concentration to the ceiling, my hand balling around the drying-out cotton ball. "I have more, though."

"Where?"

"It's a secret."

He pauses and the mattress squeaks. "So, do you want to just crash? I'm kind of tired."

I shake my head, listening to my heart thud in my chest. Even though I'm tired, if I just crash then I'll have to think about what happened and if I think about what happened I'll have to feel how I feel about it and if I feel it, I'll just want to get up and do something reckless. Then afterward, I'll be content and get tired, wanting to crash, and the whole process will start over. It's a vicious cycle. "I'm not tired at all."

He sighs heavyheartedly. "Then what do you want to do?"

I boost up on my elbows to look at him, fixing my attention on his swollen jaw instead of where his towel is starting to open up. "What do you usually do on a Sunday night?"

He reaches for a bottle of Jack Daniel's on the desk by the foot of his bed. "Get drunk and get laid." He watches my reaction as he tips his head back and takes a swig.

"Isn't getting drunk bad for you...because you're a diabetic?"

He shifts his weight uncomfortably and then looks away toward the window. "I'm fine. I don't do anything I can't handle."

I seem to be making him upset and I don't understand why. But I let the subject go, since I'm the last person who should be lecturing anyone on what's good and bad for them. I sit up and slide to the edge of the bed, planting my feet on the floor. "Well, if getting drunk and getting laid is what you want to do then you're going to have to go have fun solo," I say. "Because I don't do either of those things. Well, I drink sometimes, but not a lot." I divulge the truth to him, but not deliberately. My brain is clearly tired.

His eyes immediately snap in my direction as he chokes and alcohol sprays out of his mouth and onto the carpet, making my confession worth it. "What?" he sputters, setting the bottle back down.

"What? Drinking makes me act vicious and kind of crazy so I try to avoid it unless I want to act mean and crazy." I know that's not why he's choking though. He's choking because I said I was a virgin.

"You mean more than you already are?" he asks warily, wiping the whiskey away from his lips with his hand.

I cross my legs and the split on my skirt opens up, revealing my thighs. I notice his gaze travel toward them, his eyes blazing with something I've seen in guys' eyes many times. I can't help but wonder if Luke could be my reckless thing at the moment if I decide I want to go that route. The way he hit Preston, without so much as thinking, and the strip club fight...it makes him seem sort of dangerous, which makes me think he could feed my craving. But do I really want to get involved? Feel a connection? Because when he kissed me in the truck, I'd felt something other than numbness. I felt a spark. Life. Need.

"Yeah, so imagine how bad I can get," I say.

His heated gaze skims from my legs to my face. "It's probably a good thing then." His fingers seek the bottle again, his blazing eyes still fastened on me. He takes another swallow, peering over the bottle at me.

"Does it make you uneasy?" I ask, leaning back on my hands, amused that I'm making him tense over the fact that I'm a virgin, yet he won't comment on it. "That I am."

He sets the bottle down again and his tongue slips out of his mouth to moisten his cut lip. "Does hearing that you get crazy and vicious when you're drunk make me uneasy? Why would it when you're that way sober?"

"Don't play dumb," I say. "I know you're thinking about how I just told you I was a virgin, which is why you spit out your drink all over the floor...so does it make you uneasy, knowing I haven't had sex."

"No, but your bluntness does." He rubs his eyes with his hands to conceal whatever look is crossing his face. "I...I just don't get how." He lowers his hands to his lap. "How you..." His eyes skim up my body, lingering on my legs and then on my see-through shirt. "How you could be one?"

"A virgin." The word itself seems to make him uneasy, which only makes me want to say it more. "Why don't you get how? Not everyone wants to have sex."

"Yeah, but..." He trails off assessing me with his intense brown eyes and now I'm the one that has to work to not fidget. "You dress the way you dress and act the way you act...you fool around with guys...it doesn't make sense."

"I dress the way that I want to," I tell him, tucking my hands under my legs to try to hold still. "And I act how I need to, but I don't get why that would make you think I'm a slut... Is it because of Callie? I think she might have thought I was a whore or something."

"Why would she think that?"

I shrug. "Probably for the same reasons you think I am."

"I didn't think you were a slut," he insists. "I just thought..." His eyes enlarge and then he clears his throat. "Anyway, so if I can't drink or get laid tonight, then what else is there to do?"

"*You* can do whatever you want." I put my hands on my lap. "I just said that I don't drink or get laid."

He seeks the bottle again and tips his head back, pouring the last few drops down his throat. He gets up and tosses the bottle into the trash by the foot of the bed. I bite my lip watching his muscles ripple like they did when he was fighting with Preston.

"We could play cards," he suggests, opening the closet door. He bends down to pick a shirt up from off the floor and the towel slides lower and lower on his hips. I'm not sure if I'm so much as fascinated with his body as how my body is reacting to the sight of him. Invigorated. Excited. I've never been excited over a guy before. I've either been disinterested or afraid. With people in general.

Regardless, I want to feel it more, let it shower over me. "Cards?"

He has a tattoo on his shoulder blade, a dragon. I touch the back of my neck where my own dragon tattoo is as he stands back up and turns around with a deck of cards in his hand. "But the deal is that we can't play for money."

"Good, because I don't have enough to play with," I say, still assessing his body, but more discreetly.

"Neither do I." He sits down on the bed with his legs over the edge, so he's not flashing me, and puts the cards on his lap. "However, I never just play Texas Hold 'Em for nothing."

"Why not?"

He clears his throat. "Because it was how I was taught to play."

"By who?" I was taught to play by someone, too, and for money. A couple I lived with for about six months used to throw these Texas Hold 'Em parties and I would sit beside the table while Mr. Stronton explained the rules to me. I got pretty good at it too, but it's been a while since I played.

He cuts the deck in half and shuffles them. "By my dad." The way he says it, his voice stressed, makes me speculate if something happened to his dad.

"Where's your dad now?" I rise to my feet, adjusting my skirt.

He aligns the cards on the bed, looking up at me. "He lives in California."

I cross the room to the bed he's sitting on, the navy blue sheet balling up beneath me as I sit down and get comfortable. "Then why don't you just go live with him?"

He grips the shuffled deck of cards in his hand. "It's complicated."

"What about your mom?" I ask.

"Even more complicated." His knuckles whiten as he tightens his hold on the cards. "What about your parents? What happened to them?"

"They left me on the doorstep of the neighbors when I was six months old," I lie breezily. I've been doing it for years, making up elaborate stories to avoid the painful truth of what happened when strangers ask me. "I guess they didn't want me or something."

He cuts the deck evenly in half. "Is that the truth? Or are you making up a story?"

"Why would I make up a story about that?" I ask innocently, tucking my leg underneath me. Again his eyes go to my legs, gradually drifting up to my thighs.

He studies me unnervingly as heat caresses my skin and coils in my stomach. "To avoid the real truth."

"So are we going to play Texas Hold 'Em or what?" I aim to change the subject.

"Yeah . . . but there's a stipulation," he says. "For every hand you lose you have to tell me one thing that's true about you."

"I don't like that rule," I tell him. "And I don't like telling the truth."

"Why? Are you afraid you'll lose?" he challenges me with haughtiness.

"I'm not afraid of anything."

"That can't be true. Everyone's afraid of something."

"Fine," I give in. "But if you lose, then you have to tell me something true about you—and something good."

He fans the edge of the cards with his finger, like he's counting the cards. "What if I don't have anything good to share?"

"I'll be the judge." I stick out my hand toward him. "Now give me the cards so I can deal. I'm dealer."

He turns his hand over with the deck in them. "I usually like to deal." He puts the cards in my hand, sighing, like he's surrendering something very valuable.

I wrap my fingers around the deck. "Do you play a lot?"

"Occasionally when I need money."

I shuffle the deck, even though he already has. I was taught never to trust anyone else when it comes to playing cards. I toss the top one to the side and deal.

I lift my cards up and peek under them. "If we were playing strip poker, you'd lose after one hand since you're only wearing a towel."

He picks up his cards, pressing back a smile. "Yeah, but I won't lose."

"That's awfully arrogant of you." I flip over three cards on the bed, lining them up between us.

His mouth gradually expands to this know-it-all smile. "I know."

I turn over my cards and he gives me this strange look.

"There's no point in hiding what we have since we're not actually raising the stakes."

He smiles. "I'm keeping mine hidden, so go ahead and deal another."

I do what he says and the next card I deal is an ace. I have one, but I don't get excited just yet. Even though the odds are in my favor, doesn't mean they'll end up that way. First rule of cards. And of life.

Luke's expression is a mixture of inquisitiveness and boredom, which makes no sense since the two don't really go together. "Deal the last card," he says.

I turn it over and lay it down. None of the cards are suits and there's nothing close to a flush or run. I have a good chance of winning or at least tying if he's lucky enough to have an ace.

"What are you smiling about?" Luke wonders, rearranging his cards. "Maybe I have an ace, too."

"I didn't know I was smiling," I say, biting my lip to stop. "What do you got?"

He places his cards down and my elation instantly sinks. "What can I say?" He rubs his jawline thoughtfully. "I must be lucky."

I scrunch my nose at his cards. "How is it even possible for you to get pocket aces?"

"Any hand's possible." He relaxes back on the mattress on his elbows and the towel slips open just enough that I can see his thighs. "Now I get to ask a question."

"Go head." *It doesn't mean I'll tell the truth.* "Ask away."

His legs spread apart a little and I swear I can see his balls. "Tell me why you jumped out the window that night."

I don't miss a beat. "I was tripping on acid and I wanted to see if I could fly."

He rolls his eyes. "I've seen people tripping on acid before and you definitely weren't." He tosses his cards aside and overlaps his hands on his lap. "Come on, Violet. Tell me the truth."

I frown. "I really don't want to."

"Well, you have to. It's part of the game."

I waver, biting my fingernails. He's taking all the fun out of the moment and replacing it with pressure. "Would you believe me if I told you I was trying to fly?"

"Were you?" His body goes rigid. "Were you trying... Did you do it on purpose?"

I drop my hand to my lap. "You think I'm suicidal?"

"I don't know what to think," he says, swallowing hard. "That's why I'm asking you." His voice comes out off pitch, troubling, and I wonder why.

"I'm not. I promise." I pause, trying to shake the emerging feelings out of my body. "What about you? Why were you looking for a fight that night?"

He shakes his head. "You haven't won a hand yet, so I don't have to answer."

I lower my gaze to his cards on the bed. "How the hell did you end up with two aces?"

"I guess I'm just lucky."

"Luck doesn't exist."

We stare at each other stubbornly and then reluctantly I give up, which might be a first for me. But I'm still determined to win the next hand and get an answer from him to level the playing field.

"I was running from a couple of guys," I say as I collect the cards from the bed. *I can't believe I just gave in to him like that.* "That's why I jumped out the window."

"Why were you running from them?" He hands me his discarded cards and I add them to the top of the deck.

"No way." I scoot the cards across the bed toward him. "That would be two questions and you only won one."

He picks up the cards with a smirk on his face. "That's okay. I'll just ask you after I win the next hand." He shuffles the deck and deals out the cards, looking so pleased with himself.

I end up losing that next hand and he asks me the same question I refused to answer earlier, and then waits patiently for me to respond.

"I did something," I answer, annoyed. How the hell did he win that hand? It's bullshit. First two aces, then two queens.

"What kind of something?" He has the deck of cards in his hand and is fanning them with his thumb.

"I screwed someone over."

"That's still not really an answer."

"Well, it's the best I can give you," I say, but he just keeps staring at me, fanning the cards, over and over again, his sexy

227

brown eyes weaseling their way under my skin. "Fine." I give in for some crazy reason, the bliss I felt earlier slipping farther and farther away and I know that soon I'm going to have to do something about it. "I screwed them over during a deal a month or so ago."

He processes what I said and then sits up, chucking the cards aside. "Wait? 'Deal' as in drugs?"

I shrug with my hands out to my side. "Are you really that surprised?"

His eyes scroll up and down me. "Yeah...I don't know." He scratches his head. "Why do you do it?"

"Because it's a job," I tell him. "I also work as a waitress because I hate being in debt and school has made me get in debt a lot."

"But you could go to jail. Or worse stuff could happen." He swallows hard. "Drugs are dangerous, Violet."

"So."

"Doesn't it bother you? What could happen to you?"

"Not really. Life is just life, whether I'm living in the streets, behind bars, or in a dorm."

He frowns at me. "I had a friend that went to jail once and things weren't great for him for a while."

"Things are never great for me." It slips out and the shocked look on his face makes me want to take it back. "It doesn't really matter anyway," I hurry and say, hoping to distract him. "I don't have a supplier anymore so I won't be dealing for a while." I swallow hard at the truth.

He frees a breath, his solid, tattooed chest puffing out. "Where do you get the drugs?"

I hold up two fingers. "That's two questions and again I only owe you one."

Shaking his head, he grabs the cards and quickly deals another hand. He wins again and my suspicion rises because he has an ace and a queen and the probability of him getting such good cards three times in a row is unlikely.

"I'm not so sure these are legitimate wins," I state, putting my cards on top of the deck. It's not that I'm pissed, which is strange. I'm more intrigued than anything because usually I'm the one screwing someone over, but if he is cheating—if he's fucked me over—that'd be a first in a long, long time. "I think you might be cheating, Mr. Stoically Aloof."

"Prove it then." His lips quirk. "Now, for my next question. Where do you get the drugs?"

"From a panda bear," I say the first thing that pops into my head, not ready to fully accept he's won this hand.

His forehead creases and then he chuckles under his breath. "Oh my fucking God, you are seriously the strangest person I've ever met."

"Thanks." I shake my head and shuffle the cards on the mattress in front of me.

He puts his hand over mine, stopping me from shuffling. "No way. You still need to answer my question."

"What? 'Panda bear' wasn't a good enough answer for you?"

"Where do you get the drugs from?" He withdraws his hand from mine.

I align the cards evenly against the mattress. "From the guy you beat up today."

His lips part in shock. "How do you even know him?"

"He's my foster parent, or was from the time I was fifteen to eighteen."

"Your *foster parent*?" He gapes at me. "Are you fucking serious?"

"What do you think?" I remain as composed as I can, making him work to see if I'm telling the truth.

He firmly maintains my gaze. "I think you are."

"Okay then. You have your answer."

"Okay then." He repeats my words, his face contorting with perplexity as he takes the deck from me. "Next hand."

This time I watch him carefully, calculating every one of his movements. Everything seems flawless, until I go to pick up my dealt cards. I notice him shift his weight forward and scratch his leg. I swear to God it looks like he takes something out from underneath his ass.

"Wait a minute." I raise a finger, setting my cards down as I lean forward. "Did you just take a card out from under your ass?"

"Now why would I do that?" He lifts the two cards he has as he presses his hand innocently to his chest. "Besides, where would I put the other cards I dealt?"

"How the hell should I know," I say. "Maybe up your ass."

He blinks at me, unimpressed and I get to my feet. Without any warning I push on his arm so I can look under his ass. He busts up laughing again and I make a mental note that I've involuntarily managed to get him to laugh twice in the last few minutes. I don't know what it means, other than I must be on some comedian trip and he finds me amusing when no one really has before.

As he tips to the side, and lets me look under his ass, I get a peek of his ass as the towel slouches lower on his hip and smell the scent of booze on his breath.

There's a card hidden under him, just like I thought and I snatch it up and hold it between my fingers. "You were cheating the whole time, weren't you?"

He grabs the card away from me, a trace of a smile at his lips. "I always cheat at cards. It was how I was taught to play."

"So you knew I'd lose every hand and you'd get to ask the questions." I sink down on the bed, crossing my legs, unsure what to make of this. No one's ever played me like that. "I'm not sure whether to be pissed off or impressed."

"I'd go with the latter," he tells me, his smile growing and reaching his eyes.

"I could do that..." What the hell is my problem? I should be getting upset with him. He played me. And I kind of like it, in a weird, playful way. "But I only think it's fair that you answer some of my questions."

"Why's that fair?" he asks, tightening the loosened towel on his waist. "I should get to ask more questions for being clever enough to trick you, which I'm guessing doesn't happen that often. I'm guessing you're usually on the giving end instead of the receiving."

"I get to ask you three questions," I say, cutting him off. "And the first one I want to know is why don't you have anywhere to live?"

He's unenthusiastic about my question. "That's really what you're choosing to ask?" he asks and I nod. "Fine, but it's nothing interesting like dealing drugs." He blows out a loud breath, leaning back down on the bed, propping sideways on his hip. "I do have a place to live, but it means going back to live with my mom in my hometown and I don't want to do that."

"Why not?" I ask. "You don't like your mom?"

"Not really." He lifts up two fingers. "That's two questions, for the record. You only get one more." His voice quivers and so do his fingers. I feel bad for him because I can tell there's more to it than what he says. As much as I loved my mother, I know from my time in foster care that not all mothers are sweet and loving like mine was. Mine would read me stories, sing with me. She even taught me how to play the piano, but there are some who don't like children, who hurt them, not just physically, but emotionally, both of which I've experienced.

I thrum my fingers on top of my leg, thinking how far I want to delve into his head and my own. "Why don't you just rent a place here?"

It wasn't the question he was expecting and he's startled by the easiness of it. "Because I have about two hundred bucks to my name."

"Me, too." I lean back against the headboard and kick my feet up on the bed. "How coincidental is that?"

"Not very coincidental," he replies. "Considering we're both two college kids who just had to fork out a shitload of money to pay for fall tuition." He reorganizes the deck, moving top cards to the bottom. "You know, together we have about four hundred bucks. That's enough to get an apartment in one of the Oak Section Apartments." He winces as he says it and I'm not sure if it's because he just offered to live with me or because the Oak Section Apartments are in the ghetto area of the city, where crackheads and prostitutes live. But they're easy to get into and cheap because no one but crack heads and prostitutes want to live there.

I'm not sure what to make of his offer. My initial reaction is to reject him before he ends up rejecting me. "Nah, I don't think that'd work."

He crosses his legs, still turned sideways. "Why not?"

"Well, for starters, it'd get us a month, but then we'd be broke without food or money to pay the other bills. I still have my waitressing job at Moonlight Dining and Drinks, but I make shit and it won't cover nearly all the expenses…and I don't even know if you have a job," I say. He looks hesitant and I have my answer. "So you don't have a job?"

He frowns. "Try to look past that fact for a minute…pretend I have a way to get some extra cash. Then what do you think?"

"I think I barely know you," I reply. "And you barely know me. And it's really hard living with people you barely know. Trust me. I've done it a lot."

"It's hard living with people you do know, too." He pushes up on his elbows and turns over to put the cards on the desk near the foot of the bed. The towel opens up and I catch a glimpse of his dick.

I bite my lip, thousands of thoughts flooding my head as my heart thuds in my chest and my skin covers in tingles. When he turns around all the way back, I pretend to be examining my fingernails while shivers continue to nip at my skin.

"Yeah, I wouldn't know, but we could make it work. And it's better than living on the streets or in my truck...I think." He fidgets uncomfortably, readjusting the towel back over himself. He examines the backs of his hands like they're the most fascinating thing and for a moment he looks very vulnerable, but when he glances up there's only this rough, raw, animalistic look in his eye. "We can make it work."

"How would you get extra cash flow?" I say, nerves bubbling in my chest from the rough edge of his voice. "I told you earlier I won't be dealing anymore."

"And I'm glad," he says. "And let me worry about the extra cash flow on my part."

I shake my head. "I need to know—I need to know what I'm walking into."

"Fine, I'm going to gamble."

"There's nowhere to gamble around here. There won't be any campus parties."

"Not at the kind of the parties you've been to, but there are others."

"Dangerous parties." The words roll off my tongue like sweet-tasting honey and my nerves calm down.

"Why do you sound so exited when you say that?" he wonders curiously.

"I don't," I lie, sitting up on the bed. Can I do it? Live with him? Am I seriously considering this? My heart beats quicker, harder. Jesus. "So if we do this, then you'll actually make money, right? Not lose it."

He glances down at the cards. "I just showed you how easy I can win."

I frown, unconvinced. "Yeah, but I also caught on to your little trick."

"Yeah, but you're more observant than others."

"True."

"So what do you say?" he asks with a crook of his brow, laid-back and casual, but there's a darkness haunting his eyes. "Roomie?"

My hands are shaking, but in a good, holy-hell sort of way. "All right, it's a deal." I stick out my hand and we shake on it. His touch sends tingles up my arm and my pulse accelerates, throbbing in my wrists, fingertips, neck, and even between my legs. I wonder if he can feel it.

He frees my hand and rises to his feet, turning his back to me. He opens the towel up and I wonder what he's doing. Then he ties the towel back up and disappears for the closet. "All right, Violet, who still hasn't told me her last name. We have a deal," he calls out.

A slow breath eases out of my mouth, freeing my restless energy. Before I even know what I'm doing I open my mouth and say, "It's Hayes. My last name is Hayes."

I want to slap myself in the head for giving him my real last name. Normally I tell people I'm Violet Smith, a simple name that I used to go by when I was younger because it was better than telling people my real last name. Sometimes I'd make up extravagant names for the hell of it when Smith got too dull. Yet, I just handed over the one real thing about me to Luke. I vow that for the rest of the night I'll be as quiet as possible to avoid letting anything else stupid slip out of my mouth.

I lie down on the bed, putting my head on his pillow, which smells like smoke and cologne—like him. I focus on my breathing, keeping myself calm as night approaches outside.

When Luke wanders back out of the closet, he's wearing drawstring pajama bottoms, but he didn't put a shirt on so I'm stuck staring at his muscles and tattoos all night. He opens another bottle of Jack and takes a few more shots, which I'm noticing he does a lot and I wonder how hard it is on his body since he's a diabetic, especially after what happened in his truck. It makes me kind of nervous, thinking about the fact that he could either get really sick all of a sudden or drop dead even. As I think about the idea, it sort of hurts my heart. *Holy shit. I'm actually worried about him.*

He stands to the side of the bed staring down at me with a pucker at his brows. "So Hayes, huh?" he asks, folding his arms and jerking me out of my thoughts.

I shrug, pretending it's not a big deal when it is. "Yeah, it's just a last name, though."

"Yet, you seemed very reluctant to hand it over to me."

"Maybe, I was," I say, keeping my tone light and sarcastic. "But I guess you wore me down."

He scans my entire body and my knees slip apart, like they're giving him an open invitation. For a second I think of the porn movie I saw at Preston's and the look on the guy and girl's faces as they went to town. So content. Blissfully, lost in themselves. It kind of makes me want to let Luke do the same thing to me, see if I can get to that place.

"What are you thinking about?" he wonders as he sits down on the edge of the bed.

I bite my lip, feeling embarrassment surface, but I play it off. "Nothing important."

He seems greatly conflicted about something as he continues to stare down at me. "Do you want to borrow one of my shirts to sleep in?" he finally says.

I almost laugh at the idea of wearing something that belongs to him as I fall asleep in his room. It's too personal, then again this entire situation is getting personal and I start to get up to change beds. "I'm good, but thanks."

He nods and then with hesitancy, he lies down on the bed beside me, leaving hardly any room between us. "You can just sleep in...my bed if you want. I don't have any extra sheets or blankets."

I freeze, glancing at the mattress on the other side of the room, and then at the limited space between us. "That's okay...I can handle sleeping on a filthy mattress for one night."

He pauses, looking as uncomfortable as I do. "Just stay in my bed, Violet. If you want I'll take Kayden's old one, but I'm not going to make you sleep on that filthy thing."

I frown, considering the options. I hate sleeping with people and I know I should take the other bed or make him take it, but for some reason I find myself curious about the idea of sharing a bed with him. "Fine, we can share." I lie back down on the bed and shoot back against the wall, putting as much space between us as I can. "Just don't crowd me."

"And vice versa," he says and I roll my eyes. "And don't worry, I usually don't sleep talk, although I do sometimes sleep kiss." The corners of his lips tease upward and I'm struck by how nice his smile is.

"Don't worry, I haven't sleep bitten anyone in a long time," I retort. "Then again, no one's given me a good reason to."

"Dually noted," he says with another smile as he moves his arm above our heads to the pillow and turns on his side to face me.

I smile back, but it's tight and not necessarily my phony

one, but a nervous smile. I can't believe I'm actually going to sleep in a bed with someone. The last time that happened was when a son in one of my foster families would sneak into my room and kiss me until I fell asleep. I was fourteen and he was sixteen. Honestly I was confused because it felt so good to be kissed yet at the same time it felt wrong. Regardless of my conflicted feelings I kept letting him come into bed with me, touch me, even though we barely said ten words to each other my entire two months there. Then his mother walked in and caught us and it was good-bye Violet.

I start to sit up, deciding that I'll take the gross mattress over this because I don't think I can handle it. But he shifts closer to me, crowding me just like I asked him not to do, I feel the current of his body heat hit mine. I remember how it felt in the truck to be under him, how good his lips felt on mine, and it keeps me glued to the mattress until dark settles through the room and my eyelids become too heavy to keep open.

৵৵

It's dark. So dark. Why does it have to be so dark? My legs are trembling almost as bad as when I was downstairs, but they shouldn't be. The scary people left and I'm okay. The lady that acted like she saw me, but never said a word. I'm free. They didn't hurt me. Everything is going to be okay. But why doesn't it feel that way?

I stand outside my parents' room forever. The door is wide open, making it easy to go in, yet it seems so hard, like

I'm stepping into a haunted house and something's going to reach out and grab me at any moment. My heart hurts so bad and I want to cry, yet I don't. Why?

Finally, I lift my foot over the threshold and enter the room. It seems darker in here, yet there's more light flowing in from the window. The carpet is soft against my feet yet it stings. My teddy bear is the only thing that seems to be comforting me but it seems like at any moment it's going to vanish from my hands. Then I see my mother lying on the floor and for a second everything feels like it's going to be better. She's here and I'm not alone.

"Mommy." I kneel down beside her, stroking her head over and over again. My hands shake as I feel a warm, liquid substance coat my skin. "Mommy, wake up." She doesn't move, her body lifeless on the floor beside the bed. This isn't right. The room shouldn't be this quiet. Why do I feel so alone?

"Violet." I jump at the sound of a voice... my dad's. I leap to my feet and rush around to the other side of the bed. He's sitting up, with his hand clutching his chest, blood streaming down his arm as he breathes too loud and I can hear the pain in it.

"Daddy." I sprint to him, clutching my bear in my hand. "You're okay... you're okay..." Before I can reach him, his breathing stops.

And I'm alone all over again.

Chapter Ten

Luke

I'm screwing my whole system up, the one I worked hard to create. I spent years and years under my mom's control, cleaning up after her, listening to her rant, staying inside when she told me she was too nervous to be alone. I missed school when she asked me, listening to her play the guitar and sings songs when all I wanted to do was hang out with my friends. There were a few times when she'd let Kayden come over and I'd get to go over to his house, but they were few and far between and she'd always make me spend extra time with her. Thankfully, Kayden never saw one of her more intense episodes, but he could tell something was off, just like I knew that sometimes his dad hit and yelled at him. It was our silent agreement. I'll keep your secrets if you keep mine.

And we did, continuing to live under our parents' hold. But once I could leave the house on my own, I was done. With it all. I partied and fucked girls and hardly ever came home, sleeping in my truck most nights. I loved the taste of freedom and found it often in the endless amount of drinking and meaningless sex. It was my system. Drink and screw. Go to school. Play football. Get good grades. Excel in the important parts and cover the cracked and fucked-up parts of life. The broken parts no one's seen, the ones I buried in alcohol and doing what I do best—taking control of a girl and fucking her until I know she'd do anything for me, then walking away.

Every instinct I've ingrained into my head is telling me to do that to Violet—fuck her and run. But the thing is, if I did try to, she'd probably not give in to me and since I've never experienced rejection from a girl I'm not sure how that'd go over. I worry I'd be left with the ugliness of my need for control swarming inside me. I'd be weak, like I was when I was a kid. And I hated myself when I was a kid—I hated life.

As I lie awake in my bed staring up at the ceiling, contemplating the mess I've gotten into, the sun rises outside my window. Violet's sleeping beside me on the bed, her feet are next to my head. We were laying side by side when we fell asleep, but she must have moved in her sleep. Her skirt's ridden up and I can almost see all of her long legs and her hair is down and spread out around her, the diamond stud in her nose glinting in the sunlight. I can hear the faint sound of her breathing and I find myself comforted by it and her body heat. I don't understand it. My interest in her should be gone. She told me she wasn't suicidal and I believe her, which should mean I can let her go. Yet the more I talked to her, the more it seemed like her life was as screwed up as mine and that's making me even more

242

interested, not just to fuck her but to get to know her. I want to find out who she is, why she does the crazy things she does. Why she looks so detached most of the time and what causes the few rare smiles and the sadness I see in her eyes.

I continue to stare at the ceiling until daylight fully breaks. I start to roll out of bed to get dressed and go get some coffee, when all of a sudden Violet starts flipping out. She sucks in a deep breath, her body arching as she opens her eyes to the ceiling. She blinks and gasps repeatedly as she comes out of her daze. I'm halfway sitting up when she spots me looking at her. The detachment that's normally in her eyes is replaced with so much panic and fear I almost throw my arms around her to hold on to her. But then she quickly rolls on her stomach, shaking her head as she presses her face into my mattress. Her shoulders heave as she balls her hands into fists and screams into the mattress. I don't know what to do, if I should make her move before she smothers herself or let her get whatever the hell she's releasing out of her.

After a lot of deep breathing, she carefully turns back over and sits up. Her cheek is still a little puffy, her pupils are dilated and glossy and she looks like she's high, no emotion evident in her expression. How can that be possible, when just a second ago she looked scared out of her mind?

"Are you okay?" I dare ask and then place a hand on her knee, needing to touch her for reasons I'm still trying to figure out.

She frowns down at my hand. "I'm fine." She scoots to the side and my hand falls from her leg to the mattress.

I'm not sure whether to press or not. I know I wouldn't want to be pressed if I'd woken up like that. "Are you sure?"

She nods and gets to her feet, stretching her hands above her head. Her back arches as she yawns, her black and red hair a tangled mess running down her back. All I can think about is how much I want to grab a handful of her hair and guide her to my lips, not to conquer but to comfort. "So when are we going to head down to the apart—" She's cut off as someone knocks on my door.

My brows dip together as I get up and open the door, wondering if I'm getting kicked out. Seth comes strutting in, with Greyson at his heels, then does a double take when he sees Violet, who does nothing more than stare at him, looking bored.

"Okay, I'm so confused." He stares at Violet like she's some strange endangered species. "What is she doing here? And why does it look like you both got your asses kicked?"

Violet lowers her hands to her side and turns to me. "I'm going to leave... catch up with you later, maybe."

I stick out my arm as she tries to walk forward. "We have to get down to the apartments. We'll be lucky if we can still get one already."

"Wait a minute," Seth says, elevating his hands in front of him as he gapes at me. "You're living with her?" Seth is a very blunt person and I usually don't care because I can be that way, too, but aiming his bluntness at Violet right now doesn't seem like such a good idea.

"Yeah and it's not a big deal." I glance at Greyson, the more levelheaded of the two, for help.

Greyson steps forward and puts his arm around Seth's shoulder. He's a little taller than Seth and a little more casual when it comes to clothes, wearing darker colors like grays and blacks while Seth wears brighter ones because I think he likes to stand out.

"Relax," Greyson says to Seth. "We're all friends here."

"Not really." Seth eyes Violet up and down. "The only thing I know about her is that she can be a bitch sometimes to Callie, always making her stay out of the room when she ties that damn red scarf around the doorknob so she can have her way with helpless men."

" 'Helpless men'?" Violet asks, crossing her arms over her chest, an amused twinkle in her eye. "Are you insulting your gender?"

"No, I'm saying you're a vixen, who bosses people around," he retorts and Greyson notably cringes.

Violet moves forward, tilting her head to the side. "So what if I'm a slut? It doesn't make me a vixen." She gives me a fleeting glance that carries caution for me to keep my mouth shut about her virginity secret. A secret I tried not to think about all night, yet it was impossible.

"Yes, it does," Seth snaps. "You're mean and bossy and you don't care about anyone but yourself."

"Hey Seth, lay off her," I tell him, shooting him a warning look.

245

Violet targets a death glare at me. "I don't need you to stick up for me."

"Yes, you do," I assure her, which is clearly the wrong thing to say. Her eyes darken and Greyson gets a little worried, leaning back like Violet's about to attack us all.

Seth unfortunately doesn't pick up on the vibe, though, walking out from under Greyson's arm and crowding Violet. "Yep, you don't need anyone, right? You're perfectly fine bossing people around."

She unfolds her arms and steps forward, decreasing the space between them even more. I want to believe that she won't do anything, but I've seen her do too many crazy things to make any assumptions about Violet Hayes. I decided to step forward and again I mentally curse myself for being so drawn to her.

"Hey." I position myself between the two of them and look at Violet. "Let's go get some coffee and get down to the apartment."

"You're fucking crazy if you're going to live with her," Seth says loudly and seconds later I hear a slap, probably from Greyson slapping him on the arm or something.

Violet stares up at me without so much as blinking and her lips are set together in a firm line. I can hear the soft intakes of each uneven breath as she fights to breathe soundlessly.

"Get out of my way," she says evenly.

"Why?" I ask. "Are you going to go after Seth or try to leave?"

"Does it matter?"

"Yes."

She blinks, speechless, but then shakes her head. "I'm going to leave."

I shake my head and keep my feet planted. "Then I'm not moving."

"Okay, then I'm going after Seth," she says with a mocking attitude as she shuffles to the side. "Now please move out of my way."

I mimic her move and she glowers at me through her thick eyelashes. "Luke..."

I lean in, lowering my voice. "I'm not going to let you out of here when you're obviously upset and irrational."

"I'm not irrational," she argues and then swallows hard. "And what does it matter if I am?"

"Hitchhiking." I count down my fingers the many reckless things I've seen her do over the few weeks I've known her. "Stepping into a bar fight, dealing drugs, jumping out of windows, letting some dude get rough with you."

"I do those things when I'm rational," she mutters.

"What? That doesn't make any sense."

She glances over my shoulder at Seth and Greyson. "Yes it does...now let me go."

"Were you having a bad dream?" I whisper. "Is that why you woke up panicked?"

"I'm fine," she hisses back, sucking in a slow breath. Her eyes water over and I get lost in her emotion, my hand drifting

247

to her cheekbone to stroke her skin. She flinches against the contact as I spread my fingers over her cheek. "Please, just let me leave." She begs. "Please, I just need a moment."

Fuck. I want to kiss her so badly right now, pull her against me and just hold her. I could try and blame it on the fact that she looks so vulnerable and I just want to seize the opportunity to touch her when her guard is down, but it's not like that. I know it the moment I step back and let her go by simply because she said it was what she needed at the moment. Nothing else.

She doesn't thank me as she hurries by me and I don't turn around to watch her go. I just did something solely for someone else, tossing all of my own needs aside, and I have no idea what to do with it.

Once I hear the door shut, I pull myself together before I turn around, pretending like nothing happened.

Seth immediately shakes his head at me, flabbergasted. "What the hell was that about?"

"Nothing." I head over to my desk to clear it out. With each item I put in the box, the lighter I feel because soon I'll have some place to live and it's not back home. "She just needed a place to crash for the night."

He strolls up and leans over to catch my eye. "Not that. That weird little moment you two just shared."

"I don't share moments with anyone." I glance out the window, keeping an eye on the yard in front of the building for her to step outside.

"So you say," Seth says. "And I've never seen you do anything that would contradict that, until just now."

"Seth, maybe we should just let him be," Greyson says, leaning against the door.

I gather my pens and notebook out of the desk, along with the leather case that carries my insulin and needles and place it into a box. I relax when I spot a girl with dark hair and red streaks hiking across the grass down below. "Yeah, please drop it. I don't have enough alcohol in my system just yet." I back away from the desk toward the mini fridge. "Speaking of which." I bend down and open the fridge, taking out a bottle of vodka, hoping it'll drown out what I just did.

Greyson sits down on the bed and shakes his head disapprovingly as I tip back my head and down a much-needed shot. Seth snatches the bottle from my hand and takes a large gulp himself.

"You two are such alcoholics," Greyson says. "Seriously, this isn't normal."

"Normal is overrated," Seth jokes, handing me the bottle.

I put it back in the fridge and shut the door. "So not that I'm not super thrilled you guys randomly showed up way too early in the morning, but why are you here? I thought you were headed to your house," I say to Seth.

"Well, we were," he replies, sitting down beside Greyson. "But then I got a lovely call from dear old ma a few days ago, saying that she'd changed her mind and that she wasn't comfortable with Greyson and me staying with her, so now we're crashing in town for the summer."

"Why don't you just go to Greyson's?" I ask, crossing the room to the closet.

"Because his parents live all the way over in Florida," he tells me. "And we don't want to drive that far. Besides, I got an offer to work at the clinic and I really want to do it, being a Psychology major and all."

"You're a Psychology major?" I question. "When did that happen?"

"When I registered for fall classes and my counselor suggested I declare something other than undecided," he says, with a grin. "And since I'm so smart in the human psyche department, I thought I'd give psychology a go. And Greyson got a new part-time job as a bartender down at Moonlight Dining and Drinks. He starts in a few days."

I grab all my shirts off the hangers and put them in the box, keeping a gray one out to put on now. I don't like how unorganized I'm being, but I'm in a hurry to get down to the apartments, just to have peace of mind that I have a roof over my head. "So then where are you two living? Because getting an apartment around here on short notice is pretty much a lost cause."

"We just got a place up on Elm yesterday," Seth tells me, getting up from the bed. "Which is why we stopped by . . . it's got an extra room and we were wondering if you wanted to stay with us, since you don't have a place to stay."

I glance up as I fold the top of the box shut. "How did you know I didn't have a place?"

Seth grabs the tape from the dresser and hands it to me. "You told us the other night at Red Ink."

Me and my drunken mouth. "Well, I'm good now." I pull a piece of tape off and stretch it out over the box.

"Good living with Violet?" He exchanges a disbelieving look with Greyson and Greyson sighs. "Come on, you seriously want to live with her?"

"Maybe." My chest constricts as I say it because I do. "I can't just leave her with nowhere to go and she's got a job and everything so she can pay half the rent."

"She can get her own place," Seth says as I tug the gray shirt over my head.

"No, she can't," I reply, running my hand over my hair. "She needs help."

"Obviously." Seth rolls his eyes. "She's scary as hell."

"I'm scary as hell." I pick up my cologne off the desk and spray a little on me before adding it to another box. It seemed so hard to pack before, but it seems easy now that I know I'm not going back home.

"No, you just think you are." Seth roams around my room, collecting my watches and sunglasses I have lying around, along with loose change. He hands them to me and I add them to another box I have open next to the foot of the bed. "Just crash with us. We can split the rent three ways and Greyson knows the guy running the place and he gave us one of the furnished apartments for cheap."

"How cheap?" I clasp a leather band on my wrist that says redemption on it.

"Six hundred bucks for a two-bedroom and you'll get your own room." He smiles like it's the best deal ever.

It's about the same price as the Oak Section, yet much nicer and it has furniture. Shit, it's tempting. Way too tempting. Plus the bills would be split three ways. I fold my arms, my jaw set tight as I dig out my old self that's been hiding for days, the one that thinks of himself first because no one else ever has.

"All right. I'm in."

Violet

I'm trying to keep it together and not run out into that road. Cars crawl by at a snail's pace so it wouldn't do much good throwing myself in front of them anyway. But everything's crashing over me; opening my eyes to an unfamiliar room, Luke witnessing me spastically waking up, and the fact I'm officially alone in the world. I don't even have Preston anymore. The one person I could ever consider family is gone and now I'm standing out in front of a building, not a single person in sight. All I want to do is pick a fight, stand on the ledge of a tall building, drown in a dark pool of water. Push myself to the brink of death and maybe this time just let it take me over.

Maybe it's time. To let go. Give up. Because I'm so God damn tired of struggling to hold onto life.

I tug my hands through my tangled hair and glance around the grassy area surrounded by trees, searching for something dangerous that might give me the numbness I so desperately need. My gaze scales up to the roof of the loft dorm building, and I angle my chin up. The sun stings at my eyes but I don't blink as I observe the thin trim of the roof. *How do I get up to it?*

"Violet." Luke's voice flickers the tension inside me down a notch, enough for me to stop thinking about the roof.

I lower my eyes to see him walking across the grass and the tension pretty much fades away. He's wearing black shorts and he's got a shirt on, covering up his chest and tattoos and he has that leather band on his wrist that he always wears, the one that says "redemption." I open my mouth to say something to him that will maybe put an end to this little attachment I'm developing toward him, but for once I can't find anything to say.

"Hey," he says when he reaches me beneath the canopy of the trees.

"That's three 'heys' in the last twenty minutes." I force a smile, but it hurts.

He smiles, but his looks strained, too. "I guess that's my go-to word."

"I guess so."

The dorm building's doors swing open, the windows

reflecting in the sunlight. Seth and a guy, I think his name is Greyson, walk out, laughing about something. Seth narrows his eyes at me and shoots me a dirty look.

Luke stuffs his hands into the pockets of his shorts. "So, I have to tell you something."

"Okay..." I try not to get nervous, but I do, which makes me want to run, but I don't because I want to be near him.

"It's about the apartment." He pulls his hand out of his pocket and massages the back of his neck tensely. "Seth and Greyson were going to go to Seth's place for the summer, but some stuff happened and now they're going to stay here...and they want me to share a place with them on Elm." His arm falls to the side as he waits for me to respond.

As it clicks, my face falls, but I quickly pick myself up and my fake smile that hides the crushing disappointment rises up right on cue. "Elm's a nice place."

"Yeah, it is and I think Greyson knows the dude who owns it so he's giving them a furnished one for cheap."

"Sounds awesome." Still smiling, all rainbows and sunshine even though I feel like a fucking rain cloud on the inside.

"Yeah." He glances over at the parking lot where Seth and Greyson are climbing into a sleek black car parked near the front door. "So I was thinking," he looks back at me, "that you could stay with us, too."

My heart skips a beat, but I shove it down. "That's the most ridiculous thing I've ever heard, but thanks for the offer."

"More ridiculous than panda bears giving you drugs," he

jokes but then sighs. "Look, I know Seth's a little intense, but I asked him and he said he was okay with it."

"I don't care if he's okay with it," I tell him, backing across the grass. "I'm not a charity case. I can find my own place to live." I spin on my heels and start walking across the grass, my blood pressure rising with each step. *Stop it. Stop.* This isn't right. I shouldn't be feeling this upset over the fact that I'm walking away from some guy or that he just ruined our plan to live together. I never wanted to in the first place, yet my inner voice is laughing at me, loud and shrill. I feel like running, but I don't. I take even strides, one by one, like I'm in no hurry to get anywhere.

"Violet wait." Luke chases after me and grabs my arm, jerking me to a stop. "I know you're upset but—"

"I'm not upset." I laugh, but it sounds sharp and off pitch. "I just need to figure out where I'm going to stay."

He reels me in toward him by the arm. "Just stay with us."

"I'm good, but thanks." I tug back, but not hard enough to get me anywhere. Instead I'm drawn closer and closer to him, his brown eyes blazing like embers beneath the sunlight.

"Stay." Is all he says as the space between us disappears. I can feel the heat from his body and maybe my own as he lures me closer until our chests brush. Jesus, I think my nipples just got hard. "It'll work out...we can share a room and I—"

"You're going to share a room with me? Seriously." I shake my head. "Didn't you get enough of that this morning?"

"What do you mean?"

"I mean my crazy wake-up ritual. I wake up like that every morning."

He scans my face for something, but he's not going to find it, whatever it is. "I can handle a cranky Violet. I've been doing it for weeks."

"Yeah, but you get breaks," I say, confused. I don't get why he's being so nice and determined to help me. It doesn't make sense, not unless he wants something. "This time you wouldn't. I'd be there twenty-four/seven, while you're sleeping, eating, taking a shower."

He stifles a grin as his hand slides up my arm to my shoulder. "If you get too bad, then I'll leave the house for a while," he says and I get a whiff of vodka on his breath.

"You're drunk." It's making sense now, why he wants to help me. "I get it now."

"First off, I'm not drunk. I barely took a swallow and trust me I have a high fucking tolerance for alcohol," he tells me. "And second, what do you get?"

"Why you're determined to help me."

"I'm not determined to help you. I just want you to come live with me...us." He winces at his own words, but doesn't look away from me, our eyes bond. "Come live with me."

"I don't think that's a good idea," I say as his gaze flicks to my mouth.

"Why not?" He rubs his lips together as he moves his hand from my shoulder and his thumb grazes my bottom lip.

256

"Because I'm crazy and intense." I swallow the lump in my throat as my stomach flutters. "You'll get sick of me. I promise."

"So am I." He's fixated with my lips, tracing his thumb back and forth across them and it feels weird and wonderful and thrilling. "Jesus..." he breathes, seeming torn, an array of emotions flashing across his face, but in the end there's only conquest and confusion, a strange combination.

Before I can even take my next breath, he's leaning in and his lips are brushing mine. My breath is stolen and tossed aside somewhere, my legs instantly turning to rubber. I've been kissed plenty of times by people I hate, dislike, felt no connection with at all. This is different...even more so than in his truck...this is...stimulating. Slow and sensual...everything is slow, even my heart rate. I feel a sinking feeling drift through my body down to my toes as I slide my hands up his lean arms and grip into his shoulders to keep from collapsing to the ground. He holds my weight in his arms, again making me feel safe. I open my mouth and let his tongue slide in deeply as I press my chest against his.

"This is so much better sober..." he mumbles and I realize he does remember the kiss in his truck. He lets out a throaty groan, his grasp on my shoulder tightening as his other hand tugs at my waist, crushing me against him. Our chests collide, our body heat mixing. Everything that I'd been feeling when I walked out here is gone and is replaced by this slow burn. It only amplifies when his hand glides up my back and tangles through my hair. I hate my hair played with, but as he tugs on it roughly, it makes me want to cry out in pleasure. The idea that he could do anything to me at the moment feels so God damn invigorating. That he could keep kissing me like he is. Devour me. Have sex with me. Whatever he wants and I don't know him enough to know what that is. It's terrifying and thrilling and it's making me crave more.

I slip my hand up his back and push my palm against him, forcing him closer to me.

"Violet," he groans, dragging his teeth across my bottom lip and gently nibbling on it. "I think...I think..." He starts to pull away.

"Don't stop." My voice sounds a little more pleading than I planned and starts to jerk me back to reality, but then he lets out this low growl and his lips literally smash into mine, so forcefully I swear to God I'm going to have a bruise.

A wonderful, amazing stillness I've never experienced before fills my body as he backs me up against a tree and aligns our bodies together. He kisses me fiercely, pulling on my hair, gripping at my waist to the point that it stings. His hand starts to glide up my body, searing hot even through the fabric of my shirt. When he reaches my bra, he softly grips at my breast, gently caressing it before moving his hand to the top of my collarbone. I gasp as he folds his fingers around the base of my neck, not tight enough to hurt me, but enough that there's pressure. I'm invigorated. Stunned by how my body responds, not with need, but with satisfaction. Blissful, confounding, serenity. More than when I'm standing on the edge of a building, drowning in water, stepping out in front of cars. I want more. Need more. I clutch him, digging my nails into his skin and it elicits a groan from his lips.

He abruptly moves his mouth away from mine and starts trailing kisses down my jawline, my throat, while pressing his body up against me. I moan at the feel of him and at the adrenaline pulsating through me. Oh God, I can't believe I'm groaning. I never groan.

"I've wanted to do this since we first met," he breathes against the bottom of my neck and my eyelids flutter shut as I float from reality. I wish I could drift farther. Forget everything. I'm getting close.

"Luke, we gotta go!" a male voice shouts and just like that the moment shatters.

I slam back to the real world, the safe feeling evaporating from my body. But Luke seems to sink farther into our little fantasy, his grip on my neck constricting as his mouth travels toward my breasts.

"Luke," I pant, glancing around. "I think someone just yelled for you."

"Just a second." He breathes heavily against the top of my chest, his head tipped down, his fingertips delving into my waist, his hands trembling. I'm not sure what's going on but I sense something's off, like he's struggling to let me go.

259

Seth appears across the lawn, heading around the trees toward us, smoking a cigarette. His honey-brown eyes are full of irritation and his highlighted blond hair is sticking up. "Luke," he calls out. "We gotta go if we're going to get all your shit out of the dorm today."

Luke is still breathing against my neck, his fingers pressing deeper into my skin. I begin to wonder if I'm going to have to pry him off—and if I can—but then he releases me and pushes away. There's a glazed look in his eyes and the cut on his lip looks like it's about to split open again.

"What?" He blinks and then skims the trees, grass, and dorm building like he's forgotten where we are.

"What are you doing?" Seth asks as he arrives in front of the tree we're standing under. "We got to go. Greyson told Douglas we'd be down there in an hour to sign the lease."

Luke rubs his hand down his face, staring at me for a moment, and then composes himself enough to turn around. "I'm coming, so freaking relax," he says, sounding annoyed.

Seth rolls his eyes at him and then slants them to the side to look at me. "Are you coming, too?"

I open my mouth to say that I'm not, because it's obvious he doesn't want me to come along, but Luke turns and laces our fingers together and the rush of safeness causes my knees to buckle.

I grip his shoulders, hoping he can't notice how bad I'm trembling.

"Yeah, she's coming," he speaks for me, tracing his finger along the inside of my wrist.

Before I can react or protest, he hauls me across the yard with him. Side by side. Together. And it leaves me feeling lost because I don't feel so alone. For the first time in forever, I'm content right where I am.

Chapter Eleven

Luke

We spend the entire Sunday moving everyone's stuff into the apartment and then unpacking the boxes. It's a decent place, with tan carpet and walls, a small kitchen attached to an even smaller dining room and living room. There's two small bedrooms, one very small bath, but it's affordable. No one has any plates or anything and even though the place is furnished, we still need a lot of stuff. I'm getting a little nervous about the fact that I only have a little less than two hundred bucks in my wallet and make a vow to get out and start trying to win some money.

Violet and I barely speak the entire time we unpack boxes, rearrange the furniture, and hook up the television. Not just because we're too busy to talk, but because I can't think of anything to say and she seems to be drifting down that path, too. The room fills with awkward silence and it makes me question if this living together thing is going to work.

It seemed like such a good idea at the time, but things just got extremely complicated with that kiss and I don't handle complicated well. It makes life hard to live and I've always tried to avoid making things complicated. But now I want to let a very complex and complicated girl into my life, a girl who has a hold over me. I mean, I actually kissed her. And not because I needed to gain control for a moment, but because she looked upset and I wanted to comfort her and that was the first way I could think of. I kissed her in a way I've never kissed anyone. I kissed her with desire. It's scaring the shit out of me, especially because she seems to need me as much as I want her. All I want to do right now is go looking for a fight or find a girl to fuck and bail out on, since Violet obviously can't be that girl for me. I want to drown in alcohol. Run away. But somehow I end up hanging around the apartment all day. I fell asleep on the couch, even though I said we could share a room, telling Violet I just wanted to chill and watch television for the night. She didn't seem that unhappy about it. In fact, she seemed a little relieved.

I toss and turn all night on the leather couch, eventually falling off into a nice peaceful dream about Violet. She lies wide-eyed beneath me, her arms pinned down as I slip inside her over and over again. There's no nightmares of sticking needles in my mother's arm or seeing her come home with blood all over her hands and clothes, knowing she probably did something terrible. There's no being forced to listen to her maddening songs or her telling me how much she needs me. No cops banging on the door. No listening to her cry out in the night. There's just me...and Violet...her big green eyes filled with excitement as I kiss her, touch her, pull at her hair...

I wake up to someone tapping my shoulder. At first I think it's Seth because it seems like something he would do, but then I feel the soft touch of hair tickling my cheek.

"Luke, wake up," Violet whispers, her breath hot against my cheek.

I roll my eyes open to her hovering over me, her wavy hair hanging over her shoulders and down into my face. Her eyes are lined with black, her lips glossy, and she has a necklace on. She smells incredible, too, like soap and something fruity I'd seriously like to eat right now.

"I need a ride," she says, leaning back a little and sitting down on the edge of the sofa. There's this look in her eyes, like she's hating to ask me for help.

I gradually sit up, the blanket slipping off, but I quickly pull it back up around my waist. I sleep in my boxers and my cock is hard from the dream I was having about her. "Where?"

She bites her lip, her face twisting with animosity. "To the police station downtown."

I rub the tiredness from my eyes. "Why?"

"Because."

"Are we really going to go back to the one-word responses?"

She works not to smile, smashing her lips tightly together. "What? You think just because you kissed me that I'll be more responsive to your questions?"

"You seemed pretty responsive yesterday," I say, mentally cursing myself for starting it up again so quickly.

She fidgets with a leather watch on her wrist, but her eyes light up. "Well, maybe I'm feeling a little differently today."

"Are you?"

"Maybe."

God damn it, I need her to tell me more, but I can't just ask her. That would be giving her way too much control over me. "You're not going to even give me a little bit of a hint?"

"No."

I let out a breath, shaking my head. "All right, I can give you a ride to the police station just as long as you promise to eventually tell me why you have to go down there."

She nods once and then gets to her feet. She has a pair of black shorts on that cup her fucking firm ass and a black-and-white tube top that hugs her lean body and pushes up her cleavage. "Eventually," she says.

Damn her and her one-word sentences. It's frustrating beyond comprehension. I toss the blanket aside and get off the couch, my cock still a little hard, but I decide oh well. Her eyes drift down to my cock, then to my chest as I head to the bathroom to get dressed, feeling pretty good about myself at the moment, like I might have gotten the upper hand again.

"Give me like ten and I'll be out," I say and shut the bathroom door. I brush my teeth, tug on a black shirt and a pair of jeans, then douse myself in cologne. It's the first morning in a long time where I haven't run straight to a series of shots of Jack Daniel's, but the fact that I have to drive her somewhere makes me not want to go there just yet. I'll wait until I get home and then let myself sink into the blissful contentment of alcohol and hopefully it'll clear Violet out of my head for a while.

I run a hand through my hair then go out to the living room where she's waiting for me on the sofa, staring down at her boots. She looks exhausted and tense and it makes me want to kiss her again and try to take away whatever is making her look that way. *Yes, I definitely need shots and a fucking blowjob or something.*

I scoop up my keys and wallet from the kitchen counter and wind a path through the remaining unpacked boxes around the room. "Ready?"

She glances up at me, startled, but quickly gathers herself and gets to her feet. "Yeah." She trudges for the door without looking over her shoulder, her head tipped down, looking like someone just killed her dog.

"Are you sure you're okay?" I follow her out the front door and into the sunlight, resisting the overwhelming urge to put my hand up to the small of her back and guide her down to my car.

"Yep, I'm perfect," she says, waving me off, then she trots down the stairs to the carport, keeping distance between us like she knows what I'm considering doing with my hands.

She barely speaks to me the entire drive and I hate how

we've gone back to the place we pretty much started at. I ask her a few questions, push for a conversation, but she continues to give me her one-word responses. So I give up and ten minutes later we're pulling up to the police station, an older brick building located in the heart of the town between stoplights, parking lots, and shops. I wait a moment, deciding what I'm supposed to do. Say, see you later. Tell her I'll pick her up. Kiss her good-bye.

"What time do you want me to pick you up?" I finally ask, putting the truck in park.

She cracks the door open. "I'll call you."

I snag her elbow and stop her from climbing out. "Wait. You don't have my number."

She pauses, then she reaches into her pocket and takes out her phone. "What is it?" she asks.

I tell her and she punches it into her phone, her fingers trembling as she locks the screen and puts the phone into her back pocket.

"Give me yours, too, just in case," I say and she tells me her number, looking a little more confused with each digit.

"I'll call you when I'm done," she tells me quickly then hops out and slams the door, then winds around the front of the truck. When she reaches the sidewalk in front of the police station, she stops and stares at the sign for what seems like forever. Finally, she takes a step forward and then backward and I start to roll my window down to ask her what's wrong. But then she dashes off toward the stairs leading for the glass entrance doors. It makes me wonder why she's here. Maybe she's on probation for dealing? But she seemed too upset for it to be that.

I'm still parked in the road thinking about her when someone honks their horn. I blink my eyes away from the door and drive forward, forcing myself to stop thinking about her so much. My thoughts have been way too centered on her for the last few weeks and I need a break. I decide to hit up a little game of Texas Hold 'Em, get a few drinks, win some hands, control the game, and hopefully end up on the higher side. It's going to take some time since I don't want to throw down my entire two hundred bucks on a hand, but I'm okay at the moment with taking my time. I need some time away from the one girl I've ever let have this much control over me.

Violet

I made myself sick last night, thinking about going down to talk to the detective. I even threw up this morning before I got dressed. I hadn't even realized how psyched up I was until the sunlight hit the window and I realized that I was actually going to have to go down to the police station and talk about my parents' murder. The only thing that got me to go there was the thought that maybe, this time, their murder can be solved.

When I sit down with Detective Stephner, my dread turns to irritation. He keeps showing me mug shots I've already seen, asking me questions I've already answered. What were the people wearing, what did they look like, did they do anything that might stand out. It's all in his notes, yet he's making me retell him, making me relive that stupid fucking night that I hate thinking about, that haunts my dreams, my life, that turned me into this person, sitting here, lost in herself. I'm not even sure why he's reopening the case and it's obvious he hasn't even read their file, since he doesn't even know some of the simple details.

"Think carefully, Violet," he says. "Is there anything at all you can think of about that night?"

"Other than my parents were killed?" I reply, slumping back in a metal fold-up chair. He's got me in a small, square room with brick walls and the air stinks like cleaner and stale cheese.

He takes a sip of his coffee and spills some on his smiley face tie and down the front of his white button shirt. Seriously. Some dude with a smiley face tie is going to solve the murder of my parents that happened thirteen years ago? I lost all hope when I saw that tie and cursed myself for even having hope to begin with. "Look…" He glances down at my files, unable to even remember my name. "Violet, I know this must be hard for you to talk about, but I need you to try to think of anything at all that might be helpful."

I lean forward with my arms crossed on the table between us. "Hard for me to talk about? It's been thirteen years. I pretty much remember nothing about my parents anymore, let alone anything that happened the night they died." I'm such a fucking liar.

He gives me a look of sympathy. "I'm so sorry."

I shove back from the table and push to my feet. "Sorry for what? That I'm an orphan? That I have no family? That I bounced through foster families? That I'm the one who found my parents dead? Or that you can't figure out the person who caused all of that?" I step back from the table and the legs of the chair grind against the stained linoleum. "I don't need you to feel sorry for me. What I need is to not be here, remembering things I laid to rest a long time ago."

"Violet, please settle down and think about that night carefully," he says, rising to his feet, ruffling his blond hair into place. "Anything at all that you remember could be helpful."

I back toward the door. " 'Lean into me. Lean into me. Take. Help me. I need to understand. Help me. I can't do this without you.' "

He glances helplessly down at his stack of papers, sifting through them. "I'm sorry, Violet, but I don't understand... Is that a song?"

"Yeah, it's a song, you asshole." I jerk open the door. "The woman was singing it that night, but you should already have that in your file if you've read through it all. Now, are we done here?"

He hesitates, then nods once and I start to head out. "Wait, Violet, one more thing," he calls and I pause, but don't turn around. "I just want to let you know that you might see a few things about the case being reopened on the news."

I whirl around. "Why?"

He stacks his papers back into a manila folder. "We some-times think it's helpful to announce it to the public in hopes of someone stepping forward with information."

"No one stepped forward with information thirteen years ago," I say hotly. "Why would they do it now?"

"Time generally makes people less afraid," he states, gathering his papers into his hand. "I just want to let you know so you're not surprised if you see something."

"Well, thanks for thinking of me," I say sarcastically. And with that line, I exit, slamming the door behind me.

I slip my phone out of my back pocket as I nearly run through the police station. I dial Luke's number as I burst out the front doors and sunlight spills over me. It's the only number I've ever programmed into my phone, other than Preston's and my regular buyers. It's strange to be calling him, but a little relieving to actually have someone I can rely on. I felt sort of bad this morning that I was barely talking to him, but I couldn't help it. I was too nauseous and distracted with coming down here and I've been feeling awkward about our kiss. I've never done awkward before—I'm usually the one who makes people feel awkward.

Luke's phone never rings, going straight to his voicemail, and I shake my head at myself. "I should have known better," I mutter, pressing my finger over the end button without leaving a message. I shut off my phone, cutting off any connection we developed, then glance up the busy street and sidewalk, wondering what I should do. There's all this restless energy inside me as I'm flooded by my past.

I'm not solely focusing on my parents' deaths, I'm also remembering when they were alive, playing with me at the park, opening presents on Christmas morning, going to the zoo. Laughing and smiling in the most genuine, pure way that's ever existed. I remember being loved. God, I hate remembering that. It hurts so bad, knowing I had it once. It'd be better if I never knew what it felt like to know someone cared about me enough to never let anything hurt me, because I couldn't feel the ache over something I never had.

I massage my chest with my hand, pressing so hard it aches. I want to tear it open and pull out my heart to stop the excruciating pain. I'm tumbling into the place I need to escape, I need to do something other than continue to remember what I don't have any more, to feel that they're gone, feel the pain of everyone that never wanted me, the heartache, the abandonment, the hatred for the people who did this, the needles, the razors, the tearing at the inside of my skin. God, I need to get it out.

"I need to..." I scratch at my skin, digging and digging until lines of blood trail down my arms. "Shit." I try to wipe the blood away, not wanting anyone to see, as I hurry down the stairs to the sidewalk beside the street.

I head to the left and walk swiftly past the shops toward where the apartment complex is on Elm. The entire way that stupid song is on repeat in my head as I keep picturing the details of my parents' case play over and over again on TV. It becomes my own personal torture and I can't turn it off no matter what I try to think about. And it takes an hour to walk to the apartment in this heat, and I'm thirsty, hungry, and mentally and physically exhausted by the time I'm entering the entrance of the apartment complex. But through the heat wave, my desert-dry throat, and my grumbling belly, I still feel the clawing sensation under my skin and the nagging need to shove it out of my body, the only way I know how.

I run up the stairs to the third floor where the door to my apartment is. It's strange, knowing this is where I'm going to be living for the summer with three guys, one whom doesn't like me, one that seems afraid of me, and one that seems conflicted on whether or not he wants to screw me. If he showed up right now, I'd probably let him, since his needy, hot touch seems to have the power to smother my emotions almost as good as standing on the balcony does. But he's not here and right now I'm going to have to settle for the balcony.

I open the door, ready to dash across the living room to the sliding glass door, but slam to a halt when I spot Greyson in the kitchen with an array of baking ingredients on the counter and a red mixing bowl. He's preparing to bake cookies or something, and "Demons" by Imagine Dragons is playing from an iPod. He's fairly tall with blond hair and light blue eyes. He's wearing a gray fitted shirt and with a black shirt over it, the buttons undone.

His head is tipped down as he studies an open recipe book, but he smiles up at me when I shut the front door. "Hey."

I've only crossed paths with him at the university and a few times in my dorm room. We've never spoken and he's always seemed content with that.

I force a stiff smile and whisk by the coffee table and the boxes in the middle of the floor and head toward my room, figuring out an alternative way to regain control over my thoughts and heart. As I pass by the kitchen island, his eyes land on my arms, at the scratches, which are swollen and raw.

"Jesus." He rounds the counter and strides over to me. "What happened to your arms?"

"I got attacked by a cat," I say, still moving for my bedroom, needing to be alone and escape the only way I know how.

He lightly grabs my arm, forcing me to stop right before I reach the hallway that has a bedroom and a bath to the right and another bedroom to the left, my bedroom, which I need to be in, right now.

"It must have been a really big fucking cat," he states, examining the scratches, tracing a path up and down my arm with his fingers. "You should put some peroxide on them or you're going to get an infection."

"I will," I reply, subtly wiggling my arm away from his grip and covering the scratches with my hand. "That's actually where I was headed."

He smiles, but looks conflicted. "Well, let me know if you need anything." He turns toward the kitchen and goes back to the stove. "Do you want to help me make brownies?"

I pause. "Seriously?"

He picks up a stick of butter and begins unwrapping it. "It's just cooking, Violet. No need to get worked up." The corners of his lips tug upward as I walk over to him, curious.

"Yeah, but what about Seth?" I ask, resting my elbows on the counter as he drops the stick of butter into the bowl.

"What about Seth?"

"Doesn't it seem like he might not be a fan of you hanging out with me, since I'm a vixen and all."

"Well, since I'm not really into vixens or women in general, I'm pretty sure he won't mind." He grins and it's probably the happiest grin I've ever seen.

"That's not what I mean," I say. "I meant, because he seems to have an issue with me."

"He just likes drama," he explains, opening another stick of butter. "He'll get over it once he realizes you're not going to steal his thunder."

"Steal his thunder?"

"Yeah, you being the very colorful person that you are." He eyes me with a look that makes me feel light inside and I sort of want to hug him.

I slide down into the stool. "And colorful is a good thing, right?"

"Of course." He stabs the stick of butter with the spoon. "Besides, you and I are going to be hanging out at work when I start my job at Moonlight Dining. It's inevitable."

"You're going to be working at Moonlight Dining and Drinks?" I ask.

He nods. "Yeah, I start Tuesday."

I've been trying not to think of the fact that I only have one job now and a lot more bills. Plus, the rush I get from dealing is no longer an option. My life is changing and I'm not sure if that's a good or a bad thing. "Well, here's a little tip: It gets really slow most nights and the tips suck."

"That's good to know. I'll make sure to dazzle as many costumers as I can then. That way the tips that I get will make up for it." He grins at me. "I'm good at dazzling."

"I'm sure you are." I'm amused. "I think you and I could end up getting along, Greyson."

"You think so?" he teases in a light tone as he sets the spoon down. "You know what I think would be the perfect new roommate bonding moment? Baking some brownies together."

"I haven't baked any brownies or anything really since I was six," I admit.

He presses his hand to his heart and shakes his head. "Well, we need to change that. Granted, the best kind of bonding brownies are pot brownies, but I don't have any pot."

"Pot brownies?" I ask interestedly.

"Oh yes." He picks up the bowl and heads to the corner of the kitchen. "My parents were very hippieish and used to make them."

"And let you eat them?"

"No, but I started sneaking them when I was about fifteen

and went through my teenage rebellious phase. I'm not going to lie, I still do it occasionally when I want to relax."

"Did you wear dark clothing and write depressing poetry, too?"

"Yes, to the dark clothing." He opens the microwave and puts the bowl inside. "But no to the poetry. I was more into lyrics and music."

"Do you still write?" I ask. "Or play anything?"

He shakes his head as he closes the microwave door. "Nah, I may have been into it, but I wasn't very good." He presses buttons on the microwave and it clicks on. Then he turns around and reclines against the counter, facing me with his arms folded. "So what was your rebellious phase, Violet?"

I glance down at my dark clothes, hiding my tattoos. "I think I might still be going through it."

"And who are you rebelling from?" he wonders.

"Myself."

He laughs under his breath. "What about your parents? Did they hate—or do they still hate your rebellious phase?"

My heart drops into my stomach and I suddenly remember where I was headed before I got sidetracked with this conversation. "You know," I say as calmly as I can as I get up off the stool. "If you really want to make pot brownies, I can help with that."

His brows lift as the microwave beeps from behind him. "Oh really?"

I shrug, backing for my room. "It's up to you. I'm just offering."

He moves away from the counter and pops the microwave door open. "Well, I'm not going to pass up an offer."

I smile my fake, shiny necklace smile, the one I plaster on my face when I need to look happy. "I'll be right back." I duck into my room and go over to the boxes stacked at the foot of the unmade queen-size bed. I rifle through them until I find the prescription bottle I keep my stash in. I'm surprised Preston didn't ask for it back, but he was probably too hung over on ecstasy to even remember I had it. But I don't doubt that he'll eventually remember and come asking for it. It seems like I should care, but at the moment I don't.

I return to the kitchen where Greyson is reading the recipe book again, muttering the lyrics of the song under his breath.

"I'm going to have to tweak this a little now," he says with his finger on the page.

"Well, tweak away." I toss him the prescription bottle and his eyes widen as he catches it.

"Holy shit," he says as he twists the cap off and glances at the fairly good stash inside. "Where'd you get this?"

"I have connections." My smile is still bright like a polished cubic zirconium as I start for my room.

"Wait, don't you want any?" he calls out.

"Sure," I reply. "But I have to take care of something first."

He gives me a puzzled look, but I walk away, leaving him in the kitchen to bake his pot brownies. I won't go back and join him, not just because pot makes me evil and crazy like alcohol, but because I'm not in the mood for company anymore.

When I get back to my room, I lock the door. Then I head over to the window beside the bed and slide it open. I pop the screen off, set it down on the bed, then swing my legs out. I settle in the windowsill, staring down at the three-story drop to the concrete. I think I'd be able to survive it, but it's hard to say for sure. If I hit my head, my skull would probably crack and if I landed on my feet, I'd probably compress my spine. Bones would probably break and my blood would stain the concrete like my parents' blood stained the carpet, walls, and comforter on the bed. The fall would hurt if I survived, but for the briefest moment during the fall, I'd feel at peace, knowing that it could all just end.

Chapter Twelve

Luke

I realize as soon as I turn my phone back on that I've messed up. There's one missed call from Violet. I try to call her, but it goes straight to her voicemail. Normally, I wouldn't think anything of it, but she looked so shocked when I asked for her number. I get the feeling she's not used to having people to depend on.

I drive past the police station on my way back to the apartment, just to make sure she's not waiting there and she's not. I should be feeling good. I doubled my money. Everything should be great, yet I feel like shit. I can't stop thinking about how surprised Violet looked when I gave her my number and wondering how she felt when I didn't answer her call.

When I get back to the apartment, Seth's sitting on the leather sofa with his feet kicked up on the table, blankets piled to the side of him as he watches a sitcom on the television. Greyson is lounging on the floor with his head resting on a throw pillow surrounded by the many boxes that still need to be unpacked. Violet's standing in the kitchen pouring a glass of juice. She doesn't look up at me as she puts the juice back in the fridge, grabs the glass, and heads for our room.

I step over Greyson and cut her off as she reaches the hallway, racking my brain for the best thing to say. "Hey."

She puts the rim of the glass to her mouth. "Hey." She guzzles a mouthful, avoiding looking at me.

I crack my muscles, nervous for reasons I barely understand and don't like. "I'm sorry I completely forgot not to turn off my phone. When I go to games, I do that...and I wasn't thinking."

She stares at me with that detached look in her eyes, the one that I was first a little envious of, but now I just want to make it go away. I want to put a different look in her eyes, like the one that was there right after I kissed her. I want to make her look alive again.

She lowers the glass from her mouth. "It's fine." She starts to step past me and I brace my hand on the door frame, barricading her path.

"No, it's not. I told you I would pick you up and I should have picked you up," I say. "How did you even get home?"

She shrugs. "I walked."

"But it's hotter than hell."

"It's just a little heat. And I made it, so you can stop feeling bad."

"Violet, I'm really sorry." I sound so pitiful, but I don't care. What I care about is fixing this—fixing us. And that realization is both liberating and fucking terrifying.

"I promise it's okay." She gives me a fake, plastered on smile, then ducks underneath my arm and goes into the room, shutting the door.

"What was that about?" Seth asks as he aims the remote at the television.

I shake my head and go to the fridge to get a beer. "I fucked up."

He grins cleverly. "Aren't you always doing that?" he asks and Greyson snorts a laugh.

I pop the cap off the beer and roll my eyes. "Ha, ha, you two are fucking hilarious." I go over and drop down on the recliner, kicking my boots off. "And why are you even laying around? The apartment's a mess."

"We were waiting around for you to come clean it up," Seth says and Greyson laughs even harder. "Our own personal maid."

"Well, that's nice of you," I say. "Use my weakness of liking things organized against me."

Seth puts the remote on the arm of the chair and leaves the channel on the news. "Hey, you don't have to clean. You could leave it messy."

I look around at the boxes and balled-up newspaper everywhere and shift my shoulders at the discomfort it brings me. "I'll start taking care of it tonight."

They both laugh at me and then we settle into this quiet rhythm, watching the news while guzzling beer. Seth eventually gets up and digs around in the cupboards for food, finally coming back with a brownie. He chomps on it as I watch the newscasters talk about every bad thing within a hundred-mile radius. I'm barely paying attention, thinking about how I should just go into the room and apologize to Violet again, make things right.

My mind begins to flood with ways to make it up to her, when suddenly I hear the reporter on the television say the name, "Hayes." I snap back to reality for a moment and pay attention to the screen. The reporter quickly rattles off about the Cheyenne murder case being reopened after thirteen years and that if anyone has any question to call this number. The room gets really silent as I stare at the screen, even when it goes to a commercial. I only look away when Greyson gets up and stretches.

"I'm going to go take a shower," he announces and then leaves the room.

Seth gets up off the sofa. "I'm going to go have a smoke," he says to me. "You want to come out with me?"

I shake my head and his face contorts with confusion, because I rarely turn down a smoke break. "Okay," he says, his eyebrows raised as he leaves me and goes out onto the balcony.

I wonder why none of them are reacting like I am, but then again neither of them know the stuff I do about Violet. They might not even know her last name, since she was so reluctant to hand it over to me.

Jesus. What do I do? I mean, maybe it's not related to her, but she did just go down to the police station today and she grew up in foster homes, but wouldn't tell me what really happened to her parents. But other than that I don't know much about her, which seems so wrong at the moment, especially if she's carrying that inside her, all that death. Death is so heavy. I know this.

God, she must be hurting. I get up and go to the bedroom door. It's locked, so I knock. It takes several more knocks before she opens the door with a look on her face that rams me in the chest. She's not crying or frowning or upset. She just looks like she's drowning in a lack of emotions. There's a small television perched on the desk in the corner and the same news channel I was just watching is on the screen.

She takes one look at my face and says, "Don't ask me." Then she steps back from the door and flops down on the bed on her back. Desperation filters through her voice. "Please just don't ask me anything about it."

How the hell am I not supposed to ask her? Her parents were murdered? There's so many questions. I want to understand her life, her, and worst of all I just want to hold her and tell her it'll be okay, like I wish someone would have done for me after Amy died. But that's what I wanted and I have no clue if that's what she wants. The only thing I know is that she asked me not to ask her anything and if that's what she wants I'll give it to her.

"I'm going to go get something to eat," I tell her, gripping onto the door frame as I smother the urge to bombard her with questions. "Do you want to come with me?"

She shakes her head as she gazes up at the ceiling; her arms flopped to the side. "No thanks."

"Do you want me to pick you something up?"

"If you want."

"Okay, I'll bring you something back," I say, letting go of the door frame. "Or if you want I can just stick around and hang out."

"I want to be alone," she whispers. "Please just go. I need to be alone right now." She reaches for a purple teddy bear on the bed, hugging it as she rolls over. It takes a lot of strength not to lie down in bed and wrap my arms around her, but I don't because she asked me not to.

Chapter Thirteen

Violet

Today is turning into the shittiest day of all days in the shitty history that makes up my life. It was going fine. I got up for the twelfth morning in a row at my new apartment in my new bed and for the first time I wasn't disoriented. Good start. Then I read a book, which was relaxing, and I didn't think about my parents or their death the entire time. As an added bonus, I hadn't seen Luke all morning. I've been avoiding him ever since he found out about my parents because I don't want him looking at me with pity in his eyes. I don't want him asking questions. I don't want him learning all the details, like how I found my parents. At least the news kept that much quiet.

I've been focusing on moving forward and getting myself back to the place I was before all this happened, before the case was reopened, before Luke came along and it wasn't just me in my life anymore. I need to get my head back to where it was before, become the independent unaffected Violet again.

He hasn't even moved into our room yet, probably because

I scared him off. He did stack some boxes in the closet but I think he keeps his clothes in a duffel bag in the living room. He hasn't said anything about it either and I'm not sure how I feel about it. I keep telling myself that it's a good thing—that space is a good thing—but I find myself questioning my true feelings.

After I spend most of the afternoon reading, I go to work and it isn't that crowded because it's raining and for some reason rain keeps the crowd away. Everything is simple. Until everyone suddenly decides they're going to take their chances out in the rain. Then things get a little chaotic and I'm running around seating everyone and waiting on them the best that I can. The doorbell keeps dinging as more people file in, tracking water and mud in with them. There's this one guy who comes in by himself, which sometimes happens—random people wander in and eat alone. He's wearing a red T-shirt, tan pants, and has a creeper mustache, but, hey, to each their own.

"You want to sit at the bar?" I ask, hopeful, otherwise he's going to take up an entire table.

He shakes his head, closing his umbrella and brushing the water off his arm. "I'll take a booth."

I mentally roll my eyes at him, seat him in a corner booth, then leave him to read over the menu while I go behind the counter to get him some water. Then I hurry and tend to the register, before I head over to his table, hoping he's ready to order and not ready to waste my time.

"You're Violet Hayes, right?" he says as I press the tip

of the pen to the order book and suddenly I recognize his voice. I glance up from the order book as he says, "The Violet Hayes whose parents were murdered in Cheyenne thirteen years ago?"

A suffocating wave rushes through me and I clutch at the pen in my hand. "Are you the asshole who's been calling me?"

He notices my trembling hands. "I am." This stupid grin stretches across his face as he reaches for the water.

Fury thunders through me, along with the stifling heat of panic. My hand takes on a life of its own and I throw my pen at him.

It hits him in the face and he flinches, dropping his water on the table and spilling ice everywhere. "What the hell?" He gapes up at me like I was the crazy one, and then raises his hands in front of him. "Okay, calm down. My name's Stan Walice. I'm a reporter for Chanel 8 *News at 8* and I'd like to ask you a few questions about what you saw that night. I'm doing a piece about it."

"You can go to hell. Calling me up like some kind of psycho. Seriously. You think I'm going to talk to you?" I toss the order book at him and it lands in the water and ice and the pages are instantly soaked. I spin on my heels and weave around the tables, with people sitting around them, some staring at me. In ten seconds I've managed to go from stressed waitress, to about-to-lose-her-shit Violet. I can feel the anger in the center of my chest, a widening hole, being torn open more.

Stan follows me as I storm to the counter. "So you saw

them that night?" he asks. "The ones who broke into your house?"

I don't answer, begging myself to remain calm. That I have to. That there is a restaurant full of people, enjoying their dinners and family time and I'll be in some serious trouble if I make a scene.

"Did you find them?" he asks. "Your parents? I thought I read somewhere that you did? And that you stayed in the house for twenty-four hours before you called the cops. Why did you do that?"

I slam to a halt at the counter in front of the register where Sherry, a middle-aged waitress with a gray bob is tallying up bills. I turn around. "Go fuck yourself, Stan."

At the exact moment I say it, my boss and owner of the restaurant, Benny, walks out. "Violet," Benny hisses, glancing around at the tables and booths. His face reddens as his voice lowers. "Go in the back right *now*."

Things kind of escalate from there. Reporter guy takes off out the front door, bailing on what he started. I trudge into the back kitchen area and Benny enters seconds later. He's also the cook and wears this stained white apron that ties around his round belly. I can't stop staring at the stains as he stands in front of the oven and chews me out. The stains are red, probably ketchup, but they look like blood. Blood. Death. Blood. I start to visualize things, not just about my parents, but about me. My death. How it's going to happen. Horrible. Tragic. I picture myself on the floor, dying with my parents. For a second, I feel okay.

"Violet, I think I'm going to have to fire you," Benny says and all I do is stare at his bald head, shiny in the fluorescent light.

I probably would have just let him fire me but then Greyson walks in. He's wearing his bartending outfit, a white shirt and black pants, and has a glass in his hand. "Hey, Benny, cut her some slack. She's having a bad day."

"I don't give a damn if she's having a bad day," he replies, lifting a lid off a stainless-steel pot. "She dropped the f-bomb in my restaurant. There's kids out there for crying out loud."

"Yeah, but the guy grabbed her ass," Greyson lies, glancing at me quickly. "You have to cut her some slack. That's sexual harassment."

Benny peers up from the pot as he reaches over to grab a large spoon from the stainless-steel shelf. "Is that true, Violet?"

I shrug, knowing I should put more effort into this, but there is too much heaviness in my chest to care. All I seem to care about is the damn red stains on his apron. "I guess so."

"You guess so or no?" he questions, stirring the boiling water.

Greyson presses me with a look like *What are doing? I just gave you an easy out.*

I sigh exhaustedly, forcing myself to put effort into it, because I need my job. "Yeah, he grabbed my ass... Sorry I dropped the f-bomb."

Benny puffs a frustrated breath and points the dripping

spoon at me. "Next time come tell me before you go throwing inappropriate words around. Understand?"

"Okay."

He frowns, his forehead wrinkling, but he lets me go, telling me to take the next few days off, and get my shit together. I summon deep breaths as I nod and then grab my change of clothes from my shelf and head out back to get some fresh air. I'm going to have to lose a week's pay. I'm fuming, not at myself, but at reporter guy. I storm out the door and into the back parking lot where employees park. The sky is still gray with storm clouds, but the rain has reduced to a drizzle, and the buildings around the restaurant light up the block.

I clamp my jaw as I stride toward the middle of the muddy parking lot, my clothes clutched in my hands. Suddenly I ball my hands into fists and scream through gritted teeth: "Fuck him! Fuck!" I thought I'd gotten rid of reporters a long time ago. This one has to be here because the police are reopening the case.

Suddenly, I hear the crunch of gravel as someone approaches me. "Are you okay?" Greyson asks with concern.

I remain motionless. "I'm fine. It's just a week off work. I should be grateful he didn't fire me." I want to say thank you because he helped me, but I'm not even sure how or where to start.

"Not about that." He pauses behind me and I can hear him breathing. "I mean about what that guy said to you."

I stab my nails deeper into my palms. I should hit him. I should have hit the reporter. I need to hit something. I need to get this shaking, razor-sharp, painful feeling out of me. "I'm. Fine."

Greyson moves beside me and my muscles tighten. He's walking into a mess he shouldn't be walking into because I'm seriously thinking about hitting him, just so I can do something to get this slashing feeling inside me to stop.

He hands me a glass filled with a red tinted liquid. "It'll calm you down."

I eyeball the glass warily, feeling the anger simmer. "What is it?"

"Vodka and cranberry."

"I don't drink."

"I didn't put that much vodka in it." He continues to hold the glass out with a sympathetic smile on his face.

I snatch the glass from him and spill some on my shoe. I take a few gulps, feeling the burn of alcohol mix with the uneasy burn inside me. I'm adding fuel to the fire. I know this. And I should just dump it out on the ground and walk away.

Instead, I chug the rest of the drink down and then give the empty glass back to Greyson. "Thanks."

"You're welcome." He takes the glass and rotates it between his hands. "I get off work in like thirty minutes...you could wait around...come hang out in the bar and we could catch a bus back to the apartment together."

"Isn't Seth coming to pick you up?"

"Nah, Luke and he have a party going on at the apartment and I'm sure they're both too wasted to drive."

I turn my head and look at him, wondering just how much he heard. Did he hear that my parents were murdered? That I found them. Is there another person in my life now that knows about my messed-up past? "How much did you hear?"

"Some, but I promise my lips are sealed," he says without missing a beat

Is he for real? I stand there quietly, trying to figure it out, but I can barely understand myself let alone someone else. "Okay, I'll stick around I guess."

His smile expands. "Okay, get changed and come sit at the bar. I'll get you another drink."

I probably should have argued with him, told him that I'm not a nice person when I'm drunk, that my reckless energy magnifies. But instead I nod and follow him back into the restaurant, knowing exactly what I am walking into and not caring.

Chapter Fourteen

Luke

I'm a lucky son of a bitch. I really am, but only because I own my own luck, create it, cheat it. I've been gambling for almost a week and a half straight and I'm up to twelve hundred bucks. I probably should stop, but it's hard once I get riding a winning streak. When I sit down at the table, I control almost everything and I realize how much I've missed it.

Violet hasn't been talking to me much, spending half her time at work and the rest in her room. I try to let her be because it's clear that's what she wants but I'm starting to wonder if what she wants and what she needs are entirely different things. I can understand to a certain extent wanting to be by myself, but she's completely secluded herself from everyone, always alone. I've tried a few times to make conversation with her, just to have her back in my life and hear the sound of her voice, but she only gives me one-word responses.

I'm still sleeping on the couch, but it's getting uncomfortable and I haven't even unpacked my boxes yet, simply because she always has the door locked. I want to barge in there and claim my territory, but then I picture the look on her face when she opened the door after I found out about her parents and I stop myself, shut down my aggravation, reminding myself that it's not about me and what I want.

For the last week, I've been on the phone with my mother every other day. I was ignoring her calls, but after the thirty-something messages cramming my voicemail, I finally started picking up. She's in one of her moods, where she thinks some-one's after her—a neighbor, the mailman, the police. She did this a lot when I first went to college, calling me to tell me I needed to come home to protect her. She'd toned it down over the past few months, but I think when I told her I wasn't going home for the summer, she decided to start up again. I've been doing my best not to ram my fist into something, reminding myself that I have a place of my own and I can do whatever I want. But every time I hear her voice it reminds me of the past, then the nightmares start up, and more anger floods me.

Friday night, Seth and I decide to throw a party to cel-ebrate our new home and I'm glad because I really need a break from the stress of my life. Violet and Greyson are still at work, we got a living room full of people, music playing, an endless amount of drinks and week-or-so-old pot brownies Greyson made that Seth and he occasionally munch on. I asked him where he got the weed and he said from a friend, but I think Violet gave it to him, which makes me worry she might be going back to that douche. But I'm not going to ask her about it. If she's that stupid, then she's that stupid. Not. My. Problem. At least that's what I keep trying to tell myself, but as always I can't help think of my past and what drugs and dealing did to my mother—what it turned her into.

I put beer, chips, and some weird fruit platter Seth picked up out in the living room, but keep the hard stuff in the fridge for my own personal use. Then I get a game of Texas Hold 'Em going at the table, milking my lucky streak for all it's worth. I've got a little too many shots of vodka in my system and the kings are starting to look like queens, but I won't stop playing or drinking, because I'm too fucking relaxed.

There are five other guys at the table, including Seth, who's not very good at cards, but has fun playing. One of the guys, Jonah something or other, has a blond with really bright red lips sitting on his lap, wearing this tight leather skirt and white top with no bra. She keeps giving me these looks and I'm debating whether I want to hit on her. Jonah said they weren't dating, just friends, but it'll still be kind of weird if Violet walks in and I'm still not sure if I could fully go through with it and get what I'm seeking—a much-needed fuck, one where I'm in control over the situation. Then again, I shouldn't even be thinking about Violet. We're not together. We kissed once. So fucking what. It's time to move on. Get over a girl that has no interest in me . . . a girl that's been controlling every one of my thoughts for weeks, at least this is what I tell myself.

As I win the next hand, my intoxication blurs my thought process, and I start working my magic, flirting with the girl across from me, who tells me her name is Kenzie. After a few smiles and compliments, I get her to leave Jonah's lap and come over to mine.

"You have gorgeous eyes," she whispers in my ear, thankfully not giggling as she runs her fingers through my hair.

"You better not hurt her," Jonah says with a laugh as he takes a sip of his beer and studies his cards.

Hurt her, no. Fuck her, yes. I wind my arm around her back and she wiggles her ass a little, settling into my lap, and it feels nice, but not as good as it usually does.

"Ante up, asshole," Jonah says to me, tossing a handful of blue chips to the center of the table.

Shooting him a warning look, I reach for my chips, but pause when his eyes dart to the door. "Well, well, if it isn't my favorite fucking person in the world. What are you doing here, beautiful?"

"And if it isn't the biggest dipshit in the world. I live here, you moron." The sound of Violet's voice over the music makes me tense. I thought she wasn't going to be home from work for at least another hour.

I wait for what seems like five hours, when really it's probably only more like five seconds, then Violet comes walking past the table and turns into the kitchen area next to it. She's wearing a long skirt that sits low on her hips and this black and white top that only covers to the bottom of her ribs. I can see her flat stomach, smooth skin, and a tattoo curling up and over her rib cage and all the way down below her hip in black ink. Curvy patterns form flowers and take up half her side. It's the sexiest God damn thing I've ever seen... I want to rip her clothes off so I can see where the lines stop and begin.

She ambles for the fridge, hardly paying attention to the party going on and then Greyson appears at the table, looking red-eyed and smelling of cigarette smoke.

He flops down in a chair beside Seth, grabs a handful of potato chips and says, "What'd I miss?"

Seth squints his eyes as he leans in toward Greyson. "Are you..." He sniffs the air in front of Greyson's mouth. "Are you drunk?"

Greyson shrugs, shoving the chips into his mouth. "Does it really matter?"

Seth leans back in his seat with his arm draped on the back. "You hardly ever drink."

Greyson ignores him and starts munching on chips while my focus drifts back to Violet in the kitchen. She's hunting in the fridge for something, her head ducked down. She flips some of her hair off her shoulder, and quickly glances in my direction, her eyes flickering from the girl on my lap to me. I expected the detached look she's always so good at giving and I think she's aiming for it, but for the slightest second there's hurt in her eyes.

"So Jonah the Dipshit," she says, yanking her gaze off me. "What have you been up to for the last few months?"

Jonah the Dipshit tips back in his chair, checking out her ass. "Not a whole hell of a lot. You still up to your usual?"

Unable to help myself, I pick a chip up and throw it at him. My drunken aim is off and it hits the wall, dinging it, and Jonah doesn't even notice. Seth does, though, and so does Kenzie, both giving me a puzzled look.

Violet leans back from the fridge and closes the door with her hip, clutching a half-full bottle of tequila in her hand. I immediately sense something's wrong. She says she doesn't drink and I've never seen her drink before. I wonder if something happened, at work, or maybe with her parents' case, but how am I supposed to find out what's wrong when she won't fucking talk to me.

"Not lately." She unscrews the cap, her eyes steady on Jonah who looks like he thinks he's about to get lucky. She sucks in a deep breath, then puts the mouth of the bottle up to her lips, and angles her head back, guzzling a swallow down. Her back arches and her chest angles out as she drinks. I'm pretty sure every dude at the table, besides Seth and Greyson, watches her with their jaw hanging open.

"Vixen," Seth mutters from the chair beside me with a smirk on his face as he examines his cards.

Violet detaches the bottle from her mouth and her eyes water up as she gags. She quickly twists the cap back on and then licks the remaining tequila off her lips. "God, that burnt the shit out of my throat."

"Ta-kill-ya will do that to you," Jonah jokes like he's the world's freaking funniest comedian.

Violet tolerantly smiles at him. "Yeah, I guess so."

Jonah grins as he sets his cards down on the table. "So I know you said you weren't up to the usual, but could you please, pretty please make an exception for your favorite guy in the whole world. I need it badly, baby."

Violet holds the bottle in her hand, her green eyes darting to mine before she says to Jonah, "Follow me."

Jonah looks like he just struck gold and pushes the chair back from the table. "Sorry, guys, but I think I'm going to sit the next hand out." He scoops up his beer and circles around the table, trailing behind Violet as she breezes past me with Jonah following her like a puppy dog. They disappear into her room—*our* room. I stare at the door, my chest burning as I fight the desire to go after her. She's not mine. I don't want her to be mine. *Just let her be. It's not like she's having sex.*

"What a slut," Seth says under his breath as he reaches for a red plastic cup full of vodka and orange juice.

"She's not a slut," I snap a little harsher than I mean to, throwing my cards onto the table. "You don't know anything about her."

Seth moves the rim of the cup to his mouth. "Neither do you," he reminds me. "So how do you know she's not?"

"Because I do." But I don't. Violet lies a lot and it's hard to tell if what leaves her mouth is real—if anything. Maybe she's not a virgin. Maybe she sleeps around as much as I do. Maybe she deals drugs, sleeps around, and then does crazy shit like jump out the window.

"God damn it," I curse because this shouldn't be bothering

me. No girl ever has. Yet Violet is. I shove Kenzie off my lap and she lands on her feet but stumbles forward in her heels. She barely catches herself on the countertop.

"Rude much?" she huffs, standing up.

I rise to my feet as rage blasts through me. I have no idea what to do, but if I don't do something soon, I'm going to burst.

Violet

Drunk, evil Violet is coming out and she's bored. This is not a good combination. It more than likely means I'm going to go looking for trouble. And trouble for me usually means doing stuff like jumping out of two-story windows. As much as I love tasting death, the last time I got drunk when I was feeling like this, I ended up actually getting hit by a car. I broke my leg, too, and Preston was not happy about it. I tried to do my best to explain to him why I did it and he told me I was going to be one of those people who wouldn't be able to drink, not without severe consequences. I hate that I'm thinking about Preston and that I kind of, sort of, maybe miss him a little and the life I'd built for myself with him, because before the whole drama/groping thing it was somewhat comfortable. And I've never had comfortable before.

"Hey, do you mind if I light up right here?" Jonah the Dipshit asks as he settles on my bed, crossing his legs. He's one of my regulars who's slightly annoying and gets on my nerves, but I'm bored and need a distraction. And I'm fairly certain Luke thinks I came back here to do something with him, by the jealous look on his face. I don't like how pleased I am at the idea that he might be jealous. But he has no right to be, considering he had that skank on his lap who has so many curves her skirt and shirt couldn't even conceal them.

"Do whatever you want." I shrug, sifting through the songs on my laptop. The song titles are hard to read though and the longer I squint at them, the more bored and restless I get. Finally, I randomly click on one and "Make Damn Sure" by Taking Back Sunday starts playing. Then I decide to search out Stan Walice, see if I can get any information on him. Go kick his ass. It'd make me feel better. I run a search on him and add Channel 8, then squint at the screen. It's hard to tell which one is him...they all look blurry.

"God, this shit smells good." Jonah grins as he slips his pipe out of his pocket. He's fairly good-looking for a pothead, and not rich like most of my regular clients. He has a beanie on his head, a fraying leather band on his wrist, and a few holes in his jeans. I have the lamp on and I can see his pupils are dilated. He takes the remainder of the weed out of my prescription bottle and packs it into his pipe. I was sort of surprised when Greyson gave it back to me, only taking a little for his pot brownies. Most people would have taken it all.

Jonah says something to me as he frees the smoke from his chest, but I only crank the music up and continue my search for information on Stan Walice. But after a while I give up because the blurriness and brightness of the screen is stinging my eyes. I move the computer aside, then dig for some gum in the nightstand drawer, but all I have is a bag of suckers. I take one out and pop it into my mouth to get rid of the nasty taste of alcohol embedded in my taste buds. Then I lie down on the bed and gaze up at the ceiling. I can't stop thinking about that reporter and his questions. What if he shows up again? What if I can't handle it? Am I handling it right now? There's a calm-before-the-storm feeling inside my chest, waves ripping, white tipped, ready to rise higher as they soar for the shore. The question is where is the shore? Me? Someone else? I need to do something. I'm too unsettled.

I crank the music down and sit up as Jonah takes another hit from his pipe and smoke fills the room. I pull my knees up and watch him toke over and over again as I suck on the sucker. He says nothing, but keeps eyeing the sucker in my mouth, or my mouth—I can't tell for certain. I bounce back and forth on whether I want to kick him out so I can get my adrenaline rush solo or do I want him around? Could I use him for anything? When I kissed Luke it'd felt good and distracting. I wonder if Jonah could give me the same effect. I could try it, because I kind of need it tonight. Need to forget about my life. About my job. About Stan, the stupid reporter.

"What? Why are you looking at me like you want to fuck me?" Jonah asks with a grin, a cloud of smoke snaking from his lips.

"I'm not." I kneel up on the bed and sweep my hair to the

side as I inch closer, pulling the sucker out of my mouth. My shirt's ridden up and Jonah takes in my bare skin with a lazy grin on his face. I could kiss him and find out if Jonah is as good of a distraction as Luke. I've never been one for kissing, but maybe something's changed, maybe I could—

Someone hammers on the door. "Violet, open the fucking door." It's Luke's voice and it's full of anger.

Jonah's eyes bulge as he coughs on a breath full of weed. "Oh shit, is Luke your boyfriend?"

I roll my eyes as Luke bangs on the door again. "In the year that I've been dealing to you have you ever seen me with a boyfriend?"

He shrugs, flicking the lighter. "No, but I don't know anything about you—no one does."

I open my mouth to agree with him, when Luke starts banging on the door over and over again. Shaking my head, I get up from the bed, tripping over the bottom of my skirt when I step on it, and brace myself on the door. Luke bangs on the door again and I jerk it open. He's still in the middle of banging on the door and his fist flies toward me. I don't move and he barely stops in time, right before he hits me in the face. He lowers his fist to his side, looking startled, but then the look vanishes and he pushes past me and into the room.

"Get the fuck out," he says to Jonah in this calm, unsettling tone as he nods his head at the door.

Jonah moves the pipe away from his mouth. "What the

hell's your problem? I'm just sitting here smoking a bowl. I didn't touch her."

Luke walks up to the bed and grabs the pipe from Jonah's hands. "You're my problem. Now get the fuck out."

Jonah gets up from the bed. He's shorter than Luke, but thicker in the body. Still he does what he's asked and heads for the door, pausing before he steps out. "Can I at least have my pipe back?"

Luke shoves him out the door, and then he tosses the pipe at him. Jonah misses it and it hits the floor, spilling singed bud all over the carpet. Jonah curses as Luke slams the door and locks it. I'm tingling from head to toe as I wait for him to turn around, but he doesn't, he just leans his head against the door.

He has on a black shirt and jeans that are just tight enough to make his ass look really nice. Maybe his ass just looks really nice though. I've never really paid attention to it until now. I put the sucker into my mouth, tilting my head to the side to get a better look. When he turns toward me, I don't even bother trying to hide the fact that I was just checking him out. I'm drunk and careless and every blasé personality trait of mine is amplified.

He rubs his hand over his cropped brown hair, his arm muscles rippling. "You're driving me fucking crazy."

"You say that a lot." I roll the sucker in my mouth and his eyes dart to it.

He stares at me, his eyes large and radiating desire. "Are

you doing that on purpose?" he asks with a feral look as he nods his head at the sucker in my mouth.

The sucker clicks on my teeth. "No, I had the taste of tequila on my breath and this is the only thing I had in the room that'd cover it up."

He slumps back against the door, looking worn out. "I bet Jonah was loving it."

My lips turn upward around the sucker. "I'm sure he was."

He shakes his head and squeezes his eyes shut. "I swear to God you're trying to get under my skin."

I pull the sucker out of my mouth and chuck it into the trash. "I'm not trying to do anything to you. You're the one who came barging in here."

His eyes open, cold, sharp, and the look in them throws me back. And excites me. As the excitement mixes with the alcohol, I completely forget about everything. Where I am. Who I am. What I want.

He steps forward beside the head of the bed and I'm standing by the foot. "I was banging on the door because I was afraid of what you were doing in here."

"What? Dealing drugs? That's what I do, Luke. I already told you this."

"Well, you shouldn't be ... and that's not what I was thinking ..." His legs stretch as he strides toward me. "I thought you were having sex."

I want to back away from him, because heat and passion are pouring off of him as much as the scent of tequila and vodka is pouring off the both of us. "It's not really any of your business if I was."

"Yeah it is. Everything you do is my business."

I snort a laugh. "How do you figure?"

He crosses his arms as he stops just short of me. "Because you brought me into your life, moved in with me..." He trails off, his focus drifting to my mouth. "Kissed me."

I laugh and it's my drunken laugh, high pitched and goofy sounding. "*I* kissed you. Get your story straight. You're the one who smashed your lips into mine."

"I didn't smash my lips into yours," he says hotly, blinking his eyes into focus as he leans in. "We kissed each other together and you liked it. Admit it."

I shake my head in denial. "I won't."

"Say it."

"No way."

"Oh my God," he growls, shaking with irritation as he clenches his hands. "I can't win with you. I try and try and try to get something from you—anything—and you won't give it to me."

"I'm so sorry that I don't let you win with me like all the other girls you sleep with," my inebriated mouth says. "There's the door." I point my finger at it. "You can leave whenever you want."

He shakes his head and lets out a piercing laugh. "This was supposed to be our room, but you took it over."

"I didn't take it over, you just won't come in here."

He pauses and when he speaks again, he's calmer. "Is that what you're really waiting for? For me to just come in here? Because it seemed like you wanted your space."

"Yes, it's what I was waiting for," I stammer. Actually stammer. I never stammer. Through our little code talk I've somehow managed to lose my confident voice *and* admit to him that I've been waiting around for him to come to me.

He pauses, looking startled, horrified, then sedated, his eyes darkening as his eyelashes lower. "Say it again."

"Say what?"

He slides his foot across the floor, stepping closer, and his knee bumps against mine. "That you were waiting for me to come in here."

I shake my head, pushing my knee up against his. "I wasn't."

His gaze flicks to our knees touching. "You just said you were."

"Well, I'm a liar."

"I know, but you weren't lying."

I don't say anything at all. I think about walking by him, leaving the house, heading down the road, hitchhiking to the tallest building in the city. Get to the roof and soar. Instead I stay put, because the haziness in my head is making it okay to stay here with him. I wait eagerly for him to do whatever it is he's going to do. Yell at me. Leave me. Kiss me.

His arm comes out to the side and curls around toward my hip. I start to open my mouth as his fingers brush my skin and enfold around my waist, but suddenly I lose it and lean in, kissing him. The second our lips touch, I feel safe from all the bad in my life. I blame it on the tequila. But I'm pretty sure it's not the tequila that makes me do what I do next, only the passion I feel in the moment. As I part my lips hoping he'll slip his tongue into my mouth, I eliminate the space between our bodies, crushing myself up against him, then I raise my leg to hitch it over his hip. There's a pause of reluctance on Luke's part and then he lets out a husky groan and everything abruptly starts moving in fast motion. His hot palm slides down my hip to my thigh, fingers stabbing through the fabric of my skirt as he grips my leg and scoops me up. I hook my legs around his, locking my ankles as his tongue slides deep into my mouth. He presses up against me, moaning again as he steers us around toward the bed. Seconds later we fall. Together. We land on the mattress and it becomes concave, conforming to the weight of our bodies. We get tangled in the sheets and blanket, our legs entwined, hands all over each other, bodies writhing in harmony. I keep making these little whimpering noises, but it can't be right. I don't whimper.

Luke pulls his mouth away as I whimper for the fifth or eleventh time. He scans my face as I pant loudly, my hands cupping his shoulder blades, the warmth of his skin flowing through the fabric of his shirt.

"Why'd you stop?" I ask, breathless.

"I have no idea," he mumbles then seals his lips to mine, gathering my arms in his hands and pinning them above me.

I gasp, the desire flooding through me more powerful than my need for an adrenaline rush. I've got plenty of it in me now. Pounding at the sensitive parts of my body, throbbing in my thighs. He devours me with his mouth as he traps my wrists together and presses me down against the bed. I kiss him back with more emotion behind it than I've ever let myself feel before as I writhe against him. His free hand wanders down my body, then up my skirt, heading for the top of my thigh. It's not the furthest I've gone before, but the furthest I've gone with someone I have feelings for and the emotion behind it is becoming too much.

I start to say stop, but then his finger slips inside the edge of my panties and the words are stolen out of my lips by the startling, yet amazing tingles coursing through every part of my body. I feel like I'm going to burst and the sensation only increases when he slips a finger inside me and then another. I cry out in bliss as he starts moving them, my hips bucking against his hand, my body seeking more. He kisses me passionately before his mouth delves downward, his hand leaving my arms, freeing me from his hold.

I keep my arms above my head though, my eyes shut as I gasp for air. His other hand shoves my top up. He yanks my bra down and my nipples spring free, seconds later his mouth covers my breast. I'm gone. Drowning in a sea of desire and alcohol, falling helplessly as I lose control and my body ignites. I cry out again as I dig my nails into my palms, seeking a release from the adrenaline rush I've been craving all night. I feel myself come apart, falling into helplessness, losing control over everything as everything inside me breaks apart and my mind drifts away. When I return back to reality, I'm exhausted, drained, but content. Luke's no longer sucking on my nipple, but lying beside me with his elbow propped against the mattress and his head resting against his hand. He doesn't say anything, just stares down at me, his eyes glossy, his face crammed with uncertainty, like he's unsure—or maybe even regrets—what just happened.

"I'm sorry I had my phone off when you called me," he says quietly. "I always turn my phone off when I'm playing poker."

I want to tell him why I was upset, but even drunk, the idea of opening Pandora's box stuffed with my past doesn't seem like a good idea.

"I'm sorry I took over the room." I offer him a tired smile.

A small smile graces his lips. "It's fine. I was sort of intentionally sleeping out on the couch anyway, because it felt like you needed your space."

"I thought I did...because that's what I usually do..." I trail off, blinking through my tiredness. "But I'm not so sure anymore."

He's quiet for a moment. "If you need me...then I'm here."

I take a breath as he reaches over and then brushes his fingers along my ribs. He pulls my shirt back down, covering me up. It feels like the nicest thing anyone's done for me and I feel like hugging him, but my arms are too tired.

I yawn, the drowsiness of the alcohol taking over me. "I think I'm going to go to bed," I mumble as I flip over and practically crawl up to my pillow and collapse onto my stomach. He sits up on the edge of the bed and stares at the door. "You can go out there if you want." I yawn again. "But I wish you'd stay here...with me..." I can barely register what I'm saying, but all I know is that when I'm in his arms, it seems like all the bad is gone.

Luke

I have never done that before. Never gave a girl everything and took nothing in return. I'd always been selfish and that was kind of the point. I wanted to be selfish instead of being walked all over.

After Violet falls asleep, telling me she wishes I'd stay with her, I sit on the bed with my head in my hands as I decide what to do. I'm seriously considering lying down with her, holding her, falling asleep because I'm exhausted. Mentally. But I can't sort through my thoughts filled with the way she moaned and how all I wanted to do was make her moan again. Then she came and the look in her eyes was so content, so sexy, so amazing. There was so much inside emotion in her at the moment—pleasure, desire, want, need—and it was fascinating to watch because she never shows anything. It gave me the biggest hard on I've ever had. The next step would have been to fuck her, take back the control, get what I want out of it, yet I couldn't.

She's drunk. I'm drunk. It's not right and I don't want to do that to her—that's not how I want things to be between us.

Shaking my head, I get up and go to the door, leaving the room and her sleeping on the bed because I'm not sure I can contain myself. I feel bad for leaving, but at the same time I'm too restless to stay.

The card game is still going on, but a lot of the people have cleared out of the apartment. "Have fun?" Seth asks with speculation in his eyes as he looks up at me from his cards. Greyson has his arm around him, examining his cards. When he peers up at me, there's a concerned look in his eyes that makes me wonder if he knows something about Violet, like maybe what happened to her parents.

"As much as I ever do." I round the table, noting Jonah and Kenzie have bailed, and head for the fridge. I grab a bottle of tequila and swig it down, over and over again, letting the burn sink in, hoping to regain the person I used to be—the one I built so I could avoid being owned and controlled by someone, like my mom used to do all the time to me. But I can't find him anymore. I'm turning into someone else who I don't think I like unless I'm kissing Violet, and then it seems okay to be this way, letting go, giving her what she wants, not being the one in control, the kind of guy who does stuff for other people, who lets people into his fucked-up life.

I want Violet more than I've ever wanted anyone. I want everything I've been avoiding since I turned sixteen and I no longer care that I'm not thinking just about myself. I want

Violet so bad it burns under my skin fiercer than the alcohol burns at my throat.

At the end of the seemingly endless swallow, I still feel the overpowering urge to go back to the room—to her—so I do. I climb into the bed and nuzzle up against her, holding on to her, lying beside her, like she asked me to do. But I'm not even sure who I do it for.

I sleep with a girl for the very first time and the surprising thing is I enjoy it for a moment until I shut my eyes. Then, as usual, the past catches up with me.

ᔑ

It's dark outside, really late, but I can hear the boom of fire-works going off as they sprinkle the sky. My room is dark, but I can't sleep because I can hear my mom banging around in the kitchen. I'm about to get up and see what she's doing, because she's been acting really weird lately, taking all these pills and snorting things up her nose. But then I hear my door creak open and someone walks inside.

"Lukey, I need you." She strokes my head as I lay in bed, pretending to be asleep. "Wake up."

I open my eyes to the moonlight glowing through my room, the sounds of fireworks exploding in the distance, and my mother sitting on the edge of my bed.

"What do you want?" I ask, rubbing my tired eyes.

She stands up and wanders over to the window, staring outside at the backyard. "I think we're being watched."

I sit up. "What?"

She turns around and holds her hand out to me. "Come with me, sweetie."

I shake my head and let out a frustrated breath, but finally, I get to my feet. She sometimes acts weird like this and it's annoying, but tonight she seems more intense, her breathing really loud, her hand gripping mine too tightly as she hauls me out of the room. She drags me into the living room and we sink down onto the couch wrapped in plastic. I wait in fear for what she's going to do next, noticing the blood on her shirt and hands for the first time. Finally, she wraps her arms around me and starts to cry.

"I did something wrong," she sobs, rocking back and forth.

"Please, just let me go, Mom," I practically beg, because her grip is hurting me.

"Lukey, I can't let you go. I need you." She hugs me tighter and there's blood on her clothes. It's warm and feels wrong as it seeps into my clothes.

"Mom," I say, my voice trembling as I feel so weak inside because I don't want her holding me right now but I'm not strong enough to get away. Everything feels wrong. Her. Me. The blood on her clothes. "Why do you have blood on your clothes?"

She sobs hysterically, pressing her cheek against the top of my head. She starts singing under her breath, one of the songs she wrote for my dad when he was leaving her.

"Lean into me. Lean into me. Take. Help me. I need to understand. Help me. I can't do this without you." She sings it over and over again, all night, refusing to let me go, and I feel smaller and smaller with each word until I'm so small I barely exist.

Chapter Fifteen

Violet

I wake up the next morning, not gasping for the first time, but my head is throbbing and my dry throat burns with the need to hack. I start to get up to go to the bathroom, when I realize I'm weighed down by an arm. I roll over and find Luke sleeping beside me in the bed with his arm draped over me. Well, this is...interesting.

I sift through my memories, wincing at the protesting pain, and slowly it comes back to me in sharp images. I wince at one in particular, Luke's fingers sliding inside me, but then as I remember how it felt, my stomach somersaults, and I remember how content I felt. I could try to blame it on the alcohol—it wouldn't be the first time—but with the positive way my body responds to the memories, I'd only be bullshitting myself.

Lying beside him isn't so bad, either, which is confusing to accept. All these years, never letting anyone get that close to me, never feeling anything for anyone on a deep level. I don't know what to do with myself. Give in to the feeling or bail out.

Carefully, I lift his arm off me and duck out from under it. Then I climb over him and leave him sleeping in the room. I need to clear my head. Breathe. Think about what all this means and decide what I'm going to do when he wakes up.

I quietly pad across the kitchen, make myself a coffee, then cross the living room littered with garbage, chips, cards. I head for the sliding glass door that leads to the balcony, slide it open, and step out into the morning sunlight, a gentle breeze kissing my skin. I climb up onto the thick wooden railing with the cup of coffee in my hand and sit down, relaxing against the beams with my feet hanging over the edge. I stare down at the ground, not thinking about jumping for once, but thinking about the past.

I remember the first time I had to switch foster families. I was seven and didn't understand why at first. Yeah, I knew I was acting a little crazy and I cried a lot, but people weren't just supposed to give up kids, right? It's not like I wanted a lot, just someone to help me feel safe from the darkness that was living inside me, the memories that haunted me, the loneliness.

The look on their faces as I packed my suitcase and headed out with my social worker was one I never would forget. They weren't sad to see me going, they were relieved. They didn't want me, not like my parents did. The painful, brutal, harsh reality of life struck me in the chest that day and nearly crippled me. From then on I refused to get attached to anyone, knowing eventually they'd hand me back. It was easier not to feel anything than to feel all the bad. And I've been doing it ever since, refusing to feel anything except the one thing I can control. My adrenaline rushes. So easy to start. To endure. Much better to feel than the harder stuff, like heartache.

I shut my eyes and let the sunlight spill over me as I sip the coffee, warm my skin, knowing that what happened with Luke last night wasn't just an adrenaline rush. I felt stuff with him. Even drunk. I've been feeling stuff for him since the day he helped me get to class. He's helped me out so much and never asked for anything in return. He makes me feel safe and sometimes when he looks at me, touches me, kisses me, it feels like he wants me. All of me. The cranky, erratic, Violet that falls out windows and kicks him in the head. Who relies on him a little too much, yet he never seems that bothered. He goes against my theory about people and I just cross my fingers that I'm not wrong.

I hear the sliding door glide open and I don't open my eyes, holding my breath as I set the cup down on the railing.

"Violet, what are you doing out here?" Luke asks.

I keep my eyes sealed shut, wondering if he can remember last night or if he was too drunk. "Just thinking?"

"About what? Is it…Are you thinking about last night?" He seems nervous and I hear the door glide shut, so it's just him, me, and the open ground below.

"You really want to know?" I ask softly.

"Yeah…I do," he says, sounding strained and I open my eyes and twist around to look at him.

He looks exhausted, dark circles under his eyes, his skin pallid, almost green, and his clothes are wrinkled. He was sleeping with his head turned and his hair is flattened on one side, not the most attractive look, yet I can't seem to look away from him.

"I'm thinking about my life." I have to catch my breath because I just told the truth and the raw realness of it nearly smothers me.

He scans me over and then joins me on the railing, sitting next to me with his feet on the deck. "Yeah, I've been thinking a lot about mine, too."

"Why's that?"

"Because...you go against everything I've built...for myself."

"Yeah, you, too...for me..."

We stare at each other for what seems like an eternity, the sun beaming down on us as we refuse to look away, but not because we're challenging each other. Because we're trying to figure something out.

"Look, about last night." Luke speaks first, leaning against the beam and drawing his bare foot up onto the railing. "I think I should explain myself...I had no right to bang on that door like a fucking controlling, obsessed lunatic...I'm not usually like that."

"Actually you kind of are," I say, bringing the coffee cup up to my lips. "I've thought you were intense even before we officially met, Mr. Stoically Aloof."

"Is that why you gave me that stupid nickname?" he asks, massaging the back of his neck.

My shoulders lift and fall as I shrug. "Maybe." I set the coffee cup down.

He shakes his head, a small smile touching his lips. "You always find a way to get out of answering questions. It's like you have a gift."

"A gift for avoiding things I don't want to deal with," I say, combing my fingers through my tangled hair, which stinks of booze and pot.

His hand drops to his lap. "What don't you want to deal with?"

"Everything…sometimes life is just too hard and seems pointless to deal with."

Alarm fills his eyes as he misunderstands me. "Violet, I—"

I quickly lean over and cover his mouth with my hand. "Don't think I'm suicidal. I already told you I didn't jump out the window because of that…I'm just trying to tell you what's bothering me in the only way I'm comfortable with. I'm not a fan of getting to know people or letting them into my life. Besides Luke, you're pretty much the only person who I…" I have no idea how to finish that sentence because I'm still trying to figure out what Luke is to me. "You saw on the news…the thing about my parents. Well, after that…after they died, I pretty much didn't have anyone. It was just me and an endless amount of foster families who were pretty much giving me a roof over my head but not much more than that. So I learned to take care of myself and it's been that way for a long time. Just me and my life."

"So you only take care of yourself," he mumbles against my mouth, sounding surprisingly understanding.

I move my hand away from his mouth and slump back. "I had to. It gets hard to deal with, you know, especially when no one sticks around." I'm not sure if I'm making any sense or what point I'm trying to get across. Maybe I'm trying to scare him away or just explain why I can't keep getting involved with him.

"I actually get that," he tells me. "My father bailed out on our family when I was young and now he wants to come back into my life and it's hard."

"I've had a lot of fathers," I say, making air quotes. "And none of them wanted to come back into my life. You're lucky yours does."

"Yeah, maybe." He stares at the parking lot out in front of us. "Violet, if you ever need to talk about stuff…I'm here." I can tell it takes him a lot to say it, which makes it more meaningful.

"I'm not much for talking," I say. "But thanks."

"Still," he turns his head toward me, "know the offer's there."

I nod, unsure how to react to what he's saying—that I have someone. He wants to be my someone. "Okay."

He extends his hand toward me and tucks a strand of my hair behind my ear. "We kind of got off the subject of you and me, though, and I'd really like some answers about us, before I lose it... I came very close to losing it last night."

"I know," I say, curious what Luke looks like when he completely loses it. "I have issues with staying focused on tough subjects, though, and it seems you and I are a tough subject."

He starts to smile but then frowns, looking flustered. "Violet, I don't know what to do with us... with any of what happened... what's happening."

I frown in puzzlement. "Why do you have to do something with us at all? Why not just let things be?"

He blinks away from the parking lot and looks at me, eyes intense even for him. "Because of last night. I don't just do that. Mess around and then cuddle for the whole damn night."

"Yeah right," I attempt to make a joke to avoid the heaviness between us. "I think we already established that you were a cuddler."

He rolls his eyes, but grins. "Only you."

I shield my eyes from the sun with my hand. "What does that mean?"

"It means only you have ever been able to get to me like this. Frustrate me and yet still make me want to be around you at the same time." He scoots off the railing and stretches his arms above his head, his shirt riding up and giving me another glimpse of his abs. Then he lowers his arms and reaches his hand out toward me. "I think it's time we did something that we've been needing to do since the first day we met."

"You mean when I kicked you in the face?" I feel my

stomach spin as I remember the first night I officially met him and how much things have changed since then, in both good and bad ways. "What did you have in mind?"

He restrains a laugh as I thread my fingers through his and he pulls me to my feet. "I'm going to take you out on a date."

I choke on a laugh, but realize he's being serious. "Oh my God, you're not joking."

"Of course I'm not joking." He slides the glass door open. "I don't joke."

We enter the living room, which has a pungent smell to it due to the garbage all over the place, and then he shuts the door. The air is musty, probably from everyone smoking, and there's something that looks like wine spilled on the carpet.

"A date?" I ask as he steers me across the living room, kicking some cards and bottles out of the way. "Really? It seems a little formal don't you think? Considering we've kissed, slept together, moved in together, and then all that other stuff you did to me last night."

He presses his hand to his heart, still holding my hand so I touch his chest, too. He keeps it there as he opens the door to our bedroom. "Hey, don't pretend you didn't like it. In fact, I'm pretty sure you were the one who suggested it."

"I did not," I tell him. "But I did like it, which makes dating seem even harder. I mean, what are we supposed to do? Sit and eat dinner while we chat about our lives when everything between us is so intense?"

He wavers with uncertainty as he shuts the bedroom door behind us. "Well, we don't know that much about each other."

"Yeah, we don't," I agree. "But I generally like to keep things that way with people."

He nods in agreement. "I know, so we can either keep going down the road we're on and argue until we both lose it again, get drunk, and fool around. Or we can get to know each other and see where things go. It depends on what you want."

"You're letting me decide?" I ask, shocked.

He catches his breath for a split second. "Yeah...I think I am..."

I swallow hard as I feel the pressure of making a decision. "What if I said no? Would you be upset?"

He sits down on the bed, tugging me down with him. "I'll only answer that if you tell me the truth about how you'd feel if I said no. The door swings both ways," he says and a lump forms in my throat as I nod. Now he's the one swallowing hard. "The truth is...yeah, I would be upset. Even though you're a pain in the ass, I like spending time with you and I want to keep doing it."

"You're kind of a pain in the ass, too." I nudge him with my shoulder, the smashing weight on my chest easing up. "But I like that you've been around for the last few weeks."

He lets out a laugh and then shakes his head. "Wow, that was fucking hard."

I laugh, too, and it's the strangest, most unfamiliar sound.

He joins in and we just laugh for a moment. And it's strange and weird and...well, normal.

Then we fall down on the bed, lying side by side, our clasped hands squished between our bodies.

"So what do people generally do when they go out on dates?" I ask as he traces circles on my wrist with his fingers.

His brow arches as his fingers stop moving. "You've never been on one?"

I shake my head, pivoting on my hip to face him. "Nope. Never. I already told you I've never really had anyone in my life and going on dates would be letting people in."

His mouth turns upward into a pleased smile that looks strange on his face, yet stunning. "That's good to know. It means your expectations will be lower."

I roll my eyes and playfully pinch his arm. "Hardy, har, har, you're freaking—"

The brush of his lips silences me, my skin flooding with warmth the longer we remain together. He doesn't try to shove his tongue down my throat, he just lays there, fully content in the simplicity of the moment and I shut my eyes, falling into an easy peace.

Finally, he pulls away. "See simple isn't so bad, right?" he says, caressing my cheekbone with his finger.

I nod, agreeing, because at the moment, it's not about the adrenaline. Or how dangerous I thought Luke was or still think he may be. It's not about how intense he is. Or the escape he gives me. I'm with him because I want to be. I want to be here. And I promise to hold on to that thought all night.

Luke

I'm not even sure why I said it. I don't date, yet at the same time I don't keep chasing down the same girl, banging on doors because I think she's fucking some other dude. Violet's different. I'm different with her. And either I can keep feeling like I'm losing control or I can try to get back my structure and do things the normal, simple way by getting drunk, screwing, and bailing.

We make plans to go out and then I take a shower, change into a clean shirt and jeans and clip on my leather band with "redemption" written on it. Then I spend the rest of the day cleaning the house, while she stays in the room, organizing her stuff. I try to keep it light on the drinks for three reasons: (1) I have to be sober enough to drive; (2) I want to be aware of everything that happens, feel it, live it, because if I'm going to do this, be with her, I'm going to make it worth it; and (3) I don't want to have to make her check my blood glucose and help me with pills because I can't go without my Jack Daniel's for the night.

Although, I'm not going to just quit cold turkey. I stick to beers, and am only on my second one when Seth comes out around three or four o'clock, looking hungover, but at the same time amused.

"Have fun last night?" he asks with speculation in his voice as he gets a jug of orange juice out of the fridge.

"As much as I ever do," I say, moving a box of books no one's bothered to unpack from the floor to the coffee table.

"Yeah, but usually you go after girls who are easy." He twists the cap off the orange juice. "You were going after the vixen last night."

I tear the tape off the top of the box. "I really wish you'd stop calling her that."

He takes a gulp and wipes his mouth with the back of his hand. "And you're defending her." He puts the lid back on and opens the fridge door. "If I didn't know better, I'd guess you have feelings for the vixen."

"Her name is Violet," I say defensively as I open the box. "I don't know exactly how I feel about Violet yet, but it's enough that I don't want you to call her that."

That stuns him, his jaw dropping. "Jesus, you're being serious."

I fidget under his judging gaze as I remove a stack of books from a moving box. "Can we just drop it? I'm already confused enough and the last thing I want to do is talk about it."

He puts the orange juice back in the fridge and shuts the door. "So what are you going to do about it?"

I drop a stack of books onto the table. "About what?"

"About your feelings for her."

I shake my head, wishing he'd drop it. "I'm taking her on a date."

I hear him chuckle under his breath. "Well, that's normal of you."

"Yeah, I thought I'd give it a try. See if I like it."

"I'm sure you will," he teases. He walks into the living room, raking his fingers through his hair. "Okay, so since I know for a fact that you're an idiot when it comes to relationships and dating, I'm going to give you some advice. Take her somewhere nice and don't try to fuck her in your truck."

"I'm not a complete moron," I say. "I get that."

He leans against the entertainment center with his arms folded. "I know you're not a moron, but I've witnessed over the last year how much you like to just screw any girl that walks and how most of them are very willing to give you exactly what you want. And normally, in a normal datelike situation, that's not how things work. You have to put effort into it."

I scratch the back of my neck. "How much effort?"

He hitches his thumb toward the bedroom door. "With her, probably a lot."

"I thought you were so sure she was a slut," I remind him.

"Well, I might have been a little overdramatic. And Greyson told me last night to lay off her because he thinks she's vulnerable." He raises his hands as he backs away. "I don't get why and he wouldn't tell me, but as a good boyfriend, I'm going to oblige." He pauses at the doorway. "You should make a note of that."

I roll my eyes. "Thanks."

"No problem." He leaves me alone to unpack boxes and

the more I do it, the more relaxed I feel about stepping out of my normal comfort zone tonight.

I continue to clean and organize the house until around five o'clock, stopping at the second beer, and by the time I knock on the door to see if Violet is ready, my head is alarmingly clear. Part of me is hoping she'll bail on our date because I'm nervous and I hate it. Everything Seth said is running through my head like a train about to crash. I'm going against everything I've ever believed about relationships and I'm going into it with a girl that has problems. I've seen the vulnerable side of her that Seth was talking about, the helpless side that lives underneath her toughness, and getting involved with her means taking that on.

Can I do it?

When she opens the door, however, all thoughts of bailing out, terror, and confusion float from my head. "I was going to ask you if you were ready, but I think I have my answer."

"I thought I'd put a little effort into getting ready, seeing how it's my first date and all," she smiles, her red-stained lips ridiculously sexy, along with her hair that runs down her bare shoulders in curls. Her green eyes are framed with black and the short, red and black dress that she's wearing hugs her body so tightly I seriously almost shove her back onto the bed and skip straight to the end of the date. But that sort of defeats the purpose of keeping things simple.

So instead I offer her my elbow and, in response, she laughs.

"I thought you said you weren't a gentleman," she says, looping her arm through mine.

"You're seriously wounding my ego," I joke as I guide her out into the hallway, both of us in way too cheery of a mood for my taste, but I'm blaming mine on my momentary sobriety. "Here I am putting myself out there and you laugh at me."

This only makes her laugh harder. "Put yourself out there. How brave of you."

"It's extremely brave of me, especially with what I'm going up against." I open the door and walk outside, steering her down the stairs with me.

The sky is a pale pink as the sun sets behind the mountains. The air is warm, but I'm nervous and it's strange. I don't know what to do other than keep going forward, with her.

Deciding to keep the whole gentleman thing going, I open the door for her. This only makes her laugh more as she climbs in, not bothering to hold her dress down and I get a glimpse of her ass, barely covered by a thin piece of lacy fabric. Clenching my hand, I shut the door and hop into the truck, telling myself to calm down. That that's not what tonight's about. I start the truck and back up as she begins going through the tape collection in my truck, helping herself to my stuff. She completely ruins my organization, but I let her be, and it's complicated how easy it is.

"'My Fuck Tape.'" She reads the label with humor in her expression as she glances up at me and covers her mouth with her hands, laughing under her breath.

I grab the tape and toss it on the floor beneath my seat. "I should probably throw that one away."

"Why?" She slouches back against the door. "Are you planning never to fuck again?"

I roll my tongue along my teeth, my restraint to not fuck her in the truck right now crumbling. "That all depends."

"On what?"

Don't say it. "On how tonight goes."

"So are you saying that you're only going to fuck me if things go well," she says biting back a grin. "Or that if tonight doesn't go well, you'll go back to fucking every skank in a short dress."

I shake my head, my body vibrating with the urge to pull the truck over, throw her down on the seat, and do what I'm good at. "You know, it's saying things like that that made me think you weren't a virgin."

She rests her elbow on the seat back and rests her head against her hand, playing with her hair as she continues to chew on her bottom lip. "Maybe I only say them to get you all riled up so I can see that intense look in your eyes."

I grip the steering wheel tighter as I turn my truck onto the busy street that runs alongside our apartment. Streetlights shine down on the sidewalks, houses, and trees that border the road. The shallow mountains are shadows in the distances and the city lights flicker in the heart of the town. I drive in that direction as I turn up the music, unable to think of a response to her blunt remark.

"Oh, did Mr. Stoically Aloof just give up?" She twirls a lock of her hair around her finger with the most beautiful real smile on her lips that I've ever seen and it makes letting her get the upper hand worth it.

"I guess I did," I say submissively. "You should be proud of yourself."

Her lips turn downward. "I'm not, though."

I'm taken aback. "I thought you liked winning." I press on the brakes to slow down for a stoplight.

"I do for the most part," she tells me with this flirty look in her eyes that makes me wonder how she's managed to stay single for so long. Sure she may try to stay away from people, but it's nearly impossible not to be drawn to her. "But I was kind of hoping you'd keep going and bring that intense look out."

My cock starts to harden inside my jeans. I'm out of my element, but I dig my dusty flirting skills out, the ones I used when I first hooked up with girls.

"It's going to take a whole lot more than a few teasing remarks to get that look to come out of me," I say, turning my head toward her and flashing her a cocky grin. "A lot, lot more."

She sucks her lip up between her teeth, suppressing a laugh. "Okay." She drums her finger on her lip like she's thinking deeply and then her eyes light up with an idea. She scoots across the seat and I wait in anticipation for whatever she's going to do to win this thing she started.

She kneels up, sweeping her hair to the side, her chest at my eye level. "Light's green," she says with an arrogant smile.

I drive forward, trying to pay attention to the road, but as she leans her body toward mine I get distracted by her body heat. Then she slants her face toward my shoulder and her hair falls against my cheek. Just that alone makes my fingers tighten on the wheel. I hear the intakes of her breath as she leans down and plants a kiss on my neck. It's soft, hardly a kiss, yet it make a sweltering need blast through my body.

"Violet, I..." I trail off as she starts sucking on my neck, tracing her tongue on my skin as her fingers slide across the front of my chest. I work to keep my eyes open, on the road, at the traffic in front of me, to the side of me, but then her fingers drift downward and encounter my dick and I'm seriously about to lose it. "God damn it," I curse and she starts to retreat. I swerve the truck to the side as she pulls back, her eyes wide as she peers over at the houses beside the curb where we're parked.

"What are you doing?" she asks, looking back at me, her hair falling down across her heaving chest.

I shove the gearshift in park and reach for her waist. "All right, you win." It's all I say and then I lean over, cup the back of her head, and kiss her. So much for waiting until the end of the date.

She laughs against my lips and I shake my head, unable to pull my mouth back from hers. I keep kissing her until the sky completely blackens, until she ends up straddling my lap. I kiss her like she's the only girl I've kissed before and she sort of is, at least with any meaning behind it. I don't let my hands wander anywhere under her clothes, only over because I know once I cross that line, the date will be over. I won't be able to stop myself…Jesus, I don't *want* to stop myself. But eventually, after my lips are numb, and the heat of her body blends with mine, we pull back.

Her arms are fastened around my neck and she peers into my eyes. She looks strangely alive at the moment and I feel strangely happy that I'm the one who put the look there.

"So where are you taking us on our date?" she asks with hilarity in her voice like the word "date" is the funniest word she's ever said.

"It's a surprise." I can't help but grin when she frowns in disappointment.

"Fine, but just for future reference, I don't like surprises." She climbs off my lap and sits down beside me in the middle of the bench seat.

She leans into me as I merge back onto the road, my heart constricting in my chest. I drive down the road lost in my thoughts on how she referred to our future and how much I actually liked it.

Violet

We pick up fast food from this little dive place at the edge of the town that has the best burger, then Luke drives up to the mountains and parks his truck. At first I think he brought us here because he wants to make out more, which seems like a wonderful idea to me, especially since making out in the truck was more thrilling than standing on the edge of the cliff, debating how easy it'd be to tip forward and fall to the jagged rocks below. But then he tells me he wants to hike up a little ways, so I follow him out into the darkness, carrying our take-out bag, while he carries a flashlight from the glove box.

"You know, if I would've known you were taking me on a hike, I wouldn't have worn a dress," I say, thankful I decided against the heels and opted for my boots.

His boots scuff against the dirt as he sweeps the flashlight across the crooked path in front of us, peering over his shoulder at me. "Personally, I like the dress."

"I'm sure you do," I mutter with a smile. I'd put the dress on because I knew he'd like it. If that's one thing I'm good at, it's knowing what guys like.

He smiles over his shoulder and reaches back to take my hand. I stumble forward as he hauls me up to him, then we hike together up the path. It's late, the sky charcoal dusted with glittering stars. The moon is full and the air chilly, making me wish I'd brought my jacket. We walk silently to the top of the hill where the view spreads out in front of us. I can see the highway and the city to my side, the lights on the houses making them seem so far away I feel like I'm flying. If I didn't know any better, I would think he'd brought me here on purpose, because he knew the height and drop-off in front of us would make me feel comfortable and at peace.

Luke lets go of my hand and situates himself on the rock, positioning the flashlight on the ground so it's spotlighting the sky. I drop down beside him, set the fast-food bag down between us, and stretch my legs out, crossing them at the ankles.

"So is this what a normal first date goes like?" I ask, opening the bag.

He rests back on his hands, staring out at the view. "Honestly, probably not. Most people probably go to the movies or to dinner, but this seemed more fitting for us."

I grab a fry from out of the bag and plop it into my mouth. "Why? Because we're weird and dark and out of the ordinary?"

He sits up and rummages through the bag, taking out a handful of fries. "Yeah, pretty much."

I grab my burger out of the bag and unwrap it. "But what makes you so weird and dark and out of the ordinary, Luke Price?"

He flips the leather band on his wrist with his finger. "Lots of stuff."

I take a cup of ranch out of the bag and peel the top off. "Why do you always wear that band around your wrist?"

He raises his arm up in front of him, studying it in the light. "Because my sister gave it to me right before she died."

I start choking on my fry. My nostrils burn as ranch gets in them. "She died?" I cough with my hands pressed to my chest.

He twists his head in my direction. It's dark so I can't see anything but the outline of his face and his eyes look like two black holes, but I can picture the intensity in them. "She threw herself off a roof when I was twelve."

I have a heartbreaking epiphany. "That's why you were so worried about me when you saw me jump out the window."

He bobs his head up and down, nodding. "That and the fact that you look so detached all the time," he says and I suck in a startled breath as I realize just how much he's *seen* of me and how we have one more thing in common. Death of a loved one. He instantly reaches over and his fingers encircle my wrist. "Violet, I'm sorry. I didn't mean to be so blunt...I don't even know why I said it."

"It's okay." I exhale, telling myself that I'm not going to go down that road tonight. That I'm going to keep it together, no matter what it takes. "I'm sorry. I'm seriously overreacting." In the snap of a finger, I manage to sound calm.

His fingers dig into my wrist, right above my racing pulse. "No, you're not." It's like he understands me, even though he hardly knows anything about me.

I nod my head. "Okay, but I'm over it. I promise."

He holds on to me a little longer and then releases me. I eat my burger and he eats his chicken sandwich in silence and it's the most comfortable silence I've ever lived in. After we're done, we ball up our garbage and pile it in the bag. Then he moves it aside so we can scoot closer, our shoulders touching.

"What was your life like before you met me?" I ask, relaxing back on my palms.

He tilts his head to the side, looking at me. "A lot less complicated," he admits.

"Is that a good or a bad thing?"

"It's a complicated thing," he says and then sighs heavily. "I had this system before you came along and it was working for me, but now that system is gone…With you…you make me feel like I'm falling into this out of control world full of craziness."

I frown. "You make me sound so insane."

"No, it's not like that." He rakes his hand through his hair, letting out a grunting exhale as he sits up. "God, this is coming out sounding so weird."

"That's okay," I tell him. "Weird is okay with me and there's no one else around."

I feel him smile through the dark. "See, it's things like that that make me just want to stay here with you. Because whatever I say never fazes you."

"We could just sit here in the dark," I say, trying not to think about the many times I sat in the dark by myself. "The dark can be comfortable."

"Yeah, we could do that…" He trails off and I feel the air temperature rise as he leans into me. "Do you want to do that? Just sit in the dark with me."

"Maybe…" I trail off as his lips connect with mine. He tastes different than usual, less smoky and tasting of tequila; instead he tastes salty from the French fries. I can taste the passion of the kiss and heat pools in my stomach. I clutch his shoulders as he pushes his weight into me and forces me down on my back. My head brushes the ground below and dirt gets in my hair as our legs tangle together and he barely supports his weight above me.

He kisses me slowly this time, more deliberately than he usually does. It's like he's calculating each movement, each taste, each breath as his hands knot through my hair. He gently tips my head back so his tongue can explore my mouth more thoroughly, gradually, slowly. Jesus, he's driving my body mad. I can't think straight, my nails jabbing into his shoulder blades, his lower back, his sides, anything that I can get a hold of as my body becomes more and more impatient.

Then he's pulling away again, stroking my cheek with his finger, his other hand playing with my hair. "This is nice."

"You're starting to sound like a softy," I say, breathless.

"Didn't you accuse me of being a softy once?" He continues to play with my hair.

"I did, but I didn't really mean it."

"Well, maybe you were right all along."

"Maybe I was."

He continues to comb his fingers through my hair, his body positioned over me, and I get so comfortable I almost fall asleep in his arms, right there up on a rock. Then he lifts his weight off me and the cold seeps into my body, waking me right back up. He laces his fingers through mine as he pulls me to his feet with him.

"Where we going now?" I ask, dusting the dirt off the back of my leg.

He bends down and grabs the garbage. "How about home?"

Home. Such a strange word, since nowhere has ever really felt like home to me. "Yeah, home sounds nice."

❧

The rest of the drive home we talk about mundane things, like what his favorite food is: tacos, which I already kind of figured out, since it's his hangover food and he likes to drink. I tell him what mine is: chocolate chip cookies, the kind my mom used to make. It surprises me that I talk to him about my mom, just as much as it surprises him. Our entire conversation is so boring and normal, but the thing is I actually like it and I start to wonder if I could actually live a boring, normal, non-adrenaline-junkie life.

When he parks the truck at our apartment complex, it's still early, but Luke says we can continue our date in the house. Then he starts kissing me in the truck before we can even get out. Our mouths and hands explore each other's body until it gets too hot and then we get out and head inside. It's the perfect date, and I'm seriously reconsidering my whole theory on life, when I spot a guy sitting at the bottom of the steps that lead up to our apartment.

"You have got to be kidding me." I let go of Luke's hand as I realize who the guy is. I leave a shocked Luke behind as I storm over to the steps.

Stan Walice looks up from his notebook, looking nervous and tense. "Please just calm down. I just want to talk to you for a minute."

341

"Do I need to get a restraining order?" I ask as I arrive at the foot of the stairway.

He rises to his feet and tucks his notebook and pen into his front pocket. He's wearing wrinkled gray pants, old sneakers, and a red polo shirt, along with square-framed glasses. "Calm down. I just want to ask you some questions." His glasses start to slip down the brim of his nose and he pushes them up with his finger.

"I'm pretty sure I made it clear I'm not going to do that," I say as Luke steps up beside me.

"Who the fuck is this?" Luke says as his hand touches the small of my back, slightly calming me, but my insides still burn.

Stan's eyes dart to him, I'm sure comparing his out-of-shape body to Luke's solid, tattooed body. "I just want to ask her a few questions about her parents."

"And I already told you to go fuck yourself," I say, not with anger but with a silent plea in my voice. "Seriously, what is with reporters and being obsessed and determined to harass people?"

"I really need this story," Stan says, raking his fingers through his hair. "My job's on the line."

"She says she doesn't want to talk to you." Luke steps forward, positioning himself in front of me, protecting me. "So take the hint and fucking get the hell out of here before I have to beat your ass," Luke says and then he reaches back and grabs hold of my hand. As much as I would love to see him beat

Stan's ass, I also remember that unlike when he fought with Preston and the guys at the strip club, there will probably be consequences this time, so I squeeze his hand and hold on to him.

Stan shakes his head, panic flooding his eyes as he skitters to the side so I can see him. "Look, I know I've probably been going about this wrong, but I really need this story or the paper's going to let me go. I need something really good."

"Go find a story that's easier to get, then," I tell him, inching forward so I'm standing beside Luke. "Don't chase me down when I don't want to talk about my past."

"The easy ones are the ones no one wants to hear," he says. "Girl who finds her parents murdered and stays in that house for twenty-four hours." He moves his hand across the air, like some reporter in an old movie, making a headline. "Now that's a story. I can only imagine the things in your head . . . the stuff you saw . . . And if people knew about it, maybe it'd help finally catch the killers."

Luke's body goes rigid as flames flash through my body. He just told Luke my secret, the one that everyone wants to run away from once they know. Out of nowhere, I lunge for Stan. Luke's hands slip from mine as I raise my fist, preparing to crash it into Stan's face. I haven't felt this much fury in a long time and usually I'd find another way to deal with it, but right now all I want to do is hit Stan. Ram my fist into him. Watch his nose bleed. Watch him hurt like I know I'm going to hurt in just a few minutes.

Somehow, Luke manages to get his arms around my waist and he holds me back before I actually make contact.

"Let me go!" I protest, squirming. "I'm going to kick his ass."

"No, you're not going to." He hugs me tighter as I struggle to get air into my lungs. I need to get away from him—need to breathe. I need to run, beat Stan, do anything at all beside feel what's prickling up inside me. *My parents. Luke knows. I'm fucked up. He knows now what lies beneath my skin of steel. He's not going to want to be with me anymore.*

I push against him wriggling in his arms as he nearly crushes me against his chest. "Just breathe," he whispers in my ear, smoothing his hand on the back of my head.

I swear to God it's like he knows what's going on inside my body, like he's in tune with it. "I can't," I choke. "I hate him."

"Just try."

I shut my eyes and block out everything else besides getting air into my lungs. I can hear his heart beating steadily, and I listen to it as I try to get my own to match it.

"Get the hell out of here," Luke growls at Stan, his chest rumbling.

"I've been trying really hard to talk to her," Stan says. "If she just would, then we could get this over with."

"If you don't walk away, I'm going to let her go and beat your ass myself," Luke says calmly. "So take the opportunity to walk away now."

"You can't threaten me," Stan says. "I'll call the cops."

"Does it look like I give a shit about the cops?" Luke replies. "Now get the hell away from her." He enunciates each word to get his point across. Stan mutters something about taking his card and Luke adds, "If you try to contact her again, you won't be walking away."

Moments go by, it feels like days, before either of us move or speak again. I'm the first one to pull away, and he releases me, giving me space. Luke watches me as I search around the yard for something that will make it easier to deal with what just happened, but ultimately my gaze travels back to Luke.

"So now you know," I say and blow out a loud, defeated breath. I search for the disgust in Luke's eyes, the look everyone has when they find out, but his eyes look black against the night, the porch lights glaring behind him.

The longer the silence goes on the more I feel like I'm going to cry. Tears sting at my eyes as I battle not to let them out, wanting to be that tough girl again, the one that doesn't give a shit. I need her. She makes everything okay, even when it's not.

"I didn't know reporters were like that," Luke finally says quietly as he wraps his fingers around my arm. "He seems crazy and intense."

"Unfortunately a lot of them are intense," I reply, biting on my fingernails, desperately wishing I could read what he was thinking. "But I've never met one so obsessed like that...he's been calling me for weeks and he showed up at my work."

His eyes widen. "Why didn't you say anything?" he asks

and I don't even bother to answer. "You should have said something."

"Why? So I could tell you my sad story and you could look at me like you are right now."

"You can't even see my face so you can't see how I look."

"I know the look, though. It's the one everyone has when they hear about me. The girl who found her parents dead and then sat in the house with their bodies for a day. The fucked-up girl that scares the shit out of people." If he wasn't planning on ditching me before, I'm sure he is now.

His fingers spasm against my arm as he turns us slightly so I can see his face and there's nothing there but sympathy and maybe even understanding. "Everyone has their dark past. I have mine and, trust me, I'd be a fucking hypocrite if I judged you for anything you did. I've done plenty of messed-up shit that most people wouldn't understand."

I slip my hand out of his and hug my arms around my waist, wishing I could fold myself into myself, hide behind the steel walls that have been shrinking over the last few weeks. "Like what?" I honestly don't expect him to answer me so when he takes a deep breath, preparing to speak, my pulse stills.

"How about shooting your mom up with heroin when you were eight because she hated needles and so she made you do it for her?" he utters softly and I can tell he doesn't want to say it, but it's like his lips forced him to do it.

I don't know how to react. If I should react. If I should

hug him. Run from him. What I should do. Thankfully, he reacts for me, his fingers leaving my arm and circling around my waist.

"Do I scare the shit out of you now?" he asks and I shake my head. "And your past doesn't scare the shit out of me," he says. "Now you do, but for entirely different reasons. Ones that have more to do with me and how you make me feel."

I nod, the tears drying as he leans down to gently kiss me. And it's strange, but in a good way, because for a moment all the bad that just happened doesn't exist. I don't feel it crushing against my chest. Luke's the first person that's ever been able to lift some of the weight off me and it makes me want to cling to him as long as I can. So when he picks me up and carries me into the house, I let him. Just like I let him undress me. Allow him to pull my shirt off and slip it over my head, so I'm surrounded in the scent of him. I let him lay me back on the pillow and climb into bed with me. Then we fall asleep. Together.

Chapter Sixteen

Luke

Violet and I fall into this weird rhythm over the next few weeks. We organize our room and I let her put most of the stuff where she wants it. She has this teddy bear that she insisted had to go on the dresser, right out in the open, even though it was purple and girly. But then she told me that her dad gave it to her and I gave her a hug because it's all I could think to do. I've been hugging her a lot, partly because I like the feel of her, but partly because I'm afraid she's going to disappear.

I'm afraid she'll finally realize that I wasn't kidding about shooting up my mom and then she won't be so willing to accept it. She's subtly asked me a few times about my mom and what she's like and I give her as few details as possible, because everything's working for Violet and me at the moment.

We kiss a lot, she lets me touch her wherever and whenever I want, yet I still hold back, afraid of crossing that line and fully accepting that I've changed inside. That I'm going to actually consider a real relationship with Violet, even knowing that at any moment she could take everything away from me. It's harder than hell, though, not just to take control and slip inside her. It feels like every moment of every day I want to be inside her, over and over again. I want to see that look in her eyes again when she comes, only this time I want to be inside her when it happens.

"You've been drinking a lot of beers lately," she notes as she piles the dishes into the sink. Seth and Greyson have gone out to dinner to celebrate their three-month anniversary. They've been together longer than three months so I'm not really sure what anniversary they are celebrating, and I didn't ask. "Is it because you're trying to take better care of yourself?"

I cringe at the fact that she's subtly mentioning my diabetes—my weakness—but because it's her, it makes it a little bit easier to relax. I plop down on the leather couch and tip my head back to take a swig. "Yeah, I decided to try sticking to just beer for a while and see how that goes...get a little healthier. Plus, I think I need a little break from the other stuff."

She glances up from the sink. Her hair is pulled up, leaving her shoulders and neck exposed for me to fully appreciate. She's wearing a thin tank top with no bra and boxer shorts. I'm doing my best to keep my hands to myself, but it's hard when she's dressed like that. "A break from what?" she asks.

I shrug and set the beer down on the coffee table, reaching for the remote. "My obsession from...what did you call it... burning the shit out of my throat." I flash a grin at her, not telling her the real reason I've cut back on the hard liquor. That

I'm trying something different, aiming for a somewhat clearer head, so I can fully be aware of everything going on between us. It's hard sometimes, though, and kind of painful, now that my nerves are heightened to everything.

"Did I say that once?" She angles her head to the side, tapping her finger on her lip, pretending she can't remember. "That doesn't sound like something I'd say."

"That sounds exactly like something you say," I tell her, changing the channel.

"You sound like you know me or something," she teases with a grin as she shuts off the faucet.

"Are you saying that I don't?" I retort, picking up my beer again as I kick my bare feet up on the table.

She pauses, wiping her hands off on a paper towel. "No, that's not what I'm saying at all."

"So you're saying I know you."

"As much as I know you."

"I don't think I know you completely," I say, peeling off the label of the beer. "Not yet anyway."

She stacks some plates in the dishwasher. "You know a lot of the important parts."

I toss the damp label onto the coffee table. "I know I do."

"And you're still here." She looks down as she says it, like she couldn't care less about my reaction, but the nervousness of her tone suggests otherwise.

"Of course I'm still here," I joke in a light tone because I know it'll make her feel better. "I don't want to go back to being homeless again. Besides, where else do I get to sleep with a girl who purposely pushes her ass against my cock every night."

She looks up at me with feigned annoyance in her eyes. "I did that once and it was because I was having a weird dream."

"A weird dream about me fucking you?"

She rolls her eyes, but doesn't argue as she collects some dirty glasses out of the sink. "I'm surprised that you still want to sleep with me at all," she says. "I thought you'd be sick of my crazy gasping ritual."

I tip my head back and gulp my beer. Every morning Violet wakes up the same way she woke up in my dorm room, gasping for air. It scared the living daylights out of me for the first week, but now I just want to know what's causing it. All she'll tell me is that it's a nightmare, I'm guessing about her parents, but she won't talk about it. "What can I say, I guess I'm a glutton for punishment."

"I guess so," she muses, setting the glasses upside down inside the dishwasher. "You know, I feel like the maid around here. It always seems like I'm the only one who does the dishes."

"Hey, I clean a lot," I protest, putting the empty beer bottle onto the table. "It's Seth and Greyson who don't do anything."

"Greyson at least cooks," she remarks. "All Seth does is leave Kit Kat wrappers and energy cans all over the place."

"Yeah, I'm not going to argue with that," I say as I watch her ass stick out of the bottom of her shorts as she bends over to load plates into the bottom rack of the dishwasher. "You know," I continue, "I think if you're the one who's going to do the cleaning, we should get you a naughty maid costume."

She stands back up, straightening her shoulders. "Why bother with the maid costume, when I could just do it naked?"

I shake my head, biting on my lip so hard I nearly draw blood. "One of these days when you say something like that to me, I'm going to take the situation and make you follow through with what you said."

She relaxes back against the counter, folding her arms. "Oh, I wish you would."

My body burns with a controlling urge to touch her. I've felt it a lot the last few weeks and Jesus, she knows how to push my buttons and make it worse.

"You think I'm kidding." She moves forward to scrub the dishes in the sink, facing my direction. "But I'm not."

I watch her as she turns the water on and begins rinsing off a pan. She's smiling to herself and I start to get to my feet, ready to finally give in to my needs or hers—it's becoming hard to tell anymore. I'll take her back to the room and give her what she keeps teasing me about. But then my phone starts to ring.

"Saved by the bell," she singsongs with a grin on her face.

"Oh, this isn't over," I assure her, retrieving my phone from the pocket of my jeans. "I'm starting this right back…" I frown as my dad's name appears on the glowing screen. He's been trying to reach me a lot recently, probably because the wedding's getting nearer.

"Aren't you going to answer it?" Violet asks, putting the

pan in the dishwasher and then bumping the door shut with her hip.

"I guess," I mutter, hating that getting a simple call can ruin the entire vibe of the night. I hit talk, putting the receiver up to my ear. "Yeah."

"Hey," my father says, sounding desperately cheerful. "You haven't been answering my calls."

"That's because I've been ignoring them," I say with honesty as the rumble of the dishwasher fills the apartment. Violet leaves the kitchen and goes into the bathroom, shutting the door, taking her cute ass with her, along with the good and lightness in me.

He pauses, struggling for words. "Look, Luke, I'm so sorry about my reaction when you asked if you could move in with us," he says. "Sometimes I don't know how to be a father and I just say stuff, not really thinking beforehand. But I should have said you could move in with us. I'll even give you my bed."

"I'm good." I pick up the beer, needing the taste of it. I take a large guzzle, but it's not enough. Too mellow and weak. Too sober and unstable. *Switching to beer was such a bad idea.*

"Luke, I'm really trying here," he says. "I know I wasn't part of your life for a while, but I want to be now."

"You're really trying." I laugh harshly in the phone as something snaps inside me, the last fourteen years shoving me down farther and farther and I'm too sober and can feel it all. "Trying would have been calling me up more than ten times over the last fourteen years. Trying would have been not leaving me and Amy with Mom and her craziness."

"Your mother's not crazy." He sighs. "She just struggles with stuff."

"No, she's fucking crazy and you're fucking crazy for thinking she's not." I snap. Literally snap. All the stuff I've been holding inside me spills out as rage flares through me until all I see is white.

"Luke, you will not talk about your mother that way," he says. "Yes, she has problems but we all do."

"You're seriously defending her and you don't even get it."

"Then explain it to me. Please."

"Do you have any idea the things that she did—made me do? Do you have any idea at all the stuff that I went through… she made me shoot her up, you know. Inject heroin into her veins," I hiss, balling my hands into fists, wanting—needing the silencing burn of Jack or tequila, but instead I settle for ramming my fist against the coffee table. A few of my knuckles pop and the wood scrapes a layer of skin off. It hurts, but not as much as thinking about the past. "When I was eight, she made me crush up her cocaine, made me let her hold me while she passed out. She made me do everything with her like I was a pet. She never let me breathe. She ignored Amy." I breathe furiously, fighting to get oxygen as I throw the empty beer bottle across the room and it shatters against the wall. "She didn't give a shit when Amy died. She fucking screwed up my life so God damn badly that I have to control everything just so

I won't remember how much she controlled me..." I trail off as Violet walks in front of me, standing between the television and the coffee table. Everything gets silent as she takes in the glass around her feet.

"Luke, oh my God, I didn't—" my dad starts to say.

I press end, hanging up on him. He calls right back and I shut off my phone, tossing it onto the table, my eyes never leaving Violet. As usual, I can't tell what she's thinking which means I'm going to have to ask.

"How much did you hear?" My hand is shaking but my voice comes out even. I know she already knew some of the stuff, but she pretty much heard a replay of my entire sad, stupid, worthless life. Now she knows just how pathetic I really am.

"Everything." There's an unreadable look in her eyes as she takes a deep breath. She contemplates something and I can't take her silence. I feel like I'm about to explode.

"Violet, just say something," I say, sounding panicked and pathetic. "Please."

"We should probably clean up the glass before Seth and Greyson come back," she tells me. "Although, we could just leave the mess for them to clean up."

"Violet I..." I drift off as she tiptoes over the glass and climbs over the table beside me. Then she laces her fingers through mine and kisses my scraped knuckles softly. After she kisses each one, she looks up at me with her round green eyes, then stands on her tiptoes and plants a soft kiss on my lips. I relish in the taste of her as my hands slip around her waist. I'm confused why she's okay with this, about what she heard, about the fact that she walked into a living room covered with glass, but then I remember everything she already knows about me; how she stopped the fight at the strip club, how I told her about my mom making me shoot her up. She knows more about me than most and she's still here, kissing me and letting me be close to her.

So I kiss her back with force and passion, because I need to be with her, need to get the rage inside my chest out. I kiss her with hunger as I scoop her up in my arms and carry her back to the bedroom, bumping into walls and the door before I finally lie us down on the bed. She groans as I cover her with my body and start sucking on her neck, kissing her jawline. I only pull back to peel her shirt off, her nipples perking as soon as the air hits them. I take her in as she helps me take off my shirt and then she traces her fingers along the tattoos on my ribs and chest as she just stares at me with an almost mesmerized look in her eyes.

"Do they mean anything?" she asks, her finger sketching over the lines of a tattoo on my side.

I shrug, my fingers knotted in her hair. "I went through this phase where every time I was feeling shitty, I'd get a tattoo."

"You have a lot."

"I felt shitty a lot." I pause, running my finger down the back of her neck while my other hand travels up her rib cage, across the dark lines of the tattoo. "What about yours? Do they mean anything?"

She peers up at me through her lashes. "The stars do."

My fingers land on the spot where I know the stars are inked. "What do they mean?"

"I got them to remember my parents." She shrugs. "I read somewhere once that stars represent our dead ancestors or something weird like that."

I start to say something, but she covers my mouth with her hand. "Just kiss me."

Even though it feels like I should say more, I kiss her instead, leaning my weight into her and pulling her back onto the mattress with me. I kiss her neckline, her collarbone, the spot on her chest where her heart beats. Then I suck her nipple into my mouth, allowing all the sexual tension I've been holding in to flow out of me. She moans, her knees coming up to my hips as she grips tightly onto my shoulder blades, muttering something about doing it harder. Good God, just kill me now.

I do what she asks and move to her other nipple, sucking harder until I can't take it anymore. Then I pull away and slip her shorts off, chucking them to the side, along with her panties. Violet may love to be tough but as she lies naked underneath me I can tell that she's nervous and trying to hide it. It makes me hesitate and I've never, ever hesitated.

Before I can say anything, though, she reaches forward and undoes the button of my jeans. Then her hands slide down beneath my boxers and her lips part as her fingers brush my very eager, swollen cock.

"I think we…" I trail off, losing focus as she begins to rub me. My muscles unravel like knotted ropes as I groan. Before I know it I reach the point where I'm either going to have to stop her or settle for a hand job. With a lot of effort, I reach down and tug her hand away, and then I kick off my jeans and boxers. I grab a condom from my back pocket then throw my jeans on the floor, returning my body over hers. She has this excited look in her eyes, that I'm not sure how to interpret or if I should even try to interpret.

I start to open my mouth to ask her if she's okay with this, but she leans up and smashes her lips against mine before I can utter the words. I lose focus of everything else and before I know it I'm sliding into her. She's tighter than I'm used to which means I have to go slower than I'm used to. I grab a fistful of the sheet, fighting to take my time, inching into her gradually, but she opens her legs and arches her back, taking over, meeting me halfway. Suddenly I'm inside her all the way and I still, trying to stifle the urge to pin her down and take over. Time slips by as the connection between us builds, along with the overwhelming emotions that are consuming me.

Controlling me. But in the end I move slowly because it's not about my control. It's about her. It's all about her. Every movement, every breath, the way my heart beats fiercely in my chest, is all because of her.

Violet owns me.

Violet

I'm not even one hundred percent sure why I take things as far as I do, but once he's inside me, there's no turning back, so I open my legs and let him sink all the way in, despite how bad it hurts.

I'm trying not to quiver at the feel of him filling me, but it's difficult. It feels so unnatural, yet natural at the same time because it makes me feel safe and not alone. Like he's supposed to be in me, which is weird and I'm sure not a normal thing for someone to think the first time they have sex.

Luke stays still inside me forever, my hands braced on his tight back muscles, his head tipped down by my neck as he grabs on to the sheet. He's throbbing inside me, his skin is warm and he smells like beer, smoke, and the musky scent of cologne. It's a scent that's started to wear on me over the last few weeks, but in this unfamiliarly good way, like him, the idea of him and me together.

I'm trying to hold myself together, but the urge to move is heating at the inside of me. Everything's so still. Too still. Then he starts rocking and it sends an ache deep inside me. The ache only seems to build the more he moves, sinking deeper and deeper inside me as he breathes on my neck, trailing kisses up and down my skin, until finally he places his mouth over mine and he immediately slides his tongue into my mouth, kissing me harder as he thrusts into me harder. I lose my breath as the ache turns into something else, something wonderful that rips all thoughts out of my head. I tip my head back, my breasts pressing into his chest as he glides his hand down my back, forcing me closer as I gasp breathlessly for air.

He groans against my mouth as I cry out something I can barely comprehend, falling and flying at the same time, just like I always imagined myself doing. I clutch him, refusing to let go until I come back, adrenaline slamming against me with so much force I can barely think straight. He gives one last thrust inside me, our hips connecting completely before he slows down and his body jerks underneath my palms. Then he stills inside me. Our skin is damp, hearts slamming against each other. There's no room between our bodies as he holds on to me and I clutch him, not sure why I'm holding on anymore other than it seems like when I let go the wonderful things I'm feeling will disappear.

Finally, after a while, he slips out of me, kissing me before flopping over in the bed. He drapes one arm over his head as he uses the other to guide me toward him until I rest my head on his chest. I can hear his heart beating unsteadily as his lungs expand for air.

"Are you okay?" he finally asks, sounding breathless, on the verge of panicking.

I nod, pressing back my content smile even though he can't see it in the darkness that's settled in the room, but it's weird being happy. Plus the smile is a real one, not my fake one I always show people. "I'm fine."

"Are you sure?" he asks, seeming self-conscious. "Everything's fine? Even after...well everything."

I glance up at him, propping my chin against his chest. "Everything's fine, Mr. Stoically Aloof, now would you relax?"

"I'm relaxed," he insists. "I'm just making sure you are—that you're okay with me."

"I'm perfectly fine with you and with what happened," I assure him. And I am. For a moment, everything is absolutely perfect.

❧

"Would you shut the fuck up?" the guy shouts as the woman sings to herself over and over again. "We need to get out of here."

"Lean into me. Lean into me. Take. Help me. I need to understand. Help me. I can't do this without you," she cries as he holds her weight in his arms.

"Stop singing that fucking song!" he yells with rage and kicks one of my toys across the room. "Get your shit together and let's get out of here."

"I can't," she says through hysterical sobs. "What if someone saw us?"

"No one fucking saw us," he says, shaking her like a rag doll. "I already checked the house."

She glances around my toy room and I swear her eyes land on me in the dark corner. Does she see me? She has

361

to. Is she going to tell? "Lean into me. Lean into me. Take. Help me. I need to understand. Help me. I can't do this without you." Tears flood her eyes over and over again and I start to cry to as he starts smacking her over and over again, the lyrics and slaps haunting my head as I wait for the monsters to find me. Hurt me. Because that's what monsters do.

❧

I wake up in a panic, like I always do, my arms flailing as I sit up, my surroundings distorted as that song echoes in my head. I gasp, clutching my neck, breathing loudly as I search the dark room, my mind searching for something familiar, and finally it lands on my teddy bear on top of my desk.

Luke sits up, rubbing his eyes as he places a hand on my back. He's become so used to this it doesn't even faze him anymore. He smooths his hand up and down my back, allowing me to regain my breathing as I clutch the sheet to my naked chest, telling my heart rate to settle. I have to work not to do it the way I'm so used to doing—by seeking an adrenaline rush through danger. I know that the only reason I'm not running to the window and contemplating jumping is because he's here touching me. Calming me down. He's the one doing it now.

After I settle down, he pulls his shirt over me, slips his boxers on and lies us back down in bed, wrapping his arms around me. "I wish you'd tell me what you dream about," he whispers against my forehead as he kisses it. "Maybe I could help."

"Talking about stuff doesn't help," I whisper with my

hands on his chest. "And trust me, you don't want to hear about it."

He combs his fingers through my hair and I feel his neck muscles move as he swallows hard. "I have nightmares, too, sometimes about...about shooting up my mom...I actually really hate needles and doing that stuff...Well it still gets to me."

"But you're a diabetic?"

"Yeah, it's a great inconvenience." There's forced humor in his voice.

I rack my head for something to say, but I can't come up with anything. I could make a joke, create an elaborate story— those things are always easy for me to do. But he keeps telling me things about himself, without me even asking. Dark and screwed-up things, like the ones I've been holding inside me for thirteen years.

"It's about that night," I say and his muscles stiffen, but he continues to run his fingers through my hair. "I saw them..."

His fingers stop moving and he catches his breath. "You saw the killers."

I nod, looking down at the foot of the bed. "I did, but at the same time not really...I guess it was more like I heard them...they were noisy fuckers." My tone is light but everything else inside me feels like bricks tumbling down, crushing me, trapping me. "They didn't know I was in the room, so they didn't even bother to be quiet."

"Did you tell the police this?" he asks.

"I told the police everything; what I could remember happening, the shoes the lady was wearing...I even described the sound of her stupid voice...the way it sounded when she sang that messed-up song."

"She was singing a song?" he asks. "Really?"

"Yeah, it had some really fucked-up lyrics," I say, summoning a deep breath. "'Lean into me. Lean into me. Take. Help me. I need to understand. Help me. I can't do this without you...'" I trail off. "It's what I hear every night in my dreams."

He's silent for a while, the sounds of cars rolling by the only noise in our room. At first I think it's because he's taking in what I said, but then I realize how stiff he's gotten and how it doesn't even sound like he's breathing.

I peer up at him, wondering if it was a mistake to tell him. "Luke, are you okay?"

"What the hell did you just say?" he whispers.

I definitely shouldn't have told him. "That was the song she was singing." I push up from his chest, trying to decide whether I should bail out before he throws me out. "I'm not even sure what song it is because I've never been able to find it anywhere."

The length of his silence seems to stretch on forever. He doesn't budge. Breathe. And I grow more panicked.

"That's because she made it up." His voice cracks and then he shoves me off him.

I roll to the side as he gets up and storms out of the room. I lay in the bed for a moment replaying what he said and what he could possibly mean. Who made it up? Does he know something about the song? Does he know the person who... Oh my God... I jump up and chase after him as he slams the bathroom door shut. I jerk on the doorknob but he locked it.

I bang my fist on the door. "What do you mean 'she made it up'? Luke... Please answer me..." I hammer my hand against the door over and over again until it's swollen and throbbing. "God damn it, please just say it again. I need to know... I need to know that I heard you right."

He doesn't answer and his silence is enough to know the painful, blazing, slicing, ugly truth. I sink to the floor as things start crashing around on the other side of the door. Glass. Walls. My heart. I wait for the truth to be revealed to me, just like I waited that night, hoping it's not what I'm thinking. That Luke doesn't know the person who was there that night my parents were killed, singing that god-awful song. But deep down I know I'm wrong.

Knowing the horrible truth and the emptiness that lies ahead of me.

Luke

I hammer my fist over and over against the wall, watching it fall apart, crumble against the tile floor, turn into a pile of dust. Then once the hole is big enough, I crash my fist into the mirror. Glass shatters. My skin splits apart. I bleed all over the floor, drops of blood staining the tile along with the broken fragments of glass. This can't be happening. It isn't real. I just want a fucking decent life without my God damn past owning me. Without her owning me. A hot burst of heat burns the inside of me and I crane my arm back and ram my fist into the nearest thing still intact, which happens to be the bathtub. The tile stays intact, but my fingers feel like they break. But it's not enough. I need more. I don't want to feel like this. I can't...I can't accept it...Tears start to slip out of my eyes as I collapse to the floor. I'm bawling like a fucking weak and pathetic loser, the kid who used to do everything he was told. I'm drowning in my past, drowning in the thought that I'm going to lose Violet.

I let myself cry until the tears stop, until I know there's nothing left to do but move again. Sweaty, bleeding, and raw, I get to my feet, the glass cutting the bottom of them as I move toward the door. Violet's sitting leaning against the door and she falls onto the bathroom floor when I pull the door open. Her hair is surrounding her head as she lies there in the middle of the pieces of wall and mirror, staring up at me with dry eyes.

"When...when did this happen?" It takes more strength than anything for me to ask it. "When did your parents die?"

She sucks in a slow breath. "Thirteen years ago...the night of July third...the day before my birthday." Her eyes are blank, emotionless, worse than when I first met her. And I put that look there. This is all my fault.

I remember that night because it was the night my mother came back with blood all over her clothes. The night everything changed. The night that led to a seemingly endless amount of days filled with drugs and madness.

"I think…" I clutch my broken hand as I tremble inside and out. I can't even say it, which makes me the weakest person on earth, because she deserves to hear what I have to say. She deserves so much fucking more.

"I think I know what you're going to say, so don't say it," she tells me.

"I can't…" I struggle for words that'll make this easier, but they don't exist. "That song…my mother made up that song…" The sound of my voice hits me with invisible knives that stab at my lungs, my throat, my heart.

"She was…oh my God, was she there?" Her eyes flood as she starts crying, hysterical sobs ripping from her chest as she claws at the air, my chest, every single thing around us.

"I don't know…" But deep down I think I do because I remember that night she came home with blood on her clothes. I don't know what I should do. I want to help her, but it seems like I should be the last person to ever get to touch her. "I'll fix it," I whisper, crouching down beside her. "I'll…I'll tell someone…"

"That doesn't matter." Tears stream down her cheeks and drip down on the floor. "Nothing we do can ever fix this. Nothing. It's all gone. My parents…you and I…"

The pain in my knuckles is nothing compared to the blinding, aching pain in my heart as the meaning of her words slash open my chest. Tears pour out of her eyes and I can't stop myself, unable to fully accept reality yet. I know I'll have to let her go, because she's not going to let me hold on to her anymore. Not after this. Things will never be the same. But I can't do it just yet. I *need* a little longer before I let all of this go, my feelings for her, who I've become with her.

I bend down and scoop her up in my arms, ignoring how badly it hurts. She doesn't protest, only cries harder, gripping me as if I'm the only thing holding her to this world. I carry her to the bed and lie her down and she pulls me down to her. I let her grip me, let her cry, let her sob into my chest, never touching her, letting her take whatever she needs and wanting nothing in return.

Eventually, she falls asleep in my arms and even though I fight the urge to get up, I stay put until finally the emotional drain catches up with me and I pass out with her balled up in my arms. It only seems like I close my eyes for minutes, but when I wake up the bed is empty. I get up and look around the room, noting her bear is gone and when I open the dresser drawers her clothes aren't in them. I search the house and I can't find her or anything that belongs to her anywhere. She's gone. Everything is.

And it hurts, more than my broken hand, more than remembering, more than anything I've had to endure in my entire life. I didn't even know how much I felt for her until now, when I can't feel it anymore. I want the pain gone. I want it all gone. I need it gone.

I head to the fridge and take out a bottle of tequila. It takes a lot to get the cap off with my injured hand, but I manage. Then I tip my head back and put my mouth to the bottle, going back to the one thing I know will take everything away. I drench my throat with the burning liquid, letting it seep into every part of me, letting it drown me, until I'm so far under, I don't even want to try to breathe.

Epilogue

Violet

"So things with lover boy didn't work out, huh?" Preston asks as he drops the last bag of my stuff on his living room floor. Everything's in plastic bags, because I packed in a rush, needing to get out of there before I threw myself out the window. I would have done it, too, because the idea of everything being over sounded far better than letting the one simple, good thing in my life go. But being around him would remind me of how I got to that point, how I got to be the person that would consider throwing herself out the window.

The worst part is I feel for him, care for him, want him to be the one sitting here with me, yet I don't even think I could look at him without thinking about my parents' murder and how his mom could be connected to it. Even as he held me and I cried, the safety that I once felt in his arms was gone and all I felt was hollowness.

"He's not my lover boy…he's not my anything," I mutter to Preston, rubbing my eyes as I sink down onto the couch. My eyes ache almost as much as my heart. I've never cried that much. Never had a reason to. And I'm still trying to figure out if I was crying over the fact that Luke told me his mom was there the night my parents were killed or if it was because I knew I couldn't stay there with him, not in the way we were just moments earlier before I sang that song and broke everything apart.

After Luke fell asleep, I'd gotten up, feeling the insane, uncontrollable need for adrenaline and I did the only thing I could think of that wouldn't end badly, with one more death. I walked away and went to the only place that I have left. I'm surprised Preston even came to pick me up. I'm still not even sure why I went back to him or if I'll stick around. But right now I'm too defeated and drained to do anything else. And I'm not ever sure I'll get who I was back, the person I became with Luke, or even the person I was pre-Luke who could hold it together as long as I could shut down my emotions. Even after I tell the police. Even when—or if—they can finally make an arrest because in the end I'll still be all alone.

After Preston stacks the last of the boxes onto the floor near the hall, he shuts the door and drops onto the couch beside me. I'm still in boxer shorts and I'm wearing Luke's shirt that I can't even remember putting on, but I'm glad I have it because it smells like him.

He drapes an arm around my shoulder. "So are you going to tell me why you look like shit or should I start guessing?"

I rub my fingers over my puffy eyes. "How about we just pretend nothing happened?"

"Oh, I can't do that," he says, pulling me against him. "But at least tell me why you're crying."

"Because everything's ruined."

"Wasn't it already?"

"No, it was far from ruined."

He doesn't have a clue what I'm talking about and I'm glad. "You know, I still haven't gotten over how you talked to me before you left."

"You deserved it," I mutter and he squeezes my arm hard.

"And you never gave me back that stash," he says in a firm voice. "So unless you still have it, you owe me. Big time."

"It's gone," I say flatly. "I gave it away."

He shakes his head and presses my head so tightly against his chest it hurts my neck. "See, that's the thing about you, Violet. You never think about the future."

"That's because I'm stuck in the past."

"I know, and you need to stop thinking about the past and start thinking about moving forward, starting with how you're going to pay me back." He starts massaging my shoulder with his fingertips roughly as his other hand drifts up my thigh.

My initial reaction is to hit him, but lifting my fist up seems too complicated at the moment. Everything does and it just seems like it'd be easier to give in to him than fight back.

I stare at a spot on the floor, focusing on it instead of anything else. "Take whatever you want," I whisper. "Nothing I have left in me is worth anything anyway."

For years, Kayden suffered in silence—
until an angel named Callie appeared
just in time to rescue him.

But the more he tries to be a part of her
life, the more he realizes that it's Callie
who needs to be saved...

Please see the next page for an excerpt from
the first book in the Callie and Kayden
series.

The Coincidence of

Callie & Kayden

Prologue

Callie

Life is full of luck, like getting dealt a good hand, or simply by being in the right place at the right time. Some people get luck handed to them, a second chance, a save. It can happen heroically, or by a simple coincidence, but there are those who don't get luck on a shiny platter, who end up in the wrong place at the wrong time, who don't get saved.

"Callie, are you listening to me?" my mom asks as she parks the car in the driveway.

I don't answer, watching the leaves twirl in the wind across the yard, the hood of the car, wherever the breeze forces them to go. They have no control over their path in life. I have a desire to jump out, grab them all, and clutch them in my hand, but that would mean getting out of the car.

"What is wrong with you tonight?" my mom snaps as she checks her phone messages. "Just go in and get your brother."

I tear my gaze off the leaves and focus on her. "Please don't make me do this, Mom." My sweaty hand grips the metal door handle and a massive lump lodges in my throat. "Can't you just go in and get him?"

"I have no desire to go into a party with a bunch of high school kids and I'm really not in the mood to chat it up with Maci right now, so she can brag about Kayden getting a scholarship," my mother replies, motioning her manicured hand at me to get a move on. "Now go get your brother and tell him he needs to come home."

My shoulders hunch as I push the door open and hike up the gravel driveway toward the two-story mansion with green shutters and a steep roof. "Two more days, two more days," I chant under my breath with my hands clenched into fists as I squeeze between the vehicles. "Only two more days and I'll be in college and none of this will matter."

The lights through the windows illuminate against the gray sky and a CONGRATULATIONS banner hangs above the entrance to the porch, decorated with balloons. The Owenses always like to put on a show, for any reason they can think of; birthdays, holidays, graduations. They seem like the perfect family but I don't believe in perfection.

This party is to celebrate their youngest son Kayden's graduation and his football scholarship to the University of Wyoming. I have nothing against the Owenses. My family has dinner over at their house occasionally and they attend barbecues at our place. I just don't like parties, nor have I been welcomed at one, at least since sixth grade.

When I approach the wraparound porch, Daisy McMillian

waltzes out with a glass in her hand. Her curly blond hair shines in the porch light as her eyes aim at me and a malicious grin curls at her lips.

I dodge to the right of the stairs and swerve around the side of the house before she can insult me. The sun is lowering below the lines of the mountains that encase the town and stars sparkle across the sky like dragonflies. It's hard to see once the lights of the front porch fade away and my shoe catches something sharp. I fall down and my palms split open against the gravel. Injuries on the outside are easy to endure and I get up without hesitation.

I dust the pebbles from my hands, wincing from the burn of the scratches as I round the corner into the backyard.

"I don't give a shit what the hell you were trying to do," a male voice cuts through the darkness. "You're such a fuckup. A fucking disappointment."

I halt by the edge of the grass. Near the back fence is a brick pool house where two figures stand below a dim light. One is taller, with their head hanging low and their broad shoulders are stooped over. The shorter one has a beer gut, a bald spot on the back of his head, and is standing in the other's face with their fists out in front of them. Squinting through the dark, I make out that the shorter one is Mr. Owens and the taller one is Kayden Owens. The situation is surprising since Kayden is very confident at school and has never been much of a target for violence.

"I'm sorry," Kayden mutters with a tremor in his voice as

he hugs his hand against his chest. "It was an accident, sir. I won't do it again."

I glance at the open back door where the lights are on, the music is loud, and people are dancing, shouting, laughing. Glasses clink together and I can feel the sexual tension bottled in the room from all the way out here. These are the kinds of places I avoid at all cost, because I can't breathe very well in them. I move up to the bottom step tentatively, hoping to disappear into the crowd unnoticed, find my brother, and get the hell out of here.

"Don't fucking tell me it was an accident!" The voice rises, blazing with incomprehensible rage. There's a loud bang and then a crack, like bones splitting into pieces. Instinctively I whirl around just in time to see Mr. Owens smash his fist into Kayden's face. The crack makes my gut churn. He hits him again and again, not stopping even when Kayden crumples to the ground. "Liars get punished, Kayden."

I wait for Kayden to get back up, but he stays unmoving, not even bothering to cover his face with his arms. His father kicks him in the stomach, in the face, his movements harder, showing no sign of an approaching end.

I react without thinking, a desire to save him burning so fiercely it washes all doubts from my mind. I run across the grass and through the leaves blowing in the air without a plan other than to interrupt. When I reach them, I'm shaking and verging toward shock as it becomes clear the situation is larger than my mind originally grasped.

Mr. Owens's knuckles are gashed and blood drips onto the

cement in front of the pool house. Kayden is on the ground, his cheekbone cut open like a crack in the bark of a tree. His eye is swollen shut, his lip is ruptured, and there is blood all over his face.

Their eyes move to me and I quickly point over my shoulder with a very unsteady finger. "There was someone looking for you in the kitchen," I say to Mr. Owens, thankful that for once my voice maintains steadiness. "They needed help with something...I can't remember what though."

His sharp gaze pierces into me and I cower back at the anger and powerlessness in his eyes, like his rage controls him. "Who the hell are you?"

"Callie Lawrence," I say quietly, noting the smell of liquor on his breath.

His gaze travels from my worn shoes to the heavy black jacket with buckles, and finally lands on my hair that barely brushes my chin. I look like a homeless person, but that's the point. I want to be unnoticed. "Oh, yeah, you're Coach Lawrence's daughter. I didn't recognize you in the dark." He glances down at the blood on his knuckles and then looks back at me. "Listen, Callie, I didn't mean for this to happen. It was an accident."

I don't do well under pressure so I stand motionless, listening to my heart knock inside my chest. "Okay."

"I need to go clean up," he mutters. His gaze bores into me for a brief moment before he stomps across the grass toward the back door with his injured hand clasped beside him.

I focus back on Kayden, releasing a breath trapped in my chest. "Are you okay?"

He cups his hand over his eye, stares at his shoes, and keeps his other hand against his chest, seeming vulnerable, weak, and perplexed. For a second, I picture myself on the ground with bruises and cuts that can only be seen from the inside.

"I'm fine." His voice is harsh, so I turn toward the house, ready to bolt.

"Why did you do that?" he calls out through the darkness.

I stop on the line of the grass and turn to meet his eyes. "I did what anyone else would have done."

The eyebrow above his good eye dips down. "No, you didn't."

Kayden and I have gone to school together since we were in kindergarten. Sadly this is the longest conversation we've had since about sixth grade when I was deemed the class weirdo. In the middle of the year, I showed up to school with my hair chopped off and wearing clothes that nearly swallowed me. After that, I lost all my friends. Even when our families have dinner together, Kayden pretends like he doesn't know me.

"You did what almost no one would have done." Lowering his hand from his eye, he staggers to his feet and towers over me as he straightens his legs. He is the kind of guy girls have an infatuation for, including me back when I saw guys as something other than a threat. His brown hair flips at his ears and neck, his usually perfect smile is a bloody mess, and only one of his emerald eyes is visible. "I don't understand why you did it."

I scratch at my forehead, my nervous habit when someone is really seeing me. "Well, I couldn't just walk away. I'd never be able to forgive myself if I did."

The light from the house emphasizes the severity of his wounds and there is blood splattered all over his shirt. "You can't tell anyone about this, okay? He's been drinking...and going through some stuff. He's not himself tonight."

I bite at my lip, unsure if I believe him. "Maybe you should tell someone...like your mom."

He stares at me like I'm a small, incompetent child. "There's nothing to tell."

I eye his puffy face, his normally perfect features now distorted. "All right, if that's what you want."

"It's what I want," he says dismissively and I start to walk away. "Hey, Callie, it's Callie, right? Will you do me a favor?"

I peer over my shoulder. "Sure. What?"

"In the downstairs bathroom there's a first-aid kit, and in the freezer there's an icepack. Would you go grab them for me? I don't want to go in until I've cleaned up."

I'm desperate to leave, but the pleading in his tone overpowers me. "Yes, I can do that." I leave him near the pool house to go inside where the very crowded atmosphere makes it hard to breathe. Tucking in my elbows and hoping no one will touch me, I weave through the people.

Maci Owens, Kayden's mother, is chatting with some of the other moms at the table and waves her hand at me, her gold and silver bangle bracelets jingling together. "Oh Callie, is your mom here, hun?" Her speech is slurred and there is an empty bottle of wine in front of her.

"She's out in the car," I call out over the music as someone bumps into my shoulder and my muscles stiffen. "She was on the phone with my dad and sent me in to find my brother. Have you seen him?"

"Sorry, hun, I haven't." She moves her hand around with a flourish. "There are just so many people here."

I give her a small wave. "Okay, well, I'm going to go look for him." As I walk away, I wonder if she's seen her husband and if she'll question the cut on his hand.

In the living room, my brother Jackson is sitting on the sofa, talking to his best friend, Caleb Miller. I freeze near the threshold, just out of their sight. They keep laughing and talking, drinking their beers, like nothing matters. I despise my brother for laughing, for being here, for making it so I have to go tell him Mom is waiting out in the car.

I start toward him, but I can't get my feet to move. I know I need to get it over with, but there are people making out in the corners and dancing in the middle of the room and it's making me uncomfortable. *I can't breathe. I can't breathe. Move feet, move.*

Someone runs into me and it nearly knocks me to the floor.

"Sorry," a deep voice apologizes.

I catch myself on the door frame and it breaks my trance. I hurry down the hall without bothering to see who ran into me. I need to get out of this place and breathe again.

After I collect the first-aid kit from the bottom cupboard and the icepack from the freezer, I take the long way out of the house, going through the side door unnoticed. Kayden's not outside anymore, but the interior light of the pool house filters from the windows.

Hesitantly, I push open the door and poke my head into the dimly lit room. "Hello."

Kayden walks out from the back room without a shirt on and a towel pressed up to his face, which is bright red and lumpy. "Hey, did you get the stuff?"

I slip into the room and shut the door behind me. I hold out the first-aid kit and the icepack, with my head turned toward the door to avoid looking at him. His bare chest, and the way his jeans ride low on his hips smothers me with uneasiness.

"I don't bite, Callie." His tone is neutral as he takes the kit and the pack. "You don't have to stare at the wall."

I compel my eyes to look at him and it's hard not to stare at the scars that crisscross along his stomach and chest. The vertical lines that run down his forearms are the most disturbing, thick and jagged as if someone took a razor to his skin. I wish I could run my fingers along them and remove the pain and memories that are attached to them.

He quickly lowers the towel to cover himself up and confusion gleams from his good eye as we stare at one another. My heart throbs inside my chest as a moment passes, like a snap of a finger, yet it seems to go on forever.

He blinks and presses the pack to his inflamed eye while balancing the kit on the edge of the pool table. His fingers quiver as he pulls his hand back and each knuckle is scraped raw. "Can you get the gauze out of that for me? My hand's a little sore."

As my fingers fumble to lift the latch, my fingernail catches in the crack, and it peels back. Blood pools out as I open the lid to retrieve the gauze. "You might need stitches on that cut below the eye. It looks bad."

He dabs the cut with the towel, wincing from the pain. "It'll be fine. I just need to clean it up and get it covered."

The steaming hot water runs down my body, scorching my skin with red marks and blisters. I just want to feel clean again. I take the damp towel from him, careful not to let our fingers touch, and lean forward to examine the lesion, which is so deep the muscle and tissue are showing.

"You really need stitches." I suck the blood off my thumb. "Or you're going to have a scar."

The corners of his lips tug up into a sad smile. "I can handle scars, especially ones that are on the outside."

I understand his meaning from the depths of my heart. "I really think you should have your mom take you to the doctor and then you can tell her what happened."

He starts to unwind a small section of gauze, but he accidentally drops it onto the floor. "That'll never happen and even if it did, it wouldn't matter. None of this does."

With unsteady fingers, I gather up the gauze and unravel it around my hand. Tearing the end, I grab the tape out of the kit. Then squeezing every last terrified thought from my mind, I reach toward his cheek. He remains very still, hugging his sore hand against his chest as I place the gauze over the wound. His eyes stay on me, his brows knit, and he barely breathes as I tape it in place.

I pull back and an exhale eases out of my lips. He's the first person I've intentionally touched outside my family for the last six years. "I would still consider getting stitches."

He closes the kit and wipes a droplet of blood off the lid. "Did you see my father inside?"

"No." My phone beeps from my pocket and I read over the text message. "I have to go. My mom's waiting out in the car. Are you sure you'll be okay?"

"I'll be fine." He doesn't glance up at me as he picks up the towel and heads toward the back room. "All right, I'll see you later, I guess."

No, you won't. Putting my phone away in my pocket, I depart for the door. "Yeah, I guess I'll see you later."

"Thank you," he instantly adds.

I pause with my hand on the doorknob. I feel terrible for leaving him, but I'm too chicken to stay behind. "For what?"

He deliberates for an eternity and then exhales a sigh. "For getting me the first-aid kit and icepack."

"You're welcome." I walk out the door with a heavy feeling in my heart as another secret falls on top of it.

As the gravel driveway comes into view, my phone rings from inside my pocket. "I'm like two feet away," I answer.

"Your brother is out here and he needs to get home. He's got to be at the airport in eight hours." My mother's tone is anxious.

I increase my pace. "Sorry, I got sidetracked...but you sent me in to get him."

"Well, he answered his text, now come on," she says frantically. "He needs to get some rest."

"I'll be there in like thirty seconds, Mom." I hang up as I step out into the front yard.

Daisy, Kayden's girlfriend, is out on the front porch, eating a slice of cake as she chats with Caleb Miller. My insides instantly knot, my shoulders slouch, and I shy into the shadows of the trees, hoping they won't see me.

"Oh my God, is that Callie Lawrence?" Daisy says, shielding her eyes with her hand and squinting in my direction. "What the heck are you doing here? Shouldn't you be like hanging out at the cemetery or something?"

I tuck my chin down and pick up the pace, stumbling over a large rock. *One foot in front of the other.*

"Or are you just running away from the piece of cake I have?" she yells with laughter in her tone. "Which one is it, Callie? Come on, tell me?"

"Knock it off," Caleb warns with a smirk on his face as he leans over the railing, his eyes as black as the night. "I'm sure Callie has her reasons for running away."

The insinuation in his voice sends my heart and legs fleeing. I run away into the darkness of the driveway with the sound of their laughter hitting my back.

"What's your problem?" my brother asks as I slam the car door and buckle my seatbelt, panting and fixing my short strands of hair back into place. "Why were you running?"

"Mom said to hurry." I fix my eyes on my lap.

"I sometimes wonder about you, Callie." He rearranges his dark brown hair into place and slumps back in the seat. "It's like you go out of your way to make people think you're a freak."

"I'm not a twenty-four-year-old who's hanging around at a high school party," I remind him.

My mom narrows her eyes at me. "Callie, don't start. You know Mr. Owens invited your brother, just like he invited you to the party."

My mind drifts back to Kayden, his face beaten and bruised. I feel horrible for leaving him and almost tell my mom what happened, but then I catch a glimpse of Caleb and Daisy on the front porch, watching us back away, and I remember that sometimes secrets need to be taken to the grave. Besides, my mom has never been one for wanting to hear about the ugly things in the world.

"I'm only twenty-three. I don't turn twenty-four until next month," my brother interrupts my thoughts. "And they're not in high school anymore so shut your mouth."

"I know how old you are," I say. "And I'm not in high school, either."

"You don't need to sound so happy about it." My mom grimaces as she spins the steering wheel to pull out onto the street. Wrinkles crease around her hazel eyes as she tries not to cry. "We're going to miss you and I really wish you'd reconsider waiting until fall to go away to school. Laramie is almost six hours away, sweetie. It's going to be so hard being that far away from you."

I stare at the road that stretches through the trees and over the shallow hills. "Sorry, Mom, but I'm already enrolled. Besides, there's no point in me sticking around for the summer just to sit around in my room."

"You could always get a job," she suggests. "Like your brother does every summer. That way you can spend some time with him and Caleb is going to be staying with us."

Every muscle in my body winds up like a knotted rope and I have to force oxygen into my lungs. "Sorry, Mom, but I'm ready to be on my own."

I'm more than ready. I'm sick of the sad looks she always gives me because she doesn't understand anything I do. I'm tired of wanting to tell her what happened, but knowing I can't. I'm ready to be on my own, away from the nightmares that haunt my room, my life, my whole world.

Chapter 1

#4: Wear a shirt with color.

4 months later...

Callie

I often wonder what drives people to do things. Whether it's put into their minds at birth, or if it is learned as they grow. Maybe it's even forced upon them by circumstances that are out of their hands. Does anyone have control over their lives or are we all helpless?

"God, it's like spazzville around here today," Seth comments, scrunching his nose at the arriving freshmen swarming the campus yard. Then he waves his hand in front of my face. "Are you spacing off on me again?"

I blink away from my thoughts. "Now don't be arrogant." I nudge his shoulder with mine playfully. "Just because we both decided to do the summer semester and we know where everything is, doesn't make us better than them."

"Uh, yeah, it kind of does." He rolls his honey brown eyes at me. "We're like the upper-class freshmen."

I press back a smile and sip my latte. "You know there's no such thing as an upper-class freshman."

He sighs, ruffling his golden blond locks, which look like he gets them highlighted in a salon, but they're actually natural. "Yeah, I know. Especially for people like you and me. We're like two black sheep."

"There are many more black sheep than you and me." I shield my eyes from the sun with my hand. "And I've toned it down. I'm even wearing a red T-shirt today, like the list said to do."

The corners of his lips tug upward. "Which would look even better if you'd let those pretty locks of yours down, instead of hiding them in that ponytail all the time."

"One step at a time," I say. "It was hard enough just letting my hair grow out. It makes me feel weird. And it doesn't matter because that has yet to be added to the list."

"Well, it needs to be," he replies. "In fact, I'm doing it when I get back to my room."

Seth and I have a list of things we have to do, even if we're scared, repulsed, or incapable. If it's on the list, we have to do it and we have to cross off one thing at least once a week. It was something we did after we confessed our darkest secrets to each other, locked away in my room, during my first real bonding moment with a human being.

"And you still wear that god-awful hoodie," he continues,

jerking on the bottom of my gray faded jacket. "I thought we talked about that hideous thing. You're beautiful and you don't need to cover up. Besides, it's like eighty degrees outside."

I wrap my jacket around myself self-consciously, gripping at the edge of the fabric. "Subject change, please."

He loops arms with mine as he leans his weight on me, forcing me to scoot over to the edge of the sidewalk as people pass by us. "Fine, but one day we're going to talk about a complete makeover, in which I will supervise."

I sigh. "We'll see."

I met Seth my first day at UW during Precalculus. Our inability to understand numbers was a great conversation starter and our friendship kind of grew from there. Seth is the only friend I've really had since sixth grade, besides a brief friendship with the new girl in school who didn't know the "Anorexic, Devil-Worshipping Callie" everyone else saw me as.

Seth abruptly stops walking and swings in front of me. He's wearing a gray T-shirt and a pair of black skinny jeans. His hair is stylishly tousled and his long eyelashes are the envy of every girl.

"I just have to say one more thing." He touches the tip of his finger to the corner of my eye. "I like the maroon eyeliner much better than the excessive black."

"I have your approval on that." I press my hand dramatically to my heart. "I'm so relieved. It's been weighing on my mind since this morning."

He makes a face and his eyes scroll down my red T-shirt

that brushes the top of my form-fitting jeans. "You're doing great in every department, I just wish you'd wear a dress or shorts or something for once and show off those legs of yours."

My face plummets along with my mood. "Seth, you know why…I mean, you know…I can't…"

"I know. I'm just trying to be encouraging."

"I know you are and that's why I love you." I love him for more than that actually. I love him because he's the first person I felt comfortable enough with to tell my secrets to, but maybe that's because he understands what it's like to be hurt inside and out.

"You're so much happier than when I first met you." He tucks my bangs behind my ear. "I wish you could be this way around everyone, Callie. That you would stop hiding from everyone. It's sad no one gets to see how great you are."

"And vice versa," I say, because Seth hides as much as I do.

He takes my empty Styrofoam cup from my hand and tosses it into a garbage can beside one of the benches. "What do you think? Should we hit up one of the tours and make fun of the tour guide?"

"You know the way to my heart." I beam and his laughter lights up his entire face.

We stroll up the sidewalk in the shade of the trees toward the front doors of the main office, which is a few stories high with a peaked roof. It has a historical look to it, tan brick with a lot of wear and tear, like it belongs in an older era. The yard that centers all the buildings looks like a triangular maze with randomly placed concrete paths that cross the lawn. It's a pretty place to go to school, lots of trees, and open space, but it took some getting used to.

There is confusion in the air as students and parents attempt to find their way around. I'm completely distracted when I hear a faint, "Heads up."

My head snaps up just in time to see a guy running straight for me with his hands in the air and a football flying at him. His solid body collides with mine and I fall flat onto my back, cracking my head and elbow against the pavement. Pain erupts through my arm and I can't breathe.

"Get off me," I say, writhing my body in a panic. The weight and heat off him makes me feel like I'm drowning. "Get off now!"

"I'm so sorry." He rolls to the side and quickly climbs off me. "I didn't see you there."

I blink the spots away from my eyes until his face comes into focus; brown hair that flips up at the ears, piercing emerald eyes, and a smile that will melt a girl's heart. "Kayden?"

His eyebrows furrow and his hand falls to his side. "Do I know you?" There's a small scar below his right eye and I wonder if it's from where his dad hit him that night.

A tiny prickle forms in my heart that he can't remember who I am. Getting to my feet, I brush the dirt and grass off my sleeves. "Um, no, sorry. I thought you were someone else."

"But you got the name right." His tone carries doubt as he scoops the football off the grass. "Wait, I do know you, don't I?"

"I'm really sorry for getting in your way." I snag Seth's hand and haul him toward the entrance doors where there's a big WELCOME STUDENTS banner.

When we're in the corridor by the glass display cases, I let go of him and lean against the brick wall, catching my breath. "That was Kayden Owens."

"Oh." He glances back at the entrance as students swarm inside. *"The* Kayden Owens? The one you saved?"

"I didn't save him," I clarify. "I just interrupted something."

"Something that was about to get ugly."

"Anyone would have done the same thing."

His fingers seize my elbow as I attempt to walk down the hall and he pulls me back to him. "No, a lot of people would have walked by. It's a common fact that a lot of people will turn their heads in the other direction when something bad is happening. I know this from experience."

My heart aches for him and what he went through. "I'm sorry you had to go through that."

"Don't be sorry, Callie," he says with a heavyhearted sigh. "You have your own sad story."

We make our way down the slender hallway until it opens up and there is a table stacked with flyers and pamphlets on it. People are standing in line, staring at schedules, talking to their parents, looking scared and excited.

"He didn't even recognize you," he comments as he works through the crowd to the front of the line, cutting in front of everyone, and he grabs a pink flyer.

"He barely recognized me ever." I shake my head when he offers me a cookie from a plate on the table.

"Well, he should recognize you now." He picks up a sugar cookie, scrapes the sprinkles off, and bites off the corner. Crumbs fall from his lips as he chews. "You did save his ass from getting beat."

"It's not that big of a deal," I say, even though it does stab at my heart a little. "Now, can we please change the subject to something else?"

"It is a big deal." He sighs when I frown at him. "Fine, I'll keep my mouth shut. Now come on, let's go find a tour guide to torture."

Kayden

I've been haunted by a nightmare every single God damn night for the last four months. I'm curled up near the pool house and my dad's beating the shit out of me. He's madder than I've ever seen him, probably because I did one of the worst things imaginable to him. There's murder in his eyes and every ounce of humanity is gone, consumed by rage.

As his fist hammers against my face, warm blood pours along my skin and splatters against his shirt. I know this time he's probably going to kill me and I should finally fight back, but I was taught to die on the inside. Plus I just don't seem to care anymore.

Then someone appears from the shadows and interrupts us. When I wipe the blood from my eyes, I realize it's a girl terrified out of her mind. I don't quite understand it, why she intervened, but I owe her a lot.

Callie Lawrence saved my fucking life that night, more than she probably realized. I wish she knew, but I never could figure out how to tell her, nor have I seen her since it happened. I heard she went off to college early to start her life and I envy her.

My first day on campus is going pretty well, especially after my mom and dad left. Once they drove away, I could breathe for the very first time in my life.

Luke and I wander around the busy campus trying to figure out where everything is, while tossing a football back and forth. The sun is bright, the trees are green, and there's so much newness in the air it gets me pumped up. I want to start over, be happy, live for once.

On a particularly long throw, I end up running over a girl. I feel like an asshole, especially because she's so small and fragile looking. Her blue eyes are enlarged and she looks scared to death. What's even weirder is she knows me, but takes off running when I question how she does.

It's bugging the hell out of me. I can't stop thinking about her face and the familiarity. Why can't I figure out who the hell she is?

"Did you see that girl?" I ask Luke. He's been my best friend since second grade when we both realized how mutually screwed up our home lives were, although for different reasons.

"The one you just ran over?" He folds up the schedule and tucks it into his back pocket of his jeans. "She kind of reminds me of that quiet girl we used to go to school with—the one Daisy was dead set on torturing."

My eyes move to the entrance doors where she disappeared. "Callie Lawrence?"

"Yeah, I think that was her name." He blows out a stressed breath as he turns around in the middle of the lawn trying to get his bearings. "But I don't think it's her. She wasn't wearing all that black shit around her eyes and Callie had a haircut that made her look like a guy. Plus, I think that girl was thinner."

"Yeah, she did look different." But if it is Callie, I need to talk to her about that night. "Callie was always thin, though. That's why Daisy made fun of her."

"That was one of the reasons she made fun of her," he reminds me and his face twists with repulsion at something behind me. "I think I'm going to go find our room." Luke hurries off toward the corner of the school building before I can say anything.

"There you are." Daisy comes up from behind me and I'm overwhelmed by the smell of perfume and hairspray.

Suddenly I understand why Luke ran off like there was a fire. He doesn't like Daisy for many reasons; one being that he thinks Daisy is a bitch. And she is, but it works for me because she allows me to stay detached from feeling anything, which is the only way I know how to live life.

"I sure hope you weren't just talking about me." Daisy wraps her arms around my midsection and massages my stomach with her fingertips. "Unless it was something good."

I turn around and kiss her forehead. She's wearing a low-cut blue dress and a necklace that rests between her tits. "No one was talking about you. Luke just went to find his room."

She bites down on her glossy lip and bats her eyelashes at me. "Good, because I'm already nervous about leaving my ridiculously hot boyfriend. Remember you can flirt, but you can't touch." Daisy gets bored easily and says things to start drama.

"No touching. Got it," I say, holding back an eye roll. "And again, no one was talking about you."

She twines a strand of her curly blond hair around her finger with a thoughtful expression on her face. "I don't mind if you talk about me, just as long as it's good."

I met Daisy when I was in tenth grade and she moved to our school. She was the hot new freshman and was very aware that she was. I was pretty popular, but hadn't really dated anyone, just messed around. I was more focused on football, like my dad wanted me to be. Daisy seemed interested, though, and a couple of weeks later, we were officially a couple. She's self-involved and she never asks where all my bruises, cuts, and scars come from. She brought it up once, the first time we fucked, and I told her it was from a four-wheeler accident when I was a kid. She didn't question the fresh ones.

"Look, baby, I got to go." I give her a quick kiss on the lips. "I have to check in and unpack and figure out where the hell everything is."

"Oh, fine." She pouts out her bottom lip and runs her fingers through my hair, guiding my lips back to hers for a deep kiss. When she pulls away, she smiles. "I guess I'll go back home and try to fill up my time with boring old high school."

"I'm sure you'll be fine," I say to her as I back toward the doors, maneuvering between the people flooding the sidewalk. "I'll be back for homecoming."

She waves as she turns for the parking lot. I keep my eyes on her until she's in her car and then I go into the school. The air is cooler inside, the lights are faint, and there's a lot of shouting and disorganization.

"We don't need a tour." I walk up to Luke, who's standing near the sign-up table, reading a pink flyer. "And weren't you going to find your room or was that your excuse to escape Daisy?"

"The girl drives me fucking crazy." He rakes his hand through his short brown hair. "And I was headed there, but then I realized it'd be much easier if I went on a tour so I know where everything is."

Luke is a very structured person when it comes to school and sports. It makes sense to me since I know about his past, but from an outsider's point of view, he probably looks like a troublemaker who failed out of school.

"Fine, we'll do the tour." I write our names down on the paper and the redhead sitting behind the table smiles at me.

"You can go join the one starting now," she says shamelessly pushing her cleavage up with her arms as she leans forward. "They just stepped into the hallway."

"Thanks." Grinning at her, I strut off with Luke toward where she directed us.

"Every time," he says amusedly as he sidesteps around a smaller table with plates full of cookies on it. "You're like a magnet."

"I don't ask for it," I reply as we approach the back of the crowd. "In fact, I wish they'd stop."

"No you don't," he states with a roll of his eyes. "You love it and you know it. And I wish you'd act on it, so you could ditch the bitch."

"Daisy's not that bad. She's probably the only girl who doesn't care if I flirt." I cross my arms and stare at the nerdy tour guide with thick glasses, scraggly brown hair, and a clipboard in his hands. "Do we really need to do this? I'd rather go unpack."

"I need to know where everything is," he says. "You can go to the room if you want."

"I'm fine here." My eyes zone in on a girl across the crowd; the one I ran over. She's smiling at a guy next to her who's whispering something in her ear. I find myself entertained by the naturalness of it, no pretenses like the ones I'm used to seeing.

"What are you looking at?" Luke tracks my gaze and his forehead creases. "You know what? I think that might be Callie Lawrence. Now that I think about it, I remember her dad mentioning something about her going to UW."

"No way…it can't be…is it?" I take in her brown hair, her clothes that show her thin frame, and her blue eyes that sparkle as she laughs. The last time I saw her, those blue eyes were clouded and weighted. The Callie I knew held more darkness, wore baggy clothes, and always looked sad. She shied away from everyone, except for that one night when she saved my ass.

"No, it's her," Luke says with confidence as he flicks his finger against his temple. "Remember she had that small birthmark on her temple just like that girl does. It can't be a freakish coincidence."

"Fuck me," I say loudly and everyone looks at me.

"Can I help you?" the tour guide asks in an icy tone.

I shake my head, noticing Callie is staring at me. "Sorry, man, I thought a bee landed on me."

Luke snorts a laugh and I suppress my laughter. The tour guide huffs in frustration and continues his speech about where all the offices are as he points at each door.

"What was that about?" Luke asks in a low voice as he folds a paper neatly in half.

"Nothing." I skim the crowd, but Callie's nowhere. "Did you see where she went?"

Luke shakes his head. "Nope."

My eyes travel across the hallway, but there's no sign of her anywhere. I need to find her, so I can thank her for saving my life, like I should have done four months ago.

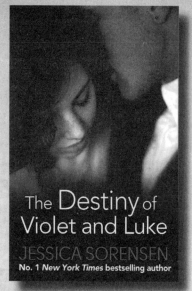